PATRICK GALE was born on the Isle spent his infancy at Wandsworth Pri governed, then grew up in Winchester. He now lives on a farm near Land's End. His most recent novel is *The Whole Day Through*.

To learn more, visit www.galewarning.org

From the reviews of *Notes from an Exhibition*:

'A beautifully written, slowly unravelling tale . . . Patrick Gale's serene and carefully crafted prose conveys a profound understanding of the workings of human relationships and the torment that mental illness causes its sufferers and also those around them'
Daily Mail

'As rich and inventive as we would expect from this brilliant author. Gale pursues the relationship between mental illness and creativity, but deftly avoids clichéd certainties . . . Its understated, tragic conclusion is as moving as anything Gale has written'
Independent

'So intimate, yet so dramatic, so beautifully written and yet such a pot-boiler . . . beautifully observed. By the end I had laughed and cried and put all his other books on my wish list. This is dense, thought-provoking, sensitive, satisfying, humorous, humane – a real treat'
Daily Telegraph

'It has a kind of quietly radiant intelligence, craft and integrity . . . [it is] a novel with a variety and freshness that is all the more powerful and surprising for being discovered in such a circumscribed and very English milieu'
Sunday Times

PATRICK GALE

Notes from an Exhibition

HARPER PERENNIAL

London, New York, Toronto, Sydney and New Delhi

Harper Perennial
An imprint of HarperCollins*Publishers*
77–85 Fulham Palace Road
Hammersmith
London W6 8JB

Visit our authors' blog at www.fifthestate.co.uk

Love this book? www.bookarmy.com

This edition published by Harper Perennial 2008
5

First published in Great Britain by Fouth Estate in 2007

A catalogue record for this book is available from the British Library

ISBN 978-0-00-726341-7

Set in Sabon and Optima by
Palimpsest Book Production Ltd, Grangemouth, Stirlingshire

Printed and bound in Great Britain by Clays Ltd, St Ives plc

Mixed Sources

Product group from well-managed
forests and other controlled sources
www.fsc.org Cert no. SW-COC-1806
© 1996 Forest Stewardship Council

FSC is a non-profit international organisation established to promote the
responsible management of the world's forests. Products carrying the FSC
label are independently certified to assure consumers that they come
from forests that are managed to meet the social, economic and
ecological needs of present and future generations.

Find out more about HarperCollins and the environment at
www.harpercollins.co.uk/green

For Aidan Hicks

If I'm on fire they dance around it
and cook marshmallows.
And if I'm ice
they simply skate on me
in little ballet costumes.

ANNE SEXTON, *Live*

Then I lie on my altar
elevated by the eight chemical kisses.
What a lay me down this is
with two pink; two orange;
two green, two white goodnights.

ANNE SEXTON, *The Addict*

FISHERMAN'S SMOCK (date unknown). Cotton. Throughout her working life in Penzance, Rachel Kelly bought smocks like these from the chandlery at Newlyn to wear, as other painters might wear overalls, to protect her clothes. (Not that Kelly ever greatly minded paint splashes or working in the midst of fertile chaos, as the large photographs of her two chief working environments behind you attest.) Neither of her studios was ever heated so the smocks may have afforded warmth as well as protection. She made much use of the pockets, once joking with Wilhelmina Barns-Graham that they were the one place she could tuck chocolate biscuits to keep them free of paint. (See postcard with cartoon below.) It was characteristic of her contrary attitudes that she despised the vogue for producing false fisherman's smocks in softer cotton, and colours other than navy blue, yet never set foot on a yacht in her life. She was wearing an even more torn and splattered example the day she died, and was buried in it.

Rachel was woken by a painting or, rather, by the idea of one. Her first response on waking was anguish such as one felt when torn from any dreaming rapture and she shut her eyes again, breathing deeply in an effort to return to sleep at once and recapture the dream where she had left off. But she was awake and her brain was fizzing in a way that would have had Jack Trescothick testing her blood and reviewing her prescription had he known.

The painting was there still, scorched on to her retinas like the after-image of something seen in a dazzle of sun. If she blinked she saw it again for a second. She saw the colours, the great, vibrating, humming globe of it but she was afraid that if she moved too soon or were forced to speak it would leave her.

She had always worked this way before, when she was young. Or younger. An image or elements of an image would come to her quite suddenly, often unprompted by anything around her, but then it was up to her and her wild brain to hold on to it long enough to fix it on paper or canvas. She was superstitious of describing the process but if forced to put it into words by a trusted friend she would have likened it to taking dictation – if one could take dictation of an image – from a quixotic teacher who could never be relied upon to repeat anything one failed to catch. Once she could find even a rough way to translate the image into crayons or pencil or lipstick or whatever lay to hand – she had once used a green boiled sweet of her daughter's – she could be fairly sure of accessing it again at greater leisure for a more polished rendition.

She knew without turning that Antony was still asleep beside her. Now that he was getting so deaf, nothing but the *Today* programme could rouse him and the radio was still silent. She listened to his breathing and heard it still had the full depth of sleep upon it. She sat up as slowly as she could. The room was still dark and she might only have been asleep a few hours. She slid her side of the duvet up and off her taking care that no shock of cold should wake him, and groped her way across the landing to the bathroom.

She turned on the light in the ferociously Teutonic bath-room cabinet Hedley and Oliver had given them last

Christmas. Blinking in the dazzle, she was amused to find last night's pill stuck fast to the hot skin of her temple.

Since her last episode, Antony had connived with Jack Trescothick in taking control of her medication. He doled out her daily dose of lithium each evening and watched her wash it down with a sip of water. Or had it changed to something else recently? Valproate? She forgot. Pills had been a part of her daily routine for so long she would have swallowed arsenic tablets without a second glance.

Only not any more. She had recently perfected a pass or two from the *Puffin Book of Magic* so he only thought he saw her swallow the pill. In fact it was glued to the underside of one of her fingertips, sticky with a quick stroke across her tongue as she opened her mouth for the pill. It worried her to flush drugs down the lavatory – pollution troubled her – so she hid the pills under her pillow then slipped them into her bedside table drawer or through a gap in the floorboards once they switched their reading lights off and Antony had turned his back.

Last night's slumber must have stolen up on her and the hand concealing the pill beneath her pillow must have ended up pressing it to her face. She smiled at the thought that its concentration of circularity might have mysteriously transferred itself through the thinnest part of her skull and into her dreams. She had thought it was a sun she saw, a dying or emerging star, but perhaps it was a planet-sized pill. Perhaps it was both?

She washed her face, cleaned her teeth, tugged a brush through her hair and fastened it back in the clasp she had been wearing so many years she took it, without even looking at it, from the place she always left it overnight.

Antony had not yet scooped yesterday's clothes into the laundry basket so they were still handily draped over the edge of the bath where she had dropped them the previous night. They weren't especially dirty – she hadn't been gardening in them – and there was no one there to see. Besides, she was worried it would wake Antony if she returned to the bedroom for the clean things she had forgotten.

It was not quite light still but that didn't bother her. She drew aside the curtains to peer out of the bathroom's narrow window. A thin drizzle was falling but it was preferable to the fog that seemed to have been blanketing the house for days. Fog did strange things to the light whereas the sort of drizzle she saw lending a shine to the slate windowsill merely filtered out the glare.

She left the bathroom and stood a while on the landing, listening to the house. The boiler was firing up, the radiators making their waking sounds, the clicks and gurgles that were probably a sign the system needed more maintenance than either of them could be bothered to give it. Even at this distance she could hear the ticking of the kitchen clock and the rattling cries of blackbirds as they hunted the food lured out by the drizzle. Antony was so deaf now that all these sounds were lost to him. He said the higher tones were going first – birdsong, children's voices, the wretched tin-whistle busker by the bank – and she couldn't think of it without imagining the frightening visual equivalent: losing all the blues, perhaps, or the yellows.

The landing was dominated by one of her paintings, so old and familiar that it hardly registered with her any more than the big one over the staircase. Usually she swept by them, preferring to keep her eyes straight ahead or on the double-height window that let so much light on to the stairs. But this morning she consciously looked at them for a few minutes each, as though she were in a gallery, and wondered at the size and energy of them and where she had found the confidence and time to produce such work with children hanging off her like fat koalas.

But this only increased the chill of excitement that had woken her so early and she moved on. The steps to the loft lay at the far end of the landing from their bedroom and the bathroom. They were so steep one instinctively climbed them as one might the ladder between the decks of a boat, with hands as well as feet. She pushed open the trapdoor. (She had nailed a double thickness of carpet underlay to it years ago so that it would fall back without a sound.) Then she climbed all the way up, shut it behind her and shot the little bolt that held it fast.

This had not been practically necessary for years – the last inquisitive child had left long ago and at sixty-nine – was he *really* that old already? – Antony had reached the age when he preferred using the intercom to climbing stairs. The click of the bolt in its catch, however, was fixed in her mind as a necessary, ritual precursor to starting work. Antony had a similar ritual involving house keys. Having once been told it was a useful habit for preventing keys being stupidly mislaid about the house, he imposed a house rule, when the children were still young, involving a Newlyn copper bowl into which everyone dropped their keys on coming through the front door. The days of children losing house keys were long past but he had confessed that because of its ingrained association with their home-comings he now found the kerchink of his own keys landing on copper whenever he came in profoundly comforting.

There was no heating up there and it was still bitterly cold as the sun had yet to warm the glass. Cold suited her, provided her hands did not become stiff with it, and Penzance rarely caught that extreme sort of weather. She poured water into the kettle from a plastic drum she filled in the bathroom and hauled up the ladder periodically, then pulled on an old sailing smock because she felt the need of an extra layer. She helped herself to a couple of biscuits, sat munching in the armchair and began to draw on the first blank page she found in the nearest of the pads scattered about the place. She drew the view of her feet, because the bunched-up extra pair of socks on them were a nice challenge. Then she brewed a big mug of builder's tea and, now the sun was up, she started to paint.

She lost track of time, as was often the case. At first she was dimly aware of the sounds of *Today* blaring out of Antony's clock-radio and of Antony getting up and using the bathroom but then, once he took himself down-stairs and entered the part of the house diagonally oppo-site the loft, she stopped hearing him and focused instead on the almost ceaseless shufflings, murmurs and squawks of the seagulls inches over her head. Visitors found the sound of them impossibly intrusive but Rachel was so used to it she found it as soothing a background to work as rain or wind.

The painting was all but mapped out on a piece of

canvas slightly under a square yard. Without taking her eyes off it, she groped for the phone on the table by the kettle, rang the carpenter who made her stretchers for her and ordered five more of the same. No. Eight, to be safe. She exchanged phone for palette – she had never let go of her brush – and laid down a little more colour. When the phone chirruped in the way that indicated Antony was calling her internally she ignored it for twenty rings or more. But he was insistent; he would have spotted the light going on and known she was sufficiently back in the land of normal people to have placed a quick phone call. She swore and answered brusquely, 'Yes?' scratching her scalp with the satisfying sharp wood of the brush handle.

'You've forgotten,' he said.

'What? I've no idea what time it is,' she bluffed. That old trick. 'Watch is in the bathroom.'

'You're due down there at eleven and it's ten to. I'll come too. Give you a hand.'

'But I . . . Couldn't the bloody woman manage without us?' she sighed.

'What was that? Rachel?'

'You're getting even deafer!' she shouted.

'I know,' he said, cheerfully enough.

'I'll be down in a tick,' she said and tossed the phone back on the table where it spilled something.

There was just a little of the cadmium yellow left so she carried on until he came and thumped on the trap-door, startling her.

'Jesus, OK. OK!' she shouted. 'I'm coming, all right?'

She had an opening that night. Only that sounded too

grand for the unveiling of a modest show in Newlyn. Forty people would come at most, the majority of them not collectors. The only critics would be from the toothless local press; older writers who hadn't actually criticized anything or anybody in years for fear of giving offence; and blithely ignorant younger ones used only to producing what Antony, pained at the neologism, called *advertorial*.

It was a small gallery, so akin to a shop in the pressures it was under to bring in customers and sell them things that the art on its walls almost took second place to its trade in earrings and handmade cards. It could never really afford to close so one show had to be taken down and another hung in the space of just half a day, the morning of the new show's opening. In Rachel's glory time, an opening involved only a brief, gracious visit to thank staff and check that everything had been hung correctly. With her star now so much lower in the sky, she and Antony performed the hanging themselves, battling with hammer and picture hooks and reels of salmon-strength fisherman's twine while all the gallery did was stick up labels on the walls giving titles, sizes and prices.

Antony enjoyed being more closely involved; he chatted amiably to the young couple still packing away some cynically naïve boat pictures and to Suraya. This was the gallery owner, surely born Susan, who had so many piercings one could hear them click on the receiver during her phone calls. She had arrived in the art business via crafts – she made something called lunar jewellery (one didn't ask) and knew so little of recent art history that she was mercifully unaware of who Rachel was or how curious it was that she should now be showing her work in a converted pilchard cannery instead of in Cork Street. Rachel suspected Suraya thought she and Antony were sweet because they were old and game and no bother.

After a few arguments, they had worked out a routine. Rachel would hold the picture at the height she thought would look best and Antony would mark the wall and tap in a picture hook. Then Rachel, being the painter, would do the hanging. And so on.

As they worked their way around the room, Rachel tuned out from Antony's conversation with Suraya who was sticking up labels in their wake as though it were a science, and brooded on the ordeal to come.

Jack would be there, bless him. Of all their friends, he was the one who most often actually bought something although she suspected he gave them away as presents later because she never saw them on his walls, not her more recent stuff.

Garfield, their eldest, would come because he was dutiful and only lived in Falmouth. Although he had the pictorial equivalent of a cloth ear, so would either ask hopelessly literal questions about the paintings or be at pains to talk about anything but what was on the walls around him. His wife, Lizzy, might come with him although, since the last time Rachel had snarled at her about something, she had developed a tendency to discover tedious last-minute crises that kept her away.

Hedley, second son, might come down from London for it. It had been known. Since he was little better than a househusband these days, he had few excuses, but she had snarled at him recently too so he would probably make do with sending flowers that pointedly cost more than the petrol would have done and she would get the message.

Her daughter, Morwenna, would certainly not be coming.

And then, naturally, there would be all the people who came to support Antony, all those friends, not forgetting the Friends, for whom she was the heaviest of his crosses nobly borne. Worst of all, there would be the enthusiasts, the self-proclaimed fans, those terrible people who would go on and on about not being able to decide between this one or that one, the tree or the leaf: the people who thought it would cause no offence when they confessed they hadn't really liked her work or even known it until the late Eighties, when she started doing pictures they could understand.

Focus, she told herself. *It couldn't matter less. By nine-thirty this evening this room will be empty, they'll all have gone home and you might even have some red dots on those labels of hers. Hey! You can even take some beta-blockers!* But all she could think about, now that she had spent an hour picking over all this work that suddenly meant nothing to her, was the interrupted canvas in the loft. And the others. Because she saw now, had seen just before the bloody intercom started squawking at her, that it was part of a series. She was starting a series that would speak a vibrant language she had never quite forgotten but had allowed to become rusty with disuse.

Her heart beat faster as she made a mental list of things she needed. At least eight more yards of canvas for the new stretchers she'd ordered and size and brushes and turps and colours, a great raft of colours she felt she hadn't used for years because they weren't found in hedges and ditches and ponds.

'Rachel?'

'I'm sorry,' she sighed. She took the picture Antony had just threaded with twine and hung it on the picture hook he had tapped in. She stood back, as if appraising the hanging but in reality looking at the picture and seeing something with no meaning or purpose at all. A nice, pretty blah.

'This is all just . . .' she started more firmly. 'It's all wrong. It doesn't mean anything.'

'Oh but it's lovely,' Suraya said, as if reassuring someone about an unwise hair colour. 'I like it. I love the one of the red trees. And those shells there are *beautiful*!'

'Sorry,' she told him. 'I've got to get back. Sorry.' And she hurried out of the gallery, blinding herself expertly to the start of his quiet protest.

She took the car. He would enjoy the walk back now the rain had stopped or Jack would give him a lift. She had things to buy and quickly. She drove fast, jumping the lights by the Newlyn Gallery and swerving over the mini-roundabout by the Queen's Hotel without giving way, so that somebody honked at her and a man with a dog had to jump back on the kerb. She sped left up Queen's Street, so as to grab a few minutes on the yellow line in Chapel Street while she bought a pile of supplies on account in the art shop there. They knew her. She was a good payer. They liked her. Oh God, they wanted to *talk*! No time for any of that.

11

Then home. Damn! No parking space. She drove the car sharply on to the pavement. Antony could park it for her later. No time now to go all round the houses looking and hoping. And then back to the loft with all her booty, slam down the trapdoor, shoot the bolt!

And relax. And deep breath. And kettle back on. And another biscuit. And more cadmium yellow. (Nice fat tube.) And start to paint.

She painted constantly, presumably for what was left of the morning and for most of the afternoon. (Her watch was still in the bathroom.) The dream that had scorched on her mind took shape on her easel and once it was safely down beyond all risk of evaporating, it took on new definition and began to evolve as she had hoped it would. She was talking the language again. Hell, she was *singing* it!

Everything else, those irrelevant pretty little daubs that had tried to shame her in the gallery in Newlyn, the sounds of Antony being shouted at by a lorry driver about the badly parked car, the sounds of lunch coming and going, of Garfield and then of Lizzy (Oh Christ! Of all the women he could have married!), and then the need to shower and wash her hair and choose a dress to wear that evening: all of it she found she could push, with an instinctive technique, to the other side of a thick, plate-glass screen where it didn't matter any more and couldn't interfere with the crucial business at hand.

'Rachel?' Garfield's voice from the landing. 'Mum? Do you want a cup of tea? Or anything?'

She ignored him and, used to it, poor sod, he went away.

12

She painted on. She snatched the phone up to have the carpenter confirm that yes, he could have those stretchers with her Tuesday. Great! What a star! She painted on.

She became aware by degrees of who was watching her. If she looked full on, of course, there was nobody there but she could *feel* her when her back was turned and from the corner of her vision, if she turned her head just slightly, she could see her outline, perched imperiously on the edge of the old armchair as if it were a throne, smoking – Rachel could smell her cigarettes now, could hear the faint sizzle of the tobacco burning whenever she took a drag – and staring at her from under that huge granite brow from those unblinking, judgemental, Old-Hollywood eyes.

So you're back, she told her, only in her head. Christ, but she hoped it was only in her head! *Do you like what you see?*

But the old girl wasn't going to speak: nothing so cheap. She was simply going to sit there, like some terrifying retired ballerina, all black headband and rigid discipline; sit there and invigilate until the job was done and done *properly*.

PORT MEADOW (1959/1960). Oil on tea tray.
Only recently identified as an early Kelly thanks to a document the new owner found among their late father's papers, this brooding study of cows on Oxford's Port Meadow in weather so bad the landscape has all but drowned, dates from Kelly's unhappy year in the city. Largely self-taught, she attended lectures and life classes at the Ashmolean when she could but was so poor she was often reduced, as here, to painting on any found object with a sufficiently large flat surface. Port Meadow shows unmistakable signs of having been used as a tea tray again after the painting was finished.

(From the collection of Miss Niobe Shepherd)

It was Antony's favourite time for taking refuge, just before dusk on a dirty February afternoon. There were no tourists, not even parties of schoolchildren. He was free to wander from room to gloomy room, studying the cases of treasures unobserved and dreamy-minded. He should have been in the Bodleian poring over the old newspapers he had ordered up to his desk that morning but his brain was itchy.

It was the first year of his study for an MPhil and he was hardly daring to admit to himself that his choice of the novels of Smollett on the thin basis of having enjoyed *Humphry Clinker* more than anyone else he knew was a mistake. Since committing to the topic he had dutifully read all or most of Smollett's other works, to find to his dismay that *Humphry Clinker* was the only one that appealed to him and even that book was fast losing its attraction under too close an inspection. He was begin-

14

ning to feel like a fraud and wondering how long it would be before his supervisor saw through him.

Security was lax in the museum at that time of day unless a school party was coming round. The few guards who patrolled the galleries seemed loath to return to their posts after the mid-afternoon tea break and would find excuses to loiter in the lobby, chatting to the woman who sold postcards, so he was surprised to find he was no longer alone.

She was tall and thin, almost gaunt. Her short, dark brown hair was swept behind her ears and tucked under a beret. She wore black slacks and black slippers like ballet shoes and a huge mackintosh surely meant for a man. She reminded him of a feminine actress trying to pass herself off as a boy: Katharine Hepburn in *Sylvia Scarlett*. She was perhaps his age, perhaps a little older; he had little experience of women and was a poor judge of age.

She was examining a case of porcelain, one of those whose contents had the irregular even haphazard look of a collection willed to the museum by a well-heeled supporter on condition it be left undispersed.

As he watched, she slid open the glass door of the case, seemingly with no thought for who might be watching, took out a small, blue and white bowl and its label then shut the door again. She didn't stuff the bowl in her pocket or bag but merely walked with it to the window to look at it more closely. Perhaps she was a member of staff but her mac made that unlikely.

He could not believe one could commit a crime with such graceful nonchalance. As he drew closer she made no attempt to hide the bowl away but merely met his gaze for an incurious moment before returning to her contemplation.

'You really . . .' he began then stopped to clear his throat because his voice had come out wrong. She was looking at him now, her boyishness revealed as a wafer-thin disguise. 'You can't simply take things out of the display cases,' he said.

'Oh but I just did,' she told him. Her voice was harsh, at odds with her appearance, her accent American or Canadian, dry, oddly theatrical. 'I had to see this in a better light; those cases are so gloomy. Look. What if . . . ? How did they do that colour? Is that truly blue, do you think, or a kind of green? It's both really. Maybe they did the colour in layers. And the background's not really white but a kind of grey-blue.'

He was sweating. Someone might come in at any moment. He glanced around them. There was laughter from the postcard counter downstairs and a flurry of steps and voices as people arrived for an art-history lecture.

'It's Ming,' he said. He came here so often he almost knew some parts of the collection by heart. She glanced quickly at the label and tossed it on the floor.

'Oh I don't care about that,' she said. 'It's the colour I'm interested in. But even this light's hopeless! How can we live with all this cloud and drizzle? We should all head south, the whole lot of us. I'll just have to look at it at home with the Anglepoise.'

She stuffed the bowl in her pocket and strode away towards the stairs and the voices.

He hurried after her. 'You can't,' he said. 'Please. I . . . Don't you see I'd have to tell someone?'

16

'Why?' She stopped and looked at him inquisitively. 'What's it to do with you?'

'Because I saw. If I didn't say anything I'd be an accessory.'

'The case was left unlocked. Nobody saw,' she said. 'It's really not that important.'

'Please,' he said.

'Oh really,' she snorted. 'You put it back, then. I've got a lecture to go to,' and she pushed the bowl into his hands so abruptly he almost dropped it.

He started to protest but she was stalking downstairs, her slippered feet as quiet on the marble as any cat burglar's. Frightened to find himself standing on the landing openly clutching a stolen artefact, he hurried back to the gallery they had left and replaced the bowl in what he guessed to be its correct place. Too late he remembered to retrieve its label from the floor and was forced to pocket rather than replace it by the return of one of the absentee guards.

Shaken to the brink of anger, he fled downstairs and, seeing her near the front of it, joined the queue that was filing in for a lecture. As an undergraduate he had swiftly become frustrated at the artificial unconnectedness of the various faculties. As a dare to himself he infiltrated a few lectures on subjects officially alien to his own, yet obscurely connected to it, on law, on zoology, on ancient history, and once he discovered that the faculties were so mixed, with students from so many different colleges that he was just another stranger among strangers and was never challenged, the dare became a habit.

This was the first of a series of lectures on Vasari's

17

Lives and the Renaissance but it might have been on double-column accounting for all the attention he paid the speaker. He was focused entirely on her. She sat in the very middle of the front row, taking careful notes yet seeming barely to glance at what her hand was writing. It could not have been the lecturer who held her attention so – he was at least forty and had a forbidding manner and an etiolated, bony elegance. So perhaps she lived for the Renaissance. He had squeezed into a place in the row behind her but she paid him no heed even when he pointedly coughed and he would have bravely given up on her as a skinny swot who stole things had she not turned to look at him, after they had all stood while the lecturer swept from the room, smiled and said,

'Bet you forgot to put the label back too.'

By the time he had recovered from his embarrassment she had left the room.

Several times in the days that followed he hung about the Ashmolean doors in the hope that she was an art student, scanning the clusters of young would-be artists as they came or left, and returned to the museum so often that one of the guards mortified him by winking at him over the postcard woman's head. He arrived at Sunday's Meeting like a drunk at opening time, thinking to lose the thought of her in prayerful silence, but the quiet of the Meeting House was no freer of her than the quiet of the various libraries where he tried to lose himself in study.

At last, a week to the day, half an hour before the next lecture in the Vasari series, he found her sitting on the Ashmolean's steps sketching something and heedless of the chill that was sending other walkers scurrying for shelter. Instead of the beret she had on a crimson head-scarf. It had the effect of making her huge old mac look glamorous instead of merely bohemian.

She smiled myopically, as though not quite sure who he was, but he sat down beside her and admitted that he had been searching for her all week in the hope of seeing her again.

'You're a virgin, aren't you?' she said, closing her sketch-book and shivering now that she was returning to the world.

'Yes,' he admitted.

She paused, floored by honesty where she had looked for indignation, then laughed, her rough voice startling some pigeons into flight.

'You're not meant to admit that.'

'Sorry. I can't lie. Never could.'

He offered her an arm but she rose unassisted.

'Are you going to the lecture?' he asked.

'Yeah,' she said, though she pronounced it somewhere between yur and yah.

'Me too.'

'Really?'

'Yes,' he said.

'For its own sake or for me?'

'For the lecture. It was interesting last week.'

'Hmm.'

They climbed the steps together as he gathered his courage to blurt, 'But perhaps you'd let me buy you a drink afterwards or . . . or take you to a film?'

She stopped just short of the doors and stood aside to let other people pass. 'Oh you're sweet,' she said. 'But I can't. I'm . . . spoken for.'

'Oh.' The last week seemed to stretch like so much elastic then smack him on the back of the head. 'Of course you are. I'm so sorry.'

'Don't. It's kind of you. I don't know your name.'

'Tony.'

'I can't call you that.'

He laughed. 'But it's my name.'

'Not with me. It's how my mother used to describe places that were high-class or fancy. *Tone-y*. Makes me think of red plush and cheap candelabra. I'll call you Antony,' she smiled. 'Give you some dignity to make up for being a virgin still.'

'OK. And what's your name?'

She hesitated. 'Rachel,' she said. 'It's Rachel Kelly.'

'What's your real name?' he asked.

'I just told you.' She flushed, he noticed.

'You hesitated as if you were making it up.'

'Don't be stupid,' she said. 'Why should I do that? Come on. We'll lose the good seats.'

Once again she pushed her way into a seat in the front row but there wasn't room for him too so he slipped in where he could, which, because he kept letting others go first, was some six rows behind her.

That week's lecture was on Donatello and, because his view of her was blocked and because the lecturer was the kind who seized attention through fear, catching one student's eye after another's and holding it, he thought he would listen and make an effort to learn so that they'd have something to talk about afterwards. He listened to a discussion of the relative values of bronze and marble in Florence of the 1530s and retained the outlines of the lecturer's points about Renaissance attitudes to sculpture from antiquity. But then the lights went out so they could look at slides and all he could think about was her face and voice. Even the memory of her voice acted like a fingernail on his skin, raising goosebumps. That the words she had spoken to him were mocking and teasingly made it clear she already had a boyfriend mattered less than that she had appeared to take an interest and had seemed to offer him friendship at least. She had given him a new name and he suspected he liked the version of himself it offered back to him.

When the lecture finished and the lecturer began to stride from the room, she pushed past people to be first out of her row and amazed Tony by running to catch up with the man. Her face was alight with enthusiasm.

'Professor Shepherd?' she called out. 'I wonder if I could just . . .' She drew level with him at the end of Tony's slowly emptying row.

The lecturer's face was mild enough as he stopped and turned but when he saw who was calling him it froze into a look of unmistakable contempt. 'Not now, Miss er . . .' he said and passed on.

Strangely she retained her expression of exhilaration, as though a public smack to her face could not have been more welcome than this dismissal. Other people had witnessed the little scene and they averted their eyes from her as they left, as though the mortification that should have been hers had become their own. By the time Tony had reached her, however, her eyes were misted and reddening with tears and she let him steer her by the elbow like an old friend.

'Let me buy you a cup of tea,' he urged. 'Please.'

'No.' She shook her head, taking the handkerchief he offered. 'It makes my heart spin. Anyway if I sat I'd be scared I'd never get up again. Could we just walk?'

'Of course.'

'You could walk me home, then.'

'Of course I could.'

He put her heavy book bag in his bicycle basket, glad he was not in his car so the journey could last longer. She struck out towards Jericho.

'My hovel's this way,' she said. Then she laughed weepily and added, 'He's in love with me. Crazily in love. He can't show it, naturally, because of his position and family. But all that's going to change very soon.'

'Really?'

'Oh yes. He'd got my letter, I could tell. He'll probably call round this evening, once he can get away. The wife's a cow. Are you shocked?'

He thought a moment and found that he was merely elated.

'No.'

'Men can be so judgemental. They know so little about compromise.'

'Have you known Professor Shepherd long?'

'Several months now. He's the reason I came to Oxford. We met on the boat that brought me to England.'

'From Canada?'

'Why'd you say that?' Her tone was sharp suddenly.

'No reason. There are a lot of Canadian students here, that's all.'

'Well I'm not a student and the boat was from New York. He'd been on a lecture tour in New England and he gave a talk during the crossing. On Rembrandt's self-portraits.'

'It's hard to imagine him not lecturing,' he dared. 'Does he ever relax?'

'Oh he's a volcano in bed.'

Tony barked his shin on a pedal and she apologized.

'It's because he's so tense, I think,' she said. 'And he suffers from post-coital loathing because he hates you for seeing him with his guard down. And in nothing but socks.' She tried to laugh at this but started to cry instead with hiccupping sobs that sounded as though they must hurt.

Tony dropped the bike against some railings with a clatter and held her, which he would never have had the courage to do were she not crying. She was only slightly shorter than him and her grasp was strong and immediate. Beneath the bulky coat she was far bonier than he had imagined, like a starving person. She smelled of shampoo and soap and he guessed she had taken a bath and washed her hair especially for Professor Shepherd's lecture and picked this red headscarf – at once passionate and demure – with a view to pleasing him.

She pulled away, sensing perhaps how much he enjoyed holding her, and walked on. 'Tell me about you,' she said. 'I need a bulletin from the real world.'

And in trying to honour her request he realized afresh how unreal the world of the university had become to him. They walked on and he told her about Smollett and his fears that he had picked the wrong MPhil topic but would be thought a lightweight if he asked to change it now. He told her about continually feeling an impostor among adults and she was shocked to discover he was only months younger than her. 'It's the lack of experience,' he said, which made her laugh without crying. He told her about the Quakers and being raised by his grandfather and about being Cornish.

'Is there more light there?' she asked.

'Much. Even when the weather's bad you can always see lots of sky. And variety in the sky. It feels odd here, having no horizons.'

'It's like being at the bottom of a weedy pond,' she snapped. 'That's why everyone here does those fucking watercolours.'

They walked on in silence for five minutes then she said, 'This is my street,' and led the way down one of the sad, low terraces that bordered the canal.

'It's nice,' he said automatically.

'It's miserable,' she corrected him. 'Though there's a wild little garden, which is good. When the sun shines. If the sun shines.'

'Are you going to be all right, Rachel?'

'Nope,' she said and smiled at him wanly. 'There's nothing you can do for me, Antony. I can't be saved.'

'Can I see you again?'

'Same time next week,' she said. 'How's about that? Another Renaissance genius, another walk home in the drizzle. Maybe I can watch you drink a cup of tea before-hand? This is my house.' She stopped on the side of the street that didn't back on to the canal, by an especially pinched-looking house. He still wasn't used to so much brick everywhere.

24

'Oh,' he said. 'All right. Your bag.'

He handed her back her shapeless satchel and must have looked especially needy or hangdog because she gave him a rapid hug and said quickly into his ear, 'I could drag you in and get you drunk on cheap wine and my record collection but it would make me feel like an old hooker and I'd hate you for it.' She pulled away and felt for her latchkey in her bag. 'You're a good, clean Quaker,' she said. 'You believe in truth and the little bit of God in all of us but I'm a miserable, hooked-on-sin Presbyterian and I'd be nothing but bad for you. Go back to the light and I'll see you for Piero next week.'

She let herself in and he was alone in the drizzly street except for an enormous cat trying to fish something out from a deep crack in the pavement.

He should have been wretched. She had rejected him, as much for youth and perceived goodness as for lack of experience. She had belittled him and treated him like a sort of provincial English eunuch who would never catch up with or understand her. But as he pedalled home to the institutional reassurances of dinner in hall and a long, lonely evening in the college library stacks with an article on Georgian pamphleteers, he swung between happiness at being taken into her confidence and the qualified promise of her friendship and excitement at being initiated into a world previously closed to him.

This euphoria lasted all week. He worked hard, wrote a long, reassuring letter to his grandfather and miraculously found Smollett funny again. The week seemed to fly along and by the evening of the next lecture he was determined to impress her as less immature than she thought him. He had read up on Piero della Francesca for a start and had found her secondhand copies of the first two volumes of Dorothy Sayers' translation of Dante. He had met a few refugees from hard-line religions and had decided that her throwaway references to their faith differences and her slightly over-dramatized sense of her moral waywardness made her the ideal audience for Dante's mix of harsh religious mythology and humane storytelling.

He arrived a whole hour before the lecture was due to start, in case her quip about watching him drink tea had been in earnest, and chilled himself waiting for her on the steps until the now half-familiar faces of the other art students began to shuffle in past him. He waited on in the lobby until Professor Shepherd appeared, with a squeak of shoe leather, then slipped in and sat in the rear row of seats, holding a place for her by the aisle in case she arrived late.

It had been raining intermittently all day and the fug of wet overcoats and Harris tweed was stifling but he found himself drawn in by Professor Shepherd. He had thought a good deal during the week about what she had told him and had decided it was a fantasy. She had met the professor on the liner, as she had said, but they were probably both with their respective families and nothing significant was said. It was a crush. One of those inexplicable crushes to which even clever girls were prone. She needed a father-figure. Perhaps her own father was weak or foolish and an eminent lecturer in her own field was safely symbolic. When he had rebuffed her so publicly, she reversed the situation in her mind to save her fragile self-esteem. After Tony's foolishly admitting his virginity she delighted in seizing the opportunity to deceive and shock him. But at bottom she had done so because he interested her and she had given him reason to hope.

Faced afresh with Professor Shepherd he was not so sure. He was younger than he had thought at first – in his late thirties, perhaps – but with the manner and dress of his elders. And even in the things that aged him there were touches of the dandy: the black shoes were polished to a mirror shine, the three-piece suit was sharply cut, the white shirt that matched the silvered gloss of his hair, brilliantly clean and creaseless, and his tie was iridescent petrol-blue. His voice, too, was at once commanding and silky. Even as it pronounced on Piero's mastery of space and precocious suggestion of frozen time, Antony could imagine it saying, 'Take off your dress and stand where I can see you.' This was not the voice of a man who loved in helplessness but that of a predator who captivated by withholding affection. So why was his latest slave not here?

Anxiety began to take hold of him until he could sit there no longer. Under cover of darkness, while Professor Shepherd was having difficulty with his slide projector, he slipped out, unlocked his bicycle and rode to Jericho through a fresh downpour that blinded him. Her little house was lit up, looking cosier than it had the week before, but when he knocked at the door an old woman answered, in a housecoat and clutching a bath sponge gritty with Ajax.

'So it's you,' she said, not letting him in, when he asked for Rachel.

'I'm sorry. We haven't met.'

'No, but it's obvious who you are. You're too late. Ambulance took her to the Radcliffe an hour ago. The state of our bathroom! You've a nerve showing up here now.'

Her husband shuffled into view in the narrow corridor behind her asking, 'Is that him?' but Tony was already back on his bike and riding up the street towards the back entrance of the hospital.

She had been given emergency treatment at the Radcliffe, then moved to a psychiatric ward across town. There was an oddly similar scene there when he finally tracked her down. He had bought flowers from a sad little stall on his way in, which was perhaps a mistake on top of the Dante. The nurse he approached took them as all the explanation she needed and was cold towards him.

'You're lucky,' she said. 'Not sure I can say the same for her. She's in the last bed on the left. You can have five minutes then she'll need rest.'

There was little more colour in Rachel's face than in her pillow. She was all sore-looking angles beneath her borrowed nightdress. Without beret or scarf her hair hung, lank and greasy, behind ears which he now saw were small but slightly protuberant. She stirred sleepily, then, seeing who was visiting her, tried to sit up, which was when he saw that both her wrists were thickly bandaged.

'Antony,' she slurred.

'Don't,' he said, pulling up a chair. 'Don't try to speak.'

'Not drunk,' she said. 'It's pills. Oh *amazing* pills. When I shut my eyes I don't dream, I just switch off like a light and the darkness is so soft and pillowy.'

She shut her eyes for several slow seconds during which he distinctly heard another woman on the ward

28

murmuring the Lord's Prayer. She opened them again, took him in afresh and said, 'You brought me *flowers*.'

'Yes. Sorry. They're not very . . .'

'They're hideous. You're so sweet. Sweet Antony.'

'And this.' He put the brown paper parcel from the bookseller on her blanket. 'But maybe it's a bit heavy going for here.' He had a growing sense of being surrounded by female patients who were all in a more or less similar state of wretchedness. She looked unimaginably lovely to him. 'What can I do?' he asked, trying not to weep but feeling tears welling up. It was as though he could feel her damaged spirit fluttering between his hands. 'Who can I tell for you? Your parents?'

'Christ, no.'

'A tutor?'

'I'm not a student.'

'Professor Shepherd, then.'

'Fuck!' she said loudly, startling him. She giggled and shook her head. 'Nobody,' she sighed. 'Just you's nice,' and shut her eyes again.

The nurse was approaching so he stood to forestall her. She took the flowers from him with a hint of disdain. 'I'll put these in a vase for her,' she said. 'Time to go now.'

'When can I come back?'

'Tomorrow. Visiting hours are two until four. You left your parcel on the bed.'

'Oh. No. That's for her.'

'Ah.' She shut the books, still bagged, in the locker by Rachel's bed.

When he visited the next day, bringing fruit this time, a smuggled bar of chocolate and a Georgette Heyer romance from the bookstall because it looked more comforting than Dante, he was waylaid by a woman doctor about the same age as Professor Shepherd and as severe as a nun, with a stethoscope where her crucifix should have hung. She was kinder than the nurse, however.

'Are you the father?' she asked.

'I'm sorry?'

'You're Miss Kelly's friend?'

'Yes.'

'Perhaps she didn't tell you. She's two months pregnant.'

'Oh.'

He sat, unwittingly confirming her assumption.

'You're not engaged or . . .'

'No but . . .'

'Hmm?'

'I can look after her.'

'Can you take her out of Oxford?' she asked. 'A complete change of scene would be best.'

'I live in Penzance.'

'Perfect. She's held on to the baby despite the overdose and losing all that blood. She's a toughie. They both are.'

'Oh,' he said, reeling. 'Good. When could she leave?'

'End of the week? She hurt herself quite badly and I want to be sure she's strong enough. The antidepressants will keep her pretty woozy. Presumably you have a doctor at home she could see?'

'Yes,' he said, having no idea because he was never ill and neither was his grandfather. He thought of his best friend, Jack, who had recently qualified and returned home but seemed uncertain whether to set up as a GP or be a painter.

And that was it. At no point was Rachel consulted. She was simply told. She was asleep that day so he just sat and held her hand for an hour until people started to stare at him but when he came the next day she was sitting up, waiting for him. She said, with the woozy slur he was beginning to find worryingly attractive, 'They tell me you're taking me home with you.'

'Well . . . They assumed all sorts of things and I just . . . I could just take you back to your digs if you like. The doctor needn't know.'

But that upset her and she shook her head and started to cry.

So it was settled. He called on his supervisor and managed to break the news in a way that wasn't a lie but sounded more of a moral imperative than it perhaps was. 'Someone very close to me, a young woman, is extremely ill and needs me to look after her,' he said. 'As she has no one else. I know this means dropping out and I've thought very hard but I can't see any other way.'

His supervisor had evidently sensed his waning enthusiasm for Smollett and research and was immensely understanding.

'If you can come back next term, let me know and we'll see what we can do but . . .'

'I think I'm probably going to have to get a job,' Antony said, which was only just dawning on him. Half the reason he had opted for research when his first degree came through was because the only other future he could imagine with an English degree was as a teacher.

31

'I suppose you could always teach,' his supervisor said, echoing what everyone at home had said when it was announced he was to study English rather than something useful, like law or engineering. And he offered to write Tony a reference should a suitable opening suggest itself.

He had a car, a Ford Popular badly rusted from living so near the sea at home. He could barely afford to keep it on the road, still less run it, and used his bicycle whenever he could, but it represented adult possibilities, however laughable, to set against the suspicion that his staying on to pursue an MPhil was somehow immature.

He settled his buttery bill and packed his suitcase and few possessions into the boot and lashed his bicycle to the roof. There was no one he felt he must see before he left. He hadn't acquired the knack of making friends. At home and at Oxford the Quakers were so sustaining they left him as lazy socially as any man dependent on a wife. Growing up with only a deaf old relative for company had left him shy of novelty and the challenges of his peers. His grandfather was so deaf now that even if he was close enough to hear the phone ring and answer it he could hardly hear what one was saying so that making phone calls to him about delicate matters was unbearable. So, rather than risk yelling at him from a kiosk an arrangement he could hardly explain to himself, he had settled for a calming, matter-of-fact letter presenting the two salient points as independent bits of news rather than a cause and effect.

Dear Grandpa, my research hasn't worked out so I've decided to cut my losses, come home and see if I can find a job, probably as a teacher.

I'll be bringing Rachel with me, a painter friend who has been ill and needs a change of scene.

She was sitting at the end of her bed, dressed and ready, suitcase standing by her feet. She had on a navy-blue duffel coat he had not seen before so that he supposed some friend of hers had called by her lodgings to bring her things she needed. The coat was fastened up to the familiar red scarf at the neck, as though she were waiting at a bus stop in the icy cold, not in a well-heated ward. She looked bloodless, blank and exhausted but she mustered a weak smile when she saw him and stood, wordlessly, bag in hand, eager to be off. The doctor intercepted them on their way out to press a jar of pills on him.

'See that she has two three times a day,' she said. 'I'm afraid it's not safe to trust her with the whole bottle. Not just yet. Good luck. Your local GP can fix her up with another prescription.'

Once they were down in the car park, Rachel became quite animated. She admired the colour of the Ford. 'I thought we'd be getting in a taxi,' she said. 'I never pictured you with a car.'

As he opened her door for her, he noticed there were brown bloodstains at the cuffs of her coat and realized her landlady must have bundled her into the ambulance with the first clothes that came to hand. Now that she was sitting, he saw they were a wild mismatch, even by bohemian standards.

'I'll need to pick up my other things,' she said. 'Do you mind?'

'Of course not. Maybe I can help you pack.'

It transpired that she didn't live in the little cottage with the faintly hostile couple he had met but in a studio at the end of their tiny garden. It was really a converted garage, basic even by student standards. There was an outside privy and hot water from an Ascot over the tiny, much-chipped sink. Presumably when sponge washing was not enough, she borrowed the landlady's bathroom. Otherwise there was a bed that doubled up as a sofa, a single rickety dining chair, a card table, a kettle and a toaster.

She saw him taking it in. 'It was the only place I could afford that had a bit of privacy,' she explained. 'Once the door's shut, they couldn't see in and I could let friends in at the window.' She indicated the room's window, which had been crudely inserted into what would have been the garage door, and he immediately pictured Professor Shepherd taking off his hat and wincing fastidiously as he climbed through it.

She had pulled out a careworn cardboard suitcase from under the bed and was rapidly emptying the chest of drawers into it. He was struck by how few possessions she had. (He was shocked to watch her casually throw her few paperbacks into the wastepaper basket.) The meagre collection of plates, cutlery and dented pans were the landlords'. The only thing of beauty was an incongruous old pewter candlestick which she thrust among her clothes when he began to show an interest in it. Her painting things stood near the window: an old easel, which he dismantled and bundled up for her, and several shoeboxes stuffed with an assortment of paint tubes, bottles of turpentine, brushes and little palette knives. When he asked her where all her paintings were, she said she had got rid of them, with a kind of flash in her voice that warned him off the subject. She clearly did not mean she had sold them.

She flung the window up and told him to bring his car round so they could load that way rather than trailing stuff through the house. Then she handed things out to him while he loaded. He had assumed she would need to leave through the house so as to settle up with her land-lords and say goodbye so was surprised when she ended her labours by climbing through the window and closing it behind her.

'But they'll think we're still in there together,' he pointed out.

'Oh probably,' she said, shivering as she got back in the car. 'I hate them. They don't matter any more. Can you drive quite fast now, please?'

He drove as fast as the car and the law allowed, which wasn't very, but she seemed satisfied and palpably relaxed as they put more and more streets between themselves and the scene of her recent troubles. Then, as they left the city and began the drive towards Swindon, she asked a few questions about where they were going, about Penzance and his grandfather. Just how deaf was he? How big was the house? Were they near the sea? Was there somewhere she could paint? She wasn't making conver-sation: she was asking questions so that he would talk so she didn't have to. And he duly talked and found he wanted to.

As if offering himself up, he told her everything. How his father had gone missing in the war and never returned and his mother effectively pined away with the stress of waiting for him.

'Nobody pines away,' she cut in scornfully. 'Did she kill herself?'

'I don't know,' he said, startled. 'I was never told.'

He related how his father's parents raised him, how his grandfather had been the town's best tailor. Her grasp of English geography seemed hazy – she thought Bristol was near Oxford and that Devon came before Somerset – so he tried to explain about Penzance and West Cornwall's proud remoteness and how it was wisest not to think of it as part of England at all but as a kind of island nation linked to it by a railway.

Thinking he had talked enough, he tried to encourage her. 'Tell me about your family,' he said. 'I don't even know where you're from or how long you'd lived in Oxford or anything.'

'I don't want to talk about that,' she said shortly. 'I never want to talk about that.'

She said no more and shortly afterwards began to cry.

She didn't sob or wail. Her grief was horribly discreet but as persistent and almost as silent as bleeding from an unstitched wound. He drove on in silence, glancing across at her, letting her cry. He believed it was healthy to let people cry – friends and onlookers were always far too ready to stifle grief with handkerchiefs and dubious comfort. But he also let her cry because her weeping somehow filled the car with the scent of her and he found it intoxicating. He noted how she didn't apologize from time to time, the way weepers usually did, as though their crying were a breach in decorum, like belching or hiccupping. Her flow of tears and occasional sniffs and nose-blowing were so regular, so placid almost, it was as though they were not simply beyond her control but beneath her notice.

After an hour, by which time her grief was threatening to mist up the windows, he stopped in a village on the pretext of buying petrol and bought her some tissues along with some ham sandwiches and two bottles of pale ale. He was prepared for her to wave the offer of food and drink away but he returned to the car to find her quite recovered and, she said, as hungry as a horse.

She ate her share of the sandwiches ravenously, poring over the road map, then suggested it might be a good idea if he gave her the pills the hospital doctor had prescribed. Remembering the doctor's orders, he shook out two of the pills into his hand and passed them over.

'I need three,' she said.

'But the label says –'

'I've been taking these, or versions of them, since I was a little girl,' she said drily. 'I think I know a little more about psychiatric medication than you do. Give me the bottle.'

He held back.

'Oh it's OK, Tony,' she said with a defeated sort of smile that gave him goosebumps. 'I won't do anything silly. Not now. Not now you've rescued me.'

She took a third pill, washed all three down expertly with a swig of pale ale, made him pause outside the village so she could relieve herself behind a hedge then fell asleep.

It was late at night, nearly one, when they arrived at his grandfather's house. Tony carried their suitcases into the dark and silent building, where his grandfather would long since have gone to bed, then gently woke her, taking the car blanket off her lap and draping it round her shoulders against the chill before he led her in. Perhaps from sleep, perhaps from pills (of which she had taken three more when they stopped at Exeter for supper) she was as solemn and wordless as a sleepy child. He showed her where the bathroom was then led her to a spare room, his mother's room, where his grandfather would expect a female guest to be lodged. She gave a little whimper of exhaustion and pleasure on seeing the bed so neatly made in readiness and started to undress so quickly he left her at once.

The idiocy of what he had done struck him only on waking from a deep and dreamless sleep. He had grown used to waking slowly in Oxford to the distant groan and chink of a punctual milk float then the muffled bell of the college clock and finally the alarm clock of the heavily sleeping research fellow in the room beside him. In Penzance the first cackle of seagulls woke him shortly after dawn. He would gladly have rolled over and slept again but nagging worry and a creeping sense of doom kept him awake and staring from his pillows at the too-familiar room, still so full of boyhood that it seemed to mock him for thinking he could become a man so easily.

He had thrown in his future for what? The thin promise of a badly paid teaching post in the town he had thought to escape and the still narrower possibility of a relationship with a pregnant woman in love with someone else?

This was a woman who thought of him, if she did so at all, as a kind of devoted page, less man than spaniel.

Thinking more clearly now than he had for weeks, he made himself sit up, listening to the creaks of the waking house and laying realistic plans. He had done the right thing in bringing her here. It was a healthier place, far away from bad associations and bad love, where she could paint again and meet other painters, like-minded souls rather than corrupt academics. He would find some useful woman, one of the Friends, to look in occasionally and perhaps cook meals. Rachel would mend. She would become the person she was meant to be, unwarped by influences and needs. For himself, however, he saw he had no further role in the happy scenario and that to linger longer than was necessary to settle her would be only to complicate matters and risk hurting both of them. He would stay on with her a week, maybe ten days, no more. He would write to his supervisor, who was far more worldlywise than he, and plead over-hastiness. His romantic folly would go understood.

Then he remembered the nurse's words about the baby and the doctor's and landlady's easy assumption that it was his. The Friends were famously non-judgemental in matters of unmarried couples and welcomed those other congregations branded, but that was only one morning out of seven. For the rest of the week she would be just another unmarried mother with all the trials and expense and disapproval to deal with and although he knew his grandfather would gladly take her in and, in time, her child, he doubted she had the strength to bear the burden of compassion.

He shaved and pissed at his bedroom sink and dressed hurriedly. She was not in her room and his grandfather was not in his. He heard his grandfather's scratchy laugh from overhead but was distracted by the smell of burning and raced down to the kitchen in time to tweak a tray of flaming toast from under the grill and tip it into the sink under a running tap. He opened windows to clear the billowing smoke then climbed the stairs, following voices.

Like several in the neighbourhood of Morrab Gardens, the house had an extra room, a kind of lookout built out of the attic. Long since retired from tailoring, half-grate-fully defeated by the arrival of John Collier's and racks of off-the-peg suits in Simpson's, his grandfather had retreated to his first love: seafaring. He spent hours in his eyrie, telescope or binoculars trained on the water, or down at the harbourmaster's office gossiping, and received a regular fee for a weekly half-column in *The Cornishman* called 'About The Bay' in which he gave details or stories of any vessels of note currently at anchor or being repaired in the dry dock.

They were laughing again as he climbed the narrow wooden steps and he thought how long it must be since the dapper and lightly flirtatious old man had entertained an attractive woman in the house.

They had all the windows flung up and his grandfather was showing her how to use the binoculars. They turned as he came up.

'Well here's the man!' his grandfather exclaimed and she hurried over, laughing and enthusing about how beautiful it all was and how the light was so strong even in winter and how she wanted to live there for ever and ever.

And before he had even climbed up off the steps into the tiny, dazzling room, Rachel had stooped and was kissing him on the lips with an eagerness that made his grandfather laugh again and clap his hands.

CHYENHAL TREES (2002). Red chalk on paper.
This late work shows a spinney of Cornish elms seen from the lane where Kelly's son, Petroc, was killed in 1986. It is characteristic of the penultimate stage in her career, when she baffled and, indeed, lost the sympathy of many critics, by seeming to reject the abstraction that made her reputation in favour of meticulous, some said populist, studies from nature. Her work from this period is rarely as simple as it seems however: empty of human life, it dwells obsessively on natural geometry and accidental arrangements and is often so bent on accuracy uncoloured by interpretation that it reveals – literally abstracts – the cold beauty beneath the natural scene. Ironically these trees stand just yards from the spot where she chose to be buried.

(From the collection of Judith Lamb)

Lizzy was talking to his father and Garfield knew straight away that it was bad news. Lizzy had a voice she only used with his parents and would become bright and twinkly as soon as she said hello, as though endeavouring to charm a child. Only this time she suddenly slumped against the fridge door saying,

'Oh no. When? I'll fetch Garfield . . . Well. Oh dear. Well of course I can. Yes.'

She had hung up before he left his chair. The air in the kitchen was thick with burnt toast fumes and the steam from drying laundry and the angry words she had been speaking when the telephone interrupted her. He made to open a window to ease the atmosphere but she was holding him now, pressing her face into his chest.

'I'm sorry I was horrible,' she mumbled to his shirt buttons.

'Tell me,' he said. 'Has she finally done it?'

'No,' she said, pulling back with a faint snort of laughter. 'After all that, she ended up having a heart attack like a normal person.'

She had never liked his mother, sensing Rachel found her too earthbound and honest. Sincere to a fault, Lizzy could not hide her excitement that Rachel had died and that she still lived, the only viable woman left in the family. She had won.

'When did it happen?' he asked, refusing to soften for her.

'This morning. He wanted to tell you but he got upset. I've never heard your dad cry before.'

'He doesn't cry easily,' he said, wondering if he could ever remember his father weeping. 'Why did he only call now?'

'I don't know. Too upset to do it before.'

'I'll go over.'

'Let me drive.'

'No. I'd . . . I think I'd rather go on my own.'

'Oh. OK.' He could tell he had hurt her. 'Don't be like this,' she added.

'Like what? How am I supposed to be? My mother's just died and my father takes all day to tell me. Sorry. I didn't mean to shout. Don't wait up, OK? I might have to stay over. There's nothing on tomorrow, is there?'

She glanced with him at the calendar.

'Nothing I can't cancel for you.'

He kissed her hair then, briefly, her lips. He was still

at a loss for how she could irritate him so much one minute then squeeze his heart the next.

'Later,' he said and grabbed his coat and keys.

In high tourist season the drive from their terrace in Falmouth to his parents' house in Penzance could take an hour and a half. But even outside the holiday seasons, when he could reach them in half the time, he saw less of them than when he had lived in London.

'Cuts both ways,' Lizzy would say. 'They see less of you too.'

But as the son, the onus to visit was surely on him. The burden of dutiful care and worry passed from parent to child a few years after that child left home. When Lizzy's father fell ill, it took little persuasion to convince Garfield they should move to Falmouth and first prop up then take on his violin workshop. Garfield was a skilled carpenter and enjoyed learning from his father-in-law. He and Lizzy had shared moral qualms about Garfield's work as a solicitor. But his covert reason for complying so readily with her suggestion was to be closer to the house he still thought of as home and to the couple he found himself worrying about during every Meeting.

So why did he see so little of them? The ill-concealed antipathy between Rachel and Lizzy was small excuse since he could always call over on his own and brave her mockery or disapproval later. In fact what he tended to do was drop by their house whenever work took him to St Ives or Penzance, so that he could honestly say he just happened to be passing, so that any emphasis on or expectations of the visit were diminished. No special meal had to be shopped for, as when Hedley drove down from town, no beds made up or rooms cleaned.

'I'm local now,' he told himself. 'I don't visit, I drop by.' But of course what he was doing was excusing his parents' lack of interest. They were always perfectly pleased to see him, at least Antony was. If it happened to be his father who opened the door he would always exclaim,

'Well look who it isn't!'

Garfield knew he meant nothing by this – it was just one of his habitual expressions, like asking 'What have we here?' when a plate of unfamiliar food was set before him – but the grudging older son in him couldn't help interpreting it as an implicit complaint that he had opened the door to find merely Garfield again and not one of his siblings.

The house lay in a Regency row of ice-cream-coloured houses one block back from the Penzance seafront. Sheltered and fertile, its long front garden was a lush, sculpture-dotted plantation of echiums, banana trees, furcraea and pseudopanax. Antony had replaced its old stone path with deep pea gravel because he liked visitors to make plenty of noise on approaching so as not to surprise him. Low-level lights, another innovation, clicked on as Garfield crunched his way to the door.

Surely it was odd, these days, for people to live in the same house all their lives? Yet this was where Antony had grown up, where he had brought Rachel when they were students and where Garfield and his siblings had been born. Garfield wondered, in a flush of guilt, if Antony would now expect them to move in and care for him the

45

way he had for his grandfather. It was unimaginable for him and Lizzy, Hedley was entirely too urban and as for Morwenna . . .

He found he could not dismiss the thought of his sister with his usual, hard-won mental shrug. Tonight the worry of her was more than usually persistent and he ran through a quick prayer that she was safe, that she was warm, that some uncharacteristic impulse might drive her to pick up a telephone or board a homeward bus.

The recent winds had tugged a rose branch free from its arch across the path. It snagged on Garfield's jersey, compelling him to take a step away to ease it free before twining it back to where it couldn't catch his father in the face.

The house looked small tonight, perhaps because Rachel hadn't left all the lights blazing. Garfield had been pulled up short by the realization that his mother would never again leave every light blazing, when the door opened.

'Oh I'm so glad it's you.'

Hedley was a sunbaked but still pretty version of their sister.

'Who else should it be?' Garfield asked, surprised to see him there so soon and thinking, *Morwenna. Wenn!*

'Oh God,' Hedley sighed. 'You know. Another of his adoring women with a bag of vegetable pasties or a thermos of nettle soup. The kitchen's heaving already. Can't think why I stopped to shop on the way down. You can buy everything in Penzance now anyway, even udon noodles, and Tregenza's have better tomatoes than we get in Holland Park and for half the price. I'm wittering.'

46

Ankle-deep in damp gravel, they hugged – another innovation – rubbing one another's backs. They had never been a family that touched. Something that at once amazed and appalled Lizzy, who insisted on kissing everyone she liked and quite a few people she didn't.

'He thought he'd rung you much earlier,' Hedley said, 'but then he said he'd left a message with a man and I pointed out your answering machine had Lizzy's voice on it. Which means he told some complete and untraceable stranger their mother's just died.' He was infallible at guessing and soothing the anxieties of others. In another life he might have made the perfect valet.

'How come he rang you?' Garfield couldn't keep the childish resentment from his voice, which made Hedley smile.

'He didn't. She did.'

'I don't understand.'

'She rang us last night. Really late – which she never does. Did. You know their nine-thirty rule. And she was ranting. Stuff about stones and beaches and Petroc and the "importance of the group". Then really paranoid, weirdo stuff about GBH and how she exerted a baleful influence on anyone who was trying to paint down here and how Wenn was cursed and . . . Oh God. I dunno. Mad stuff. I tried to ring Dad once she'd done but she hadn't hung up properly or she'd pulled the phone out of the wall or something. And of course he refuses to buy a mobile like any normal person and I couldn't sleep because she'd got me worrying.'

'You could have rung us.'

'I know. And I should. But I was due for a visit anyway

and, well, I drove through the night. She was dead when I got here.'

'Had he found her?'

'Yes. She'd spent the night in the loft. She's been working obsessively since the last show. She'd locked herself in but he broke in and found her and somehow . . .' Hedley broke off for a moment as impending tears distorted his voice. 'Sorry,' he squeaked and blew his nose. 'Sorry.' He took a deep breath then continued with a brave show of airiness. 'Yes, so somehow he'd managed to haul her down the loft stairs. I found him curled up with her on the landing.'

'Oh, Hed.'

'I know.'

'Where's she now?'

'Well I thought you'd want to . . .' He broke off and gulped and took a breath to control himself. '. . . say goodbye here so I've put off the Co-op until you're ready. She's on their bed. Happiness was never her forte but considering the state she must have been in she looks peaceful at least. Come on, Garfy. Come inside.'

At some point in the late Sixties, when their parents finally installed central heating in place of the solid-fuel Rayburn, they had removed most of the ground floor's internal walls or reduced them to piers or pillars so as to make a big, welcoming kitchen/dining/living area with a pair of sofas at one end and the kitchen sink below the rear window at the other. The décor had not been touched since so the sofas were still covered in chocolate-brown corduroy and the high ceiling was painted a burnt orange to match the swirly tiles around the cooking area. Bizarrely for such an artistically literate couple, they had acquired a matching toaster/kettle/breadbin set decorated with beige wheatsheaves which, by some miracle of careful use, was still in place.

Antony was at the kitchen table, hunched over the telephone and a list he was drawing up with the aid of a psychedelic address book even older than the kettle. The only light was coming from the smoked glass push-up-pull-down fitting over his head. As usual it was set too high for comfort and, as usual, Hedley played instinctive art director and tweaked it several inches nearer the tabletop to shed a kinder glow. Hedley had taken to admiring this light fitting as a design classic.

'Hello,' Garfield said. His father stirred.

'Well look who it isn't,' he said with a sad smile. 'Sorry about the phone muddle. It's . . . It's all a bit much.'

'I said I'd do that,' Hedley told him, glancing at the list.

'You stay put,' Garfield said, gently pressing his father back into his chair.

'Tea or something stronger?' Hedley asked. 'And there's food. God knows there's food. Just look at all this stuff. People are so kind.'

'Tea would be lovely, Hed, but I'll just go up and see her. Then I suppose we can call the . . .'

'Yes,' Hedley said and Garfield realized they had quite suddenly reached the age of talking code over their father's head as their parents used to do over theirs. 'If I tell them half an hour?'

'That'll be plenty. Back in a sec.'

Without thinking he climbed the stairs in darkness,

secure as a blind man in his boyhood home. Nothing would have moved. Like many Quakers, his father favoured simplicity so the house had never been cluttered with furniture. Even regarding what was hung on the walls or for how long – his mother's restless department – stasis had prevailed for a while. Garfield knew the feel of the banisters and every creak and sag of the uncarpeted stairs intimately. He knew he was passing under Rachel's Porthleven Series Seven and that the fiery bands of her Noon, Porthmeor loomed before him on the landing. He knew their childhood rooms – his, Morwenna's, Hedley and Petroc's – remained virtually unaltered. Hedley's old room still contained the infantilizing bunks he and Petroc had clung to through their teens and which their parents had clung to in their turn so that they had become at once a memorial and a reproach for the absence of grandchildren. Even the single beds were designed for children. Garfield knew that if he spent the night he would wake with cold, aching feet from sleeping with them dangling off the edge or neckache from sleeping with his head and shoulders hard against the headboard. At least abandoned childhood books and toys were not hoarded. Even when they were still children they were expected to conduct annual purges to help supply Quaker jumble sales.

The door to his parents' room was shut. Garfield reached for the light switch as he let himself in and the sudden glare created a momentary illusion of movement. Rachel lay on the bed, or rather his father and Hedley had laid her there. They had placed her on her side of the mattress, as though there were some chance of Antony wanting to climb in beside her still. Her hands were at her sides, her eyes were shut. She might have been asleep were it not for the slackness of her mouth and the atypical softness this lent her expression.

He reached for one of her hands but its coldness repelled him. There were bright streaks of paint on her fingers and nails and a dot of it in her ash-grey hair. That was right: she should go to her grave with paint on her since it had been her life and even lifesaver. But something was wrong. She looked wrong. He crouched on the floor beside her, staring. They hadn't suddenly put makeup on her or powdered her protuberant, shiny nose, so what was making her look so unlike herself: so kind even, and accommodating?

It was her hair, he realized. She had always worn her hair tied back off her face in a sort of silver ring with a pin jabbed through it. He had terrified Morwenna once by saying it was what held Rachel's face together and that only Antony was allowed to pull out the pin and see how she looked underneath. But now she lay there with her hair girlishly loose. He had never seen her without the clasp except on the beach so had no idea where she put it when she took it off to sleep. She had no dressing table. She was not that sort of woman. Her bedside table held the usual muddle of old newspapers, a half-empty glass of water and a chocolate biscuit with a neat record of her teeth where she had taken a bite before being distracted and using it as a bookmark. He looked in the small drawer where he remembered looking as a sugar-starved boy in search of cough sweets. There was the ladylike gold watch she never wore for long because she claimed the ticking got on her nerves and, all around it, in such absurd quantities they were almost spilling over the drawer's edges, were hundreds of pills, almost all the same size and innocent shade of white.

For a few years now, ever since her last bad patch, Antony had taken charge of her medication to ensure she neither skipped it nor overdosed. He certainly would not have known about this insane stash and it would have disturbed him. Forgetting about the hair clasp in his anxiety to spare his father further pain, Garfield set the watch aside then took the drawer to the bathroom and shook its contents into the lavatory. There were so many pills that, for a few ghastly moments, the water surged up to the lip of the bowl and began to slop over; then the blockage gave and the water lurched away with a sound like a wet cough, giving Garfield the sudden image of the bright bolus of strong medicine travelling down the soil pipe on the back of the house.

Back in the bedroom he replaced the watch in the drawer, where he found it looked somehow unconvincing and exposed. So he added a few things picked from around the room at random: a couple of paperbacks, one of her lipsticks, a few tissues. Raised to be incapable of deceit, doing this would have made him nervous even without his mother's corpse lying on the bed beside him. When he heard the stairs creaking he jumped up from the bedside and busied himself with closing the window so as to give the guilt time to leave his face.

It was Hedley with the undertakers. They'd brought a kind of zip-up stretcher with them, which they slid on to the bed beside Rachel.

'Her hair's wrong,' Garfield said. 'There was that clasp she always wore.'

'I couldn't find it,' Hedley said. 'Does it matter?'

'Maybe it's in the loft.'

'Anything you want for her – different clothes or shoes or keepsakes, or whatever – one of us can pick up in the next couple of days.' The undertaker's face was kind. He had seen this scene many times before: the stalling, the incipient panic, grown men wanting to cling to skirts and cry out but too muffled by dignity to do more than mutter about inconsequential mislaid items.

Garfield remembered the older undertaker. He had been to this house before. He was waiting respectfully for the brothers to leave the room, his stillness instructing his young assistant to do the same. Taking the hint, Garfield stepped out on to the landing. Hedley followed and, by some joint instinct, they went into their sister's room. An iron and ironing board were set out in there. An over-flowing basket of clean laundry rested on the bed.

'You could sleep in here,' Garfield began. 'I don't know why you –'

'I'm fine next door. I like it!' Hedley insisted. He pushed the laundry basket aside. He would probably come in here and sort it later. He was like that. Then he sat on the bed Morwenna hadn't slept in for years. Garfield drew the curtains then picked restlessly at things on the too-tidy desk – a ruler, a broken Penwith Pirates mug full of pens, a pile of dictionaries – where he remembered her swotting for her A Levels. The walls were hung with the huge charcoal drawings of the Merry Maidens she had made for a school art project. It was typical that she had

taken art classes just long enough to prove she was effortlessly able then given them up in search of something that
would challenge her.

'How do we let her know?' he asked.

'I was just going to ask you that. There might be an
obituary somewhere. Notice in *The Times*? She probably
doesn't read the papers but someone might who knows
her. Someone might tell her.'

Talk of Morwenna always led to talk of *someone* and
perhaps because she had withdrawn her life so far from
theirs they knew nothing and had few clues to guide them.
Garfield wondered, opening and shutting her school copy
of *Roget's Thesaurus*. 'Morwenna Middleton, Regent
Place, Penzance, Cornwall, England, The World, The Solar
System, Universe 84 (b).' The hackneyed classroom joke,
at once emphasizing and challenging her insignificance in
the cosmos, now mocked her brothers. They had no
address for her, not even an old one, no number they
could call. Garfield had long since given up on calling
friends since she had severed ties with them as completely
as she had with family.

'She's still alive, though.'

'Oh yes. She sold another of Rachel's birthday cards a
few months ago. I forgot to tell you.'

'Another one?' Garfield asked, hating the predictability
of the anger this roused in him. 'How many does she
have, for God's sake?'

There was a cough from on the landing. Hedley jumped
up, evading the issue as usual. The undertakers from the
Co-op were ready to leave. 'I'll show you out,' he told
them.

Garfield stood in his sister's doorway and watched the little procession head down to the hall. Hedley in front, acting as scout in case Antony emerged from the kitchen and saw the man and boy behind with the stretcher thing between them. It had ingenious rigid panels stitched into the black nylon that had folded up to create a kind of lightweight coffin. Presumably a harness kept her in place. He had been expecting and dreading a bodybag effect but between the four straight sides there was not even a tell-tale bulge to show which end her head was. Surely her head was at the back? Surely bodies always left a house feet first?

He came forward to keep her in view as Hedley held the front door open and said something to the under-takers about calling in tomorrow then he stepped back into the shadows before Hedley could glance up and shame him into rejoining their shattered father in the kitchen.

At the top of the loft steps was a finger-stained trap-door, now splintered at its outer edge where Antony had forced it in the night. Above the trapdoor lay a small room, barely ten foot square. The tongue-and-groove wall that followed the line of the roof's apex was punctured by a series of small doors into ingenious cupboards let into the void beyond. The other three walls were largely taken up with sliding sash windows, out of all propor-tion to the space, that gave views out across the bay and the promenade.

It had been Rachel's smaller studio. Her winter studio, she called it, although she made use of it all year round. She had a larger studio, a proper one with north-facing windows and no distracting views, in a stone lean-to at the end of the back yard. She loved the brilliance of the loft and its character even though the sunlight up there could be so bright it faded in days any work on paper she forgot to cover or tuck away in a cupboard. It was also a wildly impractical art space because the trapdoor and windows were the only way paintings could come in or out. Any canvas larger than two foot square had to be removed from its stretcher and rolled to come in or out and, once stretched, nothing larger than six by six would have been workable. Once the last of them had left home and there was less risk of noise or interruption she had worked up there more and more, retreating even from Antony's quiet, unobtrusive presence, locking the trapdoor behind her to paint for hours at a stretch. She always took a full kettle up there with her and, if she were hungry, snacked on biscuits and Cup a Soup. If she needed a piss, she used an old china potty which she would then empty through a window into a nearby gutter.

She had less strength in her arms than in vigorous youth and hated asking for help in stretching canvases. Besides, Antony had arthritic wrists so was not much stronger than she. So she had taken more and more to working on convenient whiteboards rarely larger than a biscuit tin, sometimes as small as a piece of toast. Garfield secretly preferred this smaller, tamer work. He found it more friendly and domestic but he knew it did not sell like the old stuff, or only to her few most loyal collectors.

Now, when he pushed open the trapdoor, he was startled by a cold draught. He groped for the light switch but the bulb had perished. As his eyes adjusted to the dark and the lights outside came to seem bright, he saw that one of the windows had been smashed, leaving a savage, cartoony star through which wet wind was gusting.

Stepping towards it he struck his foot on a table lamp that had been toppled to the floor. He stooped to turn it on and was shocked afresh at the squalor in which she liked to work. Floorboards, chair and table were lurid and lumpy with splashed or trodden-in paint. The not quite empty potty nestled against the kettle and an open packet of chocolate digestives. The lines had repeatedly blurred between what was for food, for artistic or personal use. A spoon brought up there for the eating of a yoghurt had lingered, unwashed, and been used to stir paint. The mouldy yoghurt pot now held a toothbrush clogged with dried-up Marvin medium. A comb, still carrying a few of his mother's hairs, had been used to spread one acrylic colour in furrows across another then been left to dry and serve whichever medium called it next – hair, paint or lifting out a teabag from scalding tea. She sat or crouched to work. When she sat it was in an old kitchen chair but there was an armchair too for occasional sprawling in, which she kept below the windows, facing her easel not the view. Two big pebbles lay on the armchair at the moment and two more on the floor behind it. There was a mark in the tongue-and-groove panelling where one had been hurled so it was not hard to deduce how the window above had been shattered.

He was moved to see she had been looking at an unfin- ished piece of her earlier work he had never seen, a big, near-perfect circle in a dazzling blue against which she had been experimenting with shades of grey when the work was abandoned. He wondered when she had done the piece. Certainly before Petroc. Since Petroc there had been nothing like this, nothing so energetically abstract.

He reached, shivering, behind the easel for a piece of hardboard that would cover the hole in the window. Sifting through the tangle of string, corks, picture wire and old felt tips in a Mint Choc Chip ice-cream carton from his boyhood, he found gaffer tape and scissors and set about making a temporary repair to keep the wind and rain out.

They were lucky with the weather. It was cold but sunny and dry. It was surprise enough that Rachel had bothered to make a will, more surprising yet that she had gone to such trouble to spell out how she wished them to dispose of her.

To the consternation of the undertakers she had insisted on a simple, biodegradable coffin made of recycled cardboard.

Lizzy was enthusiastic about this but Garfield could only worry about it turning prematurely pulpy in bad weather. Lizzy said she had once been to a funeral where the cardboard coffin had been lovingly painted and doodled on by the family the night before. Sure enough there was a second pained phone call from the undertakers to say the cardboard coffin looked well enough and was quite sturdy but that the instructions that came with it suggested asking the bereaved if they wished to decorate its plain surfaces to add a personal touch.

'You don't want to decorate it, do you, sir?'

'Erm. No,' Garfield said, alarmed. 'Certainly not.' And he took a unilateral decision not to offer the choice to the others.

Now that the coffin was being borne into the Friends' Meeting House however, he felt it looked woefully unadorned. Not even the Autumn Sheaf (assorted asters, maple leaves, some decorative seed heads) stopped the coffin looking like an outsized shoebox.

She rarely gave the environment a second thought. The only reason she had chosen this option was to have them express themselves all over her coffin. He was ashamed of his inhibitions and having connived with the undertaker's conservatism. Now what should have been grounds for exuberance merely looked like loveless economy.

Hedley could paint, of course, but he hated to fall short of perfection so took few risks. If Morwenna were there she would have understood exactly what was expected. She would have thrown a coffin-painting wake and had everyone leave their mark, however colourful or rude. She would have brought out glue and sequins and pots of coloured spangly dust. In the Hollywood version of this funeral he would find the courage to raid the box of crayons and paints in the Sunday School cupboard and hand them out right now, have everyone decorate the coffin as part of the ceremony. In the play of this funeral he would find the courage at least to stand up and speak of his shame and of how he would have painted the cardboard had he the nerve.

But Garfield had never spoken in Meeting in his life. He had often felt the prompting. Sitting in the silent circle he would find the urge to speak of joy or sorrow or of simple sudden understanding welling up in him and would even get as far as shifting his feet so they were planted firmly and evenly so he would stand with confidence. The same niggling inner voice that checked his hand above the paint box always sapped his resolve, however, by reminding him he must only speak if what he felt were true ministry and not merely a desire to hear his own voice or take issue with what an earlier speaker had said.

And Morwenna was not there. Garfield had not stopped hoping even now that she might appear, breathless, noisy and welcome. Knowing no friends who still saw her regularly, having no phone numbers or addresses not hopelessly out of date, they had placed announcements of the funeral in the *Guardian* and *The Times* adding *Please tell Morwenna* at the end. He kept up a show of being angry with her because it was easier that way. He *had* been angry when Hedley first found out about her selling the birthday cards – especially since it wasn't even her own she was selling – but now, if anyone had thought to challenge him, he would have admitted that he was more upset than angry, unhappy that she should be so desperate as to be reduced to selling something precious when she could have come to any of them for help. What anger he ever felt at her was really with himself for being unable to change the situation.

He nodded at people he knew. Lizzy was kissing, of course, Hedley and Antony were shaking hands. Then they all sat.

Penzance Meeting had no purpose-built house and currently met in a disused school from the era when a large room would be subdivided by screens and curtains for smaller classes then thrown open again for meals and assemblies. There was far more space than the Friends needed so they occupied one of the cosier subsections. The windows were placed high to avoid distracting children with views but they let in lots of light and birdsong from the surrounding streets and playground. There were the elements common to Meeting Houses the world over, the posters (for peace, for environmentalism), announcements of talks, concerts, prison and hospital visiting, the shelves of books and pamphlets. He was especially fond of this Meeting Room because of its strong, happy associations with kindergarten and school libraries. For some reason a potent silence was always especially achievable here in a way he did not often find in Falmouth.

Rachel's coffin was set upon trestles in the midst of their circle at the point where there was usually a small plain table with a faded Fifties tablecloth and a copy of *Quaker Faith and Practice*. The table was still there but moved to one side and, because this was a Meeting for Worship as well as a funeral, whoever it was who normally brought something to decorate the table had brought a clipping of a rose bush complete with glossy red hips, and set it on the table in a small glass vase.

Lizzy reached out for his hand and squeezed it briefly before settling into stillness. He glanced at her then at his father and across at Hedley, who was blowing his nose – no, crying. It struck him they had each sat not with each other but with a comforter. He had Lizzy, his father had Jack Trescothick, his oldest friend in the community, and Hedley had his partner, Oliver. He felt a pang of envy

61

at Hedley's tears. Hedley had always found his emotions easy to access, a shallow current safely dipped into then shaken off. Perhaps it was the source of his essential easeful blandness. He would rage or weep for a few minutes then move on, refreshed and untroubled. Garfield's feelings, by contrast, were a deep, forbidding pool, dark and unfathomable, stirred by sudden currents he could not control.

There were the usual sounds of a group of people settling: creaking of chairs, a squeak of a rubber sole on lino, a cough or two. Then the tick-ticking of the heater became the loudest sound in the room. He sought somewhere to rest his eyes that wasn't a person and let them come to rest on the cardboard coffin. Now that he looked at it properly it was rather fine in its simplicity and cool, off-white colour.

Someone, a woman, got to her feet then paused for a moment before speaking. Garfield recognized her but couldn't recollect her name.

'We are here to say goodbye to our dear Rachel, who was a regular attender since Antony first brought her to Penzance a little over forty years ago. For those of you who have never been to a Friends' Meeting before, this may not be the kind of funeral you're used to. The proceedings take the form of a Quaker Meeting for Worship. This is based on silent contemplation. There are two aims in our worship: to give thanks for the life that has been lived and to help those who mourn to feel a deep and comforting sense of divine presence within us. The silence may be broken by anyone, Quaker or not, who feels moved to speak, to pray or offer up a memory of Rachel.'

There was a pause while she sat and Jack stood, a copy of *Quaker Faith and Practice* in his hands. He cleared his throat and read, 'Accepting the fact of death, we are freed to live more fully.' He allowed a few seconds for that idea to sink in then turned to a place marked with a bookmark and read again. 'Quakers do have something very special to offer the dying and the bereaved, namely that we are at home in silence. Not only are we thoroughly used to it and unembarrassed by it but we know something about sharing it, encountering others in its depths and, above all, letting ourselves be used in it . . . You don't get over sorrow; you work your way right to the centre of it.'

Jack sat down and Garfield tried again to lose himself in contemplation of the coffin, and the fact that his mother was in it and that he would never see her again. Or hear her voice. He realized it was her distinctive, crackly voice with its strange, sporadically transatlantic accent he would miss most keenly. It was a voice that had often mocked him, that left nowhere to hide but which, by the same token, was utterly candid. Quakerly candid. A voice for letting you know there was no worse to come. A voice for spine-stiffening, for the be-a-man breaking of bad news, but also for the seductive invitation to break rules and say the unsayable.

When he was first old enough to join the adult Meetings and to sit in silence rather than be parked in Sunday School, she had quickly divined his horror that one or other of his parents might suddenly feel moved to speak. Once or twice she tormented him by clearing her throat and shifting in her chair as though about to stand then smiled wickedly as his eyes widened in horror. Antony was not amused. Usually, though, she was too involved for such teasing. She did not come every Sunday and elected to stay a lifelong attender rather than committing to membership. She always shied away from serious discussion of such matters yet something in Quakerism spoke to her: the lack of authoritative voices, perhaps, or the democracy. Most probably, given her unquiet soul, it was its ideal of stillness.

When he married Lizzy and Rachel was still disposed to like her, she said that she thought it a good faith in which to raise children. 'I like the way it manages to be mystical and no-nonsense at the same time – meditation in plain surroundings. It offers you the divine but it keeps it in a plain pine cupboard alongside the kettle and cookies and Band-Aids.'

He suspected that Quakers fell into two groups: the talkers and the silent. He knew that ministry was good, that it was good that anyone could feel moved by the spirit to share a revealed truth with the group but he still preferred the silence and regarded a Meeting where hardly anyone spoke as superior to those where no silence lasted more than five minutes. He knew he wasn't alone in this. Some of the older members, who never spoke, had let slip mutinous mutterings over coffee about earlier, less assertive times. They tended to blame Oprah.

He had sat in many different Meetings too so knew that some were far quieter than others. Talk encouraged talk. If no braver soul stood up initially, the timid ones were less likely to follow suit. The urge to minister went in cycles. Talky people would move away and, for a few blessed months, a Meeting would pull comforting silence back around itself.

Once he heard Rachel tell Petroc, 'Don't worry. I'll never speak in Meeting. I'm always afraid that if I stood and started speaking I'd never stop.' Which of course then made him even more afraid that one day she would break the silence and talk on and on about all the wildly disjointed thoughts that were occurring to her, on and on, for minute after excruciating minute, until people started openly to exchange unQuakerly looks or even to stare or to nudge him in the ribs and whisper,

'Can't you *do* something?'

By a small miracle nobody spoke until nearly forty minutes of her funeral had passed. He had worried there would be simple-minded praise or pointless reminiscence or even, more disturbingly, ministry that had nothing to do with the dead woman in their midst but that made some point by actively ignoring her. His mind was free to circle away from his grief into memories and fears and back to the grief again like a bird asserting its independence of a pool where its flock was drifting and feeding.

Just as he was starting to focus on the coffin again and the room and the people in the room and to think that perhaps it was sad that no one was speaking because it meant no one had loved or even liked her much, a woman he had never seen before stood up. He knew at once she was not a Quaker. She was not used to any of this but she had decided to speak because she had judged that it was important even though she had been steeling herself to it for forty minutes.

She was about his father's age, or maybe younger: late

sixties? Her coat and clothes did not fit her or go together. They looked secondhand. Her straight, grey hair was so badly cut he imagined her trimming it herself with random, spasmodic snips of a pair of kitchen scissors. She glanced fitfully about her and Garfield read and recognized the signals and knew, before she spoke, where she and Rachel had met. This was a woman who talked back to empty rooms.

Having stood and looked about her, she reached awkwardly down for a much-used plastic carrier bag.

'I got to know Rachel a long time ago when we were both in hospital, in St Lawrence's in fact. On the grid-iron. Huh! And it seemed unlikely either of us would reach our forties, never mind our sixties. I think I was more ill than she was. I mean she left before I did. But before she left she gave me this picture and it helped me and it always has and I think it says more about her lovely spirit than I can as I'm not – Huh! A very good talker. So. Erm.' She pulled off the plastic bag. 'Perhaps we could pass it round?'

She sat down abruptly, eyes bright now with mad daring and relief, and passed the small picture to the man on her left.

Nobody ever passed things around. It broke the silence in the wrong way, creating little currents of sociability and expectation. But Quakers forgive everything and, besides, it was a funeral so the uninitiated were an expected seasoning to the occasion.

Garfield too was expectant, concentration shot; a painting by his mother he had not seen before was a message from beyond the grave. He made rapid calculations as to the date it might have been done and what style she was working in then. He stared impatiently at the small, complacent smiles with which people were looking at it, then it arrived in Lizzy's hands and she placed it in his so they could look at it together.

It was small, perhaps eight inches by five, oil on board, and was almost entirely canary yellow except for a thin, uneven orange line that seemed to burn a horizon across its middle. The uninitiated might think it a painting she could have done in minutes with three or four large strokes of a paint-laden brush but he knew that it was made of layer upon layer of tiny strokes like the scales of a butterfly's iridescence and that the positioning and precise shade of the orange would have caused her agonies of indecision.

He had half-expected a daub of a kitten or a sunflower – a madhouse offering not even by her – but though unsigned, this was as recognizably hers as her own scarred wrists or thin, vulnerable neck, and it brought such a burning to his throat and eyes and a sense of loss to his heart that he could hardly bear to give it up; Lizzy had gently to prise it from his hands and pass it on for him.

He saw Oliver, who worked for Rachel's old Cork Street gallery, turning pale with desire as it approached him and made himself look up at the ceiling because he did not want to think about Hedley and Oliver or of money just now but of his mother.

And then, before the picture had quite completed its circle, Lizzy stood up, in that neat way she had, with her knees together, that made her seem to uncurl. Garfield didn't know where to look. Not at his father and brother certainly, but not at strangers either, for fear of watching their reactions. He was at once proud – 'This is my beautiful wife speaking!' – and aghast – 'This is *my* beautiful wife speaking!' much as parents must often feel when obliged to watch their children perform in public.

Lizzy was a Birthright Quaker like him and yet she claimed never to have spoken in Meeting. It was one of the things they first found they had in common. 'I think of it,' she said, 'but then the moment passes and it no longer seems right.' One of the jokes she had cracked a little too often for it to be funny any more was that there should be a neat phrase for the Quaker equivalent of *esprit de l'escalier*, for the ministry one thought of making but never quite made.

He decided to look, very hard, at his hands.

'Garfield and I have been trying to have a child for some time now,' she said and he clenched his fingers together in his lap. 'And I've been wondering whether one of the reasons it's taking us so long is fear that a child of ours might have the same mental health challenges as its grandmother. But – this sounds awful probably – but if a child of ours did have those challenges but could produce a painting like that, we'd have nothing to fear. We'd be blessed.'

She sat, less elegantly than she had stood because the chair had moved and she had to fumble for it. She laid a cool hand on Garfield's and smiled across at the woman who was now returning her precious painting to its carrier bag. 'Thank you for bringing us that,' she murmured.

The silent minutes that followed passed slowly. Garfield continued to stare at his hands, aware of the clicking of the stove and the ticking of the clock and of every sigh and breath around him. At last the woman who had started the Meeting glanced at the clock then shook her neighbour's hand and the ripple of greeting that ran round the room signalled the Meeting's end.

Everyone watched in silence as the undertakers carried the coffin out; then Antony followed them and Hedley and Garfield fell in behind as a pair, each spontaneously dropping their partner to walk together. Garfield felt he should apologize for Lizzy but found himself so clogged with unshed tears that he couldn't speak.

'I know,' Hedley said softly, his eyes as pink and small as a white rat's. 'I know.'

'You take your dad and Hedley,' Oliver said as they neared the cars. 'Lizzy can come with me.'

'Do you know the way?' Hedley asked him, blowing his nose.

'I do,' Lizzy said.

Garfield couldn't bear to look at her so stepped forward to hold open the passenger door for his father. Antony seemed to have shrunk and Garfield found himself instinctively reaching out in a policeman's gesture to prevent his father thumping his head on the door opening as he lowered himself in. He walked around, sat in the driver's seat and waited until Hedley had slipped into the rear.

'Could I have one of these?' Antony asked, holding up a tin of fruit-flavoured car sweets.

'Sure,' Garfield croaked. 'Good idea.'

They each took one. They were the old-fashioned kind, bathed in tangy icing sugar, and suddenly seemed the most refreshing thing in the world.

'I don't suppose many people are coming back afterwards,' Hedley said as they pulled out, 'but I put out
cake and tea things and whisky and sherry in case and
boiled a couple of kettles so they won't take too long to
boil again.'

This was nervous chat but Garfield could think of
nothing reassuring to say back so let it hang between them.

As they followed the hearse down Clarence Street, he
saw how Hedley reached out to give their father's shoulder
a little squeeze.

In keeping with her eco-friendly coffin, Rachel had
opted not for cremation, as had become the local norm,
but for non-denominational burial. A farmer a few miles
towards Land's End had used diversification grants to set
up both a pet crematorium and funeral service and a
multi-species burial ground so that humans might be
buried alongside their pets. His brochure boasted that he
had facilities to cremate any animal up to the size of a
carthorse and several horses had already been laid to rest
there with space reserved alongside them for their erst-
while riders. There were no headstones in the burial
ground. Instead each body or casket of ashes was laid to
rest beneath one's sapling of choice with no more permanent marker than a cardboard label tied to its trunk. The
idea was to found a new, organically spreading wood
instead of the inert space and straight lines of a tradi-
tional cemetery. Because so few mourners could bear to
settle for a quiet English native as their marker tree
however, the result was unlikely ever to seem natural in
the Penwith landscape. On their way from the parking
area to Rachel's grave they passed a few beeches and holly

trees but also flame-red acers and ironwoods, magnolias and sad, short monkey puzzles.

As Rachel's neighbour was to be an Irish Water Spaniel's swamp cypress, likely to spread with time, they had opted for something deciduous and columnar, a fastigiate English oak. It stood to one side of the waiting pit in the plastic pot which still bore the price tag and care label from the nursery that had raised it. Its long leaves had turned brown but showed no signs of falling yet. Apparently they would hold on, like a beech's, until the spring and only drop as their replacements came through. Garfield liked this idea and the way they would rustle together in the winter winds. Rachel liked a bit of noise.

Copying something he and Oliver had experienced at some friend's funeral, Hedley handed out pieces of rosemary or lavender from a basket as everyone arrived. The undertakers lowered the coffin into its hole then stood back as, following Antony's lead, the mourners tossed their fragrant sprigs in on top of it. It was less brutal than throwing handfuls of earth, Oliver had explained, made nobody muddy and left a nicely evocative scent on the hands for hours afterwards. It still felt as if they were starting the burial process though. And they were scarcely spared because they then had to stand about while a woman on a small mechanical digger pushed a mound of earth back over coffin and herbs with a brutally frank thump, so that the tree could be planted. She manoeuvred the tree out of its pot and into the hole and offered a spade to Antony in case he wanted to lend a symbolic hand but he seemed quite unmanned and merely shook his head with a brief, devastated smile.

71

People were embarrassed now, shorn of familiar form, feeling the want of a priest. Garfield stepped forward and accepted the spade instead. He tossed in one load of earth about the tree then another then carried on, heedless of the others, until it was completely planted.

'Sorry,' he told the woman, sweating now. 'Didn't want that digger going again.'

She looked frightened and took the spade back without a word. He turned away to find Lizzy had come up behind him. She took him in her arms and rocked him saying, 'There there.'

'I'm sorry,' she muttered as they turned to rejoin the rest. 'About back there.'

'That's OK,' he said. 'You spoke the truth.'

'Yes, but you're pissed off.'

'Let's not talk about it now, eh?' he said. He wanted to prolong her discomfort a little but of course she had apologized so any continuing bad feeling between them was now his fault. Never carrying the blame for long was a skill of hers.

She drove on the way back into Penzance, leaving him to ride in the back with Antony while Hedley and some carless Quakers were driven by Oliver. His father kept sighing as they drove so that Garfield was worried he was going to start crying. He wished he had some of Hedley's gift for soothing chat. Lizzy, too, was not one to say anything when she had nothing to say. It was one of their bonds. He could out-sulk her, but only just, and often gave in first only to find that she hadn't been sulking at all but merely silent.

When they arrived at the house, he realized Antony's

sighs had been suppressed speech, for the moment Lizzy was out of the driving seat and had shut the door his father seized the moment to say, 'Let's have a quick word alone, before you two head back to Falmouth tonight.'

'What, both of us?'

'Just you.'

Far more people had come back to the house than he could have predicted. Several of the women from the Meeting had taken swift command of the kitchen and tea-brewing, and extra cakes had materialized on alien china and been sliced. Far from feeling like an invasion, it was a relief. For an hour, maybe longer, the house was richly inhabited by people chatting, eating, washing up, gossiping, lapsing into tearfulness, offering comfort. All the things unsaid at the Funeral Meeting were free to bubble up now. Photographs of his mother he had never seen before were passed around. They showed her looking younger or different somehow, presenting her out of familiar context or with people he hadn't even known she knew. It was pleasant. It postponed silence and grimness. Even so it was too much for Garfield after a while and he seized his moment to commandeer the quieter of the two lavatories and stayed there longer than he needed to, reading, in an old *TLS*, a review of a book on the history of Byzantium so remote in its urgent preoccupation from his immediate concerns it was like calamine for the itching soul.

Jack Trescothick, the family GP as well as Antony's oldest friend, caught him as he came out.

'My old violin,' he said. 'Do you think you could find a buyer for it? It's a nice instrument. None of your Korean crap. I think it's French.'

73

'Sure,' Garfield said. 'Drop it off with Dad and I'll take a look next time I'm over. Maybe one of Lizzy's pupils is looking for one.'

'Thanks. Fingers getting too arthritic. And Garfield . . . What Lizzy was saying earlier about getting a child . . . Do you want tests?'

'We've had tests, thanks. The works. Nothing wrong with either of us.'

'Good. Just time, then.'

'Yes.'

'You know, inheritance is by no means certain. You turned out fine. And Hedley.' He failed to mention the other two.

'Lizzy's father suffered from depression,' Garfield explained, quietly because someone was passing them with a muted hello to use the lavatory. 'I think she worries about a sort of genetic build-up. What with Dad's mother too. Or I worry. We both do.'

'Nurture not nature, if you ask me. It'll be fine. You'll all be fine.'

Bracing talk was Jack Trescothick's speciality, as was a kind of pharmaceutical parsimony, and would always be offered first in case it could be accepted in lieu of pills. He boasted he had the fewest hypochondriacs on his books of any practice in West Penwith. 'If they can't get their sweeties, they go elsewhere,' he'd say. 'Either that or they pull themselves together.'

It was astonishing that a man apparently so unsympathetic and averse to prescribing should have proved so loyal and effective a doctor to Rachel over the years. And in a tragedy he was never slow to hand out sleeping pills.

The tea party, wake, whatever it was – half a joint of ham had appeared from somewhere, so perhaps it was supper now – lasted nearly three hours. Drifting from room to crowded room enduring an onslaught of every species of affection from sorrowful looks through hand-shakes to hugs, all of it buttered with talk, Garfield received an impression of the three of them – he, Hedley and their father – briefly upheld and protected by a loving concern that was ever so slightly stifling. The talk was to save them talking or, worse, weeping but it had some-thing of fear in it. They surely were not scared of his mother; however frightening she might have been on occa-sion, she was beyond scaring them now. So perhaps it was Morwenna's continuing absence that frightened them? Or Petroc's? Petroc's absence remained so raw and ugly and beyond consolation it had marked the family and left everyone a bit scared of them, even the most tranquil and frank of the Friends.

He overheard both Oliver and Lizzy being told in a friendly but firm manner to 'look after' them as though either partner might now be at risk of running away. At last, demonstrating his knack for nurture, Oliver began to prepare one of the healing, impromptu soups that were his speciality and the discreet scent of frying ginger and onions freed people to start leaving. As the last person left, Hedley thrust a glass of claret into everyone's hands and, helping Lizzy make toast, began a post-mortem as though it had been an ordinary party: who had said what, who had failed to come, who was wearing badly, whom he hadn't known. Where Lizzy or Oliver didn't know someone he would fill them in with an anecdotal explanation that dared them not to laugh. And soon there was laughter, and the smell of toast – so sour in his own kitchen the day she died – became cheering. How had he done it? How could one person so improve an atmosphere by force of will?

Watching them gossip and laugh, leaning against the dresser he knew by touch as well as he knew the small of his own back, Garfield caught Antony's eye and followed him out and up to the master bedroom.

Everyone had been flinging their coats and scarves on the bed where Rachel's body had lain and there was another woman's scent on the air, something sweet and floral and English. Garfield glanced at Rachel's bedside table drawer and thought guiltily of drugs and drains.

Antony was rifling through his sock drawer, carelessly spilling its contents. He produced an envelope, read its address to reassure himself then turned to face him.

'She wrote this for you,' he said.

For as long as Garfield could remember, their father had referred to their mother as *She*. Her personality was so large and pervasive that she was the first woman who sprang to mind at the word. None of them ever thought he meant Morwenna, not even Morwenna.

He began to hold out the envelope but as Garfield stepped forward to take it he held it back.

'She wrote it years ago,' he said. 'Just in case. I didn't want her to but she teased me about Friends telling the truth and she had a point. Then, when Lizzy said what she said I remembered it and thought you should, well . . . Here you go.'

He handed it over watchfully.

76

Her handwriting came as a shock. She wrote and read so little she could hardly have been said to have had a life in words. The written word was as little her medium as singing and it was always startling that someone with such a keen eye and such casually worn skills as a draughtsman should have such poor penmanship. Only her signature had confidence, because she had practised it so long and hard for her paintings it became an icon for her, a sort of pictogram for her personality. To the unfamiliar eye, the words on the envelope – Master Middleton – might have been written by a backward ten-year-old. *Master*. So she had written this when he was still a boy. Just in case.

Garfield tore open the envelope, whose glue had all but given out with age, pulled out a one-page letter and turned aside to read it, oppressed by his father's gaze.

What he read didn't make sense at first, partly because Oliver called up, 'Boys! Supper's ready!' when he was halfway down its single, spidery paragraph. He looked at his father for confirmation.

'It's true?'

Antony nodded. 'But I always thought of you as mine.'

'Did you know him?'

'Not to speak to. He was quite a bit older. He may not be alive still. There's no getting round what genes you might have inherited from Rachel but at least taking my mother out of the picture might improve the odds. Of course I can't answer for him and his family.' He nodded at the letter. There were footsteps on the stairs and Hedley's nervous cough. The smell of toast was all about them suddenly, driving off the stranger's scent.

'I'll go down,' Antony said, meaning to herd Hedley back into the kitchen. 'Let you digest it all.'

'No. Honestly,' Garfield began, meaning to say that it couldn't matter less, that it made no difference but he found Antony had gone and it mattered so much he had to sit in the tight little button-backed bedroom chair no one ever used and read the letter again.

It was dated 1960.

'My Garfield,' she had written. 'My darling, beautifully perfect. You're still a baby, only a few months old, so it's hard to imagine you reading this. I wasn't going to write anything but I've been thinking and thinking and, as always, I worry about it making me ill. I was ill for a bit again after you were born so coming back to myself to find you is so special. So I'm putting it on paper then at least it's down there and all I have to do is decide whether or not to tell Antony I've written it and whether or not we'll ever tell you. I hope I can tell you in person one day but this letter is a just-in-case. Your father, your biological one, isn't Antony. Before I met Antony I was involved with someone else. He's handsome and clever and for all I know quite rich but he was never going to marry me, whatever he said, and anyway he's married to someone else and I didn't want you born in a little circle of pain and guilt. Because you're going to be special! But you have a right to know who he is. (Antony's Quaker truthfulness is rubbing off on me!) So. For the record. His name is Simeon Shepherd (Professor).' She gave the man's address, in St John's Street, Oxford, and a phone number so short it looked antique.

Every time she had written *Antony*, Garfield noted, she

had begun to write *your* and crossed it out. *Antony*, not *your father* or *your daddy*. Was this, then, why they had always insisted on being Rachel and Antony instead of Mum and Dad, for all that their children complained that it singled them out among their friends? It wasn't, as they claimed, from a Quakerly preference of Christian names over titles or, as Antony had once suggested, to promote a democratic equality within the family. It was simply to avoid lying to a child.

Garfield thought at first she had broken off the letter with the name and address, making it less a letter than a memorandum. But as he folded it to return it to the envelope he saw she had concluded, briefly, on the paper's other side.

'Being currently of sound (ish) mind, your loving mother, Rachel Kelly.'

They didn't stay late after eating Oliver's soup. Yawning uncontrollably, Antony was plainly shattered and in need of sleep and Oliver, apologetically, was due back in London to prepare for an opening at his gallery the next day.

Something had made Garfield unwontedly horny, relief at the day's being done perhaps or even lingering irritation at Lizzy's speech at the funeral. She took it as therapy perhaps, or a burying of the hatchet, so responded warmly at first. But suddenly she yelped, which made him stop.

'Sorry,' she said, pulling away just enough to make him withdraw and the moment die. 'You were hurting me. Sorry.'

'Careful!' Rachel called but Petroc continued ahead of
her, scrambling heedlessly down the path that always gave
her vertigo if she looked anywhere but at her struggling
feet. In winter it became less path than cascade as springs
from the fields above found their ways into its narrow
channel and scoured it ever deeper. Now, in late summer,
it was a cascade of a different kind, its surface an unsteady
scree of dust and gravel punctuated by boulders at just
the angles to break a fall in the most painful way.

With their lower centres of gravity and skimpier
acquaintance with danger and pain, the children tended
to skip down it, darting from rock to rock or slithering
on their bottoms, as Petroc was doing now, laughing at
the way the gradient and beckoning beach tempted them
to start running and never stop. Garfield *had* started
running once and gashed his knee on a stone so that the
day had been ruined by him having to be taken to West
Cornwall hospital for a tetanus injection and stitches.

80

There were other beaches, more accessible, especially with small children, and just as beautiful but this remained her favourite and one she was jealous of sharing.

'Wait, I said!' she called out but he laughed at her, actually turned and laughed defiance, the scamp, before hurtling on down to the coast path and on to the stream and last rocky descent. Fighting dizziness, focusing on her inadequate espadrilles, she cursed as she slipped and stubbed a big toe. She paused, made herself look up and out at the glorious view to remind herself why she was doing this then followed him more sedately, picnic bag jouncing at her hip.

On his birthdays up till now she had simply claimed him as an excuse to snatch a day by herself somewhere he might enjoy. This was the first year he had really chosen, thought and chosen. That he had chosen to come here seemed a confirmation of the deep understanding she felt growing up between them.

With every other child there had been a sickening chasm after their birth, a blank of depression, worst with Garfield, from which she had slowly crawled to find a staring baby, ready-made as it were, thoroughly bonded with Antony and mildly suspicious of her. It was of her own doing. Her own wild indulgence. Jack had made her brutally aware of the facts by now: that the only way to avoid the depression was to avoid the withdrawal from medication she insisted on during pregnancy. But – and this she had told nobody, not even Jack – the glorious ascent before the fall and the work she could achieve in climbing made it worthwhile. Perhaps.

Yet with Petroc something had been different. Instead

of the sickening plunge there had come merely an intense interiority, a sense of her world narrowing down to a focus no larger than her baby's dimpled hand. She had barely spoken for weeks and the children had been so upset they had to be sent to stay with friends, but it hadn't been a full-blown, life-denying depression like the others.

He had been easy as a result, she was sure, so easy she had worried he might be slightly simple. He cried as any baby would, but he did not cry for long and was swiftly comforted. He did not fret and grizzle for hours on end as the others had, Hedley being the worst, but was content as soon as held so that she found she could keep him with her in the studio and work with him lying in the crook of her arm when he became restless, or strapped on her back in a papoose improvised from an old curtain and one of Antony's belts.

Her ability to use tide tables was erratic at best and this beach was far too insignificant in tourism or sailing terms to be detailed on them specifically so she had to extrapolate or, frankly, guess at a low-tide time some-where between the ones given for Marazion and Sennen Cove. Today they were in luck. The tide was out so far there were three caves laid bare for Petroc to explore and the sand was banked up in a smooth ramp from the surf.

By the time she began to clamber down over the boul-ders to reach the beach, steadying herself on the old tarry rope some kind soul had lashed to a metal ring there, Petroc was already racing far ahead, delighting in the patterns his feet were making on the virgin sand. The only other sign of life was the track where a seal had lolloped its way back into the water in the last hour or two.

Petroc was not a chatterbox like Hedley or Morwenna or strong and silent (for which read sulky) like Garfield. He talked if he felt like it but more often he was too self-contained to bother. In this he strongly resembled Antony, so that loving him was tied up in loving his father. Secretly he reminded her of the best kind of dog: amusing himself while always keeping half an eye on his owner. While he raced about at the water's edge she kicked off her espadrilles, which had never been the same since she mistakenly stood in a puddle at the fishmonger's in them. She crossed the beach to the first cave, where she changed swiftly into her bathing costume, and left the picnic in the shade to keep it cool. There was a stream which splashed down from the valley above even at this dry time of year. She slipped their bottle of apple juice into one of the pools it made, hoping to chill it.

One of the reasons this beach was special was the violent changes wrought on it from day to day and season to season. Sometimes the sand was heaped to one side, sometimes to the other. Sometimes the stream created a deep, winding gorge through the sand down which dogs and children delighted in slithering. Sometimes it carved a stealthy path feet beneath the beach surface and was undetectable until the point where it spilled out into the surf. Sometimes she would find the sand clean and pure, as she had today. At other times it would be laden with fascinating junk washed from passing ships – rubber shoe soles, plastic bottles, wrecked packing cases and once, to Garfield's and Hedley's delight, some yachtsman's ingenious heads cobbled together from a mahogany lavatory seat and an old dining chair.

For weeks on end the sand could all but disappear, visible only from the clifftop as a bank formed in the bay's broad mouth. This would expose instead the beach's rocky foundations, a mesmerizing, ankle-twisting layer of rounded boulders over a sloping granite shelf. When the sand went it was harder and less comfortable to go swimming but it had the advantage of putting off casual visitors and children. Provided one could find a broad enough boulder and had a thick enough towel to act as a cushion, it could still be a good place to muse and doze, the heat coming off the salty rocks, the stream gurgling somewhere beneath them.

'Are you coming in with me?' she asked Petroc. 'Birthday swim with your old mum?' She had persuaded him to wear his trunks instead of shorts because he could be prudish about changing in public, even in a cave. But he was content with what he was doing, attempting to divert or dam the stream by the insertion of rocks and weed bundles and merely shook his head with a fleeting smile.

She knew she should slap some sun cream on him – he had the vulnerably pale skin that went with his deep-red hair – but he hated her fussing and the sun wasn't hot yet. Besides, she had a shameful hankering to see him freckled. So she left him in peace and made herself stride into the waves, fighting the urge to cry out or flinch at the cold. She made herself dive, to get past the point where she might be tempted to run back out, and swam several strokes under water. When she emerged, gasping, she found herself in one of those mysteriously warmer patches created by the tides. She waved to Petroc, who was watching her anxiously, and he waved back. Then she lay on her back and kicked out for several more yards but the memory of swimming instruction at high school was too strong and soon she merely floated, staring up at the cliffs and sky and then out at a little plane towing a flag to advertise some attraction they would never see. Then she rolled on to her front and saw a seal watching her from only five yards away, close enough for her to hear the faint indignant snorts of its breath. She kept still, treading water, willing it to come closer although she suspected seals were not as benign as they looked. Suddenly there was another, much smaller one beside it, also watching her: a pup, perhaps, or simply a female? She glanced over her shoulder to the shore in the hope she might catch Petroc's attention without startling the seals but he was lost to his dam-building so she looked back and enjoyed a full minute's solitary communion with them before they slipped from view.

Numb from cold now, she swam back to shore and hurried up the beach to her towel. She had recently acquired a sort of beach robe, a blue towelling dressing gown with a voluminous hood. She couldn't bear to upgrade to a more matronly cut of swimming costume but the birth of four children had left her self-conscious of her increasingly pear-shaped figure and the veins on her thighs. She liked the garment, sensed it would improve as it became bleached and battered with age. She had offered to buy Petroc one as it would protect his skin and he would look adorable in it but he said no because it would look like a dress. He was probably right. She worried that boys could be turned homo with too much of the wrong kind of love but Jack had assured her it lay entirely beyond a mother's control.

She settled herself comfortably in the sand with her back against an especially flat bit of cliff. This was the risky side of the beach to lie because there were great rocks high above, barely contained in the turf and shale around them, but it caught the sun and gave the best view. She tugged her sketchpad and a pencil case out of the picnic bag and began drawing the archway the sea had hollowed out from the cliff on the beach's shady side.

It was an interesting shape but a challenge to capture with only a pencil and a few coloured crayons as it presented such extremes of light and shade. But then, working on the planes of water, the utterly still, dark pool in the sand beneath the arch and the dazzlingly white-shot blue of the open sea glimpsed beyond, she grasped an idea for a painting or a series of paintings. Layers of finely gradated colour could be built up in bands, like a stack of Pyrex saucers that had once held her fascinated in a hospital canteen. She abandoned the sketch then filled page after page with studies, leaning on her drawn-up knees.

She was faintly aware of time passing as she worked. Some people came to the beach with a dog and explored the caves, talking loudly about a bird they thought was roosting there, and passed on. Petroc padded around her and helped himself to sandwiches and a pork pie and tomatoes and some apple juice. At one point, when she had fallen back to staring at the arch in the cliff – seeing it yet not seeing it as the pictures formed and rearranged themselves on the canvas in her mind – a man walked into her vision and distracted her. He was impossibly tall, thin and old, perhaps seventy, like a Mervyn Peake illustration. She watched as he half-stripped until he had nothing on but his khaki trousers then darted like a wading bird in and out of the shallow surf, stamping his feet and stooping to catch the foam in his hands before anointing his face and neck and, strangest of all, the small of his back. She saw that Petroc, far up the beach among the high tide of pebbles, was watching too and she grinned at him. Then they watched the man stamp his feet dry on his jersey, dress and leave again, clambering back up the boulders and clay with surprising agility. His little visit had taken all of six or seven minutes, like a speeded-up re-enactment of childhood joy amid the mature pleasures of a long clifftop walk.

She began to draw a quick cartoony drawing of the man stamping in the surf but was distracted afresh by the light on the water and the entirely unwatery shapes she could see in it if she stared long enough, a kind of network of dish shapes and bending discs. Then she remembered that several of the crayons she was using were water soluble so she experimented with a corner of a handkerchief dipped in apple juice and rubbed selectively across what she had drawn. She was playing and she was working and she was entirely absorbed and happy.

Finally she broke off, when her inability to take the ideas further without paint and brushes was becoming a kind of pain, and remembered with a spasm of guilt that it was Petroc's birthday and that was why they were there together with no one else.

But he was fine, gathering and sorting stones into a collection a few feet from where she sat. He looked up, aware she was watching him.

'You're back,' he said.

'Yes,' she said. 'Sorry.'

'Do you want a pork pie?'

'Yes please!' She was ravenous, she realized, and thirsty. She drank the apple juice in her beaker, which had acquired the unmistakable sweet-wood taint of pencil and thanked him for the pork pie and tomato he brought her.

'You've done lots,' he said, looking at her pad while, unable to control herself, she briefly stroked his amazing-coloured hair.

'Yes,' she said. The sketches looked hopelessly scrappy but, with the cooler eye that followed inspiration, she could see there were enough details in them for her to recapture her ideas when she was back in the studio.

'Did you draw me a card?' he asked.

She paused. 'No,' she admitted because she couldn't lie to him. 'But you can have . . .'

'Can I have this one?' he asked eagerly. With unerring instinct he had singled out the most interesting of the ones she had blurred with apple juice.

'Of course,' she said, pleased. 'You have an eye, Petroc Middleton.'

'I have two,' he pointed out. 'You can write me something on it later.'

'Oh. All right. What are you doing there?'

'Sorting stones. I need six.'

'Show me.'

He gravely brought several pebbles to her side then

crouched to demonstrate. 'That's you,' he said, 'and that's Antony. And then Garfy, Hed and Wenn.'

'Why's she bigger than the boys?'

'Her head's so full.'

Hedley's stone was almost white, very smooth and neat and pleasing. Set upright and mounted in a block of polished wood, it could have passed for sculpture. Garfield's was black and thin, more like a length of pipe or a weapon. Antony's stone was bronze-coloured and broad.

'So we can all ride on him,' Petroc said.

Her own, she saw, was smaller than any of the others. It was black, like Garfield's, but shot through with other colours, dashes of white and pink and a kind of rust.

'It looks better when it's wet,' he said but she found herself returning, shocked, to the fact that he represented her with a stone so small and vulnerable beside those of her children.

'Look,' he said, slightly mischievously. 'I can put you in my pocket.'

'But where are you?'

'I can't decide.'

So she tucked the drawings safely in the bag where she found them the KitKats she had brought them, then they hunted for the stone that best caught the essence of Petroc.

It was one of the wonders of the beach, which nobody she knew had sufficient grounding in geology to explain for her, that the boulders and pebbles that lay beneath the sand and emerged, today, at the beach's highest point, all appeared to come from entirely different sources. Some intense heat, was it, or violent tumult within the earth there had brought forth stone of every shade? Garfield had once tried to catalogue them. Like some lost soul in the Greek underworld, he felt compelled to sort them into black, white, pink, white and black, grey and pink, grey with white streaks and bronzy yellow. The variety had defeated him as much as the lack of time between tides. He had been furious too, she remembered, that the pocket geology guide she had bought him seemed to offer no definite examples among its illustrations of any stone there.

The tide was mounting. All but one of the caves was below water. She found a stone that perfectly matched his hair but he dismissed that, perhaps as too literal. She found a lovely piece of deep blue sea glass, the colour of a Milk of Magnesia bottle, but he said it had to be stone or it wouldn't work.

'I hate to break up the party,' she said, 'but I need to get dressed again before the sea takes our things and you need to get home to birthday cake and sausages, which Antony will have had ready for an hour at least.'

He didn't protest or complain but merely kept looking and comparing and sorting as she slipped back into the cave and took a quick pee in the sand. She exchanged her robe and costume for sandy underwear, her poppy-print sun dress and smelly espadrilles.

'Found it!' he shouted.

'Well that's a relief. Let's see.'

It was the most ordinary stone imaginable, a sort of brown, earth shade with no shine and no variation in colour.

'Oh,' she said. 'Why's this you?'

'Feel,' he said and handed it to her.

It was far heavier than expected, like lead, and it fitted so exactly beneath one's clasped fingers it might have been moulded from wet clay. As the local men said when something fitted a purpose exactly, *Could've been made.* She smiled.

'See?' he asked.

'Of course.'

She had thought he would simply want to arrange the stones in the cave mouth or high on a boulder in the stream. Taught by the tedium of having to carry things home on walks, both she and Antony had long stressed the importance of leaving natural things where the children had found them *for others to enjoy.*

Petroc was insistent about bringing all six stones home however.

'They're too heavy,' she said, when the nature argument failed. 'That's a very long cliff we've got to climb and then there are all those fields to cross at the top. Why don't we put them here like this? We can build a lovely circle with them. Or . . . Or make a cairn, so people know to leave them alone for when you come back.'

But he was adamant. In fact he started to cry, which was alarming because he cried so rarely and had never been the tantrum-throwing sort, unlike Morwenna and Hedley, who were given to self-dramatization. 'You don't understand!' he shouted. 'We can't leave them because it's us!'

'Well put the smaller ones in my bag. But we can't take those big ones.'

'But they're Wenn and Antony!'

'They're just stones, Petroc. And I'm tired of this.'

With a look of thunder that would not have disgraced Garfield on a bad day, he took the two largest of the tribe, one under each skinny arm, and clambered over the boulders to the path. He couldn't always climb and hold them at the same time but had to lift them up ahead of him, climb a level to join them, then lift them up again.

Half-amused, half-curious, Rachel followed with the picnic bag over one shoulder and her feet smarting where the espadrilles, which were slightly tight anyway, were grinding sand into the sunburnt tops of her feet. The climb back up to the fields was far less dizzy-making or perilous than the scramble down but it was still slippery and arduous and her amusement turned to guilt as she watched him labouring up ahead of her with a stone under either arm. There was a big rock at the top of the climb where, by tradition, they tended to gather to catch their breath and admire the view. She took longer strides, so as to catch up with him and coax him into sitting with her. She insisted he surrender one of his stones so she could take it in her bag.

'Give me Antony,' she said. 'I'm married to him, after all.'

So all the stones came home with him.

She had thought he would introduce the rest of the family to them as he had her but he seemed oddly reticent when they reached the house, possibly because he felt he had made a childish fuss over something that didn't matter.

The stones started out on the windowsill of the room he shared with Hedley. They then migrated mysteriously to the bathroom, where one of them chipped the bath enamel. Finally they found their way, singly, up to the attic where she found a use for them as paperweights when she had the windows open. Except for Garfield, the one shaped like a pipe, which came in useful for squeezing the last dab of paint from a tube.

JUMBO JET STUDIES (1986). Ink on paper.

Kelly completed these obsessive studies of the view from the starboard side of a British Airways Boeing 747 during the only transatlantic crossing she ever made by air. This was for the one-woman show held for her in New York at Easter 1986 so triumphantly and yet, tragically, to so little purpose. Kelly hated even European flights. They frightened her and she found herself incapable of sleep in transit because, she claimed, she had convinced herself that the plane would fall from the sky if she let herself lose consciousness. Faced with the relatively long flight to New York, she occupied her mind by repeatedly making these highly finished ink drawings, complete with cross hatching worthy of Hogarth, of whatever she could see from the window beside her. The result is a modernist take on the experiments carried out by Monet at Rouen Cathedral; the essential architecture of window frame, wing and engines is unchanging from picture to picture yet the qualities of light, shadow and cloud pattern are the same in no two images. It was Kelly's idea to have the studies framed en masse like this, to suggest a stained-glass window. Interestingly nobody had noticed until the curating of this retrospective that one can tell, by comparing the nightfall and starlight pictures of the sequence with what is known of her travel arrangements, that she worked on the flight home as well as on the flight out. The assumption had always been that she was too heavily sedated on the flight home to speak, let alone to draw so beautifully.

(On loan from the Staatsgalerie, Stuttgart)

'You won't go wrecking the car, or anything?' Rachel said.

'It's hardly likely,' Hedley told her.

'No,' she said and he fancied she sounded disappointed. Antony finished stowing their suitcases and joined her at the open window. 'Wenn's got the gallery and apartment details,' he said. 'Just in case. Don't let her work too hard. Make her go for a walk or something.'

'I will.'

'And try to get Pet to revise a bit. His French oral's only weeks into term and his verbs are still feeble apparently.'

'Yes, sir.'

'Sorry.' Antony grinned. 'I can't believe we're actually going away.'

'Without us!' Hedley reminded him.

Rachel glanced at her watch. 'We're late,' she said.

Further down the platform the guard slammed a last stray door and jumped aboard as the stationmaster held up a flag and blew his whistle.

'No, you're not,' Hedley told her. 'Have a lovely time. Sell loads. When do you get there?'

'You'll have been sleeping for hours. I hope.' Antony held up a hand in farewell. Rachel had already gone to her seat without a backward glance. She hated travel, hated trains, and hated flying still more. She would be in a state until they arrived and Antony would need more than his usual saintly patience about him. Hedley hoped he had double-checked her packing behind her back. The last time they had attempted a family holiday, renting a cottage on the Gower Peninsula, she had accidentally on purpose forgotten to pack her lithium and didn't think to mention it until a week into their stay, by which time she was all but airborne and the rest of them were close to helping her off a cliff. They had to drive her to a hospital in Swansea for an emergency prescription.

Hedley waved back, leaning on the empty luggage trolley, aware of a handsome man seeing off family. He was on heat. It was pathetic. He made himself turn his back on the man and walk back to the car. Being nineteen and a virgin was sad enough without making a tit of himself into the bargain.

His gap year had been an utter failure so far, largely because of his dishonesty. Having secretly read three gay novels now, as well as dreary *Maurice*, all of them American, where he dreamed of going was New York or San Francisco. But the association with his fantasies was so close that to admit this would have been tantamount to admitting he wanted to travel for sex not culture. So he had taken a horrible job spooning filling into pasties on a bakery production line in St Just and spent his earnings on a trip to Florence and Rome instead, in the name of preparing for art school.

He had stayed in boisterously hetero youth hostels, where he was kept awake by groups of girls singing along to their guitars, walked around so many churches and galleries and museums that his feet bled and only found the courage actually to enter a gay bar rather than merely staring from a café across the street on his last night in the country. Two men had approached him within minutes, who might have been asking for lights or proposing marriage but he had been too scared and too lacking in informal Italian to do more than sort of snarl in response and drive them away.

He knew he was a man and should start acting and

thinking like one and would probably never lose his virginity until he did but he was so lacking in romantic role models that he tended to think of himself as a sort of sulky, Forster heroine, waiting to have her proud reserve shattered with a forthright kiss in a field of violets.

Now he was back, just as the Italian weather was improving, having failed to find a job out there because of his lack of Italian. And cowardice. He had landed a short-term job in the cinema which was an improvement on pasty-making, at least, but his romantic outlook remained bleak.

And now, by a keen irony, Antony had taken Rachel to New York, a trip about which the two of them had done little but complain since it was first arranged. Apparently it never occurred to them to ask him to come too.

The parking space near the house had been snatched by someone else so Hedley had to drive back to the seafront and leave the car there before walking up. Passing his driving test back in November had been the high point of his gap year to date. Not that he had a car of his own or anywhere particular he wanted to drive.

Their bedroom's curtains were still closed, puffing in and out of the open window in the breeze. Petroc had reached the age where he needed at least twelve hours' sleep a night in order to function. Judging from the crusty T-shirts under their bunks, Hedley suspected him of launching into short frenzies of masturbation whenever he found himself left alone up there. Maybe this was why he was so tired.

Morwenna was up, however, and already barricaded in by politics and philosophy revision at the far end of the kitchen table. She was cradling a big mug of tea and staring wanly at a propped-up file marked Hegel while her Marmite toast went cold.

'They get off OK?' she asked, not looking up.

'Uh-huh.'

'When are they back?'

'Not until Tuesday.'

'Fanfuckingtastic.'

'We can party every night.'

'Yeah. If you had any friends.'

The kettle boiled. He slung coffee into two mugs and filled them. Two sugars in Petroc's.

'Sorry,' she added. 'I can't talk until later. When are you at work?'

'One-thirty till nine,' he told her.

'Cool. We can do lunch.'

He stuffed a banana in the back pocket of his jeans and carried the coffees upstairs. Their room smelled like a cow byre. He twitched back one of the curtains, which brought a groan from the lower bunk.

'Here,' he said. 'Coffee. Absorb.'

Another groan.

'According to the plan on the kitchen noticeboard, you're doing French verbs this morning and *Twelfth Night* this afternoon.'

'Oh bugger.' Unlike the rest of them, Petroc had managed to grow up with a perfect local accent. He sat up just enough to sip the coffee without spilling it. 'You put sugar in this, Hed?'

'Two.'

'You stir them?'

'Course.'

'Better make it three tomorrow, then.'

Antony had claimed them an old partners' desk when the school common room was refitted so they had half each, although Petroc persisted in using his half for carpentry and making model ships and encroached on Hedley's for homework. No doubt he was readying himself for having the room to himself. His dark secret, so far shared only with Hedley, was that he planned to drop out of school after GCSEs to work for one of the boat-building firms in Falmouth. Carpentry and sailing were the only subjects that had ever stirred his interest.

There would be fireworks. Or perhaps not. Having seen three of them through school and off to university, Antony and Rachel would perhaps make an easy exception of Petroc. Rachel, certainly, would end by defending his decision against every attack. (When it suited her, she boasted about her lack of higher education.) Petroc, who so rarely did right, could do no wrong in her eyes.

Trained by her own self-discipline, Hedley took out a sketchbook from his art drawer and a couple of soft pencils and began to draw a pair of Petroc's discarded Y-fronts which had landed across a copy of *L'Immoraliste*, which he was struggling to read in the original. The hard rectangularity of the book made a nice contrast with the soft folds of the intimate fabric. You could read the pants' *Coq Sportif* waistband as clearly as the novel's title.

Rachel was angry when he had applied to art school. She said it was a complete waste of time, that she had never needed it, and that he could learn all he needed by attending life classes and would be better off apprenticing himself to a framer so as to save money later on. He shut her up by hinting that he found her sort of work old-fashioned and might prefer to learn about working with video or sound and light technologies.

'I could learn how to make installations,' he said.

This she pounced on as an even bigger waste of time before predicting that he would probably end up teaching potato printing in primary school. He knew he had to let her snarl, that his ambitions threatened her, but she wounded him. Secretly, of course, he wanted to be just such an 'old-fashioned' artist as she was, a painter, and so he did his daily drawings, like a dancer keeping limber, and was impatient and hungry for what his art masters would pass on to him. Robbed of New York, his fantasies were now coalescing around art school, fed by details Morwenna let slip about LSE and the bohemian romance of student life.

He had been feeling isolated by Rachel's scorn lately and was happy to have Morwenna home for a few weeks. At twenty-one, about to enter her final term, she remained far closer to him than she was to Garfield, who now lived and worked in London and seemed impossibly adult and distant. He still hadn't told her he was gay but he suspected he wouldn't need to, their solidarity ran so deep. It was odd. She loved Petroc more than she loved him but in the unquestioning, often maddened way a mother loved a son. Her closeness to Hedley was something she had chosen. She had long ago elected to ally herself with him rather than with Garfield, for which he was always grateful.

He loved Pet too, he supposed, but recently, especially since the abortive trip to Italy, he had detected a worrying shift in the balance of power between them. He always used to be protective of his little brother, looking out for him at school, sheltering him from the worst of Rachel's rages. But now Petroc was no longer so little – seeming inches taller than him on account of his untamed hair – and seemed to be becoming the protective one. Whereas Morwenna and Hedley had passed through school like alien children, cool and difficult and making few friends, Petroc was effortlessly social and always had little gangs of boys or girls calling round to take him shopping or surfing. (To 'play', Hedley teased him, covering his own inadequacy with envious mockery.)

It was curious that Rachel should so have favoured the one of them who was least like her, most like Antony. Antony had coped with marriage to Rachel, Hedley decided, by sustaining so many friendships outside it, through the Quakers and through the school where he taught. Hedley glanced at his father's busy diary with a kind of awe and could easily picture Petroc turning out the same way, refereeing six-a-side football, teaching carpentry, manning the Quaker peace stall or volunteering as a hospital visitor for patients with no family. These were all activities done for others rather than selfish pleasure and all generated and fostered friendships. Sometimes Hedley thought himself appallingly selfish and immoral – which was why he was currently ploughing his way through the works of Gide and Genet.

Of all of them, he was the only one to have dropped out of the Society of Friends. Admittedly he did so to get

101

confirmed and start going to St Mary's – duty of another, even parallel kind – but that had all gone sour when Father Joseph, always so sweet, lectured the church youth group about the dangerous sin of self-abuse and its toxic cousin, homosexuality. For two years now, Hedley's Sundays had been godless, a rebellion Antony, typically, disarmed with respectful silence. (And guilt at being left blissfully alone for a couple of hours every week had driven Hedley to learn to cook so that he could have lunch ready for them on their return.) Even Morwenna was still a practising Friend, though it would be interesting to see whether she and Petroc still chose to attend Meeting that Sunday without Rachel and Antony there to witness it.

As he drew on, Petroc noisily gulped the last of his coffee, slouched out of bed and went to pee, fulsomely and unsupported, in the bedroom sink, stretching and yawning as he did so. Hedley could not stop himself glancing at his brother's naked back view as Pet stooped to scrub his face with Clearasil.

He had never thought of him in a sexual light and still didn't but he admired his easy grace and the loose-limbed body that was emerging from his teenage chrysalis. He suspected that his romantic ideal would have something of Petroc's manly confidence and casual athleticism, suspected further that these were qualities rarely found in gay men and that he was thus doomed to loneliness.

He shot out a protective hand as Petroc made to snatch up the pants he was drawing. 'Get a clean pair,' he said.

'But they're my lucky ones.'

'Well, tough.'

'Bugger.'

Petroc mumbled in search of fresh underwear. It was a house law that Rachel did no laundry for anyone but herself but he had yet to master the art as Hedley tended both to clean their room and to harvest his brother's dirty clothes along with his own. Hence his acquaintance with the crusty T-shirts.

The doorbell rang. Morwenna answered it and called up, 'Petroc?' before returning to the kitchen. There was laughter on the stairs and a gang of three girls and a boy burst into the room just as Petroc was tugging on some jeans with nothing underneath.

'Rise and shine,' one of the girls said with a leer. She was Bettany Sampson, older than Petroc, whom Hedley remembered from school as a notorious slut. But then these reputations tended to be built on wounded male pride. She seemed nice enough and very keen on Petroc at the moment. She flopped on the lower bunk with one friend while the other girl climbed on the top one and the boy started flicking through their CD collection. Hedley shut his sketchbook quickly in his drawer, which he kept locked as it held his American novels, and retreated to the kitchen to plague Morwenna in turn.

The cinema prided itself on being one of the oldest purpose-built ones in continuous use in the country. Sadly it had been obliged to woo dwindling audiences by subdividing its original auditorium into three and so had lost much of its architectural charm.

Whoever was placed on the afternoon shift had to hoover the foyer and, superficially, all three studios. This

103

was Hedley's least favourite part of the job. With the house lights on to pick up the dirt patches and ice-cream wrappers, the rooms were particularly unlovely, their glamorous drapes revealed as cheap, their velvet seats as timeworn. There was a dreadful smell in the smallest studio that no amount of hoovering or fresh-air spray would remove, as though a dead animal had been tacked behind the stapled ruched fabric that masked the sound-proofing or someone had died during a screening and not been discovered until their bodily juices had soaked into one of the seats. The perk of the job – the chance to watch each new film for nothing – quickly palled and he doubted the place would retain any magic for him if he returned as a paying customer.

To his surprise, however, he discovered that he enjoyed the part of the job that involved dealing with the public. He had always thought himself shy and awkward, a typical schoolmaster's son, too well-spoken and obedient ever to fit in. Having a reason to speak to people, even if only to say, 'Enjoy the film,' or 'Small, medium or jumbo?' lent him confidence. People came there to be happy or to escape, which was infectious, and he found he wasn't trying to roughen his accent, the way he usually did, but presented himself as a sort of genial host or cheerful young priest. He had a role – a reason to speak – and saw that people responded if he was mildly flirtatious, perhaps because having the ticket counter between him and them cut him off at the waist and desexed him as effectively as a silly uniform would have done.

When there was a children's film on he enjoyed catching the eyes of exhausted mothers and teasing a smile out of them. The men were harder, unless they were on their own when they could be surprisingly talkative. If they were handsome, he liked being extra helpful, warning them to sit near the back if the film was very loud or reminding them there was a licensed bar upstairs if it was very long and had no interval. There was a wistfulness to his encounters with the handsome ones because it was in the nature of cinemas, unlike pubs and bakeries, that few customers could be described as regular and – pensioners aside – none was likely to return within a week or so.

It being the Easter holidays, there were two children's matinees showing the previous year's Disney cartoon, *The Black Cauldron* at one-thirty and *Young Sherlock Holmes* at two. Children always bought masses of sweets, drinks and ice-creams – the cinema's chief source of income he was sure – so the displays and fridges all had to be restocked after each intake. Then he had nothing to do until the teatime screenings but sit behind his counter selling an occasional advance ticket and watching shoppers on Causewayhead pass the window. He was meant to sell ice-creams out of this window, which could slide back, but the management offered nothing that couldn't be found more cheaply in the Co-op and it wasn't yet warm enough for ice-creams to appeal to anyone but a filmgoer. Besides, Hedley did little to encourage custom as he had encountered enough mannerless, sticky-coined brats for one afternoon. Because the window was small, people were too distracted by the film posters farther along the building to pay it much attention. No one thought to look in and he could stare with impunity.

A young man with a whippet on a rope appeared out of the crowd. He had on a suede sports jacket of a kind Hedley coveted and short hair, which was why it took him a second or two to recognize him as Troy Youngs. The last time he'd seen him, Troy still had big, New Romantic hair because he was emulating Simon le Bon on a tight budget. The new look was a great improvement. He tapped on the glass and Hedley slid the window back.

'All right?'

'Troy! How are you? Good jacket.' Hedley was in work mode and forgot to blunt his enthusiasm and Troy was a bit startled.

'What? Oh. Thanks. Yeah, well, Wenn said you'd be here.'

Morwenna had a longstanding thing going with Troy's even dodgier younger brother, Spencer. Never quite a relationship, never allowed utterly to peter out, it had its roots in her late teenage rebellion. He regarded her as posh arm-candy, something to set off his latest motor, she regarded him as a source of uncomplicated fun. She claimed he liked it that she had no romantic expectations but Hedley suspected the truth was that Spencer thought she was easy.

'So how's Kirsty? How's grown-up married life?'

'Didn't work out,' Troy said. 'Didn't happen, did it?'

'Oh. I'm sorry.'

'Yeah. Well. Women, Hed. What can you do? We're having a bit of a party tomorrow night.'

'Yeah?'

'D'you fancy coming? Spencer asked Wenn and she said you were still around so . . .'

'Yeah. Sure.' Hedley remembered to be cool and not to ask what time and should he bring a bottle.

'Cool.' Troy didn't smile. He never smiled. Not smiling was his thing. 'See you then.'

'Yeah. See you.'

Hedley shut the window. The cartoon, adverts and trailers were done for the two o'clock screening and the feature had started so Candy, the usherette, had returned to the foyer where she liked to perch on a stool, watch the passers-by and smoke, if the owner wasn't around to see her.

'Who was that?' she asked. She hardly ever bothered speaking to him, having decided he was too stuck-up or too young or too gay to be worth noticing.

'Troy Youngs,' he said.

'What? Spencer's brother?'

'That's right.'

'You known him long?'

'Since we were kids. We were at school together. They give good parties.' He felt himself rise a notch or two in Candy's estimation and set about polishing the chrome ticket dispenser, enjoying giving her no more information and ignoring her for once. She had a mean little mouth like a rat trap and a prim way of stubbing out her cigarettes that implied she felt smoking Lambert & Butlers made her more interesting. Petroc, who was a mine of lowlife gossip because he had friends on the Treneere estate, said she had three children by three different men and was a notorious slapper in both senses.

Hedley wished he could ring Morwenna to gossip but he knew he couldn't without being more honest than he felt ready to be. Besides, the phone was set up for incoming calls only, which went straight through to an answering machine that enthused at tedious length through the week's programmes. Then he remembered that Morwenna had set Troy up to ask him in person, when she could simply have passed on the invitation herself. Perhaps this was confirmation that she knew more than she was letting on.

She had started hanging around – she scorned to call it *going out* – with Spencer Youngs in her idle months before going up to LSE, when she was eighteen to Hedley's sixteen. Usually he had picked her up in his car and taken her back to his father's rundown farm but occasionally he had come into the house, every inch the unwelcome bad boy, and spent an hour or two in Morwenna's room, where they played their music so loud Rachel would start thumping on the attic floor or would storm out to the studio or to visit Jack, raging that if Morwenna got pregnant and ended up on the Treneere estate instead of going to LSE, that was her affair.

There was no fireplace in Morwenna's room so they'd invade Petroc's and Hedley's so as to smoke joints up the chimney. Spencer decided Hedley was cool because of this and got Morwenna to bring him with her to the next party at Bosviggan, which involved horrendously risky lies about visiting perfectly innocent friends who were actually on holiday in Brittany.

Which was how Hedley got to know Troy, who had actually left the school long before Hedley was old enough to notice him. Spencer's big brother, an impressive five years older than Hedley, was thin where Spencer was stocky, and had rusty blond hair, prominent cheekbones and a mouth like a line. He smiled so rarely that it was rumoured his teeth were as crooked as his hero's, David Bowie. Despite the Duran Duran hair he was cultivating at the time, he looked like a sexy ferret. With astonishing bravery, possibly born of his Bowie fixation, he had let it be known he was bisexual. There was never any proof of this, nothing with a pulse, but there were no steady girlfriends either so the revelation, or rumour, effectively lent him a tantalizing odour of sophistication that went some way towards counteracting the squalid, borderline poverty in which the Youngs lived.

You couldn't say Troy singled him out – he would never have done something so obvious – but Hedley rarely went to Bosviggan without Troy finding a minute or two alone with him, longer if people were drinking and inattentive. In his cool, interested-but-not-really way, he drew Hedley out and found out about him, about how he was different from his brothers but not precisely why. They talked about the pressures of family expectations, of the lack of privacy and of where they'd rather live than Penzance.

It was Troy who, casually, and saying, 'Don't bother to give it back as I won't read it again,' passed him a battered copy of *Dancer from the Dance*, which he claimed a *bloke on a train* had given him.

It was gay. Completely, undeniably, lock-it-in-a-drawer gay.

Hedley would have been hard-pressed to summarize the plot even when the book was fresh in his mind, as it seemed to be nearly all parties and nightclubs, but it conjured up another world, a drug-fuelled, hedonistic subworld of New York where a shifting crowd of men fell in lust and danced and wore wonderful clothes and occasionally fell deeply in love. It could have been designed to instil a yearning for big city life in provincial closet-cases too timid even to land a kitchen porter's job in an Italian hotel. And probably was.

Because of the terrible holiday on the Gower Peninsula, he didn't have a chance to talk to Troy about the book for weeks and when he did, Troy was maddeningly vague and unfocused beyond dismissing it with a shrug and saying, 'Yeah, well, but it was all a bit gay, wasn't it?' So that Hedley wondered if perhaps he was astonishingly stupid and had read the book with little understanding and passed it on with even less of the significance the gesture might have had.

But then, because Morwenna was off sofa-surfing with Spencer somewhere and wasn't around to see, he accepted some girl's offer of a toke on her joint one night, found after a few stoned minutes that the girl had wandered off to dance and been replaced by Troy, and it all came splurging out.

With hindsight this was probably exactly how Troy's being bisexual had become such an open secret. They had not talked for long, because the police turned up soon afterwards to complain about the noise and Morwenna had insisted they leave but Hedley had said enough to wake worrying that Troy would now tell the world. Or at least Spencer, who would tell Morwenna.

Nothing was said, however, and when he was next up there he found Troy was now all questions. So what was it like, actually being gay? How did it feel? What was he going to do about it, since he wasn't, you know, just bisexual like Troy? They were questions that struck to the heart of Hedley's teenage frustration and insecurity.

But then, once he was drunk enough to deny all knowledge later, Troy said, 'You could kiss me. If you like. Just to see how it feels, you know?' And they had gone out, minutes apart, to the biggest of the empty barns, stumbling on God knows what in the darkness, and kissed and kissed. No talking, no groping – Hedley didn't dare without encouragement – just kissing. Then some people had come out into the yard from the house and Troy had got nervous and slipped away.

It happened three times more, again in the barn, now with no more preamble from Troy than a muttered, 'You . . . you know?' and a minute inclination of his sexy ferret face towards the back door.

Hedley would go home, walking as often as not, cheeks on fire from Troy's stubble, more worried that he reeked of Troy's Blue Stratos than that anyone might smell dope or beer on him, but exhilarated in a way that had nothing to do with the man he had been kissing and everything to do with the possibilities of a future that seemed a little bit nearer.

Then Morwenna had gone up to LSE and Antony, in a hideously embarrassing little exchange on the stairs, said, 'I don't want you spending time up at Bosviggan any more without Wenn to keep an eye on you.'

And a few days later, Petroc let slip as they walked to school that Kirsty Spiers, the big sister of one of his mates, had got engaged to Troy Youngs and how her family were dead against it as they had hopes for her but it was going to happen anyway. And then Morwenna had decided she was in love with someone in London and had hardly come home at all for a while.

The audience from the one o'clock screening came out, bringing with it a great gust of pent-up sugar and excitement and stale air scented with artificial fruit. Hedley smiled blandly in case anyone looked his way while Candy sat on, legs twined tightly around her stool as though it was rats not children surging past her. She then smacked on a single rubber glove and slipped off to walk around the studio just emptied and throw the worst of the litter into a bin liner. Hedley followed the last of the children out and propped the doors open to draw in some fresh air off the street then retreated behind his counter. Candy came back to the foyer, slung her half-full bin liner into a cavity behind the freezer then stood just outside the doors where she smoked a cigarette, watching the late shoppers with alternating expressions of scorn and blank incuriosity that showed exactly how she must have looked at Petroc's age, three children and three fathers ago. She squished the butt with a neat swivel of a toe then resumed her station on her stool.

She affected to read the Film Society brochure then asked him lightly, 'So Troy Youngs, right?'

'Yes?'

'Is it true he's AC/DC?'

'It's what they used to say,' Hedley told her. 'But it's a pack of lies.'

'Really?' She perked up and unconsciously touched her hair. 'You know that for a fact? Because a friend of mine's quite interested in him.'

'He's gay,' Hedley told her. 'Now that is. Totally gay. Kirsty Spiers broke off with him because he wouldn't, you know, satisfy her.'

'Oh,' she said, comically deflated.

'Still,' he breezed as the first group arrived for the teatime screening of *Pretty in Pink*, 'one girl's loss'll be some boy's happy day.'

MING FROG BOWL (1960). Oil on board.

Dating from the early years of Kelly's marriage, when economy forced her to recycle her materials, this tiny painting is worked on the back of a larger work (artist unknown) which she sawed into pieces. Bowl with Greengages (1960) and Milk Bottle with Corn Cockles (1960) were painted on other fragments of the same work. It shows the interior of an Early Wanli dish, dating from around 1580, showing a toad – not a frog – sitting amidst plants and on a cloud of what may be toad spawn. Such porcelain dishes were made in the late Ming era for export to the Japanese market. Utterly unlike her later work, it displays a precocious academic flair. Careful examination of the light reflections on her bowl's surface reveals the distorted representation of a couple standing between the bowl and a nearby sash window. Perhaps Ming Frog Bowl represents a tentative step towards painting of obvious commercial and decorative appeal. Kelly certainly retained a sneaking admiration for the exquisite still lives of William Nicholson at a period when they were quite out of fashion compared to the abstracts of his son, Ben and this work could be read as a homage to his. Kelly is not known ever to have possessed or had access to such a valuable ceramic so it is assumed she worked either from a postcard or from memory. A remarkably similar bowl formed part of Oxford's Ashmolean collections until it was accidentally broken in 1970.

(Lent by the Warden and Fellows of
Christchurch College, Oxford)

They had exchanged letters. Garfield wrote to Simeon Sheperd initially, attaching a photocopy of Rachel's letter, explaining that Rachel had recently died and that he desired nothing but to meet.

'I quite understand how awkward this will be for you,' he wrote. 'And that you may wish to have nothing to do with me. I feel sure you are as curious as I am, though. I know you probably have family and will perhaps prefer not to introduce me to them or in any way alert them to my existence.' As an afterthought he enclosed a fairly recent photograph Lizzy had taken of him when they were out on a friend's boat. It revealed little about him, of course, other than that he was in his forties, capable of smiling, possessed of good teeth and all his hair, but he hoped it might make the receipt of the letter less alarming, stop it, at least, from seeming the work of a crank.

A card came back almost at once. It was of some porcelain in the Ashmolean.

'My father is beyond correspondence these days,' she wrote. 'And is probably too confused to understand who you are. You are welcome to come and look at him whenever you like. We never leave home but the late afternoons are best, between four and six o'clock. Yours sincerely, Niobe Shepherd.'

It seemed to be the only house in St John's Street that had not been restored and cosseted in recent memory. Garfield had researched Simeon Shepherd on the Internet and found that he was an art historian who had published no articles for twenty years and no books for thirty. He had found a copy of his monograph relating Uccello to an Iranian artist of the same period and had tried to read it on the train but, with baffling assumption of knowledge, it had no illustrations and seemed to be more footnote than text. What he had learnt led him to expect

115

severity and elegance. This house must once have had both but now looked down-at-heel, even shifty. Its tarnished brass knocker was of an odd, possibly Masonic design, a kind of triangle suspended from an eye. The rust-coloured paint was flaking so badly from the door he could see patches of bare, blackened wood. He knocked too vigorously and a large paint flake fluttered to the ground.

A sharp-nosed, middle-aged woman opened the door, took one look at him and exclaimed, 'Christ! Sorry. That was a shock even after the photograph. You'd better come in.'

'Thanks.' He stepped into the gloomy hall. It smelled of gas and damp and he noticed the woman was wearing two cardigans.

She gave a quick smile that revealed nothing. 'I'm Niobe Shepherd,' she said. 'My father's upstairs.'

His half-sister. And she said *my father* not *our* or *your*. Garfield's mind was working so hard at missing nothing he found it hard to speak.

'I'd keep your coat on,' she said. 'The boiler's packed up again and he's got the only fire. I've just made tea. Do you want a cup?'

'Yes, please.'

He followed her into the kitchen. It was like an advertisement from 1952 and did not appear to have been redecorated since then. There was a sour, lemon colour on the walls. The torn curtains were decorated with a frenzied 'kitchen' pattern of spice jars and bay trees. There was the kind of gas cooker that lit with a wand on a greasy hose and, beside it, slope-fronted cupboards with

116

striped glass doors that slid in unclearable crumb-clogged grooves. A saucer on the floor held a half-eaten sardine, another, some yellowing milk. An enormous, off-white cat glared from discomfitingly yellow eyes on a blanket-covered chair in the corner.

The table was barely visible beneath a thick typescript and an array of open shoeboxes filled with little cards. He picked a stray one off his chair in order to sit down. In a tiny version of her handwriting it read, *Slater, Montagu* and gave a list of page numbers.

She took it from him with a muted, 'I knew I hadn't lost that,' and tucked it into one of the boxes then poured him a mug of tea. 'Is it very tarry?' she asked.

It was tepid. 'It's fine,' he assured her. 'It'll wake me up.'

She sat across from him and ferreted out a packet of gingernuts from under the pages of typescript she had already turned. 'Indexing,' she explained. 'It means I can work from home and save paying someone else to be here.'

'Oh. I see. Interesting.'

'Not very. Dull books are easier on the whole. If they send one that threatens to be interesting I have to read it backwards to avoid getting too drawn in to do the job properly. I should computerise but I can't face it.' She stared at him again and laughed shortly. 'You do look amazingly like him.'

'Really? Don't you?'

'Not at all. I take after my mother.'

'Is she . . . ?'

She shook her head and dunked a biscuit. 'She died

years ago. She coughed nervously. 'He was always very independent, luckily. Until fairly recently.'

'Ah.'

They both drank their nasty tea.

'You probably want to see him now,' she said abruptly just as he burst out with, 'My letter must have been a shock.'

They each apologized and made *no, after you* gestures then she said, 'Not greatly. You're not the first.'

'Really?'

'He seems to have been both extraordinarily fertile,' she said, 'and careless.'

Was this his voice in her? This cool, drily amused superiority?

'We have two half-brothers,' she added. 'That I know about, that is. The others are both younger than you. Both American. He did several lecture series there after my mother died. I was boarding and it paid handsomely compared to what he made here. They don't look like him like you do. But there's an interesting pattern emerging. Your mothers all kept a secret until they died and you've all said you don't want anything. Which is lucky, given that there's so little to be had. This is rented.' Her economical gesture took in the house about them. 'In case you were wondering.'

'I wasn't.'

'We have it on a long and intractable lease. His attendance allowance and disability benefit help and the council and university do their bits.'

'What's wrong with him?'

She sighed, stacking index cards into neat piles and, as

she bent her head forward, he noticed a bald patch on her scalp, perhaps four inches across. She had attempted to disguise it by growing the rest of her hair long and pinning it across in an artful disarray but as she fretted and rubbed at it, the habitual gesture she made now, the artifice was steadily pulled aside.

'He had a stroke,' she said. 'At first that was all and he lost most of his speech. Then he had another one and lost the use of his right leg. Now I think it's just advanced crumble and multi-infarct thingy. I used to be able to understand what he was saying but most of the time now it doesn't make sense. And he's stopped reading or writing, which is a bad sign.'

'Did he meet the others?'

'Oh yes. He had quite long talks with both of them and was signally unimpressed. You'll have a much easier time of it. Shall we go up?'

Was there some mischievous pleasure for her in all this? Some grim amusement to be had at this futile hunger in her male half-relatives for a meaningful connection to an absent and faithless father? The cat jumped off its chair with a malevolent growl and led the way upstairs. As they climbed past dim etchings Garfield could barely decipher in the half-light, the sounds of a television drew closer.

Simeon Shepherd's room was stifling after the tomb-like chill downstairs. An oscillating fan heater was competing with a Western. The old man in the wheel-chair was asleep, his head to one side. He had thick, white hair and sharper versions of Garfield's features. Now it was Garfield's turn to swear under his breath.

Niobe looked from one to the other. 'Sinister, isn't it?' she said. 'Like the last scene of that stupid Kubrick film. He'll turn into an embryo next. Pa? Pa!' She gave her father a vigorous shake. 'Bit deaf too,' she explained to Garfield. 'Sit. Please.' She muted the volume on the television.

Her father, their father, was looking around him and blinking as deliberately as an owl.

'This is Garfield Middleton, Pa. His late mother was another of your girlfriends.'

Simeon Shepherd seemed to focus on Garfield a moment or two then murmured something indistinct.

'I'm so sorry,' she said. 'I've forgotten your mother's name.'

'Rachel Kelly,' Garfield said.

'The painter?'

'Yes. I thought I'd told you.'

'Good lord. He should have married her and made some money that way. Silly fool. Rachel Kelly, Pa! The abstract painter! You know? Cornwall! Patrick Heron!'

He made another gargling sound and looked quite definitely at Garfield now.

'Ah,' she said. '*That* got through. He hates abstract art with a passion. I'll leave you two to get acquainted.'

'Oh, but . . .' Garfield thought to ask her to stay and interpret but she was too brisk.

'You can't stay long,' she said. 'He has the concentration span of a gnat and he'll probably fall asleep again in a bit. I'll be back in the kitchen.'

She left them alone with the cat, which leapt on to the old man's lap where it seemed to double in size as it reached almost to his chin. Garfield had been wondering how such a thin, bookish-looking woman found the strength to haul her father in and out of bed and bath but he saw now the man was even slighter than she was, a human husk. There was a kind of winch contraption over the bed and, presumably, similar machinery in the bathroom.

The old man was still staring at him, stroking the cat as a reflex.

'Hello,' Garfield said. 'My mother died a couple of months ago. She'd written me a letter that explained you were my father, otherwise I'd never have known . . .' He heard this explanation tail off foolishly. Abashed, he looked about the room.

The paintwork and carpet were as threadbare as else-where but there were things of beauty in here; a small Flemish painting of a young woman hung over the fire-place and there was a gilt-framed landscape behind the sofa of an avenue of poplars that looked French. They went badly together but perhaps represented the only things of worth father and daughter had not yet been obliged to sell. He hoped at least one of them would survive for Niobe. In their brief, strange interview he had begun to feel affec-tion for her. He glanced at the television.

'*The Searchers*, isn't it?' he asked. 'I like Westerns too. Ford's almost like a painter, isn't he, the way he gets his cameraman to draw the beauty out of those landscapes? He composes them and makes you look.'

Still the stare.

'I wonder if you ever saw any of my mother's paint-ings? Rachel Kelly? Was she painting yet when you . . .

knew her? They were amazing. She lost her way a bit after my . . . The earlier ones, the ones from the Seventies, I think they'll stand up for themselves for a while yet. I live in Falmouth,' he added. 'With my wife Elizabeth. Lizzy. She's a violin teacher and I mend violins. Well any stringed instrument. I had to rebuild a double bass last year after someone put a foot through one. That was a challenge! I didn't always do this. I was working as a solicitor. In London. But so many of the clients were crooks and . . . My wife . . . It wasn't right somehow and then I helped out in her father's violin workshop and he taught me before he died and it sort of happened. I read your last book. Well, I did my best. Not really my field.'

He stopped talking. This was pointless. Simeon Shepherd's expression had altered so little Garfield wondered if he were actually asleep again but with his eyes open. He thought of how Antony would behave in such circumstances and made an effort to sit in companionable silence instead. There was a waist-height, glass-fronted bookcase against one wall, and on it a cluster of silver-framed photographs. Even at this distance, by the indirect light from the standard lamp a few feet away, he could distinguish the stereotypical formats of a wedding photograph and a studio portrait of a mother and baby. There was also a portrait of a man in uniform.

'Can I see?' he said after a second's hesitation and went to pick it up. 'Was this you?' Of course it was. It might have been a younger version of himself in fancy dress with a particularly cheap and savage haircut. The young man was smiling. Was this, Garfield wondered, the smile that had seduced Rachel? Or had she seduced him?

It was impossible to imagine. She had always been so wild and exuberant and risky. And so mad. Yet everything in this house, in the book he had tried to read, in the bleakly dutiful daughter downstairs, spoke of sanity, reserve and withdrawal: the antitheses of a passionate life. The young man in the photograph was handsome enough but it was hard to see him as a serial seducer. Perhaps he had simply been the passive-manipulative sort, adept at projecting a veneer of helplessness so that women couldn't help responding to him. He thought instinctively of Lizzy and her insistent baby hunger. Perhaps Rachel and the others had been decades ahead of their time in coolly appraising Simeon Shepherd as the ideal oblivious donor, his cheekbones almost as high as his IQ.

There was a trembling in his pocket from his mobile. He took it out, apologizing, and saw it was a text message from Lizzy saying simply, *Well? L.x.*

An idea occurred to him. He should take a picture to show her and any child they might eventually have. 'Would you mind if I took your photograph?' he asked. 'To show my wife?'

Simeon Shepherd was staring at the television now, confused maybe at the lack of sound. Garfield lined him and the monstrous cat up in his mobile's viewfinder, moved the standard lamp so that it cast a better light over them, then took the picture.

The mobile's camera made a tiny noise, the sound of an old-fashioned camera shutter and film winder, as pointlessly nostalgic as the pseudo clockwork tick added to some electric watches. It was a tiny noise, far quieter than the purring of the cat, but apparently it reached the old man and enraged him. Or perhaps he had indeed been asleep with his eyes open and was always bad-tempered on waking. For whatever reason he was suddenly bolt upright, focused and angry. He shouted senselessly and shook his hands at Garfield. The cat yowled, jumped free and ran hissing from the room.

'I'm so sorry,' Garfield said, alarmed. 'It's just a tiny camera. I took your photograph to show my wife. Look. You want to see the picture? You don't? Oh. Well. Shit.'

He took up the remote control and unmuted the television so the room filled again with the sound of surging film score and whichever Californian landscape was doing duty for the Wild West. Then he hurried out, shutting the door behind him.

Niobe Shepherd was deeply involved in her indexing again and evidently inured to outbreaks of noise from upstairs because he stood in the kitchen doorway without her looking up and he ended by clearing his throat and saying a vague, 'Well, I should be erm . . .'

She gave one of her ambivalent half-smiles and came to see him out.

'Sorry,' she said. 'That probably wasn't quite the cosy reunion you'd pictured.'

He shrugged, feeling desolate now. 'I don't know what I'd pictured. But meeting you was . . . Here. Let me give you my details. Ah, but you've got them already. Of course you have. Falmouth is a lot closer than America.' He added, 'You're always welcome to visit us and, well, let me know how he gets on. And perhaps you would post me the other names? Of the Americans?'

She was giving him no help. He was the third she had watched writhing like this. Perhaps there would be more? She merely kept that look of possibly malicious amusement about her and opened the front door for him. It was seizing up and she discreetly braced herself with a foot against the jamb as she tugged it open.

'Let's keep in touch,' he said.

'Let's,' she said and something in her manner stopped him offering a hand, as Hedley would have done, or even a friendly kiss such as Lizzy would have mustered. He found himself almost ducking out of the door. 'Bye,' she added and shut the door behind him with a thump. Pausing, dazed, on the pavement, he heard her lock it and tug a bolt across.

The sense of desolation that had stolen up on him in the hall intensified as he realized he was now a prisoner of ill-laid plans. Lizzy had suggested he come alone. She was going to a concert in Truro with Antony and Hedley, who seemed to have taken root in his old room and had not been home to London and Oliver since the funeral. At her prompting Garfield had taken a room in a hotel for the night. It was possible he would be asked to spend the evening with his new relations, she said, or that they would want him to fit in a second visit on the Sunday.

He glanced at his watch. There was no longer time to catch the train to Reading that would let him pick up the last bearable train home of the evening. There was always the sleeper, of course, but that didn't arrive in Reading until well past midnight and there could be no certainty of finding a berth free. His days of making the overnight journey slumped in a seat to save money were long over and besides, such a late journey still obliged him to find some way of filling the evening. He used to know people in Oxford. At least one friend from law school was a legal-aid barrister here somewhere. But he had made no preparatory phone calls, not knowing how things would transpire at the Shepherds', and had not thought to bring his address book with him.

He began to walk back towards the hotel and thought that of course there was no reason not to ring Lizzy and ask her to look numbers up for him. But then there was always the risk that a reunion with friends with whom he had exchanged no more than Christmas cards since his wedding might prove just as dispiriting as his meeting his natural father.

There was nothing he wanted even slightly to see at the cinema. He scanned the posters but it was half-term and they all seemed to be for films aimed at children or at adults who had yet to grow up. Like a fool he had brought nothing to read but Simeon Shepherd's monograph. He had spotted a tempting secondhand bookshop earlier but all the shops seemed to be closing or already closed for the weekend. He would simply have to break two habits of a lifetime: eat on his own then spend an evening watching television. (They only had a radio at home.) If he caught a train immediately after breakfast he could be home by mid-afternoon, unless there were to be Sunday disruptions on the line.

Just then he spotted a familiar poster and realized the handsome building he was passing on St Giles was Oxford's Friends' Meeting House. He doubled back and checked the details, although Meeting for Worship would be at eleven the next day, just as it would be in Falmouth and Penzance. It was not the first time he had wished Meetings happened more often than on Sunday. He felt badly stirred up and quiet contemplation with a group of Friends would have afforded some calmer, clearer thinking. Perhaps his hotel room would be quiet enough for him to turn out the lights, lie on the floor with his head on a pillow and meditate.

He had chosen to stay at the Randolph purely because it was offering a special weekend rate. Loomed over by so much brocade and high Victoriana, he felt underdressed without a tie and wondered if this would give him sufficient excuse to eat in his room rather than suffer the ordeal of a table for one in a restaurant with lighting too romantic to read by.

He wanted a cup of tea and wandered in search of one only to find waitresses wheeling away trolleys of cakes and tea things.

'Afternoon tea finished half an hour ago,' one of them explained. 'But you can get just a cup of tea if you ask in the bar.'

The atmosphere in the bar felt quite wrong for tea and his resolve weakened at the smell of newly chopped lemons and the sound of ice on glass. He ordered a pint of Graduate instead, because he had a raging thirst, and a whisky chaser because his coat was too thin and his aimless walk through the streets had left him chilled.

He found a dark corner table where he could nurse both drinks and think. There had been no revelation. He had felt no sudden imperative of love for his true father, felt nothing for him in fact. But there was no denying he was the old man's son and he had come away from his wretched household with something he had not possessed before: a kind of permission. He was no longer a Birthright Quaker. He could not pretend that all his upbringing had vanished at a stroke but he now had, it seemed, a different, thornier inheritance with which to balance it.

His father was no longer a pillar of rectitude, a good man on whom, effectively, people had been congratulating him for as long as he could recall. His father now was a man who had shown no loyalty to his wife, sired at least three children with other women to whom he gave no support and had probably made little, if any, provision for the daughter who was inexplicably caring for him in old age. His house had an aridity about it, with no signs of friendship, no suggestions of faith.

He remembered he had not rung Lizzy to make a report and knew, even as it occurred to him, that he wouldn't. He hardly ever drank. Lizzy was a teetotaller. It was one of those articles of faith, like her vegetarianism, he had absorbed and adjusted to when he met her. Were she somehow able to see him there with spirits as well as beer on the table before him, she would have assumed he was recovering from bad news. It would not have occurred to her that he might be relishing a small step towards independence from principle, even from her. He had just received a small but potent vaccination against goodness, against his family, against something and the alcohol was a first symptomatic reaction.

Guiltily he took out his mobile and pressed 1 to call her. She was out of range or had hers turned off in anticipation of the concert so he left a quick, calm message inviting no response and saying he'd see her the following afternoon and would ring her from the train. He turned his mobile off and slipped it back in his coat pocket then took a long, good draught of excellent bitter.

When he looked up again, a woman was smiling at him from the next table.

'Job done?' she asked.

'Is that how it looked?' he said.

She shrugged. 'Pretty much. I'm getting another. What are you having?'

'Oh, I . . .' He saw to his surprise that the pint was almost gone and surprised himself further by letting her buy him a second whisky. She bought him a double and sat across from him at the table.

'That's very kind of you,' he said.

'Not at all. You probably haven't noticed but this bar is a shark pool of predatory males.'

'I hadn't. Well I'm safe.' He flashed his wedding band.

'Me too,' she laughed, and flashed hers. 'No,' she went on. 'Don't introduce yourself. I could tell you were about to. If we get each other's names we start fishing for connections and thinking of associations and, well, let's just not.'

'All right,' he said. 'So you're here on your own?'

'Yes. Twice a year I escape my life with the perfectly good excuse of seeing my dentist. I've always come to one here. She's good and causes me no pain and, since it's only twice a year, I could see no pressing need to change when we moved away. And it's far enough from home that I can come for a night and enjoy a little break.'

'Your husband never wants to come too?'

'I've never suggested it. But no. He's too busy and my going away makes him busier still. Sometimes I coincide with a touring opera company but this time I planned badly so I've got a quiet night in ahead of me. You?'

'Oh. Yes. Quiet night for me too.'

'I meant why Oxford?'

'Sorry. Family research. I came to meet the man I've just discovered is my biological father.'

'God! Was it strange?'

'Very.'

'Will you see him again?'

'Probably not. He's pretty sick and frail anyway. I live a long way away and my life is very different.'

'So what do you do? Remember this is your chance to lie and impress me.'

'I can't lie,' he admitted. 'I'm congenitally incapable.'

'You never lie to your wife?'

'No.' He smiled into his glass. 'I don't think I'd do it very convincingly.'

She laughed quietly and he saw just how attractive she was. She was slight and almost oriental-looking, with very straight, dark hair that swung forward across her face whenever she looked down. She had shrugged off her suede coat to reveal a neat, subfusc outfit like a woman barrister's on television. Her silk blouse was undone one button further than she probably realized so that one cup of her bra kept moving in and out of view. She wore a double rope of plump pearls; her husband was busy to some purpose. Garfield was a bad judge of age but placed her on the kinder side of fifty but the other side of motherhood.

'Do you make a practice of talking to strange men in hotel bars?' he asked.

'As I say,' she said, 'only twice a year. Are you going to eat? My anaesthetic's finally worn off and I could eat this beer mat. Can we eat together?'

'Yes.'

'Good.'

'Why not?' There was no harm in eating and the company of a good-looking woman was preferable to room service and the cultural wasteland he gathered constituted Saturday night television.

He could not, after the event, have said how exactly she ended up in his room. He did remember her cheekily admitting she had not yet got around to checking in when she spotted him in the bar. Perhaps it was the way the waiters treated them, with that sly, suggestive deference they never showed people dining alone? Perhaps it was the grisliness of their fellow-diners that made them feel subtle and attractive by comparison?

Or perhaps it was the name thing? He had heard often enough how prostitutes held back from allowing clients to kiss them. It was always presented as something disappointing and impersonal, as in, 'Of course, they never let you kiss them.' As though this somehow made the sex they offered fake. It seemed to Garfield that evening that, by withholding kisses, prostitutes were cannily playing on the sexiness of noncommitment. It was precisely because they didn't kiss the clients that the clients could depersonalize them to the point of asking for anything. Withholding names was akin to withholding kisses; with no exchange of names, however casual, however fake, there was not even the pretence that these were the early hours of a relationship. Not even a purely friendly one.

By instinct they ordered generic hotel food, rich but safe: a crab thing, steak with béarnaise sauce and sauté potatoes, more wine instead of pudding. And they talked. With a judicious lack of geography or specifics, she told him about her life. Her husband was a consultant urologist but had based her and the family in deep countryside. They had three children, all away at boarding school. She taught the oboe to a handful of pupils, usually in their schools, sometimes at her house.

'Do you love them?' he asked. 'Your husband and children?'

'I'd die for them,' she said. 'Is that love? I wouldn't even have to think about it. If it was a matter of taking a bullet or swallowing poison or walking into a burning room or whatever. If they could live, I'd do it. Although I'm scared of pain. I'd probably crack under torture and betray them.'

'You've thought about it.'

'Over and over,' she said. 'But,' and her smile fell. 'One of my children, one of my sons, I find I don't love as much. In fact, as he grows up and becomes more and more his own person, I find I love him less and less.'

'He's a teenager. It'll pass.'

'They all are. It's not that. He's simply become someone I wouldn't think of getting to know if we weren't related. I'd still die for him but . . . I don't *like* him. Did your mother like you? Of course she did. I'm unnatural.'

'Actually I'm not sure,' he said. 'She was ill so often when we were small and her illness could make her pretty scary so when we weren't looking after her we were being frightened by her. Not much room in that equation for like or love. And now that I know she was pregnant with me when she married, I think she probably resented me when I was a baby. If I hadn't come along, she'd have been free.'

'Not every maiden's prayer back then.'

'No, but she wasn't your average . . . She ended up so hemmed in by marriage and kids and . . . She was such a wild child. I don't know why she stayed, when I think about it.'

'Did she have affairs?'

'If she did, she was very discreet. Everyone knows everyone else where they lived.'

'Was she happy?'

'She was bipolar so happiness didn't come into it. She was often high, often wildly elated, which could make her fun to be around but I don't think she was ever steadily content. Especially later on, once we'd left home.'

And prompted by deft questions, he told her a little of the saga of the Middletons, about the crises Rachel suffered after all but one of her births, about the trips into hospital, the painting, about Petroc, about Morwenna. He didn't go into much detail – he knew of old that people unfamiliar with the story tended to be shocked if told too much so he sketched things in and left a lot out. But he was still surprised to notice tears in her eyes.

'Sorry,' she said. 'That's so sad.'

'I suppose when it's all you've known it seems fairly normal. Well, no. Not normal but . . . acceptable.'

'Children are shockingly durable. Mine have had such

133

an easy ride so far that I worry. They need a few shocks to toughen them up and make them less vulnerable. I bet your wife thought she was rescuing you.' She leant forward, resting her keen, clever face on her hands in a way that made him resent having to talk about Lizzy, which in turn made him spiteful and he found himself telling all about Lizzy and her campaign to get pregnant.

This seemed to embarrass her in a way that the earlier details had not and she sat back and steered the conversation into cooler waters.

Not long afterwards there was a pause during which he stared at her in a way that wasn't conversational and she stared right back. Then she said, quite simply, 'Shall we go up?'

They had paid for the meal with a pair of cards, earlier, so they left the table almost at once and headed upstairs. It was only when they were climbing the stairs and he asked what floor she was on that she admitted to having no room of her own yet.

'Oh,' was all he could think to say and continued to his room where he let her in and they fell on one another without another word.

Of course it was unlike the sex he normally had because it wasn't with Lizzy but it was different too in that the woman insisted on total darkness and silence whereas Lizzy liked a light on, however dimly, and tended to talk a lot. She was taller, too, and thinner. The darkness was strange. It was the utter darkness of a well-curtained hotel room and yet he rapidly found that he was effectively seeing her with his hands.

'Christ,' she sighed when it was over. 'Does she like it like that?'

'Like what?'

'Well . . . You're pretty rough.'

'Am I? Sorry.'

'No. It's just that . . . You've been married a while and . . . There are other ways.'

And at the point where he would usually have given Lizzy one last kiss then fallen asleep, she began to kiss and touch him in a way that got them starting all over again. She kept the light off only this time she talked. In fact she proceeded to teach him several explicitly practical lessons.

When he woke thirsty a few hours later and stumbled to the bathroom for a drink, he found his cock and balls were aching from use in a way he had last experienced in the first solitary frenzies of adolescence.

When he woke again, the curtains were half-drawn and she was singing quietly to herself in the bath. He was shy of going in there to join her, although the husky sound of her voice, or the quantities of water he had drunk at the sink earlier, were making him hard again. He pretended to doze as she dried herself and dressed but she wasn't fooled because she came and sat on the end of the bed eventually and spoke to him as though she knew he was wide awake already.

'Will you tell her about this?'

'God,' he said, sitting up. 'Morning. Probably.'

'Why?'

'I never lie to her.'

'Ah yes. Congenitally incapable. But why?'

'I owe it to her.'

'So that she can be upset? It's your problem surely, not hers, if you feel guilty. Why spread it around?'

'So you won't tell your husband?'

She chuckled. 'Of course not. He'd be terribly upset and so should I. I think it's a peculiarly male syndrome, this need to tell. When you still love your wives, that is. It's totally illogical, when you stop to analyse it. Anyway.' She held one of his feet that was sticking out from the bedding and gave it a gentle shake. 'You're man enough to carry the burden on your own. I'm going in search of breakfast. Thanks for a lovely, unexpected evening.' She bent over to kiss his big toe. 'I've left cash for my share of the room.'

'But . . .'

'I insist. It's a dignity thing. Bye.'

She gave his foot another squeeze and left.

He climbed out of bed soon afterwards and was shocked to see it was already ten o'clock. He had missed the first train that connected through to Penzance and, unless he wanted a long wait in Reading, there was no point walking down to the station until past noon. He bathed, breakfasted on the room's ration of instant coffee and shortbread fingers and checked out, causing some confusion by his insistence on paying part of the bill with the notes the woman had left behind.

He thought about dropping by the Shepherds' house once more to say a second goodbye to the waspish Niobe then realized there was no point. Old instinct diverted him instead into the Friends' Meeting House. It was about two minutes before eleven so he just had time to slip into

NOTES FROM AN EXHIBITION

the Meeting Room and take a seat in the circle before the door was closed. It was far better subscribed than Penzance Meeting. There were perhaps thirty people in the room. Including her.

He saw her almost at once, probably because she had seen him coming in and was still looking at him as he automatically ran his eyes around the room on taking his seat. She smiled at him then looked down at her hands which she held loosely clasped in her lap. He felt a jolt of panic at first, but as he breathed deeply and began to listen to the room growing quiet about them he saw there was nothing to fear. Nobody here knew him and it was quite as possible that she was a stranger here too. And even if they were known, there was nothing to connect them. They were among Friends.

He couldn't resist looking at her again, less obviously. She was not beautiful, he saw, but she had a sort of clean clarity to her. If one were casting actors to play Quakers in a film, hers was the kind of face one would look for. She was not a voluptuous seductress nor was she a hypocrite. If asked, she would have admitted that she spent last night with a man who wasn't her husband because it felt good and (perhaps) she liked him but insisted that this had no bearing on her love for her husband or the truthfulness with which she aspired to lead her life.

It crossed his mind that she was so matter-of-fact about their casual adultery she was capable of standing now and sharing with the Meeting her deep sense that the pleasures of sex were God-given.

But of course she didn't. In fact no one spoke. It was

one of those rare, lovely hours he cherished and when he finally reached home that night he would tell Lizzy about it. About the serene pleasure of sitting in a roomful of thoughtful people for a whole hour without a word being said. A roomful of strangers.

When the hour finished and suddenly people were shaking hands around the circle, Garfield found his mind had become completely disengaged from the room and had been thinking intensely about Rachel and what her life must have been like before his father found her in this cold, landlocked city. He readjusted to his surroundings slowly with the almost sickened feeling of someone abruptly woken from deep sleep, and was one of the last to stand and be sociable.

Trained by Antony's example, it was normally a rule of his to accept a cup of coffee and make the effort to talk to at least one stranger before leaving. But he was anxious about his train. He was about to slip away when the man who had been sitting beside him and who shook his hand at the end caught him gently by the elbow and said, 'Now do you two know each other?' and brought him face to face with the woman.

'Oh yes,' she said with a kind smile. 'We're old friends.'

'How are you?' Garfield asked her as she shook his hand.

'I'm very well,' she said. 'Thank you. And you?'

'Me too,' he said and found he was grinning. 'I have a train to catch,' he added, as much to the man beside them as to her.

'Of course you do,' she said. 'Now you're not to worry so. Everything will be fine. You'll see.'

'Will it?'

'I'm a bit of a witch,' she said. 'Trust me. Go well.'

He had a powerful sense of her blessing as he left the building. It was as though she had tucked something warm into his breast pocket and its benign heat suffused him as he walked and induced a mild euphoria. When his mobile vibrated and it was Lizzy to say she had just left Falmouth Meeting and was missing him he said, 'Me too,' and found he meant it.

They chatted on the phone about this and that as he walked past Worcester and through the abruptly less charming, traffic-clogged area around the station. When she asked him about meeting his real father and he told her she said, 'A bit of an anticlimax, then.'

He said, 'Yes and no. It's changed things a bit. I think I want to go back into law. Do legal-aid work around Falmouth and Truro. Would you mind?'

She laughed. 'Of course I wouldn't.'

'But your dad's business . . .'

'Was his, not yours. And it was failing anyway when you took it over from him. You must do what you're best at.'

'You're sure? You're not just saying that?'

'Course not. It was London and all those fat-cat clients that didn't suit you, I think. Not law.'

'Everything's going to be fine,' he said.

'What? You're cracking up a bit.'

'It'll be fine,' he said. 'You'll see.'

FROM THE STUDIO SOFA (1960).
Indian ink and watercolour on paper.
Dating from the first year of Kelly's marriage, this evocative work is a neat illustration of a turning point in her career as an artist. The work is still figurative, almost neurotically so in its detailing, and depicts the view from her studio sofa across the yard to the back of the Middleton family home in Penzance. The dresses drying on the washing line are recognizably those in photographs 6 and 8. She has detailed the house's brickwork with an almost autistic precision. And yet the colour overlay is entirely non-naturalistic, non-figurative. If one edits out the ink drawing, as shown in the digitally enhanced scan below, the watercolour element bears a striking resemblance – in its use of interdependent shapes and wilfully inharmonious colour choices – to her first experiments in abstract work (see exhibits 10–15). Significantly the small painting she shows then hanging beside her studio window is Geometry Series 42 by Jack Trescothick, also her doctor and a family friend, whose influence is generally credited with launching Kelly into modernism and a wider public. He also saved her life on at least one occasion.
(From the collection of Dr Madeleine Merluza)

The months leading to Garfield's birth were the happiest Rachel had ever known.

The weather was glorious – she had no idea anywhere in England could be so sunny and even hot – and she found herself seduced on several fronts. She fell in love with West Cornwall, not just Penzance and St Ives but the coastline and coves, and the strange, haunted villages inland. She fell in love with the house, which managed to be at once older than anywhere she had ever lived and yet entirely innocent of bad atmosphere. It was as though the sunlight washed it through every day, rinsing away any particles of regret or sorrow that might have gathered in the corners. This was partly thanks to its layout, which seemed designed to attract the sun and minimize the sense so many buildings gave her of smothering you as you came in and closed the door but it was partly to do with her third seduction, by Quakerism.

Antony's faith, which he had only slowly revealed to her, passed on from Michael, his dear grandfather, and his great grandparents before that, was not a covert, Sunday thing, detached from his weekday life, but a part of the fabric of the place, like its chopping board or window seats. Antony's and Michael's openness, their way of giving everything and everyone their due weight, of avoiding sanctimony but abhorring glibness too, was embedded in the fabric of the house because the buying of a mug or looking glass would be approached with the same self-questioning care as the question of whether or not to support a certain cause or what to take someone in hospital. Schooled in her parents' unthinking hypocrisy, scorched by Simeon's cynicism, she was beguiled.

When they took her to her first Meeting for Worship and she witnessed the potent combination of quiet contemplation with the lack of Christian paraphernalia she had long dismissed as nonsense, she found herself marvelling that Quakerism had not become the dominant world faith. It seemed so accessible, sane and adaptable.

Their wedding day was unlike anything she had imagined. Yes they made their vows before witnesses, and signed a register, but there was no white dress for her or penguin suit for him, no paternalist piffle about being given away, no sense that she was losing her identity. (Arguably she had done that already . . .) Instead there was a group of Friends silently focusing on them and their hopes, perhaps, but also holding a Meeting for Worship as they would on any Sunday.

'You don't have to come to Meeting with us, you know,' Antony told her. 'Plenty of wives have husbands who don't belong and vice versa.'

But she continued to go and wanted to, even though she suspected she would never formally become a member of Penzance Meeting. She went because she found the weekly experience recharged her and improved her mental focus.

She and Antony didn't share a bed at once. She made her way to his room when she couldn't sleep one night because of a thunderstorm, about two weeks into their marriage. She found him very attractive but sex was not a great success at first because he was inexperienced, which in turn inhibited her. But it felt right and, as their joint technique improved, began to feel good in a way that spilled over into their daylight hours.

As the baby swelled within her, she started painting and drawing again. On the tiny income Antony was earning as an English teacher in the boys' grammar school they were too poor for her to indulge her hankering for large canvases but she economized with ingenuity, blowing the last of her savings on paint, paper and pencils and working on everything from old pieces of marine ply she found discarded to overpainting old pictures and even

Woolworths' canvas-look reproductions she picked up for almost nothing in junk shops.

Antony was out at work all day and Michael spent most mornings strolling around the harbour and town, passing time with friends or researching his shipping column so she was left a good deal to her own devices, which suited her.

She was befriended by Jack Trescothick, a boyhood friend of Antony's who was now one of the town's doctors. His real love was painting and his abstract work, which secretly she found a bit dry and scratchy, had won him the respect of the Hepworth circle in St Ives and a place in the Penwith Society of Artists. Jack puzzled her, though. He kept a symbolic distance from his exalted friends by choosing to base himself in Newlyn rather than St Ives and he kept a distance on art by continuing to practise as a GP. She teased him that it was the Quaker in him, unable to give himself over to something self-indulgent when he could use his training to help others but she suspected he did it because he was scared of failure. By using that old English stand-by of posing as a gifted amateur, he sought to spare himself from judgement. By degrees she discovered that the Fred he fleetingly referred to was his lover, stoutly independent, a fisherman and even less openly homosexual than Jack was. Jack was so very discreet, in fact, that she had at first been tempted to flirt with him.

Knowing his grandfather was out most mornings and dozing off a beer lunch most afternoons, Antony must have asked his friend to keep an eye on her, to check she wasn't going to pieces again. She didn't mind because she so quickly warmed to Jack, who was a little like the brother she had never had, but it was hard to say whether Jack kept more of an eye on her in his guise as doctor or as artist. As doctor he calmly monitored her pregnancy, testing her blood pressure and making sure she remembered to eat properly. He also gave her the courage to reduce then stop entirely her intake of antidepressants, for the sake of the baby.

As artist, he helped her carve out a studio from the junk-laden outbuilding at the back of the house. Set across a little yard, where she used to hang the washing, this had once been a laundry. It retained a copper, where Antony's grandfather remembered his wife and mother cooking puddings as well as boiling linen, and a system of pulleys in the high roof to lift poles on which sheets were dried. Antony's mother had briefly tried using it as a greenhouse during the war. When she was widowed, Michael had put in the larger window for her in the hope that an interest in raising seedlings might save her from morbid introspection. Since her death it had been the one blighted part of the property and become a dumping ground for things potentially useful but unwanted. An old pram, whose fabric had rotted in the sun, a bicycle with a bent wheel, quantities of bamboo canes from when the garden had been given over to vegetables and so on.

Encouraged by the others, Jack helped her clear it out and sweep away decades of cobwebs. They spent two days sloshing its walls with whitewash, cleaned the window with vinegar, moved back in the decrepit chaise longue they had been about to put out for the dustmen and suddenly she had a studio almost better than his purpose-built one on the edge of Newlyn.

She began to paint every day, with no particular view in mind other than perfecting whatever idea had seized her. She walked a lot, although the great bulge of her baby made this tiring and drew disapproving glances from women who thought she should be at home with her feet up. She drew and painted small works in situ, on beaches and in fields.

She discovered she was not a terribly good housewife as a result, frequently forgetting to do anything about food in the evenings. But Antony was forbearing: happy, presumably, that she seemed healthy again. Michael was a plain but reliable cook, used to fending for himself and feeding Antony, so would often rescue her by cooking them all chops or sardines or sausages.

When the pregnancy finally defeated her and she was obliged to lie down more and more to rest her aching back and legs, the old man enjoyed fussing around her, although he could hardly hear a thing she said and would often just smile rather than ask her to repeat a remark. Antony would come home from teaching to find her listening to the radio, being fed bloater paste sandwiches by his grandfather and amusing local gossip by Jack. They were all very merry together and she saw no reason to think life should not continue like that.

The baby started on September the fourth. She was checked on by Jack then driven by Antony the few hundred yards from their front gate to the little lying-in hospital on the seafront towards Newlyn, with Jack pedalling his bicycle alongside them and shouting encouragement.

Childbirth was at once far more painful and far simpler than she had been led to imagine. Nothing, least of all reading the copies of Truby King and Dr Spock from the lending library, had prepared her for the sensation of her body taking over so entirely from her mind, an effect heightened further by the midwife kindly giving her laughing gas when the pain and the language it was drawing from her threatened to become too much.

But the baby was perfect, to the point where just looking at him made her cry but in a happy way and she could quite see how some women thought the pain was worth the reward and had baby after baby until they were worn out. They gave him the room across from theirs, which she had already painted blue with a frieze of little clouds, and laid him in a cot donated by a Quaker household that had no further use for it.

But then the shadows came for her.

First Michael shocked them by announcing he was moving into a nursing home. There was nothing wrong with him apart from his deafness and a touch of angina, but he was adamant, saying he had friends there and preferred to move in while he was still compos mentis. It was clear he felt the house belonged to a young family now and that he would be in the way and a burden. But the reverse was the case, not least because he didn't mind cooking, and Rachel found she missed him painfully.

The baby was now not so sweet and cried for hours at a time and Antony seemed to think she could stop it just by being its mother, which was far from the case. So they were short with each other and had their first proper arguments. And Jack was away, taking one of his semi-detached holidays with Fred in Tangier, so she could not look to him to tease her into better cheer.

All this would pass. She knew it would. She knew babies grew up and couples rediscovered harmony. She knew she would have time to paint again in a while and that her breasts would not always hurt so. She knew the weather would not always be so blustery and dark.

And yet the darkness that stole upon her was like no darkness she had experienced before. It had no real cause and it came upon her with devastating speed, like a storm across bright waters. Quite suddenly, in the space of little more than a day, whatever little gland provided hope or a sense of perspective ceased its merciful function and she woke from the afternoon nap that Truby King insisted mother and baby take in their separate rooms and Garfield was crying through the bedroom wall and softly, from the drawer where she kept the pills Jack had weaned her off during pregnancy, a second, malign baby was whispering to her.

She left Garfield to cry, fearing to look on him, and took the pill bottle from the drawer. It felt wrong to die in a house that was so good and where the good baby, the innocent one, was lying so she pulled a fisherman's smock over her jersey and her thickest coat over that and gathered up the pills and a bottle of sloe gin Fred had made for them and took herself out to the studio. There she swallowed the pills, in several painful fistfuls, washing their gritty bitterness away with great, greedy glugs of the sour-sweet liqueur. Then she lay back on the broken-down chaise longue with a blanket over her and waited for death.

A delicious calm came over her and for a few minutes an extraordinary clarity of vision, so that she could see every detail of the familiar view of the house's rear, its windows, its drainpipes, the patches of rust, the fern growing from a crack beside the drain, the washing lines. But she could simultaneously see the shapes these elements made purely as shapes, uncluttered by meaning, and the way the sunlight, falling on those shapes without understanding or preference, simply as sunlight, released colours and patterns that only she could see. Even Garfield's jagged crying, barely audible through his open window, and then only to his mother, had a shape and a colour.

Part of her saw all this and thought, *Wait! Let me see it long enough to get it down!* And the other, stronger part spoke with her mother's voice, soothing but controlling too, tucking the thick, death-blanket about her, and said,

'No, dear. Don't try to speak. We can just sit here a while and be nice and calm.'

THE GODFATHERS (1972).
Pencil and coloured crayon on paper.
SYMPATHETIC BLUES (1972). Oil on canvas.
Never shown until now, although named and signed as if for exhibition, The Godfathers surfaced among Kelly's numerous papers and sketches after her death. The setting is the artist/doctor Jack Trescothick's Newlyn studio where he is shown on a sofa with his fisherman companion, Fred George. The child between them, his face hidden in a cat mask but clearly identifiable from his clothes, is Kelly's third, her son Hedley. The reason this tender picture, in which Kelly's affection for the three and their fondness for one another is so evident, is strange is that only Trescothick was Hedley's godfather. Fred George was drowned when *Amazing Grace*, the fishing boat he was working on, mysteriously sank on a calm summer night a year before Hedley was born. The informal photograph taken on his fifth birthday (see below) shows how his mother's drawing simply replaces her and his father on the sofa with Trescothick and George. Executed in the same month, Sympathetic Blues is surely an abstraction of elements in the same image: artist, lover and godson are echoed in three shapes whose shades pick up exactly the shades of blue the three are wearing in The Godfathers and whose arrangement – two larger forms bending protectively around a much smaller third – suggests an emotional intensity from which the figurative work holds off.

(Both works on permanent loan from Antony Middleton)

Hedley had not meant to stay on so long after the funeral. With disastrous timing, long-booked builders had arrived in his and Oliver's house in London to rip out, extend and

149

re-fit the kitchen and Oliver was too busy at the gallery to oversee the work with the necessary attention to detail. Oliver could date a picture frame from only its back view and tell a real Kokoschka from a fake virtually by smell but he was quite incapable of stopping an electrician placing a socket several inches out of place and affected a kind of snow blindness when faced with fabric swatches. By rights Hedley should have driven back to London two or three days after Rachel and her shockingly undecorated card-board coffin were laid in earth. Nearly a fortnight had passed, however, and he was still in Penzance.

No one but he seemed to realize how much there was to be done. Sorting Rachel's clothes had taken days, for a start. She had always been a spendthrift clothes shopper and seemed never to throw anything away. As child after child had left home, she had simply extended her storage territory into the wardrobes and drawers they left empty. She never emptied her pockets when she put things away, either, so he kept finding things she would have long since forgotten losing: bracelets, cheques from galleries, house keys. Many of these finds would involve leaving the room to go to her desk or in search of yet another sombre consultation with Antony. Some of the clothes – old bras, pants and tights and numerous things ruined by paint – could be bundled into bin liners without hesitation. Others were good enough for charity shops but needed washing or dry cleaning first. Others – usually barely worn suits or dresses, purchases made in her high-spending bouts of mania – were grand enough to count as vintage and there-fore be sold for charity through a dealer.

This was all time-consuming enough but then there

was the way so many clothes were so evocative that Hedley would find himself remembering or weeping or simply sinking into little bouts of unconstructive reverie before stuffing them, no decision made, back into a cupboard.

He was crying a lot still, which was unlike him. He had thought experience had left him thicker-skinned.

He had pictured her death, and even wanted it, often. The reality had proved far easier and less traumatic than anything he had imagined: no hospital, no messy suicide, no drawn-out guilt trips or deathbed speeches. It was the unexpectedly quiet exit of such a histrionic woman that had unmanned him, he decided. He loved her, he had always loved her, but it was a love in which he had grown used to thinking of her as the tireless adversary. For as long as he could recall, their every conversation had been a skirmish, their every affectionate moment freighted with protective irony.

She required his worship and would have hated him to see her reduced by a common or garden heart attack, would have hated him for seeing it. He had long suspected that, for all her bohemian credentials, she thought him less of a man for being gay. She was certainly made insecure by his living with a man who worked at Mendel's, the gallery that had always represented her to the world. She had asked him to end the relationship and, when that failed, had tried to have Oliver fired. (Oliver's mourning was purely sympathetic and professional.) That it was made plain that she was now less valuable to Mendel's than Oliver was had not endeared him to her.

Apart from all the clothes and belongings, there was the loft window to fix. Hedley called a glazier out to replace the broken pane up there. While waiting for him he took a bucket out to the garden below and picked over the flowerbeds, pots and gravel, retrieving all the pieces of shattered glass he could spot. He found one and then another of the six big pebbles she seemed always to have kept to hand there and, not far from them, snagged on a yucca's needle-sharp leaves, the missing circlet thing she had sometimes worn about her wrist but more often used as a hair clasp when she tugged her hair back out of her face.

He showed the glazier up to the attic then took the hair clasp to Antony. He found him in his usual chair, which caught the sun until noon. Hedley saw at a glance that he had failed to finish even the first of the letters he had set out to write that morning. He had probably not read the paper either but had completed both the day's sudoku and cryptic crossword instead.

'Look what I just found,' Hedley said, as he felt he had been saying for days, as he handed this or that memento or keepsake found in drawer or pocket.

Antony took the thing and turned it over, opening and closing its crude clasp. 'She always said this was by GBH,' he said. 'Though I don't see how it could be. She never made jewellery, did she?'

'Not that I know of. Did they even know each other?'

'Barely. She met her when she did some teaching . . .'

'Hard to imagine that!'

'One of her colleagues was having an affair with some artist nobody remembers now and the three of them used to slope off to rather wild parties, nude swimming and jazz and a lot of the usual boho willy-waving while the girls sat around adoringly.'

'You never told me this. Where were you?'

'Oh. Minding Garfield, probably.' Antony looked back at the hair clip. 'They got on at first but then Rachel had another bad spell, after Morwenna was born, and lost touch. But GBH was like that: she'd pick people up, having sudden enthusiasms, then drop them as soon as she felt they'd let her down. Morwenna should have it,' he said, handing the clasp back. 'Where was it?'

'In the garden. She seemed to have thrown it out of the window she broke.'

'She was in a bad way. The noise she was making! She cried out and . . .'

'What? Dad?'

'Nothing. It's nothing, really.'

'Dad?'

Antony looked up, his face infinitely kind. 'She had no record of a weak heart so I keep wondering if she scared herself to death.'

'Surely not?' Hedley sat on a nearby chair.

'She used to see terrible things, when it was bad.'

'The baby.'

'What?'

'I remember once her going on and on about a baby,' Hedley told him. 'She made you stop the car and made us all get out so she could be sure it wasn't in the car with us.'

'Don't remember that.'

'So what else?'

'She never told me. She used to say telling me would make them too real.' Antony's face closed down again and he looked back at the letter he had started and sighed.

'I should get on,' Hedley said.

'Are you leaving us already?'

'No, no.' Hedley noted that unconscious first-person plural. 'But I've got things to get back to. You know.'

Hedley also had to cope with the various tardy obituarists needing facts confirmed and dates checked. Nobody could quite grasp the idea that Rachel's own family had so little knowledge of her life before she met Antony. They had a birth date and knew she was probably Toronto-born, although people often said she had a Massachusetts accent. There was no copy of the marriage certificate, nobody knew her parents' names and she had trained them all so early never to ask about her past that it had become a sort of habit to act as though she had none.

Then there was an ever-growing stack of letters to answer, now spread across a couple of breakfast trays. At first Hedley had thought this the ideal quietly therapeutic task for Antony and for a few days after the funeral his father kept busy writing deeply considered replies. But after that he seemed to give up. Days passed, with the piles swelling as acquaintances noticed the obituaries, with only two or three responses written and it became clear Antony was being defeated by the effort. So Hedley sorted them into relatives, close friends and mere acquaintance. The mere acquaintance and relatives, at least, he felt he could write to on the family's behalf.

Even without all that needed to be done, Hedley didn't feel he could leave his father yet. Friends called round, especially Jack, and Antony would sit with them for as long as they cared to visit but he was not encouraging. He made no phone calls and, Hedley noticed, had taken to hiding behind the answering machine which still had a message mentioning Rachel. He suggested Antony record a new message and Antony started but then he gave up, defeated by technology, and so they were left with an answering machine that simply beeped at callers, which was still more off-putting than suggesting they might wish to talk to the dead.

When the glazier had gone Hedley slipped up to the shops with the wicker basket Rachel used to carry. He loved all this. The gentle queuing at Tregenza's for fruit and veg and coffee beans, then at Lavender's for bread and cheese and ham. He loved the walking down one side of Market Jew Street for the paper and the post office then up the other for the olive stall. People said hello as he passed them. Three others stopped him for news and a chat. All the things that in adolescence made him itch for London – the slowness and charm, the lack of anonymity, the languid measuring out of the day in meals and drinks and little snacks – were dear to him now. The astonishingly parochial gossip – whose niece the nice postman had married and what the less nice postman had done to enrage the man in the lampshade shop's unmarried sister – came to seem more vital than anything in the national newspaper. The sitting companionably across the room from Antony of an evening doing nothing more exciting than reading, having eaten early because Antony suffered acid reflux if he went to bed on a full stomach, the going to Meeting with him, the chatting with everybody at length afterwards: all these things were suddenly what he wanted, what he felt he needed most. With every undemanding day that passed since the funeral he found it harder to contemplate abandoning them. This was disquieting because it implied that his usual life was lacking whereas he had got into the habit of thinking his life was more or less as perfect as life was going to get.

On his way home down Chapel Street he made a short detour into St Mary's to light a candle for Rachel then paused on a bench in the graveyard to admire the view of the bay.

Scrupulously good in most ways as a boy, his only major act of rebellion had been to sign up for confirmation classes at eleven to join the C of E. Rachel took the blame. She brought him into St Mary's the previous year to shelter from the rain once when they were shopping then sat back and watched, hugely amused, as he was seduced by all its high church gewgaws and statues that were such a contrast to the plain severity of the Friends' Meeting Houses that were all his experience of religion so far. When he pestered everyone with questions for days afterwards Antony ended by insisting Rachel bring him to a service by way of answering them. She had started it, he said, and it was more or less the faith of her youth after all. So she brought him back for a service and he was lost. Hymns, readings, a choir singing mass, bells and incense, lace and ceremonial, the mysterious business of the Eucharistic rite. Compared to the inward contemplation and occasional, formless declaration of British Quakerism, the service presented a drama.

He signed up for classes and was confirmed six months later. Thereafter, when the rest of the family went to Meeting he usually elected to come to Eucharist on his own, in his school suit and only non-school tie. Garfield and Morwenna teased him at first but desisted when Antony had a sharp word with them about religious tolerance.

He never entered greatly into the church's society – he grew into an inhibited teenager – but he took money for the collection, followed the readings in his Bible and took, for a while at least, to reading his scriptures every day and exploring the novel discipline of formal prayer.

The difference in his sexuality was never discussed – they were not that sort of family – and even with Morwenna, to whom he was closest, the subject was always skirted – but the flamboyant difference in his selected religion provided its convenient metaphor.

Hedley was not a high-flyer academically but he got by. All that ever really interested him was art so he went to art school in Falmouth where he was quiet but fairly popular and continued to drift in the upper half of the underachievers. He moved to London to share a cheap flat with two quiet girls who were abandoning painting for picture restoration and, thanks to a conversation struck up with an admiring older man after a service at St James's Piccadilly, landed himself a job in a small gallery several minutes to the cheaper side of Cork Street.

It was a quiet job. The vast majority of the gallery's sales – it specialized in discreetly homoerotic works of the late nineteenth and early twentieth centuries – were by catalogue. All Hedley had to do was dress nicely, sit behind a Biedermeier desk all day, sending off catalogues when requested, describing works in detail in answer to telephone enquiries and charming the occasional browser to the point where they felt so guilty at leaving empty-handed they at least bought a handsome catalogue or subscribed to the mailing list.

Once a week he had the fun of buying and arranging new flowers for the vase on his desk and of choosing a picture to sit in pride of place on the little ebonized easel in the window. Once every two months it fell to him to organize and often host a little Friday soirée to launch the latest show. Since nearly all their artists were dead, there was never a private view as such, so there was no need to court the press or placate painterly egos. He had merely to be sweet and modest and funny and occasionally gravely grateful. He became first an expert bluffer then something of an expert on Tuke, Burra, Vaughan, Minton, Cocteau and friends.

Oliver came to one of the launches, charmed Hedley before Hedley could charm him, and bought a tiny painting to justify further monopolizing his attention. It was an eight by four Duncan Grant watercolour of a man in a jewel-bright forest clearing. He, too, was an expert bluffer and Hedley had no inkling he didn't buy such things on impulse all the time and was actually spending several months' salary. Clients often asked for advice on hanging and because Hedley had a good eye and was wildly inquisitive to see how other people lived, he was happy to offer advice as an aftersales service. Oliver's street was an awesome one in Kensington and it was disarming to find that he actually lived not in one of its vast cream houses but in an eccentrically converted stables behind one which he only rented for a pittance from a distantly expatriate ex and which had only one room beside the bathroom.

The spot that was perfect for the little picture just happened to be over the bed, where Hedley proceeded to spend all weekend.

They were such a perfect fit he worried at first that they should be best friends not lovers. They were both middle sons. They each had a dead sibling. Luckily there were enough differences to pique one another's interest. Oliver's family had rejected him, or he them; the story changed according to his audience. He was entirely atheist with the proud rigour only a lapsed Catholic could muster. He played poker. He was only four years older than Hedley but had worldly abilities and an ease around moneyed, straight men that made him feel much older. Crucially he had a past whereas Hedley had enjoyed no significant relationships. This difference became rapidly obvious and Oliver began not to hide his history exactly but to reveal it with tactful caution, piecemeal and only as occasion demanded. Someone would come up to them at an opening and talk to Oliver with slightly too much hunger for recent developments while tossing unsettled glances at Hedley. Later on that evening Oliver would confirm that he had once been involved with them, but would do it in a way – often with some small, unflattering detail – that gently negated the person as a threat.

When he discovered who Hedley's mother was and that he painted too but had begun to neglect it, he encouraged and hectored him and then astonished Hedley by selling his small works to friends and clients for far more than Hedley would have dared demand.

Oliver had only been marking time in the gallery where he had been working when they met. By the end of a year he had been taken on at Mendel's. He took out a huge mortgage, bought their mews house off his ex, spent a fortune on taps, lighting, orchids and heritage paint and sold it to an American banker for so much they were able to halve the mortgage and buy a sort of cottage with two bedrooms that was in Holland Park but only if you persisted in the delusion that Shepherd's Bush Tube station wasn't five minutes nearer. That was twelve years ago.

'If we were straight,' Oliver joked, 'we'd have two children in boarding school by now.'

They had a good life together. They entertained and were entertained, they travelled and the friends they had in common now outnumbered Oliver's scary exes. Oliver persuaded Hedley to give up his job at the little gallery so he could paint full-time but now Hedley seemed to spend most of his days contentedly shopping and cooking. He was still enough of a Birthright Quaker for their material comfort, or rather the degree to which the material comfort mattered, to trouble him.

There were times too when, joking apart, he felt worryingly like a wife. People still bought his little paintings when he found time to do them but they bought them directly from him, not through a respectable gallery, and it tended to be the wives who did the buying. They said things like, 'I loved your last one, the apple, so much I keep it in the kitchen so I can look at it every day. Could you maybe do me another one of a pear but facing the other way and with the same background?'

Women took him out for lunches to pick his brains about curtain fabrics. Men tended to chat with him but talk to Oliver. He had become lightweight by default.

Hedley's only strength within the family was Morwenna. From the year she dropped out of university, he had been the only one of them she sought out. *Maintain contact* was too reassuringly regular a term for her sporadic appearances. She sought him out just twice in his three years at Falmouth. Quite by chance the second time was when he already knew where he was going to share a flat with the two quiet girls. Thereafter he left a scrupulous trail for her, like breadcrumbs in a fairytale wood. A tiny bit of her brain that wasn't garbled by drugs or madness or whatever it was that had driven her from the paths of normal people, retained his address and phone number the way a sleeping bird clutched its perch.

He never saw her for long though. The last time, a couple of years ago, he had persuaded her to eat supper with him and Oliver and stay the night but she had broken his heart by being gone before either of them woke up. She wasn't sleeping rough, or not frequently. She often had no or little money. She always had people with whom she was travelling or volunteering or about to stay. She seemed to have become a kind of Buddhist. Or perhaps it was that she was the best Quaker of them all, striving to create the fewest ripples as she moved through life and being a constant service to others, never to herself? He longed to ask her questions – how she lived, what she was trying to achieve in all this restlessness – but instinct warned him off and he forced himself, the way he used to with Rachel in her worst periods, to keep the conversation in a studiously calm present tense. Was she well? Did she need any money? Where was she living? And of course he pressed her with family news in an effort to keep her sewn to the rest of them, however slack the stitches.

The first few times she contacted him he had squeezed an address or a phone number out of her but it seemed the very act of giving out such information made her suddenly itch to move on so it was self-defeating. Instead he had learnt to encourage her to regard him as a poste restante, a safe, still point in her bewilderingly shifting world. If all else failed she could count on him, reverse the charges wherever she was, beg for money, a plane ticket, his company, whatever she needed. He would pay or, rather, Oliver would.

Keenly aware as he was of his material comforts, he was astonished at how she had managed to possess nothing but the clothes on her back and in whatever piece of luggage she was living from at the time. Her only things of value were small pictures of Rachel's: two startlingly lovely pastels Rachel had given her when she left home for LSE, and birthday cards Rachel had painted over the years. Of these, Morwenna had retained not only all her own but all the ones done for Petroc and several of the others, traded in their foolish youth for urgently needed trifles. (Easter eggs, in Petroc's case.) This booty she carried with her for the first few years. Then, after he had moved to London, she outraged Rachel by selling one of the cards at auction. It fetched nothing like its real value and he begged Morwenna to entrust the rest to him for secret safekeeping. If she wanted to sell anything more he could do it for her through Oliver and Oliver's contacts, securing her a better price and sparing Rachel's feelings.

Several thousand pounds' worth had now passed

through Oliver's hands into the art collecting ether. What happened to the money was a mystery. Quite possibly she gave most of it away. She lived with some nuns in Yorkshire for a while as a kind of postulant – unpaid servant, basically – and after that had a year or two in a scrupulously Marxist commune in Cologne, where everything had to be shared. She retained traces of her old, sharp humour, could laugh at nuns and communards, so he did not agree with Garfield that she was mad. It felt more as though she were under some huge obligation, a curse even, that kept her watchful and exhausted, so that her familiar intelligence was blunted and her wit made dim.

The first times she sought him out he was so relieved to see her he couldn't resist telling the others but once it was clear she was never going home and seemed to have cut off Garfield as much as their parents, Hedley began to keep quiet about seeing her beyond reassuring them from time to time that she still lived. He didn't want to seem to be saying that she liked him more than them. And quite possibly that wasn't it. Perhaps she only kept in touch because, as the guardian of her art collection, he was like her banker or trustee: a necessity, not an intimate.

And in a way she had brought him and Oliver together. He was still shaken by a recent, horribly swift and jangled phone call from her to the work number when they met, and found himself forgetting his obligations to his other guests as he told Oliver all about her. Oliver's dead sister had been schizophrenic and he knew all about relationships that had to be lived in the present tense.

'Just be grateful it's still her coming to you,' he said, 'and not the police.'

Morwenna dropped out of university in the middle of her finals. Worried friends reported her having behaved erratically before melting into the crowd on Waterloo Bridge and never returning to her hall of residence. Shortly afterwards she sent Rachel and Antony a plain white postcard on which she had written, 'I'm not dead or anything. Couldn't cope. Sorry . . .' She didn't write love. She didn't write her name either but her handwriting was distinctive.

It was when Hedley started at Falmouth that autumn and was living back at home but hardly there that he started to miss her. His life was filling with new experiences and new friends, so he shouldn't have done. If she were still at university she wouldn't have been at home anyway but the knowledge that she had cut herself loose and might be anywhere was terrible to him. Obsessive even in childhood, she had taught him the power of pledges with fate when he was quite small. 'If I do without chocolate until Sunday, the cross-country run on Monday will be cancelled,' or 'If I hold my breath to the end of the road, I'll get the questions I want in the maths test.'

It had become part of his habitual thinking. Throughout his first term he found himself routinely thinking, *If Rachel dies then I can have Morwenna back.* But Rachel was making herself especially hateful to him at this period, so perhaps she wouldn't be a tough enough sacrifice to satisfy the Fates.

*   *   *

Days later. The house was cleaner, the wardrobes emptier and the piles of letters still largely unanswered. Hedley had still not gone home.

'Is all well at his end?' Antony asked after Hedley hung up from Oliver's daily phone call.

'Hmm? Yes,' Hedley told him. 'Everything's fine. So have you chosen your password and written it down somewhere?'

Antony had finally decided to admit a computer to the house and Hedley had already spent hours setting it up for him. Rachel had always hated televisions and tarred computers with the same brush so had never allowed one to be bought although both Hedley and Garfield had repeatedly tried.

'I hate the dead black way their screens look when they're off,' she'd say and that was the end of the matter.

Ever since retiring from his teaching post at Humphry Davy, Antony had been involved in adult literacy. His basic technique remained the same while politics and funding changes altered the organization around him, but finally his patience had worn through when Jack Trescothick had urged him to call in on the adult learning centre for the first time since Rachel's death. The equivalent of a headmistress had duly offered condolences and welcomed him back, then announced they now needed him to go on maths and computer courses 'so as to arrive at a fuller understanding of the plight of the adult learner with basic skills challenges'. He had told them he was too old to retrain and given up.

This had depressed Hedley as he thought a sense of duty to his students, many of whom were such hopeless cases they'd been coming to him for years, was the one thing likely to shake his father out of his mourning torpor. But then, after yet another obituarist – this one from some feminist mag in New Zealand – had rung up with queries about Rachel's origins, the idea took hold that perhaps Antony would start researching the gaps in the family tree.

Antony had spent a frustrating morning in the reference library and an even more frustrating one on the phone to the US and Canadian embassies in London and to various record offices and genealogical societies listed in a book the library had found him. Genealogy had become such a national obsession apparently that official sources had become jealous of wasting phone time on it. Today he had announced that he needed a computer and Internet access if he was to make any progress without packing a bag and leaving Penzance for Toronto.

He claimed he was quite used to computers from the ones at the adult learning centre but Hedley was beginning to suspect he only learned how to use one as a glorified typewriter and then only when a colleague or student had already set the word processing program running for him.

He typed in the password Antony had chosen – the unexpectedly jaunty Quakerman – pressed 'enter' and clapped with genuine relief as the modem obediently clicked awake and proceeded to dial. The complications of a broadband connection could wait until the computer had proved itself indispensable.

But Antony was not so easily distracted. 'So everything's fine,' he asked. 'With you and Oliver, I mean?'

'It's fine, Dad. Honestly.'

'I feel bad you staying down here so long. Doesn't he miss having you around?'

'He's probably relieved to have the place to himself for a bit.'

'Eh?' Antony cocked a hand to his better ear. He was becoming so deaf it could only have been scrupulous political correctness that had made the literacy place hold on to him so long.

Hedley tapped his father's glasses back up his nose and Antony took the hint and manoeuvred their built-in hearing aid back into his ear.

'Everything's fine,' Hedley told him finally. 'Now look. When you dial up, this little icon appears in the bottom right-hand corner. If you can't see that, you're not connected. OK?'

'OK.'

However grim of itself, Rachel's death had provided a welcome distraction and an excuse. When she made her last insanely jabbering phone call to him, on the attic handset, he had been entering a crisis of his own.

This had a face and a name. She was called Ankie Witt. She was a Dutch painter who had moved back to Europe after a spell in South Africa where she had dropped art in favour of politics and worked for the ANC. She produced the sort of work Hedley loathed that seemed to be all about ideas and very little about paint: close-ups of parts of her body variously wired to car batteries or Bibles, wilfully childlike images of her being abused by her father, huge squares of canvas on which she had painted, with stencilled letters, rambling accounts of same abuse unpunctuated by insight, wit or punctuation. She wasn't especially young, perhaps thirty-eight – but she retained a young woman's confidence and a child's self-belief. She wasn't especially attractive – she had disconcertingly large, square teeth and a bovine brow – but she had a room-stilling sexiness that had something to do with a sense she conveyed in seconds of being unafraid and unshameable. She was a talented self-publicist and a hot new thing and, even when being bored or offensive, assured journalists of good copy.

It was a coup for Oliver to have brought her to the gallery; the painters with whom Mendel's had made its name in the Sixties and Seventies were now so Establishment that it was in danger of becoming a dinosaur park. Oliver's brief was to bring in artists people could actually afford for a year or two, whose work sold for thousands not tens of thousands.

He effectively represented several younger artists, not just painters, and was in regular, supportive contact with most of them but his role with them had professional distance. Apart from mounting their shows he acted as a kind of agent and matchmaker, introducing them to collectors who were likely to favour them, brokering occasional commissions for site-specific work. But unlike some gallery men who collected artists like big-game trophies, he preferred not to become too close. He claimed it made it easier on both sides for money to be discussed if the relationship remained professional.

Ankie was different. Overnight, seemingly, she was his new best friend. Had she simply come to three dinner parties in a row, Hedley would not have cared, but she started dropping round without warning – only ever when Oliver was home – or turning up at Mendel's when he was about to leave so that he drove her home with him or, worse, changed his plans to fit in with her wishes. Hedley would already be cooking when Oliver would ring to say, 'Ankie's dragged me to this amazing bar she's found. Do you want to join us?' or 'Ankie says I've got to see this Korean film at the Curzon. Come too and we can go somewhere afterwards.'

So assertive with others, Oliver seemed to be incapable of saying no to her. He always tried to include Hedley at least. Ankie never did. Hedley might not have felt so threatened by her had she at least had the subtlety to go after him on a charm offensive. From their first meeting, when she let her eyes slide off his while saying, 'Oh, hello,' when Oliver introduced her, she had barely acknowledged his existence.

The few times she rang and he answered she said only, 'Is Oliver there?' She bypassed that problem entirely once she had Oliver's mobile number. She ate the food he cooked, without comment, looked in on his studio without comment. If she found herself sitting by anyone who wasn't Oliver or famous, she ignored them to talk to Oliver across the table. She was not above simply taking his neighbour's seat when they left the room for a minute and laughing off any objections.

Ankie laughed a lot and made people laugh. Had her voice not had a buzz-saw edge to it one could have found her swiftly in a crowd by the telltale sign of a circle of people laughing and not saying much. She could be very funny, as monsters so often could, always at the expense of others, usually at the expense of others within hearing range. Just as there were people who did not feel a night out was complete without someone passing out or throwing up, so Ankie did not seem to feel socially fulfilled unless someone, usually a woman, had left the room in tears or, better yet, attacked her with words or a wineglass. Then her eyes would shine and a kind of moist satisfaction stole over her. If she was ever sweet or kind it would be in the hour after some such scene, as though some hunger in her had been answered and she could finally spare some attention for others.

Hedley tried. Of course he did. Because he loved Oliver and would have walked over broken glass to please him. He always liked Oliver's friends, at first simply because they liked Oliver and then in their own right. Many of his best friends now were friends they had in common. But Ankie defeated him. He tried but even when he laughed at her jokes her laughter would dim slightly and she would turn aside as from a bad smell.

So he tried objecting. He told Oliver she was offensive, but that was like pointing out that rain was wet and Oliver merely shrugged and said what could he do, she was his highest-earning artist and so on. So he tried pointing out that she had no boundaries, that she clearly fancied Oliver and wanted him for herself.

'Well sure she's insecure. But who wouldn't be after what she's been through?' Oliver said. 'She knows I'm not available.'

'Has she said so?'

'She's been here. She's met you. Look, what is this, babe? Are you jealous?'

Raising the subject at least meant that Oliver realized Hedley didn't like her but then he merely stopped bringing her back to the house or involving Hedley in what were now effectively their dates.

Rounds one and two to Ankie.

Alone too often, frustrated and feeling he had mishandled the situation, Hedley attempted retaliation and began to see something of a handsome and flirtatious ex of Oliver's who had begun to hover like the proverbial chicken hawk. This made matters worse in that the ex became extremely keen, scenting encouragement and when Hedley, tempted, put him off, he threatened to tell Oliver they were already sleeping together to help him make his mind up.

Hedley finally cracked at the end of that rare thing, a quiet night in with just the two of them. It was their anniversary and Oliver was very attentive and full of rather sweet nostalgia and, best of all, managed not to mention Ankie once all evening. They resisted the lazy, anaphrodisiac of slumping comfortably in front of the television and, with one accord went to bed early and were making love of a kind that quite put the flirtatious ex out of Hedley's thoughts when the phones rang, first Oliver's mobile, muffled in a distant jacket, and then the land line, just inches from the mattress.

They both manfully ignored it, Oliver even smothering it with a pillow before returning to the matter in hand, but then the answerphone clicked on in the study. Soon the unmistakable tones of Ankie were burbling through the open doors to where they lay.

171

'Oliver? Ollie! I know you're there. Listen, you handsome fucker, pick up the phone. Pick it up now!' And so on.

Unfortunately the machine was set up for taking long, involved messages from fretful artists so had no time limit fixed. She hung up eventually but not before the mood in the bedroom had cooled to the point where she might as well have been there between them.

Hedley lost his temper so rarely it was like a violent fit coming upon him.

'Why don't you sleep with the silly cow just to shut her up?'

'Not this again.'

'It's what she wants! Isn't it?'

'No. She's . . .'

'It's harassment, Oliver. Plain and simple. Can't you see that? She's coming between us and I'm not strong enough on my own, not with you off schmoozing her.'

'She's a friend, Hed.'

'Isn't that a bit unprofessional?'

'Fuck off.' Oliver had never said this to him, not in anger. They both fell silent, possibly equally shocked. Then the phone started to ring again.

'If you're not man enough to tell her when to back off,' Hedley began.

'No!' Oliver tried to get to the phone first but Hedley pulled him aside so furiously he struck his skull on the headboard.

Well good, he thought. *Serves you right.* He tossed aside the pillow and snatched up the phone. 'Listen, you talentless bitch . . .'

'What?'

'Rachel?'

'Petroc?'

'Sorry I . . . It's Hedley, Mum. Petroc's dead. Why are you whispering?'

'She mustn't hear me,' Rachel hissed. 'She's under the table there and – oh, fuck. Hedley, are you still there?'

'Yes,' Hedley sighed.

'The stones. How many should there be for it to be perfect?'

'Which stones, Mum? Where's Antony? Have you had your pills?'

And so began the last forty-minute phone call of Rachel's life.

By the end of it Oliver had draped the duvet over Hedley's shoulders, pulled on a dressing gown and gone to watch television. Hedley looked in on him once he had tossed a few things into a bag. 'I'm sorry about your head,' he began.

Oliver said nothing.

'She's really bad again. I'd better drive down. I don't understand it. Maybe the valproate isn't working as well as the lithium did or she's changed back or . . .' He realized Oliver wasn't looking at him so he left.

He seethed most of the way down, speeding like a madman on both motorways. He turned on his mobile when he stopped for petrol or coffee in the hope that Oliver had left a message, only to seethe afresh when he saw that he hadn't.

Finding Rachel dead blasted all those thoughts aside apart from a momentary, low, childish voice that said, *Well he'll have to be nice to me now.*

Oliver was scrupulous. He bought crazily beautiful flowers as soon as he heard the news and had them sent to Antony and they were from him, not the gallery. The Mendel's ones were considerably less special but then she had made them no significant money in years and hadn't had a solo show there since the mid-Eighties. He came down for the funeral, bringing Hedley a choice of suits and a shirt and black tie bought for the occasion. He stayed one unbelievably weird night below him in Petroc's old bunk then drove back early with the parting instruction, put with warm sincerity, that Hedley was to take as long as it took.

Since then he rang every day and even sent a few postcards. Together they sustained an illusory continuity of their normal life together, exchanging dull bits of information about what they had done or who they had spoken to. He loved Hedley and missed him, he said. He couldn't wait for him to come home. Oh and which fabric should they use on the old kitchen sofa, the soft pink stripes or the pinky brown weave or the taupe stuff that felt like suede? And if he posted Hedley a bundle of catalogues, could Hedley choose the light fittings for the new bookcase?

And then, that morning, with lethal quietness, like the scene in the horror film where the audience suddenly spots the killer crossing a doorway behind the heroine's back, Oliver let slip a *we*.

'I think,' he said, 'we're going to see another Gong Li film tonight.'

Hedley kept his responses light and neutral and hung up soon afterwards but when Antony started asking him if everything was all right between them he had to leave the house for a while. *We* might have referred to several people, but Oliver only saw Korean films with Ankie. Then there was the little matter of that *another*, which began to suggest they had been taking in a whole season of the things in Hedley's absence.

He needed to speak about it with someone. Morwenna. If only. Even in her adult strangeness, she remained a good listener and would take his side with the reliability of magnetic north.

Antony wouldn't begin to understand. If Hedley could not fathom Ankie's motives, how could he expect his father to? Spite was not in his vocabulary. Besides, contemporary London life having lain so far outside his sphere of reference for so long it would have been like explaining house music to William Penn.

Garfield was no better, but for different reasons. He was too much the older brother, always so high-minded, so fixated on pleasing Rachel and Antony it was a wonder he had focused on any girl long enough to convince her to marry him. And ever since he had thrown in law for his Joseph the Carpenter act, the fog of inhibition that came between the brothers had been thicker than ever. Oliver's theory was that, for all that Garfield meant well, he found the idea of having a gay brother deeply distasteful so got around it by treating Hedley as though he had never grown up. The insulting implication of this being that he thought gayness a stage out of which Hedley would eventually mature.

The solution came in a phone call Antony took while

Hedley was out: Garfield had invited them over for Sunday lunch. Hedley would talk to his sister-in-law.

Hedley drove Antony over to Falmouth for Meeting, then they went back to Garfield and Lizzy's house for the rest of the day. Spring was in the air. The trees were greening up and, in the daffodil fields, the unpicked flowers were nearly all spent and browning. As if to chime with the clamorous birdsong outside, the Meeting seemed extraordinarily talkative.

Garfield seemed happier and less brooding than they had seen him for weeks and he announced over lunch that he was going back into law. The man he had introduced them to after Meeting worked for one of the numerous firms in Truro based around the county courts and thought he could find an opening for him on a six-month trial basis. He would wind up the instrument repair business and start there in a month. The understanding was that, as a sop to his conscience about making money from other people's trouble, he would only work on pro bono, legal-aid cases.

Antony was pleased about this but not, Hedley could see, as pleased as Garfield could wish. Garfield always wanted more than either parent could give and had not spent enough time with Antony lately to have learned how subdued all his reactions had become since Rachel's death. Hedley knew he ought to resent the speed with which Garfield had backed away and left all the sorting out of Rachel's things to him but actually he had been glad of it. Garfield had a sentimental way of relating everything back to his own emotional history that would have made sorting out even a box of her old shoes an interminable process.

This represented a complete volte-face on Lizzy's part – she who had always been so set on saving Garfield from Law and London, and who had seemed to seize on the maintenance of her father's ailing business as a kind of sacred trust. He glanced across at her and received a sharp look back that told him to wait until later.

He liked Lizzy, against all the odds. He had enjoyed a swift understanding with her from the day Garfield first brought her to visit them in Penzance and did not need to look at her to know, when the others talked about going for a walk up to Pendennis Castle after lunch to enjoy the perfect weather, that she wanted him to stay back with her.

She was an archetypal good girl, the sort who kept a towelling band in the bathroom so she could keep her hair up while giving her forehead and neck a thorough scrub. She reminded him of Laura and Midge, the clean-living picture restoration students whose flat he used to share. Nice girls like that, girls who assumed the best of people and thus made one strive not to disappoint them, had become rare in his life.

The house had a pretty first-floor sitting room. As soon as Garfield and Antony were walking down the garden path for their digestive stroll, Lizzy took him up there with coffee and the chocolates Hedley had brought knowing she would have no chocolate in the house because she found it irresistible.

'I think it's wonderful what you've been doing for your dad,' she said at once. 'Garfield really appreciates it, I know. You're much stronger than he is. Emotionally, I mean. How is Antony, do you think?'

'Better. Definitely. He's started researching the family tree a bit, which is fantastic because it's given him a goal.'

'Doesn't he know it all already?'

'His side, yes, but hers is a mystery. I had all the obit-uarists after me and I think that's what got him out of his armchair finally. He's logging into all these New England and New York websites now in search of her. But with Kelly not exactly being unusual among Irish immigrants, he'll have his work cut out.' He took a chocolate then remembered to offer her one, which she waved aside.

'So. When do you head back?' she asked.

'Oh . . . you know. Soon, I suppose. Though it's sort of fun just bumbling along with him. I used to look around at all these sad men who end up living with their mothers and think how did *that* happen and suddenly I can see.'

They laughed.

'Oliver must miss you, though,' she said.

'Hmm.'

He planned on easing into the subject but Lizzy's face was so pure and sympathetic he couldn't resist shocking her a little.

'Actually I think he's having an affair and he's glad to have me out of the way.'

'No. Hedley, are you serious?'

'Oh it's probably nothing. I want to hear about you two. What's with Garfy going back into law?' He patted the little sofa beside him. All the furniture there was slightly doll-sized because it was one of those houses where the rooms looked perfectly big enough until you furnished them or opened a door. Hedley thought guiltily of the twelve-foot, bed-depth monster he had recently ordered for their sitting room in town then found himself picturing Ankie Witt sprawled on it. Lizzy had joined him and he was all set to start telling her then saw a difference in her expression and a sly hint of a smile.

'What?' he asked.

'You won't believe this,' she said. 'But at long bloody last you're going to be an uncle.'

'No! Oh Lizzy, that's fantastic news!' He hugged her. 'When did you find out?'

'A few days ago, actually longer than that. But we were only certain yesterday. Garfield rang to ask you both over as soon as we heard.' She laughed. Her happiness was uncontainable and transformed her. He marvelled at her control at keeping it tamped down all morning and all through lunch.

'Do you think he's telling Antony now?'

'Of course. You know Garfield. *Look what I did, Daddy.*' Her quick assessment of Garfield's nature was no less devastating for being delivered in a loving tone. 'We had half a mind to keep quiet a while longer. I didn't want it upsetting Antony, coming so soon after Rachel.'

'He'll be over the moon. Of course he will.'

'Oh good.'

She laughed again and gave him a glimpse of how full and satisfied motherhood would make her. He ate another chocolate but still she waved them away, already controlling what the child would eat, poor thing.

'But what about you?' she asked. 'I want to hear all about everything. You weren't serious about Oliver?'

179

'No no. And there's nothing to tell,' he said. 'Everything's lovely, the extension's going to be lovely, Oliver's lovely, I'm lovely.'

She accepted it and poured him another cup of coffee.

When Garfield and Antony came back Antony was almost as happy as the mother-to-be and Garfield was impossibly pious in his effort not to appear smug. And Hedley smiled on them all and made his face a mirror to give them each the version of himself that would least unsettle them. It was a trick he had learnt in boyhood: in a family of committed truth-tellers, someone had to tell a few kind lies to keep the whole thing together.

That night he settled Antony by the computer with a great box of Rachel's papers he thought might hold some clues for his family research then took himself quietly off to her loft.

No one had been up there since the glazier's visit but it needed doing. In many ways it remained the best room in the house, certainly for someone living alone, and would be wasted as a morbid shrine. Inspired by some fabric he had found, which he liked, although it was quite unsuitable for him and Oliver, he had a vision of the loft tidied up, repainted and carpeted and converted into a delightfully sunny room where Antony could sit and read and doze. It was a room in need of reclamation.

They would have to do something about the ladder-like steps, naturally, and the silly trapdoor, which were quite unsuitable for an elderly man who would one day be unsteady on his legs. It needed proper stairs, with a banister. It needed a radiator for the cooler months. The incredible accretions of paint, splashed, trodden or smeared on the floor and the one unwindowed wall were too thick merely to paint over and would have to be burnt and scraped and sanded away. The floorboards, he noticed for the first time, were handsomely broad. They were probably old ones reclaimed from some wrecked ship's timbers when this eccentric lookout was first erected. They could be sanded back to cleanliness and waxed, then he could find a few Turkish or Iranian rugs; even modern ones would fade to tastefulness in the sunlight.

Hedley fetched a large cardboard box from the stash he had gathered in supermarkets for the purpose, some bin liners and a broom. The least spent of her paints and better brushes he put in the box to take to London and add to his own stocks. The rest, the wrecked brushes, the mangled tubes of colour, the spoons and palette knives she had used so brutally they had bent beyond usefulness, he swept into bin liners. He dismantled the easel, which she had in any case broken, perhaps on her last terrible night, and carried it downstairs along with the similarly shattered chair. He emptied the kettle out of the window and tossed it in with the rubbish along with the biscuit tin and paint-streaked teabags and filthy sugar lumps. Sentiment stayed his hand over throwing out the tray as well because it was one Petroc had made for her in carpentry class. Liberal use of paint stripper and beeswax might be enough to salvage it but quite possibly Antony would want it with the paint splashes left on, a memorial to mother as well as son.

At last the space was clear and fairly clean and he could begin work on the hive of cupboard spaces let into the back wall between the chimney stacks.

As he had been tidying, a sort of mental dialogue took place between him and Rachel. The mess was so her, the impulse to tidy it away so him. He was a very tidy painter. It was a superficial symptom of what would always keep his work at the purely decorative end of the artistic spectrum. But as soon as he started emptying the cupboards, her undeniable voice took over and his kindly fussing one was silenced.

He emptied the first two smaller cupboards then suddenly, painfully wished Oliver or, better yet, Morwenna were there to help him. There was so much and most of it was of such high quality. At first he found only notebooks and sketchpads. She was an inveterate draughtsman and maintained a lifelong habit of throwing off drawings from the life as a preparatory exercise before beginning her work with paint. She drew used teabags, ruined brushes, paint tubes squeezed and doubled back on themselves. There was a sketchbook meticulously recording and transforming much of what he had just carried out to the dustbins.

She drew, too, when she was waiting or ill. Some psychiatrist or occupational therapist long ago must have taught her to use her skill with a 2B pencil and scrap of paper to suspend her mind when it threatened to become too busy or to divert it from irritation whenever circumstances – a traffic jam or delayed appointment – threatened to fill her with pointless anger. She threw many of her sketchbooks away – once filled they were of no more value to her than empty paint tubes – but in the dusty heap of them he had salvaged, he found quick drawings of them as babies or children, of

Jack Trescothick's waiting room and countless ones of views through the car windows. She had always kept a sketchbook in the car. There would still be one in the glove compartment right then if he went out to look. There were drawings without number of her right hand (she was left-handed) and several, only slightly cruder, of her left.

Done fleetingly, with no view to preservation or selling, these images tumbled across one another, over-lapped or undercut. A good one would be ruined by a failure that slewed across it or by her spontaneous mischief in adding some element of caricature or cartoon. But their cumulative effect was to summon up not only her prodigious, careless talent but the maddening truth that art was the one thing that stilled and focused her impossibly restless personality; art won through where her family failed.

There were no drawings from her depressions, only fleeting records of the periods of descent or recovery. She must have destroyed most of her hospital work before leaving hospital each time. She joked once that she never picked up a pencil when she was depressed because some thin, surviving bit of her healthy brain retained what she had been taught about depression and sharp objects not mixing.

And then he found finished pictures. Several perfectly sellable ones from her extended, figurative, post-Petroc phase which, for some reason, she had held back from framing. The pictures Mendel's had never wanted. Here were the familiar, meticulous studies of shells and fruit and Cornish hedges and a sequence of ominous black

183

birds – rooks? ravens? – he had never seen. Even discarding a third of these there was enough for a good-sized posthumous show in the Newlyn gallery that had remained loyal to her later phase. But then he opened other, bigger cupboards, which he noticed for the first time resembled funerary vaults, and found fascinating near-duplicates of familiar works that had long since found homes in various collections, works that, hung alongside their better known 'finished' counterparts, would reveal how meticulously plotted were her apparently spontaneous creative processes.

The night she died Garfield had mentioned spotting an old abstract work of hers from the Sixties and Hedley was impatient to see it for himself. Garfield had mentioned a big disc in shades of blue and grey. It was half off or half on its stretcher and had been shoved so violently into the cupboard the stretcher had actually broken in one corner. Perhaps she had started to stretch it afresh, thinking to finish it, or, in a fit of economy, to scrape it down and paint over it.

He spread it out, astonished at its freshness, and saw at once this wasn't an old work at all. It was a new stretcher, of a construction she had only been using for ten years or so. The colours were those on the palette he had just thrown out. He saw them afresh, slightly smeared where, as usual, she had laid cling film across the palette to stop them drying out overnight.

It was big compared to the work she had been doing since Petroc, the sort of thing she used to do when she still favoured the studio at the back and wasn't constrained by what could be fitted through trapdoor or window or what was small enough to be economically priced for tourists.

He wished Oliver were there to marvel with him, to help and advise. It was staggering. Entirely undomestic. Only a metre square perhaps but still a big, grand statement for a museum or a rich man's house. Excited, he went back to the cupboards and found eight more, this time with undamaged stretchers. These were finished and roughly dated on the back as well as signed on the front. She had been working like someone possessed for she had completed these in just a month before she died.

He spread them out about him like so many exotic rugs. They were a sequence of sorts, in that they were all variations on the idea of a disc. There was a fiery one, a sun in effect, and one the precise off-white of her newest medication. The other six were less perfectly round, more organic. He stared at them for ten minutes or more before he recognized the precious pebbles she seemed to have had about the loft for ever and which he had just tidied away to the bathroom.

She had painted them in such close detail and so much larger than lifesize that they had become abstracted. Or perhaps she had merely revealed the abstract art that nature had worked on them? Stone which a glance showed as merely brownish, seen closer to revealed swirls of pink, blue and deepest purple. And yet they weren't just the pebbles. She had added something or revealed something.

Hedley sat back, aware of the sounds of Antony moving about downstairs again but reluctant to tear himself away. He could see how these big, triumphant canvases would look hung in a sequence in a space light and generous enough to let their colours vibrate off the walls like a line of cathedral windows. It was too soon to go worrying Antony about them but these paintings needed to be seen and not merely sold. Oliver would know how to proceed. Hedley set about carefully sliding them back into storage. His mind was spinning ahead. Were these cupboards entirely dry? Was the household insurance enough? When could he persuade Oliver down to see them?

The thought of Oliver inevitably led back to a mental image of Ankie and all at once Hedley could see why he had been so powerless in the face of the woman. It was because she was so like Rachel. Sensing her foe's weak points by instinct, she had touched on his boyhood conditioning never to threaten or upset Rachel's delicate equilibrium however badly she behaved. Like Rachel, Ankie was powerful, dismissive, erratic, a threatening, clamorous, emotionally hungry presence and deep down he wanted to appease and please her. But she was not remotely as talented and therein, just possibly, lay his chance to overcome her.

Not that he had ever overcome or even withstood his mother. He had simply withdrawn from the field.

Once the last painting was tidied away he should have gone downstairs and set about making something small but nutritious for Antony's supper. He got as far as opening the trapdoor and turning out the light but then he sat back in the old, defeated armchair where his mother had spent such tormented hours, defeated himself but drawing thin comfort from the possibility that proximity to the greater predator would protect him from the lesser one.

Morwenna was alone in St Ives with Rachel because it
was her tenth birthday and that was the tradition.
Considering she was so abnormal in other ways, not always
bothering to dress properly or wash her hands or brush
her hair, eating pills more often than she sat down to
normal meals, considering she was a painter, considering
she painted paintings which weren't actually *of* anything,
considering she sometimes cried or laughed for no reason,
considering she was mad, Rachel was surprisingly

187

insistent on traditions. The night before Christmas they could only use candlelight, even in the bath, because it was a tradition. On Midsummer Day they had to have all three of the day's meals out of doors, preferably on the beach, and always the same beach, even if it was high tide, even if it was raining. Tradition again.

And when it was anyone's birthday they had to spend the day with Rachel. Not Antony, of course, because he was married to her so that would have been silly. But the rest of them. The idea was it was your day and, within reason, she had to go and do and eat whatever you wanted. Garfield was even more of a traditionalist than she was and always wanted exactly the same thing: crab and chips then ice-cream and chocolate sauce in Bailey's then a film. Being a boy he took real pleasure in commanding Rachel, knowing she had to do stuff, had to eat pudding – which she affected to despise – and watch a film – which would have her twitching with impatience. Hedley was only eight, so was only just starting to take full advantage of his birthdays and would dream about them and plan them in such detail and change his plans so often that the big day, when it came, was bound to disappoint him. Petroc, being really small still, had birthday outings that were actually an excuse for Rachel to go off on her own somewhere and just take him along like a giggly parcel.

Morwenna adored Petroc. The look, the sound, the smell of him filled her with a kind of hunger so that she wanted to possess and control and sort of crush him with love – a feeling neither Garfield nor Hedley ever inspired in her. She was ashamed that when Rachel got into the car with her that morning and said, 'Your day. Just us. What'll we do?' she really wanted to tell her mother to take everyone else away somewhere and leave her alone with Petroc for a few hours. But she had once been as deeply in love with Rachel as she was with her little brother so it was easy enough to shrug and say, 'It's being just us that matters. What do *you* want to do?'

So they had driven to St Ives because there was an exhibition at the Penwith Society Rachel wanted to see. This filled Morwenna with foreboding. She liked St Ives. It had proper beaches, unlike Penzance, and people went there on holiday so, even though it was barely half an hour away, going there tended to feel a little like being on holiday too. It was the mention of art that unsettled her.

Rachel never said as much but it was obvious she thought Morwenna more talented than her brothers. When they brought paintings home from school, she'd dismiss them with a 'very nice' or an unconvincing burst of enthusiasm, whereas whenever Morwenna did or whenever Morwenna picked up her crayons at home and drew things, Rachel took it as seriously as she might them forming letters correctly or doing maths. She would ask impossible questions like, 'Why did you use that colour instead of this one?' or 'What makes you draw the tree from that angle?' and if she came across Morwenna in the act of drawing or painting she could never refrain from correcting the way she was applying a colour or demonstrating an effect she could improve by holding her pencil at a different angle. The result was to make Morwenna self-conscious and nervous about art by introducing rights and wrongs into something that would otherwise have been a kind of play.

Similarly Rachel would ask her opinion of grown-ups' paintings – as if the opinion of a little girl really mattered to her – then would weigh up Morwenna's responses in a way that made it clear that it wasn't enough to be honest and say, 'I like this' or 'I don't like that.' There were right and wrong responses. Morwenna loved her mother's paintings. She liked to sit close to them and stare without blinking until the vibrant colours began to blur and shift. They made her feel things as strongly as music did but whereas you felt quite safe saying, 'This piece makes me think of snow falling on lily pads,' or 'This piece is like a giant marching through the forest breaking trees,' you couldn't specify what Rachel's paintings suggested and it was a grave error of taste to say they reminded you of things like clouds or boats or birds. The only thing more frightening than Rachel's anger was her disappointment when you said something stupid like, 'That blob's the lady and that blob there's her husband.' She looked at you and simply turned aside in a way that felt like the sun going behind a cloud, only for ever.

Antony said they all had to be careful not to hurt Rachel's feelings.

'She feels things more than we do,' he explained, 'so we have to treat her gently.'

Luckily she never asked Morwenna's opinion of her own pictures but she was sure to ask in the Penwith Society. Morwenna did not understand the details but she knew that to enter this small gallery together was to enter a minefield. There were friends of Rachel's and Antony's in the Society, like Uncle Jack, who it would normally be right to like out loud but Rachel was not a member of the Society for some reason. She said she wouldn't want to be, in a way that implied she wanted to be very much but that the Society had said no.

The drive over started well. The sun was shining and the trees on the edge of town were dazzling in their finery. They stopped in Rachel's favourite lay-by, high up beyond Badger's Cross, so they could get out and admire the view of St Michael's Mount far below and so she could take Morwenna's birthday photograph. As they drove on, plunging down into Nancledra, Rachel made her giggle by saying it was the kind of place where people married their sisters and as the car laboured and coughed up to Cripplesease and the steady descent towards the back of St Ives, Morwenna saw that for once Penzance and St Ives were sharing the same weather. Perhaps the day would go well after all.

'Isn't this great? Just us girls together?' Rachel called out and Morwenna said yes it was and asked Rachel to tell her about when she was a baby, because this always put her in a good mood.

'You were the tiniest baby,' Rachel began. 'You were so tiny you hardly made a bump so a lot of people just thought I'd been eating too many Jelbert's ices. And I carried on wearing my normal clothes for ages with no beastly maternity smocks until the very last month. And I was painting as usual. I did some really good work while I was waiting for you to show up. It was a beautiful autumn day, just like today, and I was painting.'

'Was it a circle or a square?'

This was the only permitted joke on the subject of Rachel's art and Rachel laughed.

'It was a square, cheeky. You know it was because I had it hanging in your bedroom for ages.'

'The purply one with the green line.'

'That's the one. So I was working on that, listening to the radio, and suddenly I can feel you starting. So I call out to Antony and say put the suitcase in the car because it's time. And he went out to get the car started and to turn the heater on, because it was quite chilly and windy even though the sun was shining, and then he realized we needed petrol so he drove to the Co-op to buy petrol and to drop Garfield off with friends, and by the time he was back . . .'

'I was born!'

'You were born. The only one of you to be born at home. You were so tiny, you'd slipped out of me like a pretty little fish and I'd hardly had to puff and pant at all.'

'Not like with Hedley.'

Morwenna said this for the pleasure of seeing the little, false thundery expression she knew it would bring to her mother's face. Sure enough there it was and Morwenna giggled, forgetting she wanted to be at home with just Petroc.

'Hedley?! Hedley was another matter entirely. Hedley took two whole *days* to arrive in the Bolitho Home and your father began to say maybe we should just leave him where he was because he sort of liked me the size of a mountain.'

Morwenna loved Rachel again. Rachel was doing what

she so rarely did, making you feel you were the thing, the person, whatever, at the front of her mind. Most of the time she was being distracted by all the clamour and demands and bother of family and even under that surface level of irritable chat you knew she wasn't seeing the room at all but was staring away inside her head at some painting she'd left half-finished or some other painting she hadn't even begun yet.

It would be a good birthday after all. Sliding into double figures had felt ominous, a first significant pace away from childhood and towards a time when more and more would be expected of her. But laughing with Rachel, daring to admire her now that she was staring straight ahead, she decided all would be well.

'If we pass three women with wicker baskets before the bottom of the hill,' she told herself rashly, 'it'll be fine.'

This was cheating slightly because wicker baskets were a far safer bet than nuns, or policemen on bicycles and even as she formed the thought, or possibly just before, she counted off her first one: a smart young woman with a wicker basket over one arm chatting to a friend on a doorstep. The second came swiftly after: an older woman pulling a basket on wheels in which a pile of library books was plainly visible. But there was no third. As the bottom of the hill drew ever closer and The Stennack turned into Chapel Street and then Gabriel Street where they had to turn left among the shops, she paid less and less attention to what Rachel was saying in her anxiety to see one. Even a cat basket would do. Or a log basket.

Please, she thought. *Please?*

But there was nothing. Only prams and string bags and one fierce-looking woman with a bag made from Black Watch tartan. And now they had turned the corner and it was too late.

'What's the matter?' Rachel asked, irritated at being ignored probably. 'What is it?'

'Nothing,' Morwenna said. 'I . . . I thought I saw a girl from school, that's all.'

There was no cheating fate. By the time they were parking on the Island, which usually gave Morwenna a small thrill even though she knew it wasn't really an island but just a promontory with a car park on it, the sky had clouded over and Rachel's mood was darkening in sympathy.

'So,' her tone glittered as Morwenna brought her back the ticket for the car park. 'We'll just call in at the Penwith Gallery then buy the things Antony asked us to get.'

'Whisky and double cream and lemons.'

'Yes. Then we can get fish and chips and then . . . Then we'll see. Just look at that sky!'

Morwenna glanced up. It was grey, with darker grey clouds around which a threatening hint of pink was showing.

'What colours would you paint that with?' Rachel asked.

Morwenna knew a child would say grey and red so she said, 'Purple and black. Maybe some deep blue. Clouds are hard. They work best if you make the paper wet.'

But Rachel wasn't listening. 'We needn't go in for long,' she said. 'It's just so I can tell Jack we went. After all, it's your day, not mine.'

She was getting nervous, Morwenna knew the signs. She was winding herself up like a spring with razor edges. She had always seemed more attuned to these impending states in her mother than her brothers were, the way a dog could foretell thunderstorms. The mounting tension was infectious and she hated it the way she hated Garfield stretching rubber bands too far or making balloons squeak. At least with a balloon or a straining rubber band you could reach out and make the bad bit happen sooner.

The gallery wasn't huge, like a museum – it had just one big sunny room tucked behind a row of houses near Porthmeor Beach – but neither was it like the galleries where pictures were for sale, because they had to pay to go in. Something that made Rachel mutter under her breath.

Rather than walk slowly round the room like her mother, interrogating each picture, Morwenna made directly for the paintings by Uncle Jack. There were only three. She recognized them at once because of the way he always framed his canvases first then painted over the frame as though the picture's exuberance wouldn't be contained. In fact exuberance was a word she had learned when Antony and Rachel were discussing him once. There was a bluey-green he used, too, which he must have mixed himself because she never seemed to see it anywhere else. Perhaps he put something in it that wasn't paint. Soup, maybe, or melted sweets.

She couldn't have said why she liked his pictures. Perhaps what she liked was the fact of knowing him and liking him so that spotting his pictures in a gallery was like seeing a friend in a crowded room. She felt proud when she saw his pictures on a gallery wall whereas when she saw Rachel's there was always a stab of worry. *Why wasn't anyone looking at them? Why hadn't they sold yet?*

They were no more *of* anything than Rachel's paintings but something about them suggested a narrative, the titles perhaps. These three were called Because You Left Early, Missing George and Witching Hour. There was a happy quality to their use of colour that made them seem to sing where their more rigid neighbours merely spoke or whispered. Perhaps she was confusing the character of the painter with his work, but in this austere setting Uncle Jack's paintings seemed to be kind.

He wasn't really her uncle. They just called him that.

She became aware that Rachel was moving round the exhibition towards her. She had thought to keep several steps ahead of her and so avoid the difficulty of a discussion but she was pulled up short by a sculpture.

It was made of some sort of close-grained wood. It was roughly cylindrical only its ends were rounded off, like a gentle, pointless bullet, and it bulged slightly in the middle. It wasn't solid. There was a kind of split in it, a cleft like the gap in a rock where you might find baby crabs. If you peered closely you saw that the cleft opened out into a sort of cave where the wood had been left rougher, paler and unpolished. The rest, the outer wood and the edges, the lips, of the opening, had been rubbed as smooth as a piece of sea wood and waxed or oiled until it shone and you could see every line and whorl in it.

Morwenna knew you weren't allowed to touch but she

had never found touching so hard to resist. Or smelling. She wanted to seize the thing in both hands and breathe it in the way she would the skin of a ripe melon or a peach, or Petroc when he had just had his bath and had his hair standing in tufts and was huggable in pyjamas. It was quite simply the loveliest thing made by a person she had ever encountered. The paintings around it seemed flat and sterile by comparison, even Jack's, an effect heightened by the sculpture being the only thing of its kind in the gallery. Like a cat in a bookshop, its advantages were all the greater for being unfair.

'Darling?' Rachel only called them that when she was impatient or on edge. Morwenna knew better than to linger and ran to join her at the door. 'What did you think?' The inevitable question slipped out as they walked up the lane.

'It was interesting,' Morwenna told her, using a word that had proved safe in the past even though it encouraged further discussion.

'Hmm,' Rachel said. 'The usual suspects. Did you like Jack's?'

'Of course,' Morwenna said. 'I saw them as soon as we walked in. You can always tell which are his. Is he very different?'

'You tell me.'

'Well . . . He must be or they wouldn't be so easy to spot but . . .'

'What? It's OK. You can say whatever you think. You don't have to like his work just because he's our friend. That would be facile.'

'What's facile?'

'Like the French for easy only insulting. Too easy. Too simple.'

'Like Terry Stephens' boat pictures?'

'Ssh!' Rachel giggled. 'Yes.'

Morwenna hoped this meant they had moved on. Rachel was inspecting a butcher's shop window. Piles of sausages and lamb's liver and crouching chickens and skirt for making pasties: the kind of display that made Morwenna feel queasy if she looked too long, mainly because of the nasty plastic grass fringes that had been arranged around each tray of meat. But no. Rachel was relentless.

'So. About Jack. But what? You said but.'

'Well . . . If his paintings are so easy to spot, does that mean he's just doing the same thing over and over, like Terry Stephens?' She thought of Because You Left Early and Missing George – even this soon after seeing them they were muddled in her memory and indistinguishable. She compared them in her mind's eye with the amazing sculpture. 'They're all colourful. They're all cheerful. They're a bit like sweets, really, aren't they?'

'Don't try to be clever-clever. It does something odd to your face.'

Rachel's swift reproof, delivered almost casually, seemed to sting more than one place at once and left Morwenna unable to walk and think at the same time. As usual, Rachel seemed unmindful of the strength of her words.

'Come on,' she called back cheerfully as she walked on. 'I just need some things from in here. You said we had to do whatever I would be doing.'

It was a stationer's, really, selling everything from writing paper and bottles of Quink to cheap paperbacks and packs of cards. Encouraged by local painters and illustrators, however, it had branched out in a small way as an art supply shop. There were racks of oil paint in tubes and watercolours in the little, tempting, paper-wrapped packages that made them look like expensive toffees and strange pencils that weren't coloured and weren't HB either. There were artist's pads, drawers of special papers and a revolving rack of seductive books Rachel loudly despised with titles like *How to Paint Seascapes* and *Drawing Horses is Easy!*

Hedley had bought a huge tin of Swiss crayons here with his birthday money from Uncle Jack but seemed so awed by its size and smartness once he got it home that he did little but arrange its contents in different ways or make very neat sort of diagram pictures with each crayon in turn represented by a square coloured in with painful precision.

Morwenna admired some prettily packaged bottles of Indian ink while Rachel made a pile of paint tubes on the counter with her usual decisiveness. 'We were going to get you one of these for your birthday,' Rachel called out. She was holding up one of the shop's little wooden models designed to help artists get people right. Morwenna loved them although secretly she'd have preferred the expensive one like a horse.

'Yes, please!' she said.

'It's not a toy, though.'

'I know. It's to help with proportion.'

'Well pretend you didn't see and remember to act surprised when you open it. I just wanted to be sure it was the right thing.'

The threatened rain arrived when they were still two streets from the chip shop and they had both dressed equally foolishly, lulled by a sunny morning. They sheltered in a little supermarket where Rachel suddenly remembered she had promised to buy things but not what they were. Morwenna reminded her and held the art bag while Rachel put several other things besides cream, butter, whisky and cornflakes in her basket. She was like a magpie in food shops, drawn to glitter and colour and quite capable of buying something they didn't need and would never eat, because she liked its packaging. Antony had trained Morwenna and her brothers to be firm when they were with her.

'Admire things with her,' he said, 'but then put them back. She won't mind. Not if you do it kindly.'

Rachel was admiring some packets of saffron when a terrifying old woman came up to them. At least her face looked old, as craggy as cliffs and as furrowed as a field, but she had a good figure and a big gash of amazingly red lipstick, so perhaps she wasn't that old but just very battered. She was just the way Morwenna imagined Hansel and Gretel's witch would look. Her hands looked as spread and strong as a road-mender's. Morwenna could picture her tucking Petroc into a casserole with carrots and onions and a bottle of wine then thumping a lid on him so heavy he couldn't escape as she slid him into the oven.

The woman was peering up at the shelf where Rachel's whisky had come from. 'What? Up here?' She shouted to the lady behind the counter. 'No, there's nothing here but Bells and Famous Grouse. I ordered it. I always do. You had no business to . . . Oh.' She had spotted the bottle in Rachel's basket and came close. 'I'm sorry,' she said, not shouting any more but still not very politely. 'But you've got my bottle there. I buy it on account and it's normally put aside for me with the other things but the new girl didn't know. Do you mind?' And she reached into the basket and took the bottle.

'Barbara?' Rachel said, letting her take it.

'Yes?' The woman didn't seem pleased to be talked back to, especially not by her Christian name. She had her bottle and now she wanted to leave. Now she was closer, Morwenna discovered she smelled like an ashtray. Neither of her parents smoked, or not at home, but Morwenna had sniffed ashtrays and cigarettes out of curiosity at other people's houses. Jack smoked a pipe but he used peppermints afterwards, which didn't make it not smell but made the smell a bit better.

Rachel was putting on her party voice. 'Of course you won't remember me after all this time. Rachel Kelly. We met at the Artists' Ball ages ago. And then I went swimming with Jack Trescothick and the gang and you –'

'Oh yes,' the witch said to shut her up but Morwenna could see she either couldn't remember or hadn't cared to be reminded. She was glancing over Rachel's shoulder for an escape route and Morwenna half-thought to step aside and hiss, 'This way!'

'We were in the Penwith Gallery just now.' It was one of those times when Morwenna wished Rachel had a normal accent or rather no accent at all. Her curious mixture of American drawl and la-di-dah English had a way of becoming grotesquely exaggerated when she was

201

nervous. She could tell she was nervous now from how busy her fingers had become. They were fretting with her buttons, with the handle on her wire basket and the paint-splashed leather of her watchstrap. 'Morwenna's been admiring one of your lovely vulvas.'

Morwenna wasn't quite sure what a vulva was but she suspected it was rude because the Witch blanched and another woman who was passing them with, too late, a wicker shopping basket gave a sort of indignant cough and hurried away knocking a can of beans off a display.

The Witch stared at Rachel for a moment then said, 'Oh yes. You've been ill, haven't you?' Then she crouched down to Morwenna's height. It was frightening. She had an even stranger face close to, with a huge brow like Queen Elizabeth the First's and the deepest wrinkles Morwenna had ever seen and she was rather furry and smelled so strongly of cigarettes and something else not very nice that it was a bit like being too close to a clever, dangerous monkey, the sort that bit if you made the mistake of pushing food through their bars when they asked for it.

But Morwenna was fascinated too, because the sculpture had been so beautiful, and wished Rachel wasn't there being embarrassing.

'So what did you think?' the Witch asked, only of course she wasn't a witch, Morwenna realized now, but Dame Barbara Hepworth.

Morwenna thought of Hansel and Gretel again and of how Gretel stands up to the witch by being a bit rude and witchlike herself to match her. 'I liked it,' she said. 'I liked the way it was smooth and rough at the same time. It made me think of secrets.'

'Secrets? Good! Show me your hands? Are you strong?'

She set down her whisky bottle and Morwenna gingerly offered her hands, which weren't very clean actually. Dame Barbara took them firmly in hers and spread out the fingers then turned them over to look at the palms. Whatever she found there she kept to herself. Her own hands were quite worn and rough, not a lady's hands at all but maybe dames were different. With a new gentleness she folded Morwenna's fingers over on themselves, as though she had passed her a secret note and was tucking it away, then she sort of handed her hands back to her. 'I'll tell you something, Morwenna,' she said. 'Life can be bloody sometimes but then suddenly it's bloody marvellous.' She took her whisky, stood upright again and only glanced at Rachel in passing before walking away.

Nobody was ever rude to Rachel. They tended either to be too scared or to concerned. Certainly nobody ever mentioned her 'illness' so openly and in public. Morwenna was torn between a deeply instilled urge to protect her and a worrying, entirely new temptation to cheer.

Somehow Rachel appeared not to mind having been first insulted then ignored. She took down a different brand of whisky from the shelf, carried her basket to the counter and paid calmly enough. Once they were back on the street, however, she walked through the puddles so swiftly Morwenna almost broke into a run to keep up. Worse, she started muttering to herself. Morwenna only caught snatches that made any sense, like 'Stuck-up old huckster' and 'Who does she think she is' and 'So drunk she could hardly stand'. Passers-by were staring and even stepping off the pavement to avoid them.

Suddenly Morwenna noticed they had passed the fish and chip shop and interrupted her without thinking, because she was hungry.

'What about lunch?' she called out.

Rachel stopped abruptly and looked down at her in much the way Dame Barbara had looked at herself minutes before, as though she couldn't quite place her and resented the need to try.

'What?' she asked.

'The chip shop,' Morwenna said in a small voice, hoping she wasn't about to cry. Rachel hated it when any of them cried; it felt like failure. 'We just passed it.'

Rachel looked back up the street the way Morwenna was pointing then looked back at her for a second or two, wearing what Garfield called her ticking face, meaning the face she wore when you could hear her brain ticking like a cooling car engine, then she turned on her heel without a word and strode to the shop. Her tone was strenuously cheerful again but not friendly.

'Remind me what you like. Cod or scampi?'

'Scampi's expensive.'

'It's your birthday. Scampi and chips, please,' she told the man.

'Anything for yourself?' he asked.

'No. Lunch makes me sick.'

'Anything to drink?'

'Anything to drink?' she relayed to Morwenna.

'No, thank you,' Morwenna said to the man, although she badly wanted a fizzy drink to help the chips go down.

Scampi was a terrible decision, of course, because it meant a longer wait. Morwenna spent the time trying to find scampi on the Fish of the World poster and trying to take her mind off the way Rachel was staring at other people who came in.

The parcel eventually handed down to her was hot and sent vinegary fumes up her nose that made her want to rip it open at once. Eating in the street was bad manners, however; it was a rule. So she clutched her lunch close under one arm as they walked. Instead of striding on muttering to herself, Rachel now strolled, apparently lost in thought, as though she were all alone. It was like a punishment for greed: walk slowly while clutching cooling chips and forbidden to eat them. When they finally reached the car again Rachel remembered it was a special occasion and drove them to the far end of the car park to give them a sea view.

'I almost forgot,' she said. 'Your card. It's in the glove compartment.'

Morwenna looked in the glove compartment and took out that year's card. As always it was wrapped in newspaper and done up with string. Rachel never gave them cards from a shop but did them tiny versions of her paintings on stiff, cream-coloured board which she folded in two. This was another of her traditions. Garfield said it dated back to when she was in hospital after Hedley was born and couldn't buy a present on his birthday so did him a picture instead. Morwenna cherished the five she had been given already – Rachel didn't waste them on children under four – and had acquired several of Hedley's and Garfield's in rash exchanges for Easter eggs or comics. She knew Rachel's big paintings sold for quite a lot of money and that these tiny ones were also worth something so weren't really a cheat's way of not buying a present. She kept them in a drawer and liked to take them out occasionally when she was on her own and spread them around the room pretending it was a grown-up gallery. She liked to place them in order of merit too. They were all abstracts, of course, but they were friendly abstracts, somehow, perhaps because they were so small: pictures for very modern doll's houses.

That day's was a bit of a cheat, even so. It was orange. It looked as though Rachel had simply taken her biggest brush and dragged orange paint from one side of the card to the other. She hadn't quite covered the card, though, and she had painted in a sort of fringe of yellow. She had signed it with the signature she used on her proper paintings and inside she had written 'For Morwenna on her tenth birthday, love from Rachel.'

But Morwenna looked at it and knew it had been done last night in a resentful hurry, probably after a reminder from Garfield or Antony, because they were better at remembering birthdays than Rachel was. 'Thank you,' she said. 'It's lovely.' And she leant to kiss Rachel's cheek.

'I can't believe you're ten already. Now. Put it out of harm's way and eat your chips before they get cold.'

The chips had become soggy and the scampi were tasteless and gluey and sort of sliding out of their batter coating. The vinegar appeared to have evaporated for all the tang it lent the spoiled feast.

The desire to cry was becoming stronger and stronger, not because the food was ruined, fish and chips were still a treat even when past their best, but because the day was, in a way Morwenna could not have defined out loud.

Rachel had begun to talk again, prattling on about Dame Barbara and some long involved story about Uncle Jack swimming naked, a smelly fur rug and a bracelet made from a tiara. She was talking as though she had a crowd of adults to show off to, not just Morwenna, and the bleakness creeping from Morwenna's heart caused her throat to constrict and made the stodgy food harder and harder to swallow and she began to wish she had been brave as Garfield would have been and demanded a Coca-Cola in the chip shop as her birthday right.

At last she could bear it no more and she scrumpled the rest of her lunch into a ball inside the paper. She was crying before she had opened the door but she managed to hold back any proper sobs until she had slipped out and slammed it shut behind her.

She had not meant to cry. It was pointless with Rachel. It was different with Antony but tears never reached their mother. They seemed to confuse and freeze her. Laughter reached her. And affection. Had Morwenna laughed at her and hugged her she would have caught Rachel's attention like a finger-click.

She knew this was not normal. She had observed other children's tears and seen how, depending on the sort they were, mothers reacted to them with shock or irritation and ultimately with an attempt to comfort. Rachel would simply be staring at her or, more probably, talking to herself or looking the other way. Morwenna remembered her discomfort when Garfield, always a crybaby even when too old for it, cried at a hideous children's party when some boy kicked him over on the gravel. Other mothers had stared when Rachel ignored him but continued to chat and laugh with one of the fathers. She was probably laughing now at Morwenna's absurdity.

She tried to control her tears, hiccupping and snorting, fighting to keep hold of her handkerchief and the left-over scampi and chips at the same time. It was spasmodic, out of her control and all surgy, like being sick. The day was ruined. Her special day. It was her fault for trying to be grown-up and clever rather than coming up with a list of things she wanted to do. But it was Rachel's fault too for not understanding this and not remembering to treat her like a child on her birthday anyway. She was like a stone. A horrid, sharp stone.

A gust of wind caught her handkerchief and blew it to the grass. Morwenna bent for it, missed then had to dash after it. The effort and ungainliness cured her crying and left her merely angry instead and, having snatched back the handkerchief, she took out her fury on her lunch instead. In a single, savage movement, she shook the news-paper parcel open into the wind. Chips and scampi flew up and away from her and suddenly the air about her was loud and white with swooping gulls seizing the morsels even before they landed on the rocks below the car park. They were forbidden to feed gulls, especially at home where they gathered, if encouraged, and made a noise on Rachel's studio and attic roofs. But it was as though she had conjured them out of thin air with a single gesture and it felt dramatic and immensely satisfying. Rachel responded to big gestures far more readily than she did to crying and would quite understand one's jumping out of the car in order to summon a shrieking flock of herring gulls.

You're ten now, Morwenna reminded herself. *You're nearly a woman.* She dreaded being prised apart from her brothers by femininity the way she had seen it happen to other girls in other families. It would be different, perhaps, if she had a sister, but you couldn't have a sisterhood of one and Rachel would be no help.

Summoning a sense of purpose, she folded up the greasy piece of paper and walked to stuff it into an overflowing concrete rubbish bin then turned back to the car feeling thundery but recovered and grateful, now that her face must be blotchy and her eyes piggy with weeping, that she could rely on Rachel to pay her little outburst no heed.

Sure enough, as she drew near the car again she saw Rachel was smoking one of her very occasional cigarettes in the dramatic way she had and concentrating on something she was drawing with the special tortoiseshell fountain pen that lived in her handbag.

She barely registered Morwenna's getting back in the passenger seat beyond a low, thoughtful, 'Hi,' as she made a few more quick scribbles. Morwenna helped herself to a barley sugar from the glove compartment and thought about the drawing model in the bag at her feet which Antony would be giving her at teatime. He would give it after Hedley's and Garfield's presents and whatever they pretended Petroc had got her. She would never use it for drawings. She might try dressing it up or making it hold things in its little arms, then one of the boys would borrow it for some violent game even though war was wrong and it would end up lost and broken or subjected to experimental surgery like her variously maimed dolls.

And just as her unfinished, unappetizing lunch had become the focus of her angry disappointment so the gift-wrapped wooden mannequin came to stand for all the sorrow and discomfort of becoming another year older, the enforced attention of a birthday and its equally brutal removal with the opening of the last present. At least at Christmas the fever and disappointment were shared.

'There,' Rachel said, screwing the cap back on her pen. 'I added a little something extra.'

She passed over the birthday card. It looked much the same. Still abstract. Still orange. Perhaps Rachel had not been drawing but writing. Perhaps she had written an extra message after the *love, Rachel* about tears and disappointment. Perhaps she had written an apology? Morwenna looked inside.

The writing was unchanged but on the left, on the reverse of the orange picture, she had drawn something.

Rachel could draw just like Rolf Harris. It was one of her dark secrets. She could do grown-up drawings and filled notebook after notebook with the exquisitely shaded pencil or ink images she usually threw off to warm up before she started painting or when she was merely struck by something she'd stumbled on. But it was her cartoons the children loved. They were well drawn but immensely funny somehow, the more so for the seriousness of most of Rachel's work and the demonic speed with which she threw them off.

She had done a cartoon of the little supermarket they had just been in. There was the narrow aisle, its sides stacked high with everything from biscuit tins to bleach, only she had added in funny things like a crocodile and

NOTES FROM AN EXHIBITION

a coffin. There were the whisky bottles, by which she had added a dangling sign which said *HOOCH!* And there was Morwenna, wearing exactly the tartan skirt and best white shirt and black shoes she had on today and there was Rachel, beaming so crazily there was a star glinting off her teeth. And there, in pride of place, was Dame Barbara, complete with high, deeply scored forehead and pushed-back headscarf. She was pointing at the whisky bottle in Morwenna's basket and apparently offering a small sculpture in return. There was a caption underneath. *A Brush With Greatness*, it said.

It was very funny and Rachel's self-portrait was better than any apology. What did she have to apologize for anyway? She had given up a working day to Morwenna. They had seen an exhibition, met a famous sculptor, had fish and chips by the sea. They even had a funny story to carry back to the others. In some ways it was a vintage year.

'Thank you,' Morwenna told her. 'It's brilliant.' She closed and opened the card again to appreciate it afresh.

Rachel tugged her over and kissed the top of her head. 'My only girl,' she said and started the car to drive them home.

They talked all the way back or, rather, Rachel asked questions and made Morwenna tell her things. She asked her about school and who her friends were and what her favourite and least favourite subjects were and what she wanted to do when she grew up. (To which Morwenna had to say, 'I don't know!' as if the question was silly, otherwise she'd have had to say I want to be just like you, which was something she had never said aloud and

211

which was an impossible thing to admit.) It was odd. Rachel asked the questions as though they didn't see each other every day, as though she were a visiting godmother or something.

As they pulled back over the hill above Nancledra and paused again to say ooh at the view from Cornwall's Best Lay-by, Morwenna realized it was because the day must be a kind of treat for Rachel as well as her, a chance for once to avoid having to share or be shared and the thought filled her with a kind of sticky, homesick feeling, like the smell of tears behind your face when you'd finished crying.

They wound down around the hillside, past the first few houses, past the sign to Polkinghorne that always made Rachel laugh and intone the name in a deep, slow voice, past the succession of backyard washing lines where Garfield and Hedley always played a competition as to who won out of pants or bras, and up to the junction with the seafront. There was nothing coming. Morwenna was trained, as they all were, to look left at junctions and say *clear left, clear left* for as long as it was safe to pull out. But Rachel left the car where it was and asked, 'You don't often cry like that, for no particular reason, do you?'

Morwenna was too embarrassed to turn round. She just kept on watching for traffic from the left and when she said no it came out all squeaky. 'Just checking,' Rachel said and drove on.

HAIR CLASP (1963?).

Silver, tungsten florist wire and steel.

This ornament is said to have been made by Dame Barbara Hepworth as a bracelet for a fancy dress party. It was part of Kelly's strong signature 'look' when worn as a hair clasp to keep her hair out of her eyes as she worked. The story of its origins seems unlikely. Hepworth was not known as a jeweller even of occasional pieces and there is no documentary evidence of her having known Kelly, let alone liked her well enough to make her gifts. If the story is true then it seems Hepworth made (or acquired) the piece as part of her costume for the St Ives Borough's Artists' Ball of 1963. A fundraising event, this set out to ape the more genuinely bohemian Arts Balls organized a decade earlier by Hepworth and colleagues to raise funds for the Penwith Society of Arts they had formed in 1949 as a modernist rival to the traditionalist St Ives Society of Artists. The two semicircular plates are made of silver (not hallmarked) bound together with what appears to be the thicker grade of florist's wire. On closer examination, the hoop-ended steel pin which then fixes the two halves together around hair or wrist is a kitchen skewer of a type then commonly available, with its pointed end sawn off.

(From the collection of Morwenna Middleton)

Rachel had never worn her hair so high. The style was not a beehive but it had required a little cushion to be pinned in and her hair piled up and lacquered over it by the girl in the salon. She had hoped to look a little like Julie Christie but it felt artificial, like a dead animal arranged up there, and she disliked the smell of lacquer so had tried spraying on scent to cover it.

213

She had bathed with extreme care, terrified the creation would collapse into absurdity, then dried herself, dusted herself with talc and dressed as though a bowl of water were balanced on her head. It probably wasn't half as fragile a structure as she feared but she was unused to such things. They never went to grown-up parties. In fact they never went to parties. Supper or lunch at people's houses was as festive as they tended to be and she sometimes felt she had moved from her late teens to her early thirties without a frivolous stage in between.

The theme was Gods and Goddesses so she had found a pure white, backless dress that was perfect. It had a loosely gathered bodice held up by a chunky, mock-silver chain that went around the neck. It fell in folds that were romantic, if not strictly Grecian, and she paired it with silver sandals that were so cheap it didn't matter if they fell apart.

She had spent all morning making herself a diadem out of stiff cardboard wrapped in aluminium foil and stuck with small silver Christmas tree decorations. She gave it a quick shake to check the glue was holding and all seemed well so she lifted it up and tucked it over her head. She looked at herself critically, front and back, in the house's only full-length mirror, teased down a couple of long strands of hair and decided the effect was rather good. If not quite Julie Christie.

Giving her little pupils at West Cornwall Girls their weekly art class that afternoon – she had them drawing dandelion clocks – she had been giddy and let things get a little out of hand so that Miss Binns, the young history teacher across the corridor, had looked in to ask if something was amiss. Then she had spoiled Garfield when she picked him up from school because he looked so sweet in his uniform. She bought him an ice-cream sundae in The Buttery and listened happily to his earnest talk of school and hadn't become impatient with him the way she sometimes did when he went on and became tedious. And all this sprang from a real happiness, not a sick one, because finally she had the right pills.

When she had her last breakdown and a neighbour had spotted her, passed out in the studio, and called Jack in time to save her life, Jack had pulled strings to have her seen by a specialist. Vernon Wax took into account the patterns of her behaviour when she was apparently well rather than merely treating the effects of her break-down. He diagnosed manic depression. It was chemical, he said, not causative, despite the contributory factors in her history, and needed a permanent chemical treatment with lithium carbonate. Dosage varied from patient to patient, metabolism to metabolism and it would take regular blood tests to ensure the dosage was then main-tained at a level that would even out her moods without damaging her kidneys. The only immediate side-effect was a metallic taste in her mouth but that would come and go and she would adjust to it because everybody did. She had to cut out or at least cut back the caffeine and salt in her diet and she had to be wary of doing anything that would make her sweat so much the sodium level in her body dropped below the lithium one. The antidepressants she had been prescribed before were, Wax said, the worst possible thing for her as they would have increased her chances of a rapid descent into suicidal behaviour, which was precisely what had happened, abetted by her natural tendency to post-partum blues.

This was fairly new science, apparently, and the reason the drug worked was still not understood. Jack had read up on the subject, she being the only such patient on his books, and the salt of a ground metal had become as much a part of her daily routine as insulin injections for a diabetic. And it was working. Her moods evened out, although the short temper was revealed as temperamental not chemical, she became easier to predict and live with and when she was happy or sad, it tended to be for good reason. No more nights broken by fizzing anxieties she couldn't name, no more strange fears, no more mania. She was not mad. She had a chemical imbalance that was controllable.

At first the relief was so great the news seemed all good. She returned to motherhood, painting around its edges when Garfield let her and more, once he started in playgroup. When Michael died, she found herself able to support Antony for a change instead of the other way around. He began to make a little more money. Garfield started primary school. She painted more and, with Jack's encouragement and introductions, began to put her work into local, semi-professional exhibitions. She sold some. She took a part-time job at West Cornwall Girls' School in the art department which paid enough to keep her in materials.

Something had changed, however. Something had fallen away. Now that she had a diagnosis she was less of a victim and she became aware that her marriage had been founded on a vulnerability and an inequality that were no longer there. Antony was too equable and rational to be threatened by this change but she was and began to be oppressed by it and the careful life he had built around her. Worse, she noticed a falling-off in her work and felt she now approached it coolly whereas her old turbulence had brought with it moments where she felt she was accessing a white heat of inspiration, something this new controlled safety had closed off to her.

She emerged from dressing to find Antony still in his day clothes. He had agreed to wear a silver beard and carry a lightning bolt, both of which she had made him but there he was, hunched apologetically over a heap of marking, pleading exhaustion. His compliments on her appearance didn't help as they only made her feel silly and overdressed and her mounting excitement as she drove across the moor to the north coast was fired by irritation and an unformulated need to strike back at him.

Having handed over her coat and accepted a drink she felt exposed without a partner. Happily Jack was there and feeling similarly spare. He never appeared in public with Fred, although everyone knew about them and their adjoining cottages. It was never discussed. She could see Fred's appeal but their relationship was obviously so entirely about sex she had found herself at a loss for how to make conversation with him.

Jack was wearing a dinner jacket but had a small tin skillet on the back of his head like a helmet and when she looked blank he explained he had come as Pan.

'Oh lord,' she said, looking about them.

It was a measure of how restless Rachel had become and how stifled she had started to feel that, in preparing for a Gods and Goddesses Ball to raise money for the arts in the district, she had so completely forgotten the likely reality of such an event. The St Ives Guildhall was not the Ritz and its main rooms, even when decorated with twined garlands of ivy, laurel and bay, were not a ballroom. Local councillors and librarians still looked local in fancy dress or more so, if possible, exposing flesh untouched by the sun or stripes where it had touched too much.

There was a band, too small confidently to fill a large acoustic and compete with the chatter of the crowd. Rather than playing standard ballroom stuff, the players were trying to be with it, playing Herb Alpert arrangements like *Spanish Flea* and *Tijuana Taxi* with much po-faced maraca shaking. Only a few brave souls were attempting to dance to it.

'Your hair is amazing,' Jack said.

'Don't,' she told him. 'I think it's the highest hair in the room. I don't know what I was thinking of. I feel like Marie Antoinette.'

He looked up at her hair once more, without saying anything, which didn't help.

'This is ghastly,' she said.

'Isn't it? They wanted to revive the old Arts Ball idea but nobody in the Society could spare the time to organize it and it was left to the council. And the old affairs were pretty ropey, looking back at them. No Antony?'

'He's being a saint and minding Garfy.'

Jack caught her eye.

'He had marking to do,' she admitted. 'I wasn't happy.'

'Oh dear.'

'And I think he wants a bigger family.'

'Well. It is a bit tough on Garfy being an only.'

'Yes but . . .'

'Hmm.'

It was uncanny sometimes how Jack, who smoked a pipe and played cricket for his village team, could occasionally think like a woman and let her leave things unsaid because he instinctively understood what she was getting at. They paused in their walking around to watch some particularly brave dancers, the tallest of whom seemed to have misread the invitation and had come in a rabbit costume. The band had launched on a Beatles medley, though still to a Latin beat.

'Of course,' Jack went on thoughtfully, 'and speaking as your GP, if you did decide to have another, you'd probably have to come off the lithium while you were pregnant.'

'Wouldn't that be risky?'

'Of course, but people do it. A calculated risk. There's so little research on the effects of lithium on unborn children. There's little enough on its toxicity in adults. I'd keep an eye on you. It may even affect your fertility.'

The thought this planted was still in Rachel's mind as they collected fresh drinks from a passing waitress and continued their slow circuit of the room. Jack discreetly tucked his pan behind a flower arrangement and tidied his hair. He had padded the pan's inside for comfort but said it was cramping his style.

They said hello to a colleague of hers from West Cornwall Girls, a young English teacher who had dressed, rather vampishly, in a man's suit to which she had pinned

219

a sort of gallery of men cut from knitting patterns and postcards of Old Masters.

'Hims Ancient and Modern,' she explained. 'Love the crown. Who are you?'

'Juno,' Rachel said. 'And this is Jack,' leaving the colleague confused.

'You'd better think of someone else to be,' he muttered, as the colleague left them to greet someone. 'GBH has come as Juno too.'

'Who's GBH?' she asked but he was nodding and raising his eyebrows indicating she should turn around.

Barbara Hepworth – Dame Barbara Hepworth as she had become in the last few years – was in black, not white, which matched the severity of her style. She had made herself a tinfoil coronet remarkably like Rachel's, only without the Christmas tree baubles. She had what could only be called an entourage, all male, some of whom Rachel recognized as better-known members of the Penwith Society. They were walking in a cluster a few steps behind her, which enhanced the queenly air of her progress. She greeted Jack with a quick, affectionate expression and they kissed then she turned her attention quizzically on Rachel.

'Well this isn't Fred,' she said.

'Barbara, this is my old friend, Antony Middleton's wife, Rachel Kelly. Rachel, Dame Barbara.'

Rachel took Barbara Hepworth's extended hand and briefly felt the strength in it.

'Why aren't you Rachel Middleton?' Dame Barbara asked.

Rachel longed to retort *Why aren't you Barbara*

Nicholson but instead she explained, 'It's my maiden name, the one I paint under,' and only just fought the impulse to drop a curtsy.

In photographs Dame Barbara always looked like Bette Davis playing a Yorkshirewoman but in the flesh she was smaller and livelier than the pictures suggested. Her voice sounded like a woman on the BBC: she pronounced Jack as *Jyeck*. However there was an unexpectedly sexy edge to it from cigarettes and stone dust, presumably and, rumour had it, drink.

She took in Rachel's white dress and crown. 'I know Jack came as Pan,' she said, 'but what are you?'

Jack nudged her too late as Rachel said, 'Oh, I'm Juno.'

'Oh, but I'm the Queen of Heaven,' Dame Barbara said. 'There can't be two of us. Tell you what, let me just rearrange this a little.' And she tweaked off Rachel's crown, folded it smartly in two, creased it down the middle into a sort of tiara, shedding a couple of baubles in the process, and set it back on Rachel's head. 'There,' she said. 'You can be Diana the Huntress and wear a half-moon.'

Rachel's face must have fallen because Dame Barbara looked back at her and stopped performing for her entourage.

'God I'm sorry,' she said. 'Did it take ages to make? I know mine did. Here.' She swiftly unfastened a sort of silver buckle she wore around one forearm and fixed it to Rachel's instead, conveying an unexpected kindness in the gentle way she took her hand to do it. 'Now you're complete. I made this yesterday but it looks much better on someone young and pretty.' And she passed on.

'Your face!' Jack laughed, once she was out of earshot. 'I don't know whether to be pleased or furious.'

'Well that's always her speciality. She tried to bully me into being one of her assistants once. Can you imagine? Let me take that off you. It'll never stay up like that.' He removed the crumpled crown, folded it further and dropped it with a smile on a passing waiter's tray.

The evening unfolded in a way it never would have done had Antony not stayed home with his marking. Dame Barbara left soon after making her circuit. The younger members of her entourage, sweeping Jack and Rachel and the colleague *en travesti* with them, abandoned the ball shortly afterwards. They went to a noisy pub then for a moonlit swim on Porthmeor Beach.

The sea was surprisingly warm. Or perhaps that was just the effect of drinking. Rachel's expensive hair collapsed, which was a sort of relief. The little cushion thing floated away into the darkness. The sudden nakedness of them all didn't feel sexual, possibly because they were in a group, but when she stood shivering beside Jack as they both attempted to dry themselves on the one handkerchief they had between them, she felt they had passed for ever beyond some transitional stage and that he was now as deeply in the weave of her life as Antony. Maybe even deeper.

Dressed again, she was battling with her hair when he suggested she use the Hepworth armlet to hold it back and helped her do it, pipe clamped in his chattering teeth for the suggestion of warmth.

'Jack?' she asked as he fiddled to fasten the thing behind her.

'Hmm?'

'If I did have another baby, would you be its godfather?'

'Of course,' he told her. 'Honoured. But only if it's a boy.'

Apparently by prior agreement, they all then went up the hill to Trewyn Studio to thaw out and keep Dame Barbara company. It was a simple, two-storey building with a garden and workshops beside it where Jack said she had worked for years but to which she had retreated full-time since the end of her marriage nearly fifteen years earlier.

Everyone knew everybody else, even her colleague, who turned out to be having an affair with one of the married artists, which would have scandalized their strictly Methodist employers at the school. Rachel was shivering still and Dame Barbara draped her in some kind of animal fur which reeked. The booze – neat spirits – flowed freely. Two of the artists produced bottles from their coat pockets and the multiple conversations became rowdier and more opinionated but Dame Barbara's pronouncements cut through everyone else's. Rachel's own opinion was rarely consulted.

She was fascinated to see this other side to Jack, which was entirely in abeyance in his doctoring life, among these artists for whom he was a painter who pursued medicine as a sort of eccentric sideline, not the other way around. But more, she was fascinated by their host. At least thirty years older than the rest of them sprawled on her floor, she had dropped the queenly air she wore around the town councillors and was arguing and gossiping as if among friends and matching them drink for drink with fewer ill effects. Rachel found herself drunkenly fixing on the extremities of the Hepworth accent so that she caught single phrases but no sense from what was being said. *The Enyetomy of Myenne. The Gawgeousniss of the way we re-ect.*

And then Dame Barbara was suddenly on her feet, dismissing them with a yawn.

'Help me clear up, could you,' she told Rachel and Rachel found herself alone in the studio with Britain's Greatest Living Female Artist as the others stumbled out into the night.

The overhead lights were back on – they had been drinking by candlelight – and their harshness was probably as cruel to her as it was to Dame Barbara. In the end there was no *help* involved: it was she who walked around the place collecting glasses and bottles on a tray and she who washed up at a rather dirty sink while Dame Barbara perched on a stool watching her, scowling and smoking. And interrogating.

'So you paint?' she said.

'Yes,' Rachel told her.

'Do you sell?'

'I'm starting to.'

'Where?'

'The Newlyn Gallery. Jack's introduced me to –'

'Oh it's no good being like Jack – a gentleman amateur. Women have to work harder at this game. Are you married?'

'Yes.'

'Children?'

'One.'

'Only one. Well that helps. If you're serious, don't have any more. Don't let anything get in the way, not children, not your husband. Nothing. What did you do with the bracelet I lent you?' she asked abruptly.

'Oh I, er . . .' Rachel glanced down at her arm, forgetting Jack had put the thing in her hair.

'Doesn't matter. It's probably here somewhere. It's silver, mainly. Do you know Jensen's work?'

'Who?'

'Oh never mind. Shut the door firmly when you go, would you?'

She had walked back up to bed, cigarette in hand. She was old enough to be a grandmother, maybe even was one, and yet she was living in squalor like a kind of student. Charming at first, with its curious combination of lush potted plants, bashed-up antique furniture and the maquettes for sculptures, the place became desolate when you reminded yourself she actually lived there and wasn't eventually going home to somewhere more comfortable. Tipping the contents of an ashtray into the rubbish bin, Rachel imagined her peeing in the gaunt little bathroom then climbing into bed with only a last splash of Scotch to warm her and lying there, staring up at the high ceiling from those judgemental, Bette Davis eyes. She was probably thinking, *Christ what a pointless evening!* Or, no, probably clearing her head at last of meaningless chat and thinking about the work that would have been occupying a part of her mind all evening, tugging on the skirts of her concentration as she would have never let children do.

Rachel had drunk far less than the rest of them and had made herself a strong and nasty instant coffee in the studio. The startling strangeness of the evening's end had sobered her up still further. As she went in search of her car she found Jack sitting on a garden wall, smoking his pipe. Far too drunk to drive. She led him back to the Morris and drove home with him snoring lightly against the passenger door.

The house was silent, of course, when she finally let herself in. She looked in on Garfield, gently tugging the bedding back over his shoulders, then slid into bed beside Antony.

'God you're cold,' he mumbled as her feet woke him.

'Sorry.'

'And you're sandy! Where on earth have you been?'

'Swimming. With Jack and his friends. Sorry. Too tired to wash it off.'

She pressed against him then, when she rolled over, was glad to have him roll over too and press himself against her.

'Jack introduced me to GBH,' she said.

'Who?'

She giggled, remembering Jack as she led him back to his front door and fished his keys out of his pocket for him. 'It stands for *God! Barbara Hepworth!*'

His arm came around her as he settled back to sleep and she held it close, wide awake now but wrapped in warm relief.

NORMAN MORRISON (1965). Oil on canvas.

In November 1965 a Quaker called Norman Morrison doused himself in gasoline outside the Pentagon and burned himself to death in protest at America's continuing involvement in Vietnam. The strength of his pacifist demonstration was rendered ambiguous however by the fact that he was clutching his infant daughter at the time whose life was only spared because he was persuaded to throw her clear of the flames engulfing him. The news and equally shocking photograph soon reached Penzance, where Kelly had barely recovered from the second of her post-partum breakdowns. This painting, with its searing use of scarlet and vermilion tones within a block-like structure of greys and blacks, has often been taken as a literal translation of newsprint into oil paint. However Sir Vernon Wax, her consultant at St Lawrence's, Bodmin where she had herself admitted within hours of finishing the painting, recalled in his memories: 'What had engulfed her was not the fact of the suicide but the danger in which it had placed Morrison's child. In a lucid moment, she likened his flames to her own insanity licking about her own infant daughter.' After her recovery she presented the painting to the hospital and, on the occasion of its hanging there, told Wax it wasn't about Morrison at all but about heroic love. '"See that little grey square that seems to be holding the whole thing up?" she told me. "Don't tell him, but that's my husband."'

(Lent by Cornwall NHS Health Trust)

There were intervals, usually in daylight hours or at times when she would have taken herself off to paint, when Antony could almost forget she was dead. They had lived such independent lives within their marriage, even after his retirement, that he had been deeply conditioned to spending days on end with her only nominally present. She kept such erratic hours, often being seized by a sudden need to work or read or go for a walk late at night or in the hours after dawn, that he was even used to waking to find himself alone in bed. What kept betraying her absence was the unaccustomed tidiness everywhere. And the calm.

The tidiness was as much to do with Hedley's contribution as with the absence of Rachel's. Having him on this extended visit had become something like having a wife again but of the 1950s school. He made beds and aired rooms. He dusted and hoovered. He set good meals on the table at regular hours and provided charming conversation with them. His presence was a delight but Antony could tell that, in the name of being a good son, he was actually deferring for both of them a time of necessary recognition, perhaps even the time of full mourning.

When his nerve had cracked at last, an hour after all the shouting and banging gave way to silence, when he broke into the loft and found her cold, it seemed that all his feelings would be released in a merciful rush. Alone with her body he had cried and raged and brooded. He kissed her and shouted at her and held her, free to do as he liked because she had not died in a hospital with all the family around her. But then, once she was buried, a kind of numbness stole over him, abetted by Hedley's housekeeping, and he found he was missing the honesty of sorrow and unsettled by the ambiguous feelings that insinuated themselves in its place.

Was the absence of her not like the calm after days of violent weather? Did life not feel easier now he no longer shared it with such a difficult woman?

Jack gave him Prozac in the first flush of crisis to help him cope. Antony had come off it now, not liking the way it kept his feelings so muffled and hoped this would bring them flooding back, but it hadn't. In his shrewd way Jack had been more help than anyone, Jack whose life had been so shaped by the loss of a loved one. Jack had been without Fred for far more of his life than he had been with him but had never loved again – or not publicly – and, notoriously, had abandoned painting in the throes of grief and barely resumed it in the decades since. He maintained the gentlemanly pretence that medicine had been his vocation, art a mere hobby. He had work in the Tate – a small painting of his was regularly hung in their St Ives gallery and was one of their best-selling postcards there – but time had made the pretence a fact.

Jack called in every day for a few minutes, checking on his patient on his walk home from the Morrab Road practice he now shared with several much younger partners who did almost all the work. Grief was a kind of illness, he maintained, and ran a course as predictable as measles or the common cold. Its fever always abated, given time and management, leaving the luckier among them with scars where love had been. He had been just as supportive after Petroc and even that grief, shockingly, had receded in time.

When Antony hinted that Hedley's continuing presence was threatening to turn him into an emotional invalid,

Jack gently reminded him that Hedley was mourning too and pointed out what Antony had missed. 'That boy's always been the family glue, stopping you going to pieces, keeping the peace. With Rachel gone he's out of a job. He needs time to adjust. That's assuming all's well with him and Oliver. I can't think why else he'd end up spending all these weeks in a single bed.'

Even as he dismissed this and said that things with Oliver were fine, Antony realized that perhaps they weren't. Hedley had always presented his home life so smoothly that it compelled an equally smooth acceptance and certainly didn't invite discussion. Worried now, Antony waited until Hedley was out grocery shopping then rang Oliver at the gallery. Possibly he had been tactless because there being a problem between them seemed to have no more occurred to Oliver than it had to him. Backing off from meddling further and embarrassing them both, Antony turned the conversation to whatever paintings Rachel had left behind and the possibility of a show and it transpired that a (fairly junior) Tate curator had already been making discreet enquiries. On safer ground, Oliver agreed to come down to look at them at the first opportunity and take photographs. A friend of his was rather keen to see Cornwall, he added disconcertingly just before they ended.

When various obituarists had rung with queries about the details of Rachel's life, Hedley had dealt with them. They had agreed on the formula: *Hinting at some unhappiness in her family background, she preferred to keep all details beyond her date of birth and Canadian origins a mystery*. It had been Hedley's suggestion that, now that she was dead, there could be no harm in a little investigation.

Antony had accepted long ago that it was not something she wished to discuss.

'If I'd told you I was adopted,' she liked to say, 'you'd have left it at that. Just pretend I was adopted. Pretend I was a foundling. It's really very dull.'

Had she suffered from conventional depression, there was no doubt she would sooner or later have taken a talking cure and been encouraged by a therapist to dig over her life before coming to England. As it was, with Jack and the other doctors so certain her problem was purely chemical, her only therapy was chemical-based, which always worked in the end. Perhaps, too, because he had been all but denuded of family when they met, he had not been led to wonder much about hers.

When the funeral was announced and the obituaries began to appear, he began to wonder idly if some relative of hers, or someone claiming kinship, might not emerge from the shadows but they had heard from no one. It was not unlikely that her relatives were all dead. End of story. But it began to irritate him. He began to feel stupid telling people that he didn't know. It almost suggested, it struck him, that he didn't care.

And so, encouraged by Jack, he tried researching in the town's libraries and when that failed he gave in to pressure from Hedley and admitted a computer to the house.

Once connected to the Internet, he actually knew far more about surfing genealogy sites than Hedley did. Literacy students not referred by an employment agency often denied they had a problem and would make their first overtures to the centre as a request to learn about the Internet. Their failure to form sentences in an e-mail or their heavy reliance on the computer's spellchecker could gently be used to convince them that perhaps there was something beyond computing they needed to learn. In the hope of luring them into writing some extended prose that could be used for a detailed analysis of where their literacy problems lay, Antony's ploy with some of these was to suggest they therefore use the centre's computers to research their families. He knew all the genealogy sites, as well as the ones for tracing people students had been to school with or known through work.

With no great expectations and largely to satisfy Hedley, he pursued the usual channels. He listed Rachel as his wife and the mother of the four children on a couple of family tree sites, specifying that she had come to England from New York in 1959 and been born in Canada. Nobody contacted him apart from a slew of American Kellys who hadn't read the bit about Canada. Then, hunting through their bedroom bookcase in search of a copy of J. T. Blight's *A Week at the Land's End*, he was shamed by finding several out-of-date National Trust members' handbooks to fetch a box and, Hedley-fashion, do a little weeding out.

The box was half-full when he came across a small Bible. It had slid behind the other books and, to judge from its thick coating of dust, had lain unconsulted for years. There was a Collins School Bible on the kitchen bookshelf, abandoned by one of the children there and used as the house reference copy for crosswords ever since.

This one was inferior even to that. It was a cheap, Gideon Bible stolen from some hotel drawer. He was shocked to see how Rachel had scrawled illegibly over page after page of text, in different coloured inks that soaked through and with cheap biros that often punctured the paper. It was like coming across a cruel snapshot of her at one of her lowest ebbs and his immediate impulse was to toss it into the box.

But it fell open at the front page. In a small oblong of clean white paper, which Rachel seemed to have protected from her own insane scrawls by outlining it when the Bible first came into her possession, a childish hand had written, 'Ray Kelly, 268 Gerrard Street East, Cabbagetown, Toronto. Please return on pain of death!'

She had never called herself Ray, even when they first met. It certainly wouldn't have suited her and must have been one of those phases so many children went through of trying on different names as they experimented with signatures or ways of answering the phone.

He threw the book away, seeing it was both distressing and unusable but next time he was at the computer he thought to add the shortened name as a nickname on the entries for her, in case it would make her more familiar to someone who had known her in childhood. With Hedley's help, he also had the earliest photograph he had of her scanned on to a disk at the copy shop in town. It was taken by his grandfather and showed the two of them side by side on the doorstep. She had hated it at the time, saying it made her look old because she was wrinkling her forehead but he had kept it in the back of his sock drawer, along with a few precious early postcards written

by the children, and now he felt it made them both look
pathetically untested and young. He had thought her so
sophisticated and urbane at the time, a woman of experience, but to look at her now she seemed little more than
twenty or twenty-one. Some four years younger than she
actually was.

When he brought the disk home, Hedley used the
computer to enlarge and enhance the picture then, at
Antony's insistence, cropped him out of it. They then
attached it to the various genealogy sites. Especially seeing
it enhanced like that, Antony felt it was unmistakably
how she had looked at that age but he still felt he was
lowering a small and untempting piece of bait into a very
deep lake.

A response came in just two days. Encouraged by
Lizzy, who was full of talk of just think what fun it
would be when his grandchild was old enough to e-mail
him, he was getting into the habit of checking and
replying to e-mails once a day. He did it after taking in
the real mail and before reading the paper. He logged
on, thinking to find nothing but the usual nonsense about
enlarging his penis or acquiring a degree by simply
writing a cheque, and there was a real message for him
from winnie@simplegifts.com.

'I was at school with the woman you call Ray in Toronto
and knew her from when she was small. I didn't know
her by that name though. Then we lost touch, which
saddened me. I'm so happy to hear she had a family and
was happy. Here are some pictures for you. Could I see
some more of yours?'

He double-clicked to open the attached file without

preparing himself and suddenly there was a picture of a black-haired toddler in a snow suit and another of Rachel, unmistakably Rachel, in school uniform at about twelve, looking furious but striking, recognizably herself as it were. He zoomed in on the pictures until their details broke up into little cubes. He stared until his eyes ached.

Hedley had gone to tidy Jack's overgrown garden for him. Some Quaker friends were driving Antony to a Peace Lunch way over in Come-to-Good. From there he was going to be collected and taken to Falmouth by Lizzy and then Garfield was driving him home after they'd given him supper. It was going to be one of those days when the kind wishes of others made him feel like an elderly parcel and he felt a need to take some action and achieve a little for himself by way of compensation. So he marched into town, to the place where Hedley had helped him buy a computer, and bought himself a scanner. It proved light to carry and ludicrously easy to use and within an hour of getting home he was scanning and attaching pictures of his own.

He sent Winnie a favourite picture of his, one he kept on his bedroom chest of drawers, of Rachel and the older children helping Petroc blow out the candles on his fifth birthday cake and a much more recent picture of her taken for an article in *The Cornishman* for her last Newlyn exhibition showing her leaning on the promenade railings and looking a bit ferocious because the photographer had taken too long. He filled in a bit of detail for Winnie, who he guessed could not be an art lover: how Rachel had settled in Penzance with him and become a successful painter and loving mother despite living with the burden of bipolar disorder. For good measure he scanned in a copy of the most readable, if least accurate, obituary that had appeared to date. The Quaker friends were collecting him at eleven so at ten-fifty he checked his e-mail one more time. She had responded.

'I woke up at dawn and couldn't sleep (yet again!),' she wrote. 'I'll be in the UK next week and I think we should meet up. I attach my picture, so you can see I'm not some psycho. Best. Winnie MacArthur.'

He guessed she was a little younger than him,' though having that North American knack for self-preservation, she could have passed for late-fifties. Yet to have been at school with Rachel, she must have been older. Her hair must once have been blonde and now was dyed but she had allowed enough silver through for her hair to match her finely lined skin. She was dressed with quiet elegance and was laughing in the picture because a large dog – a Newfoundland? – had jumped up to greet her. She appeared to be standing in the doorway of some kind of furniture shop.

She was also, without question, Rachel's sister.

'PS,' she had added under the picture. 'Her name was Joanie, back then. Joanie Ransome.'

For as long as Winnie Ransome could remember, she had dreamed of an extra sibling. Brother or sister, either would have done. She simply needed one to spread the pressure a little and mop up some of the attention. With just her and her older sister, Joanie, the situation was intolerable. Among friends, groups of four were held to be good, unlike groups of three, because they could split into pairs. But four in a family meant your parents had only the two of you to weigh in the scales of justice so invariably one would always be down when the other was up.

Joanie came first. She was almost exactly a year older and was so tough and strong-natured she'd probably have withstood being an only child. But as soon as Winnie arrived and there was a point of comparison, their parents decided that Winnie was the good one, the little angel,

237

no trouble at all and Joanie was the miniature hellcat, the hothead, the problem child. It was almost as though Mom needed this one of each thing to make her life complete. Like having a nest of tables. And if you took a girl and told people, in her hearing, that she was good, that was who she felt she had to be. Always. Or perhaps Winnie's problem was that she was a born conformist? Maybe if she'd found the courage to break the mould earlier on she wouldn't have felt so constrained now that she was within a year of leaving school and finding the avenues open to her so few.

Joanie was dark and bony – skinny Mom called it – and striking despite her big nose. Her eyes were green, true green not just pond-coloured, and she was quick-witted and funny, though their mother called it sharp. Winnie, by contrast, took after their mother and was a Dutch blonde, curvy and blue-eyed and invariably standing two steps behind and staring at her feet while Joanie shot her mouth off. Winnie was undeniably pretty, china doll pretty, with a little tiptilted nose and tiny hands and tidy little ears and a neat, if rather too rosebuddy mouth.

But it was a prettiness that seemed to require inactivity. As a little girl, much admired by relatives, her reward was to be buttoned into dresses she must not tear or get dirty, so she had to sit still indoors while Joanie ran wild climbing trees with boys. Now she was a teenager she had more say in what she wore and since Dad had been promoted and they had moved to the new house in Etobicoke she actually had a clothing allowance. Boys had taken to calling her a doll, which was a compliment but again seemed to require a kind of waxen passivity.

Joanie was talented and clever. She scored well in class, when she could be bothered, and maddened the Havergal staff by her habit of answering back questions in a way that made the whole class laugh and the teacher feel stupid. She loved Katharine Hepburn and sat through *The Philadelphia Story* over and over until she could imitate her funny accent and angular way of talking and drove their mother crazy pretending that was now the only way she could talk. And Joanie was an artist. She had been winning art prizes and illustrating the school magazine since she was fourteen or so and it didn't matter if she was so rude and wild that no boy would marry her, because she had a future. Admittedly Mom thought being an artist was an unladylike ambition and there was an ongoing battle because Joanie wanted to go to Ontario College of Art and draw people with no clothes on whereas Mom wanted her to be a commercial artist, and get a job painting glamorous gowns and pots of makeup for one of the better magazines or working for an advertising agency, like Lauren Bacall in *Written on the Wind*, only not so vampy.

Winnie, by contrast, had no talents beyond gymnastics, which had got her into the cheerleading squad but would never prove a ticket to the wider world. If she could be any film star it would have been someone sweeter than Katharine Hepburn; she favoured the ones that sang without showing too much body – Kathryn Grayson or Debbie Reynolds. She had a sweet, true singing voice in church but was too terrified of singing solo ever to do anything with it. She was invariably placed in the lower third of her class and would be lucky if she even made it to secretarial school. (She had glanced at a shorthand manual and thought it looked impossibly strange and difficult.) She had recently decided that her only realistic option was marriage and motherhood.

'And where's the shame in that, I'd like to know?' Mom asked.

And there lay the problem. Havergal was a good school. For girls it was probably the best and they were very lucky to be sent there. Through its prestige, through the friends with brothers, through sports events and carefully policed interschool dances, she was meeting the pick of the local boys, boys with old money behind them and futures all mapped out. And her family were going to let her down. Her father was only middle management in a pharmaceuticals firm. The boys she was meeting had fathers who were on company boards or they were surgeons or judges or, at the very least, political. Dad worked every hour God gave then came home and simply wanted to eat with his family and watch TV. He didn't belong to any clubs because he didn't see the point. He didn't even play golf. Secretly she loved him for all this, for his lack of push, but right now it was not what she needed. Her mother was no better, since her ambitions were too naked and her clothes and background, Winnie was coming to realize, were all wrong. The only thing she did right was attend the right church, i.e. not the Catholic one. And it was through church, not Havergal contacts, that Winnie had met the boy she thought she stood some chance of marrying. Josh MacArthur was handsome, but not too clever. He was assistant captain of his school hockey team and, unless he was offered a sports scholarship to a college in the States, likely to skip university to go into sales for the MacArthur family business, which was hotels.

He always talked to her after church, even walking her home or to their car if the weather was bad. If he saw her on the street or in a store, he came right over to talk. He liked her, she could tell he did. He paid her compliments. She even had it from one of her friends via her friend's brother, who played on the same team, that Josh thought she was a doll. But he had never asked her on a date. The nearest she had come was when she was out with a group of girlfriends and they had met him in a group of boys. But that didn't count as, being a good girl, she didn't have the sort of friends who paired off under such circumstances and necked in the backs of cars. He was currently available, having been dropped for the team captain by Diana Holberton a whole year ago. Her friends said he was dumb but she didn't care. He was polite. He was a gentleman. He would never make her feel stupid or pious. He was perfect.

The problem, she decided, was Joanie. Since graduating from Havergal, Joanie had been running wild. She had started drinking and smoking. She had crashed her car – amazingly not hurting anyone. She had stopped coming to church. Worst of all, she had a reputation as a tramp. Joanie had never dated anyone, or not for long enough for it to be serious. She tended to treat dates as a handy means of getting out of the house and into a party, where she could then lose the date in question and have fun. Behaviour like this threatened other girls and,

Winnie was certain, was where the bad reputation had arisen, not from anything more sinister.

But this summer things had escalated. There was a huge fight with their parents one night because she was offered a place at art school but Mom was disgusted when she found this was on the basis of a portfolio containing detailed drawings of naked women in 'graphic' poses. (Winnie wasn't allowed to see the originals but Dad, who had been drinking a bit, said, 'Let's just say their legs weren't crossed,' at which Mom hit the roof.) Mom had then worked on Dad and forced him to agree that Joanie could only accept the offer if she agreed to attend secretarial school for a year first, at which Joanie had called her a *fucking self-righteous bitch* and stormed out, stealing Mom's car and worried everyone sick by not coming back until lunchtime the next day. Then she cut her dresses and her hair short, both badly. And then she stole money from Dad's wallet before, the last straw, she was brought home by a policeman. He had 'found' her at some party where people had been arrested for smoking marijuana. Luckily he didn't go to their church.

Joanie swore up and down she hadn't smoked it herself but Winnie discovered this was a lie because all the time Joanie was grounded she kept seeing her, bold as brass, leaning out of her open window so as to smoke reefers without the smell giving her away. She burned filthy incense all the time, too, which could only have come from Chinatown and which even Winnie knew was a sign.

The atmosphere at home was terrible. Joanie was either seething in her room playing loud music or storming off slamming doors. (Grounding her had proved hard to enforce.) Mom was either haranguing her through her closed bedroom door or weeping hysterically or getting sozzled on Old Fashioneds she clumsily disguised by mixing them in coffee mugs, although they gave her breath like a flamethrower.

Dad began to work late and Winnie would happily have learnt shorthand if it had meant she could join him at the office.

The sad thing in all this was that she never stopped loving Joanie. But her admiration for her died, her envious admiration, and Joanie sniffed this out and began to hate her for it. She had always pretended to hate her, calling her Little Miss Perfect or God's Dolly but this had been only to get at Mom, because she would come into her room later on and be friendly and sweet and talk about them being united in adversity. But now if she saw Winnie she just sneered or looked right through her or barged her out of the way. Winnie had come to stand for everything she hated, which was so unfair. She couldn't help being conformist: she did it because everything else scared her so. And she couldn't help the way she looked. The smooth, blonde perfection that still smiled blandly back at her from the bathroom mirror was no effortless blessing but took work to achieve and tension to maintain. It took so much tension that the effort to pull herself together in the morning and get herself to Havergal for classes began to give her sick headaches and sometimes she had to excuse herself from class and lock herself in a washroom cubicle and just sit there breathing deeply.

Her friends began to fall quiet when she rejoined them. She saw the MacArthurs, as a family, cross a street to

243

avoid her. Word was getting around. Ronnie Fleming, the friend's brother who had agreed to be her date for the Prom, began to look hunted and then suddenly wasn't taking her after all because he was taking Dede MacLean and blushingly let on that his arrangement with Winnie had never actually been agreed, had it, and he had a prior promise to Dede. Like hell he did.

Jesus was no help, although Winnie didn't give up on him. On the contrary, she began to demand more of him and started taking herself off to weekday Communion services and even Bible Study. It was on the way home from Bible Study that she saw Joanie in another boy's car with a whole gang of them, all boys except her, driving into the Flemings' place.

The Flemings lived in one of the older houses, on the edge of Etobicoke really – a place whose original land must have been carved up when the area was developed. They had money. They had a cleaning lady, twice a week, and a kind of rec room for the *young people* built on the side of their garage in what had once been some kind of servants' quarters or stable block. They were just the sort of people Joanie despised, especially in her new, ultra-rebellious persona. So it was incongruous to glimpse her in their midst, all in black, with her insane Beatnik haircut and trampy lipstick while they were all dressed like only slightly updated versions of their fathers and might have been on their way to a country club dance. One of the boys, one Winnie didn't recognize, had been swigging from a Jack Daniel's bottle and it was perhaps this inconsistency and the crazy speed of the car that made her pause halfway to her parents' house and turn back, Bible in hand.

Night was falling and it was easy enough to slip into the Flemings' drive unobserved. It wasn't like her to be so bold and brave but they had been studying the story of Deborah and she saw how a sense of righteousness could be like a flaming torch or a sharpened steel.

There were lights on in the main house, not many, and she saw Louisa Fleming carrying a casserole out from the kitchen. There were lights on in the rec room too, but not so brightly, and there was music. The car she had seen was parked there, not over by the main house. She heard boys whooping. It was some kind of party.

Curious, she drew closer, sliding between the car and the hedge. The curtains were drawn but there was a gap. She peered in.

The scene was so confusing, so unlike anything she had seen before, that it took her a second or two to make sense of it. The boys were standing, huddled together, drinking and passing a reefer between them, vaguely watching something on the television. Joanie was on a sort of day bed a few yards away. Winnie only spotted her because the light from the television was flickering across her bare legs. There was a boy on top of her. When he climbed off her, she saw Joanie's breasts were bare and glimpsed her face. It looked blurred because her lipstick and mascara were all smeared but she seemed to be laughing. Then a second boy, unmistakably Ronnie Fleming, came over, unzipping himself as though he were about to use the bathroom. He dropped his pants and, fumbling with his underwear, took the other boy's place and started pumping.

Winnie only watched long enough to recognize two of her friends' brothers then she turned and ran home.

The house was empty when she came in. Her parents
were at some boring drugs company party to mark a
retirement or something. She turned on lights. She felt an
urgent need for lots of light. She went directly to Joanie's
room and started to go through her things. She felt sure
all the answers she needed would be there.

It was a mess, of course, unlike *her* room. Clothes and
makeup were everywhere but also records and books and
art things. For a few minutes it felt as though all Winnie's
life, all her good-girl years, had been leading up to this
so that at this crucial juncture where her sister needed her
to be strong, she could act with absolute, unquestioning
authority. She felt as if she was a force of light dispelling
a darkness that had been allowed to gather too thickly in
one place. She found a tin with pot in it and cigarette
papers. And pills with no proper box or wrapping on them
. . . She found a school folder full of photographs of people
of all ages exposing themselves. Some were of tribespeople,
torn from Dad's *National Geographic* collection, some
were of white women, presumably torn from *Playboy*,
which she had seen in his briefcase occasionally, and some
were of men and women in the underwear sections of
mail-order catalogues. The juxtapositions disturbed and
puzzled her. Then she found a stash of drawings.

Most of Joanie's art was in a couple of portfolios at
the foot of her bed and was familiar. The naked women
drawings had been torn up by Mom. But now she found
another stash, hidden under Joanie's mattress. These were
of naked men. Boys. Boys they both knew, some of them.
Boys from the Flemings' rec room. And they were touching
themselves or . . . *offering* themselves.

If only her parents had been at a dinner instead of a cocktail party, things would have turned out differently. She would have had time to calm down or maybe even taken herself off to bed and seen the situation more clearly in the morning. Instead, they came home while she was still weeping in a huddle on the stairs and she had no sooner seen their worried faces looking up at her than she felt a child again, not remotely a teenager, and everything had come spilling out in a confused tumble. If Mom wasn't sober when she came in, she sobered up in seconds and within half an hour had packed a bag full of Winnie's things and driven her to her grandmother's farm an hour outside the city.

Winnie liked it there and was relieved to escape the tensions at home, the need to be an adult, and even to have the perfect excuse for avoiding the humiliation of a Prom night with no date. Missing graduation was no big deal either, since she graduated but with predictably mediocre results. Her grandmother was all kindness and simplicity, feeding her, setting her to collecting eggs and gathering kindling, asking no awkward questions.

When Mom fetched her back a week later she explained very carefully that Joanie was ill, in her head, and had obliged them to place her in the Clarke. She wouldn't go into details, she was too ashamed, but she had evidently decided to blame the whole affair on drugs and made Winnie promise that if ever some boy tried to get her to smoke marijuana she would run straight to the police.

Dad was only slightly more forthcoming. Driving Winnie into town one day he admitted that Joanie had lost control and started to see things that weren't there.

Nobody said anything about the pornography or the drawings, which presumably were all burnt. Winnie wasn't about to confess that she had kept one of the drawings, the one of Josh MacArthur, for herself, having stuffed it under her sweater as they came through the door that night. She had uncreased it by pressing it between books beneath the spare room mattress at her grandmother's. Now that she had got used to its startling contents, she had to admit it was beautiful, even though it was beauty of a dangerous sort she could never share with anyone.

She visited Joanie in the Clarke a few times but hated going there. The staff members were so kind and clearly cared for her sister and it was nothing like the asylums in horror films but she blamed herself for putting her there and for the things they were doing to her: the drugs and the electric shocks.

This guilt only intensified when Josh MacArthur suddenly asked her on a date after coming up to commiserate most politely after church one Sunday. It turned out he had been keen on her for months but was shy because he thought she disapproved of him.

'I always found I could talk to Joanie,' he said. 'Seeing as she talked to me first. But I never wanted to ask her out. Only you.'

She sat with his sisters now to watch him play hockey. Actually the violence of the sport was so unbearable she tended to spend a lot of the game watching through her fingers or playing with her gloves and listening to the terrifying, slick sound of the boys' blades on the ice and the bloodthirsty yelling of the crowds. She became a regular guest at Mr MacArthur's table and she had let

Josh go beyond kissing her face to kissing her breasts, one and then the other. He was scrupulously fair in dividing up his attentions but she doubted she would ever have the nerve to ask him about Joanie's drawing of him.

When Joanie suddenly hissed at her, during a visit, to bring in her driver's licence for her, it seemed like a chance of making amends. Not least because it involved doing something behind her parents' backs. She didn't think she would use it for one moment but she had seen enough of Joanie's life on the ward now to understand how such a small symbol of independence could be precious there. It would help remind her of who she was.

Then the bleak midwinter Sunday arrived when a police car pulled up outside the house while they were entertaining the MacArthurs to lunch and they had heard, just like that, that Joanie was dead, pushed in front of a train by some crazy Irish girl with whom she had escaped.

'But I don't understand,' Mom kept wailing until finally her father asked her *what*. 'How she got her driver's licence.'

'She took it with her everywhere,' Winnie told her, briefly catching Josh's eye. He was standing there, still holding her by the arm as if he felt the tragedy would sweep her out of the house like a hurricane if he didn't. 'She liked to say that way she could just take off if somebody asked her.'

The crazy Irish girl was never traced and had either melted into the crowds at Niagara or crossed the border and joined all the psychos and druggies drifting around New York. Her mother came to the funeral. She was a tiny woman, apparently so shocked and ashamed she had lost all power of speech. Winnie coped, probably because she had Josh to support her now. He had asked her to marry him and she had said yes. They were keeping it a secret until after a decent interval but it helped her stand apart from her parents and not feel implicated in the whole sad mess of them any longer. She also liked to think that, in dying, Joanie had somehow given her a bit of her strength of character. She wasn't so scared any more or so pious. Her faith in Jesus had gone under the train wheels with Joanie, though she was saving that bombshell for after a decent interval too.

Then, out of the blue, she received a postcard of the Empire State Building. It was unsigned and had taken months to reach her because rain or snow had blurred the number and it had been delivered to an empty house far along her parents' street which had only just been sold to a young family. All that was written, apart from the address, was *Boo!*

It was probably a silly joke from some girl from Havergal she never saw any more, one of those girls with the dirty-minded brothers but, although all the evidence was to the contrary, she liked to think it was from Joanie. Joanie, she liked to pretend, had escaped them all and gone to live out her rebellious destiny somewhere wives didn't enthuse about Betty Crocker and husbands had more to talk about than life insurance and sports. She kept the postcard in the attic, in the same cardboard box as her wedding veil and the drawing of Josh with nothing on but a boner.

She liked to think it was Joanie's way of saying she forgave her.

It was one of those perfect Manhattan spring days she
realized were familiar to her entirely from their Hollywood
facsimiles and they were finishing a long and delicious
lunch in a little bistro. The leafy square behind them bore
all the hallmarks of recent gentrification: clean pavements,
fresh paint, an organic bakery and a civilized coffee bar
with red leather club chairs and the day's newspapers.
They had paid for their own flights but the gallery had
put them up in the tiny apartment Thalia Koralek maintained for guests in a new condo development in what
had been a derelict school. Thalia had explained that the
district, derelict school and all, had been a no-go area
only a year or so ago, a network of crack dens and sordid
squats, a fiefdom of some drug gang on which the new
mayor had waged a protracted war. The new colonizers
of the district had retained just enough touches of the
square's bleak past – and what Thalia called *street* – to

lend a teensy trace of danger to flatter the incomer's liberal heart.

Now tree blossom blew down upon grass untainted by dogshit or hypodermic and well-fed children played in a remarkably clean sandpit. The city was still recognizable but barely tallied with the grim place she had passed through on her way to Europe.

'That's because you're considerably richer than you were back then,' Antony told her, catching their waiter's eye and scribbling in the air for the bill. 'God knows where you stayed then and I doubt you did much shopping.'

The show didn't open until that night – they had finished the hanging only yesterday – but already a third of the pictures had sold thanks to a catalogue-mailing.

She wondered for a moment how he would cope at the opening but of course he would cope beautifully because he treated everyone the same. He would confess to being a schoolmaster not an artist in a way that would disarm even the most status-conscious collector and would pay the toyboy handing round canapés the same attention as the banker with a Nicholson over his fireplace. She was far more nervous than he was and it would only get worse as the evening approached. She had beta-blockers to stop her stammering or sloshing her wine-glass when Thalia introduced her to yet another intimidating journalist or moneyed stranger.

Antony's gift was that he could never be intimidated because he didn't care, or he cared only about the things that carried moral rather than social weight. Listen as she might to his calm good sense, she could never emulate him and supposed it went back to childhood conditioning; she was the product of her mother's pathetic self-consciousness while he came from a line of men who accepted everyone as they found them and guilelessly assumed they would return the courtesy.

He paid the bill and idly fiddled with the scrap of paper. She reached out for his hand and stilled it and, before she knew it, they were holding hands across the tablecloth in a way they'd never have done at home.

'Couple of middle-aged honeymooners,' she said and he just said yes and smiled to himself, turning his hand round beneath hers to caress and then gently grasp her wrist in a way that made her want to go back to the tiny bachelor pad with him and draw the curtains. Only it was too minimalist to have anything but white roller blinds, which would let in too much light and leave her, at least, frozen with inhibition. So they would probably do no more than lie there and fall asleep then wake all muddled and cross.

She was still jetlagged but in a pleasant way that simply left her feeling unreal and floaty, as though her actual body were several blocks away leaving this lightweight dream self to drift pleasurably along behind. They had spent the morning walking – because it was too lovely a day to lose to museums and Antony had read that sunshine on the face was a way of helping the pineal glands adjust to a new time zone. They had strolled here and there, stopping for coffees and consulting an amusingly humourless architectural guidebook borrowed from the guest flat. Then they had taken one last look at the hanging and reassured Thalia they were still in the country and would show up in time to meet the people she wanted them to meet. At once egged on and made nervous by hearing about the advance sales, Rachel had gone shopping for a new outfit to lend her courage.

Everyone they encountered there, male and female, seemed immaculately groomed. Hair, nails, makeup, shoes: nothing was left to chance. The money they could have spent on food they blew on looking as if they earned double what they did. Antony assured her it was good to stand out as the artist and that a less kempt appearance would be a badge of distinction and Englishness but, as the morning wore on, she became more and more conscious of her bashed-up shoes and broken nails and unnurtured, provincial hair. Even the vast women climbing down from an out-of-town tour bus were manicured and coiffed. So she had bought the most expensive dress she had owned in her life, some bargain shoes to match and made an appointment at three to see to her hair and nails.

'But you won't have talons like Thalia?' he asked her.

'Fat chance,' she said, 'with ruinous stumps like these. But they can sand them down or something and give me some clear lacquer and do something with all the dead-looking bits of old skin around the edges.'

'I'd never noticed those.'

'Neither had I!'

They had laughed a lot. They were lighter together here, easier, and it wasn't until they sat down to lunch, exhausted from all the walking and shopping, that she saw it was because they were temporarily childless. Apart from the occasional day trip, they never went anywhere as a couple. She hated travelling and he loved being at home so it never happened. Being on their own at home when Petroc was out with friends didn't count because the house and its clutter was so insistent a reminder they had a family. Freedom for her had long since come to mean solitude in the attic or out in the studio. It came as a pleasant surprise to find she could enjoy this sense of airy detachment with Antony at her side, could actually share it with him.

'I used to worry, you know,' she told him as they walked back across the square past the children on swings and the young men playing basketball, 'that it would feel strange when they'd all grown up and left home. I used to think I'd cling on to Petroc for dear life. But now I can't wait, bless him. I mean I can but . . .'

'I know,' he said and gave her arm a little squeeze above the elbow as he steered her over the road.

He held her to him in the little lift, burying his nose in the front of her hair, and, with only a token mumbling from him about *feeling a little tired*, they went directly to bed and made love without even pulling the blinds. She mutely encouraged him to take her from behind, which she preferred these days as she felt her back was ageing better than her front, and he readily obliged so perhaps he felt the same about keeping her eyes averted from his sliding perfection. And they fell into a delightful, jetlaggy sleep with his arm still flung about her chest and her toes still pressing the tops of his big feet. She fell asleep smelling the good smells of him and clean bed linen and hearing the bouncing of the ball against the metal mesh of the basketball court and looking at her smart shopping bags lined up neatly on the bedroom armchair full of reassurance, like young but competent maids.

She did not hear the phone ring. She woke on her own to the sound of the bedroom door shutting and the realization that Antony was talking next door.

'No!' she heard him say, and the complaint of a kitchen chair being roughly sat on. 'Where?' and then, 'What time was this?' and then 'Where are the others?'

She pulled a borrowed dressing gown about her before opening the door to join him, robbed of abandon by a completely unfamiliar edge to his voice. He sounded frightened. Raw.

Hearing her open the door, he turned. His expression made her dizzy. Suddenly the floor seemed unwalkably slippery and she slumped on to the nearest chair, just as he had, as he said, 'Tell them we'll be on the first flight we can, Jack.'

As he hung up, there was nothing for her to ask but, 'Who?'

Silence settled on the room, as familiar and comforting to her as certain hymns to other worshippers. Morwenna glanced around her before yielding to it. It was a large, first-floor room with meticulously maintained 1890s decoration. There was a small jungle of tall potted palms and dracaenas in the deep, rounded bay window that marked the building's corner. Because of the height, the view was a soothing one of trees in the square's central garden: chestnut, plane and lime.

She would never get used to the ceaseless novelty there. Brussels' hybrid culture and constant stream of passers-through was reflected in its Quaker Meeting, which was polyglot, well-dressed and rootless. Ministry was often made in heavily accented English in a room where she sometimes suspected she was the only native English speaker. There were the unchanging elements of Friends' Meeting Houses the world over – the table, the flowers, the books, the noticeboard and the sense of a heterogeneous group united by a hunger for something more than mere life, the stuff of things, could offer. There was that slightly séancy atmosphere and the dim anticipation of weak coffee and biscuits. (Only the coffee there was real and instead of biscuits, there were often warm, sugared waffles or sweet and bendy stroopwafels if someone had been to Holland that week.) But the handsomeness of the art nouveau building – owned by the Quaker Council for European Affairs, who paid for its upkeep by renting out rooms for meetings and parties – and the muted elegance of the Flemish regulars and the quantity of new faces every week made it strange. No doubt a Quaker growing up with weekly exposure to the arrangements at the Square Ambiorix would find the relative poverty and quiet sameness of a Cornish Meeting extreme by comparison. She had heard that Meetings in Africa or Central America were different again, some of them involving exuberant music, some of them more overtly Christian, some of them so profoundly meditative and unstructured that they lasted all day, not just for an hour between breakfast and lunch.

Roxana caught her eye and smiled. Oh God. She knew she should smile back but feared it would come out as a sort of simper or, worse, a sneer so she dropped her eyes to her lap, opting for demure over honest because she was a coward.

Roxana had fallen in love with her months ago, that

much had been obvious, but had only made things awkward by declaring herself the previous night, which meant Morwenna would have to move on for fear of hurting her gratuitously.

People fell in love with Morwenna all the time, both men and women. It was not a thing she could have predicted and certainly not a thing she deserved. She looked pretty odd much of the time, she knew, so it wasn't primarily a physical attraction. It was because they could not believe the simplicity of her – the lack of home, or job, or possessions, the routine lack of money – and projected mysteries and secrets on to her. And it was these that ensnared their hearts. Had she invented a persona to match other people's, given them the usual litany of career, expectations, relationship history – crucially those expectations – the banality of it all would have put people off and simplified her life. But that would have involved lying, which was something she wouldn't do. She had taught herself to withhold information but never to falsify it.

Garfield thought she was mad. A lot of people did. Largely this was because their idea of sanity was so enmeshed with property; economic and social stability with its mental equivalent. She was bipolar. She was intelligent and well-educated and had diagnosed herself and read widely in the subject long before any doctor pronounced the diagnosis over her. It was a kind of curse, the obvious inheritance from her mother backed up by the gloomy genetic parcel from her father, whose mother had proved herself suicidal but had possibly been mildly unhinged as well. She had tried medication and rejected it. For personal reasons which her coolest, most rational

259

moments showed her to be justified, she had chosen to surrender to her illness as she was surrendering now to the silence of the circle of men and women beside her. It drove her this way and that and was steadily wearing her out. She was like a plant rooted in too windy a spot. It would kill her sooner rather than later but death held no fears for her and suggested only the blank bliss of sleep. Were she not a Quaker, she would have killed herself years ago. Insofar as she deserved to die, though, living was a fit punishment for her.

She had only tried to kill herself once and her depressions had rarely been as deep since. They were terrible and seemed to go on for months but after surviving one, she knew she would survive more. She didn't always know she would survive at the time, of course, since depression of its very nature made such knowledge hard to believe, but she had learnt to manage herself. When she was entering a high but was not yet in a dangerous, hypomanic state, she stored up messages for herself to help pull her through the dark times. She wrote stories, poetry or simply long letters to herself, e-mailing copies of them to an address maintained for her by a convent which had once taken her in, which she only accessed in times of great need.

Through this process, much of it self-exploratory, she had become a writer. Nobody knew it yet; she certainly hadn't reached the stage of describing herself as a writer on forms. She had sold a few of her stories to magazines and websites and one of her earlier poems, written when she was living in Potsdam with a rock musician, had achieved a kind of immortality as the lyrics to a song.

The musician had stolen the poem after parking her in a Berlin A&E department, changed its *he's* to *she's* and passed it off as his own so she received no royalties from it. But she heard it being played in shops or bars sometimes, especially in Brussels – where its lines about belonging to a mongrel race had struck a chord – and, like her letters to herself, it was cheering.

She was writing a series of long letters to Petroc as well, unposted naturally, which, provided she only looked at them from the corner of her eye, seemed to be coalescing into a kind of novel. But the novel's ending was so inescapably death that she only wrote the letters when she was feeling especially brave or strong. Not that death frightened her. It was just that she felt more ready for it on some days than on others. She liked to repeat to herself a Stoical exchange from the teachings of Epictetus in which the worried pupil asks, 'Shall I, then, exist no more?' and his master replies, 'Thou shalt exist, but as something else.' For a long while she had cherished a bookmark, now lost, on which one of her nun friends had penned her a quotation from *Religio Medici*: 'We are in the power of no calamity while death is in our own.' (They were Anglican nuns, so relatively openminded about suicide.)

She could so easily have loved Roxana in return. The temptation to shout down the voices telling her to move on was terrific. Roxana was the only woman she had been involved with in this way – allowing it to progress as far as bed rather than tearful conversations. Blonde and sturdy, what Henry James called *vaccine* in looks and manner, she was not obviously attractive. However she had that Flemish sexiness that was partly to do with her smokily slurred accent when she spoke English, partly with her cool acceptance of absolutely everything that caused no suffering. She was politically a radical, who had only left the radicals because they refused to reject violence and she wanted to be with people who got things done. She had carved a living in Brussels as a lobbyist. She was a natural Quaker – a refugee from her parents' post-Lutheran atheism – and had taken Morwenna under her wing a year ago when Morwenna stumbled into her first Meeting at 50 Square Ambiorix, nearly catatonic with sleep deprivation and evidently, grubbily, homeless. She had an attractive apartment – a sublet of a sublet – in an unrestored 1880s building between the Oude Graanmarkt and the canal and a fridge as bottomless as her heart was warm.

That they had stayed together longer than Morwenna had lasted with any man was less to do with unacknowledged lesbianism than with the fact that Roxana had never raped her, drugged her or stolen her clothes or poetry or abandoned her, penniless and gibbering, in a public place. Morwenna didn't think she was a lesbian but then she didn't think she was anything at all. Sex with anybody tended to leave her feeling panicky and stifled but at least with men one was required to give nothing back. Roxana, bless her heart, needed feedback, reassurance, more than merely a companionable heartbeat and a body's simple warmth.

She had not made the mistake of trying to make Morwenna see a doctor – she liked her beer so knew all about self-medication and respected her choices – but, through one of her useful network of Low Country exes, she found her a job that would suit her, stimulating and wonderfully solitary, in an archive of botanical art. It would mean regular money, security, taxes, having somehow to track down what Morwenna called her notional insurance number.

'And hey,' Roxana said, with her characteristic down-turn of the mouth, 'archivists are hardly normal but it would be a kinda passport to the world of normal people, yes?'

There was no pressure; she had a whole fortnight in which to decide. It was more than Morwenna deserved. Since dropping out of university her CV had consisted of nothing but waitress and chambermaid jobs and, once, folding shirts in a laundry.

She glanced up again. Again Roxana sensed she was looking at her and looked right back and blessed her with a private, no teeth, smile. Morwenna held her gaze this time, gave her a kind of smile back then wrenched her gaze away towards the open window and the view of trees. At the stop near the front door a bus's doors closed with a hiss and a rubbery thump. She felt the too-familiar churning in her belly that had been nagging her for days like a thing waiting to be born.

She made a quick mental tour of Roxana's flat. There was nothing crucial she could not abandon there. Having no identity card, she always carried her passport. She had the scant remains of her birthday card money in her wallet. She had on the stouter of her two pairs of shoes and her warm suede coat because the morning had been chilly. There wasn't enough cash for a train any great distance but there was plenty to stand breakfast to any lorry driver who gave her a lift.

Twelve o'clock came and she slipped away the cruellest way, with not even a veiled explanation or goodbye, under cover of going to the lavatory while Roxana was helping brew coffee with the boys who ran a bookshop. She would write to her, she decided, once she knew she wasn't coming back. She had tried to leave once before – using the cover of feigned shock when they had first slept together – but hunger, lack of impetus and a disarming curiosity had driven her back after a day or two.

She jumped on the first bus that came and rode it along Rue d'Archimède to the European Commission, then caught the Metro to De Brouckere, which felt horribly close to home. She then jumped on another bus, an 87, which took her way out to beyond Berchem-Ste-Agathe and a particularly horrible shopping mall near the ring road. There she had to wait on the windswept fringes of the lorry park for nearly two hours before someone pulled over who didn't want a prostitute. Sundays were quiet and she suspected there was a bylaw limiting goods vehicle access to the city.

It was a rule of hers to trust in fate when hitching, especially when all that mattered was to leave a place. Italy. Germany. Holland. She took care to have no preference in her mind when he wound down his window but swiftly racked her mental dictionary for a shrugging Flemish 'wherever?' in case he was one of the rare, cussed ones who wouldn't speak French. *Ik ben gemakkelijk?* Or was that sexual? *Ik geef niet?*

He was Scottish, headed to Dunkirk for the boat crossing to Ramsgate then on up to Dundee. His lorry announced a firm specializing in logistics, which left her none the wiser as to its load. She had heard that lorry drivers engaged in smuggling, especially the smuggling of people, were always happy to have a properly passported woman passenger join them in the cab as women were thought to convey an air of the wholesome.

So England it was, then. For the first time since she had fled Hedley and Oliver's house two years ago.

The driver was fifty-something, a recent ex-smoker – that she was a non-smoker too was a condition of his giving her a lift – huge and pasty-skinned with sandy hair cut convict-short. With well-trained eyes she took in the wife and child snaps tucked into a vent in the dashboard and the little fire extinguisher she could use to cosh him if they were no more than a cover. He talked incessantly, showing no curiosity, which was a blessing, largely about people in his home village. He talked well, even amusingly, and she was beginning to think that, since she had never been north of Edinburgh, now might be the time, when he abruptly started saying how his wife had allowed him no sex for nearly a year, despite his long absences, and how he was wondering if she had turned lesbian and, if she had, did Morwenna think it would be within his human rights to ask at least to be allowed to watch.

So she deflected his enquiry amiably enough until they were safely through passport control and on to the boat, then she bought him a pie and a pint and locked herself in the ladies and read a discarded magazine until drivers were summoned back to the vehicle decks.

There were queues of cars at the other end, and lorries. She had no plans at all beyond her itch to keep travelling and could equally have hitched a lift back to the

Continent or walked inland to Canterbury but then, as she began to cross the road to follow the few foot passengers struggling with their shopping into Ramsgate, a lorry parked outside the customs offices made her stop. *T. H. Thomas, bulbs, seeds and nursery sundries, Madron, Cornwall* its flank proclaimed, and there was the dialling code of her childhood. Being virtually an island, the west of Cornwall seemed to contain nothing but Cornish culture, Cornish lorries, Cornish people, Cornish names and numbers when you were there but they were so deeply diluted as you moved away to even halfway up the county that coming across the 01736 code or someone called Penberthy in Brussels or even London caught her attention like a waving flag. As ever she was trapped between a sharp swell of infantilizing homesickness and a keen desire to deny the familiar and walk stiffly past. The lorry was blue with sunshine-yellow, unfancy lettering. There was a painting in the same innocent yellow turning a stylized Cornish map into a cornucopia from which a bunch of daffodils was spilling.

'Where are you headed?'

Seeing her staring, the driver had wound down his window. He looked about twenty, barely old enough to have charge of his own lorry, but perhaps it was his father's.

'Oh,' she said, instantly exhausted. 'I don't know. Nowhere really. This reminds me of home. I grew up in Penzance.'

She had not been back there for over ten years. Had the time come finally? She felt breathless with indecision. Was this how it was supposed to happen?

'Well we're setting off as soon as the wife's got the paperwork sorted in there. We've room for a third.'

'Are you sure?'

As answer he opened the passenger door.

'I . . . I might not go all the way there,' she began but he was already deep back in the cab, out of hearing. She hesitated but then the wife appeared, who was even younger than him, with furry boots and a pierced nose and was so sweet and encouraging Morwenna joined them.

Having invited her to ride with them they were oddly shy of involving her in their quiet conversation. She tried to stay awake, it had always seemed a common courtesy as well as a safety measure to stay conscious when being given a lift, but the setting sun was warm on her face and bright in her eyes and the cab air was thick with the scents of dog and air freshener. She fell into a shameless sleep.

She woke a couple of times to find they had pulled into a motorway service station. The second time, the wife returned with a bacon roll for her and a cup of tea. Morwenna thanked her, unable to tell her she had not touched meat in years. The bacon was delicious, salty and slightly burnt, just as she remembered it. Fed, she fell asleep again – it was night now – and didn't wake again until the woman, girl really, tapped her on the forearm to say they had passed Whitecross and were nearly at the turning for home.

'Are you going to be OK from here?'

'Of course,' Morwenna said. 'I'm sorry. I've been so rude. All I've done is sleep.'

'That's OK,' the girl said. 'Paul's brother's been on the

road for a couple of years now, so it's good to do what we can. Might bring him back, you know? Karma and that.'

She thinks I'm homeless, Morwenna thought. *I suppose I am.* 'You're very kind,' she said. 'Thank you.' And she repeated, 'Thank you,' to the young husband. As she opened the door and climbed down into the lay-by where there had always been a man selling 'fresh' mackerel from the back of his car, she shivered. The night air was sharp.

'Here.' The girl handed her down the remainder of a packet of flapjacks.

'But I . . . No.'

'All right? See you.'

The lorry pulled away with a toot of its horn and she was alone. Stilling fear with food, she tugged the little plastic tray out of the cake packet and found the couple had tucked a ten-pound note inside where a flapjack would have been. Morwenna tucked it into her pitiful wallet, ate a flapjack then began to walk.

She was just above the roundabout from where roads led off to Marazion, Helston and Penzance. Walking on the verge of a road designed only for cars, she took the Penzance route. It was half-past three in the morning, not an hour to go banging on doors and frightening people. But now that she was walking, the night was less cold and familiar sights began to draw her on. At the next roundabout she took the turning into town and again at the third so that she was soon on the pavement above the train tracks, where the miraculous fig tree had grown up from the embankment rock. Finding little changed, she walked on, following the seafront past the car park and the inner harbour – nowadays the only harbour – over the Ross Bridge, past the Scillonian and the light-house museum, past the lido, past the older houses clustered below St Mary's. And there, all too soon, now that the promenade to Newlyn stretched ahead of her beneath its chains of white lights, she was at the turning for her parents' house.

She could have woken them. After such a long absence of course she could, or simply slept in the garden or even searched in the old hiding place for a latch key, because theirs was a door that was never double-locked. But she found she was walking on above the quietly breaking waves and now she knew what she had come to do.

She walked on along the deserted road to Newlyn, where there were already signs and sounds of activity towards the harbour and fish market. The quick route now would be to turn inland as if for St Just, then to turn left at the junction with the Land's End road – the network of roads remained as bright in her mind as a diagram in a child's textbook – but she knew she had to take the route he was taking so she went towards Sancreed the long way, up the steep hill towards Paul and then inland along the narrow lane through Chyenhal.

As the road plunged down into a valley, trees reared over it – big trees for that part of the world, their branches black against the starry sky. She walked past the spot at first, because she was too busy admiring the branches and marvelling how much you could see in the real country darkness once you got used to it. She had become too used to the never-quite-night of Brussels and had forgotten the velvety quality of true darkness and its unexpected gradations. She had forgotten how moonlight could cast a shadow.

She realized she had passed the spot when she reached the steep curve in the road which Spencer had taken so fast they nearly rolled over. She turned back. It was all more recognizable going in that direction: the oak tree and the old concrete shelf where milk churns used to be left out for collection. She touched the tree. If she had a torch she knew she would find the frowning face formed by patterns in its bark. She touched the concrete shelf. Then she sat and then lay on the concrete, just where he had ended, though huddled up for warmth unlike him. She cushioned her head in the crook of her arms and closed her eyes.

She breathed deeply and focused on the silence that was never quite silent once you listened to it. She exerted again the discipline learned in girlhood, imagining a light somewhere above her, a warm, sweet-smelling light like the kind thrown out by the finest beeswax candles only more searching and insistent. First she held Roxana in the light, imagining her soothed and healed and comforted. Then, for the first time in years, she dared to hold Petroc there.

This was far harder. Like so many woodlice disturbed at the lifting of a log, the old if-only's skittered through her consciousness. *If only I had paid more attention to what he was telling me. If only we had offered him a lift. If only I had acted my age and not been such a stupid little slut.* And behind the if-only's came the still unanswerable questions. *Was I wrong to testify against them? Was it really honesty that made me say no, he's lying because I was there with him and yes we were drunk and yes we were out of our tiny minds . . . Or was it simply vengefulness spurred on by shame?*

She heard again Rachel's devastating rejection of her, delivered in a toxic little hiss on the station platform so that no one else would hear or judge her.

And then, just when she was breaking under the effort, the warmth reached her as she held him in it, and quietened her and without even noticing it she slipped into sleep and dreamed of things too long unregarded.

She was woken by a pick-up speeding past with dogs barking in its open rear. The sun was up but hadn't roused her because she'd ended up asleep with her face buried in the crook of one arm. She ached all over and was shocked to find how she had seized up from moving so little. And yet, sitting up with her legs dangling off the churn stand, combing her hair back off her face with her fingernails, she felt almost refreshed and certainly in better spirits than she had been for weeks.

It seemed she had refound a sense of purpose, if only temporarily. She breakfasted on the last flapjack and apple then sat on for a few minutes concentrating on the image she had formed of the young lorry driver and his wife and holding them in the light. But her blessing lacked the radiance it had achieved the night before; she was already preoccupied by the task ahead.

She stood, shook the crumbs and leaves off her clothes, stamped the feeling back into her feet and performed some yoga stretches, smiling serenely at a startled driver who rounded the corner and passed her, staring. Hedgerow sleepers were not the commonplace they had been once.

Then she set out again in the same direction she had

been going the night before, away from Chyenhal, past one of the inland views beloved of Newlyn School painters and up to the junction with the main road at Drift. From there it was a twenty-minute walk up the Sancreed lane behind Drift which skirted the reservoir, then down a steep track into the neighbouring valley with Bosviggan's fields on either side.

Approached from the rear like this, the farmhouse was hidden by trees but even before she could see it clearly, a violent change was evident. When they had all spent so much time there years ago, this had still been a working farm. Both Spencer and his older brother had dropped out of school to take it on from their father, who some degenerative illness had incapacitated. The business had not been thriving before – it was said that the family were stranded gypsies, not born to the land, more used to seasonal labour than the relentless slog and responsibilities of agriculture. (This had amused Hedley, who said that Troy and Spencer had television names which didn't work in their favour locally either.) Under the sons, who had seemed so streetwise to her then but of course had been little more than teenagers showing off, the farm stumbled from crisis to crisis, propped up by the generosity of the father's friends one month, hobbled by Troy's latest get-rich-quick scheme the next.

The yard was invariably ankle-deep or deeper in filth from the cattle sheds and lent a lurid soapy fragrance whenever the washing machine was used on account of a burst waste pipe. There were always cars being repaired or customized – one of Spencer's sidelines – always a few whose owners appeared to have abandoned them to the rust and brambles and cat life and always pieces of half-dead farm machinery held together with fibreglass tape as much as ingenuity. There were always half-crazed, useless dogs, occasionally ferrets and, for one memorable summer, a buzzard with a broken wing. It was an appalling mess and the place every teenager with pretensions to cool wanted to be. The brothers were godless, as good as parentless, had limitless space for casual guests and, because they were friends with at least one drug-dealing fisherman, threw anarchic parties with a reputation for sin.

They were every parent's nightmare so, for a couple of heady years, both she and Hedley had fallen under their spell. Even as the bit of her that slaved for exams and paid rigorous attention in class knew, as Spencer didn't, that he was just a phase she would soon leave behind for better, more adult things, the soft, inexperienced part of her needed him to stamp her with credentials school and the Quakers couldn't. Life beyond Penzance secretly scared her and Spencer helped her overcome that, not least because she knew she was using him.

Shockingly the mess had all gone now and, with it, any trace of the brothers and their crippled father in his caravan. The wrecked cars had gone and the ruinous farm machinery, the semi-feral chickens and the dogs. In their place were a handful of clean, new cars on smart gravel where all the muck had lain. There were window boxes and tubs all neatly planted out and a kind of wishing well where there had used to be a treacherously leaky manhole over the dairy's old urine pit. The barns and pig shed had all been converted. Pretty sash windows were dressed with blue gingham curtains and little slate signs

indicated the entrances to Bosviggan Farmhouse, The
Barton, The Old Dairy, Mowhay Cottage and The Byre
respectively. Sure enough, a little way up the drive she
came upon a smart notice, in a heritage blue to match
the gingham, announcing Bosviggan Holiday Cottages and
giving a St Ives phone number.

She felt she must turn back at the sign and stare a
while to convince herself the huge change had really
happened. Had the father died and the boys escaped at
last? Had Troy finally got rich quick? It was all far more
tasteful and tidy than anything she could imagine them
achieving on their own so perhaps they had been obliged
to move out? Perhaps the bank had finally heard one
feeble excuse too many and forced a sale?

She was startled by a deep, rumbling bark and the
appearance at her side of a thickset brown dog, like a fat
Rottweiler or a cross-bred Labrador.

'Oh,' she said. 'Hello.' She was not used to dogs, rarely
comfortable around them, and hoped it would move on.
But it crouched beside her, panting merrily and began to
take long, deliberate licks at her calves and feet. 'No,'
she said and made to walk on in the direction from which
the dog had come. She was in jeans – bare legs would
have been worse – but something in the animal's interest
was oppressive and she feared its worship might turn
without warning to something nastier. Its panting had
revealed stacked teeth like a shark's and, sure enough,
when she moved it sort of bounced at her and made a
playful snapping movement at her jeans' trailing hems.

'No!' she said more firmly.

'Keeper!' someone shouted. 'Here! Keeper!' It was a

NOTES FROM AN EXHIBITION

boy, at that unreadably leggy age between twelve and fifteen. 'Sorry,' he told her, gruff with embarrassment. 'He don't often meet strangers. Sorry. Keeper!'

He had been walking on a path she hadn't noticed, off the track and under the trees and now plunged off it towards her, all outsized trainer and overstretched leg. He ducked his head as he fumbled to get a collar and lead fastened on the dog, which had now decided to play and was bouncing its meaty paws in a circle with Morwenna as the tree in the middle.

'Someone doesn't want to come,' she said, relaxing now.

'Telling me,' he muttered. 'Bloody animal. We were meant to be going the other way, weren't we?' He had on a baseball cap over a thatch of red-brown hair, and baggy shorts worn low on his hips but his stab at cool was let down by his cruelly skinny arms. As he succeeded in catching the dog at last, she stole a glimpse of his face under the brim of his hat.

It surprised her so much that without thinking she said, 'Petroc?'

He looked at her properly for a second, long enough for her to see it, then the dog took off in the direction they had come, tugging him in its wake.

'Wait,' she said. 'Please. I just . . .'

She was unfit, quite unused to running, so couldn't keep up. And the boy couldn't stop, although he glanced over his shoulder at her a couple of times. Perhaps it was a routine with the dog to walk so far every morning in return for being allowed to race home afterwards? Perhaps it knew there was food waiting for it? For whatever reason it all but towed him along the track and through a gap in the trees and then she heard a door slam.

She drew closer to where he and the dog had vanished and found a little outpost of the Bosviggan of her youth. There was an extraordinarily unadorned bungalow, whose once white rendering someone seemed to have been using for target practice, a couple of caravans propped up on breezeblocks and a cluster of cars, none of which looked roadworthy, one of which was missing its windscreen. Someone was chopping logs nearby. She could hear the rhythmic thumping of blade on log. She could hear the dog barking too, frantic with excitement, somewhere in the house and the boy yelling at it, his voice cracking.

It had been a delusion, of course, of a sort to which she had never become sufficiently inured to dismiss them as such as they occurred. She was hungry; her blood sugar was crazily low. He was just another boy and it was purely the strong memories stirred by returning to this place that had made her see something in his face that wasn't there.

She had come much closer to the bungalow than she had intended. She turned away and was startled to find a man only feet behind her. He had several days of stubble and was dramatically bald so she didn't recognize him until he spoke.

'What the fuck are you doing here?' he demanded and she said nothing, as she struggled to align the hostile man before her with the confident boy she remembered. She stared at his right hand, which held a hatchet, and recognized the little bluebird tattoo above his thumb. She remembered kissing it. He had many other tattoos now. Less kissable ones.

'I wanted . . .' she began. 'Spencer?'

'We don't need you around here no more. You did enough damage, all right?'

'Is that your boy I saw?'

'You stay away from him and all. Go on.' He took a step towards her. 'Piss off.'

Frightened, she staggered around him and the oiled gleam of the blade and hurried away along the drive, not daring to look back in case he was following her and took her fear as provocation.

Soon the drive spilled out on to the road and she felt safer, away from the brooding trees. But then there was a car engine close behind her and the parping of a horn. She didn't dare look round in case it was him and turned her face submissively towards the hedge, hoping he would drive past her. But the car paused right beside her, engine still running, and a woman's voice called her name.

She turned. The driver was a woman, a battered thirty-something, crazily thin with long, dyed black hair and a silver ring in her nose to match Spencer's gold one. 'Are you OK? It's Bettany, remember? Petroc's friend?'

'Oh,' Morwenna said. 'Yes. Yes of course you are.' She stared at the henna tattoos on the woman's wrists.

'I can give you a lift into town if you like.'

'Oh. Thanks.'

Dazed, Morwenna let herself in on the passenger side. It was one of the less hopeless cars from the bungalow. A cat had left muddy pawprints all over the windscreen but either Bettany wasn't bothered by them or the wipers weren't working.

'Haven't seen you for ages,' she said.

'No,' Morwenna admitted. 'I . . . I've been away.'

'Sorry about back there. Spence gets a bit paranoid sometimes. He may not even have known who you were, you know?'

'Oh I think he knew. But I'm sorry. I wasn't snooping. I just took a walk and found myself there and then I met . . . Is it your son?'

'Rocky. Yeah.'

Her skinny hands on the wheel showed every tendon. She had the kind of skin that would bruise at the slightest pressure. She had so many silver rings on her left hand it made Morwenna feel uncomfortable looking at it. The biggest ring had a skull design with two little moonstones in the eye sockets. Death grinned at her and Morwenna stared at her own hands and out of the window instead. They had passed through Sancreed and were on the main road towards Penzance.

'So have you and Spencer been together long?' she asked, still looking out of the window.

'Since he got out?' Bettany said. She phrased every sentence as a question.

Morwenna remembered how that had grated on her nerves and how furious Petroc had been when Antony suggested upspeak was a symptom of moral relativism in the young. 'When was that?' she ventured, looking round but studiedly casual.

'Eight years ago?'

The maths was no great challenge, subtracting the years from what she guessed was the age of the boy with the dog. Rocky. Short for Petroc? She couldn't ask.

'Are you home for long, then?' Bettany went on.

'Maybe,' Morwenna said, trying the idea on for size. 'Probably not. But don't worry. I won't bother Spencer again.'

The girl was suddenly focused, distraught even. 'What did you want? What did you hope to get out of seeing him?'

'I . . . Nothing. Closure? Isn't that what it's called? I had a chance to come home so I took it and then I found I needed to see Bosviggan again.'

'Yeah, well, it's all change there, isn't it?'

'The holiday cottages. Did Spencer do those?'

'You must be joking. He and Troy were only ever tenants and they had to move out when . . . Their dad bought the bungalow before he died so we'd have somewhere.'

'Where's Troy now?'

'Auckland.'

'God!'

'Yeah. Making a mint with a nightclub? So there's just Spencer and me. Look I know what you're thinking. Why's she been so sly and secretive? Why didn't she tell us anything? But it wasn't like that. I was in such a state afterwards and, well, I just needed a fresh start, you know? I was scared your mum and dad would want to take him away or sort of take us over. Shit!'

'What?'

'I hadn't meant to tell you.'

'That's OK.'

'He's Spencer's boy, OK? He thinks that. Spencer thinks that. And, well, most of the time now so do I, frankly.'

'That's OK.'

'You won't tell them?'

'No.'

'Why're you smiling, Morwenna?'

'I'm an aunt.'

'Yeah. Well. Not really. Forget it. Best that way. Just forget I told you?'

'You were sleeping with Spencer back when I was, then?'

'Search me. Yeah. Sorry. It was only casual back then, though. We were just kids, weren't we?'

'Yes,' Morwenna admitted. 'I suppose we were. Anywhere on the front's fine, thanks.'

'OK.'

They were driving through Newlyn and Bettany pulled over as soon as she could, keen to be rid of her difficult passenger.

'Bye,' she called out, inexplicably cheery now. 'Take care, Morwenna! All right?'

Morwenna stood on the pavement a moment or two, taking stock. Across the road several boys were flying back and forth on the skateboarding ramp, jeans miraculously hooked round their hipbones in the look Rocky had been aiming at. She crossed over to be nearer them without a moment's thought and was almost hit by a lorry, which blared its horn, then by a car, which swerved to avoid her. The car driver screamed abuse at her through his open window but she walked on.

Someone somewhere was shouting her name.

She watched the boys.

It had always struck her that their shortening of their names in childhood were all puns when you listened to them. Head. Pet. When. Only Garfy, out on a limb as ever, had two syllables and a name with no meaning.

The boys whizzed noisily back and forth, practising their turns and jumps and appearance of effortless agility. One of them was much too old to be playing with the others, but perhaps this wasn't play to them but something more important, like sport.

'When! When?'

She began to walk swiftly as she pondered, only dimly aware of people having to dodge out of her way. The revelation that Petroc had fathered a son, that she was an aunt, had been followed so swiftly by the harsh ban on further contact that all she was left with was death. Death had been following her all morning, she realized. Longer than that. Death was the belly-churning she had been mistaking for the return of her old friend, mania. Death was the skittering, chattering questions and if-only's at her back. And death had whispered her away from Roxana. It had been waiting patiently beside her as she slept in the lane. It had walked beside her as she made her way to Bosviggan. It had been there in the thudding of the axe and the barking of the dog and the boy's startled thinness and his mother's terrible rings. And now it was impatient and chasing her, running to catch up. And she was ready at last, ready to greet it like a lover.

'Wenn! Wait!'

There was a firm touch on her shoulder. She started with a gasp then found it was Hedley. Little Head! Even as she asked him why he was there and not in London where he belonged, tears sprang to his eyes and she knew that death was using him to reach her.

'Come on,' he said, after trying to explain. 'We can run you a nice hot bath and find you some clean clothes – something of mine might fit you. Then we can get you something to eat.'

She let him lead her back across the road and up to their parents' terrace. She held back, frightened at the sudden sight of the house in daylight but he pulled her along with him, as a child might have done, and she realized that death was as much outside the place as in it and that she might as well surrender control.

We are in the power of no calamity, she recalled.

'I'm so tired,' she told him. 'I might not talk much.'

'That's OK. Antony's over in Falmouth with the others so we can be as quiet as you like. Oh, Wenn. I'm so glad.'

He took her hand then. He wasn't the boy she always remembered when she thought of him but a man, almost middle-aged. She wondered if she seemed equally old and unfamiliar to him.

They were halfway up the path to the front door and he hugged her suddenly, almost violently. She found she couldn't hug him back. Her arms were like lead, like arms in a dream. So she told him, 'You're an uncle, you know. Pet had a baby.'

'Ssh,' he said. 'Don't. We can talk later. Once you're rested. So much to tell you . . .'

So perhaps she wasn't making much sense. That happened sometimes, when she was at a low ebb: her words came out fine in her head but outside they just made people stare or look away.

UNNAMED STUDY (1967?). Wax crayon on paper. Because of the inferior medium used, this small work is thought to date from one of Kelly's enforced stays in what was then Cornwall's only psychiatric hospital, the defunct St Lawrence's in Bodmin. (Once the size of a small town, now largely demolished or redeveloped as housing, the hospital's records for their distinguished patient have been lost or destroyed.) There is no date but Kelly is known to have been treated there for nervous breakdowns following the births of three of her four children, in 1960, 1964 and 1967 and during a further breakdown in 1965. At least two of these involved suicide attempts and all were almost certainly brought on by her insistence on taking no medication of any kind when she was pregnant. By a cruel irony, she produced some of her greatest work in the periods of almost frenzied activity – and mental instability – in the weeks preceding the birth of each child. Unnamed Study (1967?) gains its putative date from the distinctly Op Art or Rileyesque ways in which the orange-coloured squares are made to vibrate or throb by the subtle application of contrasting greens between them. Another reason it is thought to have been executed in hospital is the lack of any finished, larger work produced from the study.

(Lent by a private collector)

'Today I am seven,' Garfield wrote in his diary. 'I am seven and my sister Morwenna's still only three and the baby, who doesn't have a name yet but's a boy, is two months old. Our mother is in hospital so this birthday won't be quite like the others as we're going miles in the car to visit her. We will see how things turn out!'

He hated the diary. It was a tyranny. It was a lockable

one, which he liked because it made it a secret as no one else had the key or knew where he hid it. However it was a five-year diary so it would last until he was twelve, which was ages away. Nobody had managed to give him a satisfactory explanation of what it was for. Holiday diaries were different. Everyone knew about those. You stuck in a postcard or something every day of the holiday or did a drawing in it or a painting and you wrote what you had done. Then you all took them into school on the first day of the Christmas term and there were prizes for the best ones. He complained about having to do holiday diaries but they were easy really, especially if the exercise book wasn't too big so the postcards used up half a page. And it was only eight weeks or less. Two months. And you put public things in it because people would be reading it.

The five-year lockable diary, though, was like a small, leatherette conscience.

'Just put your thoughts in it,' Rachel told him. 'The things you like and the things you don't. Don't just say what you had for meals as that's boring but you can say what you did and how it made you feel.'

'What's it for, though?'

'When you're older you'll be able to read it and see how you used to think when you were little.'

'But I'll remember.'

'You won't remember everything. You're forgetting things already.'

He tried, because he was the eldest – especially now he was to have a little brother – and had to set an example. But he felt uncomfortable writing things down unless he knew they were true, like the dates of battles or what

Humphry Davy invented or Isambard Kingdom Brunel. But feelings weren't like facts. And how did you know they were true? Or right?

Some things he had written down then wished he hadn't. He wanted to tear them out but he didn't dare. He bought some special ink eraser instead, which you dabbed on from a little brown bottle with a plastic applicator in the lid. It smelled funny but it sort of worked only once it was dry you could still see what you'd written but in very pale yellow instead of blue Quink washable.

It had only recently occurred to him that he could simply leave days blank. Since he held the only key, nobody would know. But he had learnt to take nothing purely as it was presented to him. He was told the diary was private, secret, but that could change. He might suddenly be asked to hand it over, unlocked, or he might fall ill without much warning, like Rachel did, and leave it unlocked, readable by anyone who was passing his room. Nobody could resist reading a book of private things. It was wrong but irresistible, he could see that.

When Morwenna was old enough to keep a diary, he would have to warn her to hide it somewhere without telling him. She was only three but she was already showing a worrying lack of caution. She shared and showed everything. She ate chocolate or ice-cream or biscuits in an unguarded, open way, vulnerable to any passing dog or seagull or unscrupulous child. She shared things with thoughtless generosity she only regretted once it was too late.

'Garfy?' Antony called up the stairs. 'Are you ready?'

'Coming!' He locked the diary, which he hid under his

mattress and reached up into his bedroom fireplace to tuck the key on to a sort of sooty shelf in the chimney. Then he hurried down to the hall where Antony was buttoning Morwenna's cardigan for her.

The hospital where Rachel went to have the baby was in Penzance, on the seafront. It wasn't really a hospital because no one there was ill, just having babies. It was a sort of house, called the Bolitho Home. St Lawrence's, the hospital she was in now, was miles away in Bodmin, which was nearly in Devon it was so far.

Garfield tried to sit in the front, in Rachel's seat, but wasn't surprised when Antony told him to get out and sit in the back because Morwenna was too little and might have opened her window or her door when they were driving fast. Not that they ever went very fast. The car was a Morris 1000 Traveller and cream-coloured, with woody bits. It was very old, nearly antique, and Garfield often heard Antony telling people it would go on for years so long as they treated it carefully and didn't overtax the engine. It was so old it had indicators that popped out from the sides to flash, rather than just flashing like a normal car's, which Garfield liked. But the seats got hot and sticky in summer and stuck painfully to his calves if he was in shorts, like today. Also the back seat stank because Rachel had forgotten a pack of Anchor butter once and it had melted into the upholstery leaving just the dried-up paper and a terrible smell that actually smelled like carsickness. It was especially bad on hot days and today was hot because they were having an Indian summer. Garfield and Morwenna breathed through their mouths to avoid smelling it too much. If they opened their windows instead, Antony would complain they were creating too much drag and making him waste fuel. Which was bad for the planet, like not turning off light switches or having too deep a bath.

As he drove, Antony told them the baby was going to be called Hedley, after his grandfather, who was Michael Hedley Middleton. Then he told them all about why Rachel was in hospital in Bodmin. He always told them the truth about everything because it was important and what Quakers did. He didn't always tell them right away, though. Garfield had known she was in a different hospital for days, from listening to conversations, and had been waiting for his father to tell them about it.

Other people, even including other Quakers, were not as truthful as Antony, Garfield had noticed. They dropped their voices, thinking he couldn't hear them, or spoke to him as if he was about five to say, 'Mummy's not gone away for long. She'll soon be back. She just needs a rest after having the baby.'

But Antony said she was sick. Not like when you'd eaten too much lemon mousse but sick in her head so she'd been hearing and seeing things that weren't there, like having a dream but with her eyes open. She'd also got sad. Very sad. In spite of having the new baby to think about. So she was in the hospital so that she and the baby could be made well and happy again. They weren't to be worried by what other people said. She wasn't mad. There were poor people in the hospital who were mad and were probably never coming out because they couldn't cope on their own. But calling even them mad or loony wasn't polite or even medically correct. They were ill, like Rachel, but more so.

Garfield decided the baby had to be with her because of milk.

'Can we catch it?' he asked. They had been doing coughs and colds at school. Steve Pedney, a rather rough boy whose father was said to be in prison, was told off for blowing his nose by simply blocking one nostril with a finger while emptying the other smartly on to the playground tarmac. They all laughed because it was so disgusting but clever too and Garfield thought it might be nicer than spending the day with a soggy handkerchief in your pocket to surprise you when you put your hand in. But Miss Curnow said that was how tuberculosis was spread. Steve Pedney still did it though. *Coughs and sneezes spread diseases.* Madness and sadness might be spread too.

'No,' Antony told him, wrinkling his eyes in the rearview mirror in the way that meant he was smiling. 'It's just inside her, like a tummy ache. You can't catch it by being near her or hugging her. In fact she'd probably like a big hug when you see her. She'll have been missing you. But she's on very strong medicine too which might make her seem a bit quieter than usual or a bit sleepy. Don't worry. Just be yourselves and ask me afterwards if there's anything you don't understand.'

At that point Morwenna started singing one of her aimless, rather tuneless songs so they both stopped talking and listened to her. She picked music up like a sponge – songs from *Play School* or advertisements (at other people's houses because ITV wasn't Quakerly), hymns from kindergarten and Sunday School, even carols from the Salvation Army band – but she sort of melted them down and transformed them so that unless you knew in advance what she thought she was singing it could be hard to guess. Garfield listened closely and decided that today it was the woman on the Shredded Wheat advertisement. He tested his guess by joining in and singing the real version alongside her.

'There are two men in my life.
To one I am a mother.
To the other I'm a wife.
And I give them both the best . . . with natural Shredded Wheat!'

It was an odd song because it didn't go anywhere. It was truncated – like the tail-end of something longer – but oddly haunting. He had only watched the advertisement a few times at a friend's house and to his knowledge Morwenna had only seen it once, when they watched it together in an electrical shop while Antony was buying batteries. But her memory was like that. It was almost frightening.

The other thing that was strange about the advertisement was that you didn't actually see the woman, just people on a sad-looking beach with the sun going down, but you felt you knew what she was like. You could tell she cared. She gave a lot of thought to how she fed her husband and her son. It was odd that she called her son a man because he obviously wasn't but perhaps she was a bit shy of him. Perhaps he was strict with her like his father and food was her only way of reaching him. Food instead of hugs. Like some of the women friends from the Quakers who kept coming to visit while Rachel was away in her hospitals, the ones who called her Mummy instead of Rachel and who lied and said she was tired when they obviously knew she wasn't but that they mustn't say she was mad. They gave Antony cake and stew. But mainly cake. Garfield looked at the back of his father's neck and thought of the Interflora poster on the flower-shop door in Market Place that said say it with flowers. Say it with cake.

Morwenna caught his eye and smiled and sang more in tune so he knew he had guessed right. They kicked their legs in time and sang the jingle together, more confidently now there were two of them. It was funny.

> 'There are two men in my life.
> To one I am a mother.
> To the other I'm a . . .'

'That's enough, now,' Antony said, quite firmly.

Garfield shut up at once but Morwenna carried on, louder and faster, giggling, not understanding because she was only three and a half.

'That's enough, Wenn,' Garfield told her and tapped her knee so that she looked at him. 'Ssh,' he told her.

'Ssh,' she said back.

'Who's this?' he asked, picking up her doll. She snatched it off him, as he knew she would, and lost herself in a quick fury of love, correcting the doll's skirt and hair and squeezing it harder than any mother would. She didn't really love her dolls, she just possessed and controlled them. She spent ages telling them off in language he couldn't always understand and sometimes encouraged him to pull their heads off with a sick-making rubbery pop that made them both laugh. She laughed even more if he muddled the heads up when he put them back but then she tended to panic and he had to calm her by changing the heads round the way they should be, and fast.

They drove on towards Bodmin in relative silence. Some of his friends had parents with radios in their cars but all the Morris had were maps and Rachel's sketchpad and a red tartan picnic blanket that smelled of beaches and seaweed.

Rachel wasn't a mummy and she certainly wasn't like the Shredded Wheat lady. He thought it most unlikely she had been missing him and wanted a hug. Sometimes, especially if she was painting, she hardly knew you were there. And when she got angry it was really frightening. She never smacked them or hit them – Antony said that wasn't right, which meant it wasn't Quakerly – but she shouted and she hit things instead.

It was worth it though for when she was happy. When she was happy she was better than any stupid mummy because she was like someone your age, like a sister but a sister who could put you in the car and say, 'Let's escape, let's not go to school today.' When she was happy and did things like take Garfield on a train ride or out for a long walk when he was meant to be in school or going to the dentist for a filling, Antony got cross but she just got crosser and then laughed at Antony, which was very shocking because he wasn't someone you laughed at, being a teacher.

When he was older Garfield might have to be in Antony's English class at Humphry Davy, which was something he secretly dreaded as he would not know how to behave and imagined it would make things awkward around the other boys. His father must have a nickname, like Fishface or Wingnut or Dr Death that all the boys used. It would be so terrible he had even wondered about failing the Eleven Plus on purpose so he'd have to go to the other school, the bad one full of boys like Steve Pedney who never used handkerchiefs. Only that would not be Quakerly.

He had recently stopped always going to Sunday School and started occasionally sitting with the grown-ups in Meeting instead. The power of the silence impressed him and what was Quakerly and what wasn't was often on his mind. Wanting more pocket money now that he was older wasn't. Being nice to Steve Pedney, even though other people weren't, was. We all had a little bit of God or goodness in us, even Steve Pedney, like a tiny candle you couldn't blow out however hard you tried and however bad you were and when you sat with the others in silence you had to think of that candle and try to make it shine brighter. Or you had to think of the people who needed it, not just Steve Pedney but children in Africa or Rachel in St Lawrence's or your new baby brother, Hedley, who you weren't sure you were going to like much and imagine holding them in a kind of warm light made by all the people in the circle. It was quite hard work, a bit like magic, and he enjoyed it. When they had assembly at school and all mumbled the same prayers together and it was all about God and Jesus and everyone saying exactly the same thing, it seemed shockingly noisy and so perfunctory it was hard to see what the point of it was. Antony said it was up to him what he believed, that he, Antony, believed in God and Jesus and would probably call himself a Christian and that Rachel didn't entirely but that they both believed in goodness, the little candle inside everybody, even Steve Pedney. Even Steve Pedney's mother, who Garfield had seen in the Co-op once, who had arms like roast pork and looked awful.

St Lawrence's was big: lots of large old buildings and

quite a few smaller ones. It was like a little town behind its own wall. It wasn't like a hospital because it didn't have ambulances coming and going and there wasn't a queue of people with blood coming out of them or taps stuck on their toes and bunches of flowers to give to friends. It seemed very quiet. You only knew it was a hospital because it had those coloured signs with white capital letters that only hospitals had. RECEPTION, the signs said, as if they were shouting. THERAPY UNITS. DRUG DEPENDENCY UNIT. REHABILITATION UNIT.

They were a little early. Visitors were only admitted from two until four so they had to wait in the reception area and sit quietly looking at magazines until it was time. There were a few other visitors waiting too: a man with some books in a basket, an old woman with a bunch of grapes already arranged on a plate, a man and woman who murmured together in a corner and looked really worried as though they'd come in secret and hadn't expected anyone else to be there. The murmuring woman started to cry and Garfield had to whisper to Morwenna not to stare. Morwenna was still too little to know what tactful meant so he was surprised she didn't loudly ask why, the way she usually did. She fell to drawing on ladies' faces in a copy of *Woman's Realm*. Garfield pretended to read a copy of *Motor Sport*, which was a man's magazine, but he was really watching Antony.

Antony was normally very serious and calm. You didn't really notice his moods because he didn't have any. He was always the same, the unchanging pavement under Rachel's weather. But today he was different, even nervous. He kept looking at his watch, as though he didn't trust the clock on the wall above the nurse's head, and turning his wedding ring round and round as though he wanted to unscrew his finger.

He had seen the baby before. They hadn't. Not really. Children weren't allowed to visit the Bolitho Home in case they gave the babies germs or tuberculosis so Garfield had been made to wait on the pavement outside, holding Morwenna's hand although she was wriggling like a fish and her hand was all sweaty and she kept asking why. Then Antony had appeared in a window, as he said he would, and held up the baby.

'Look,' Garfield told Morwenna. 'Up there. See? That's the baby. That's our brother. See?' But she had just started crying *Anty Anty* which was how she said Antony. She hadn't been interested in the baby at all. Which wasn't surprising because at that distance it looked as if Antony was just holding up a bundle of white blanket with a lamb chop inside it. When Garfield asked him what Hedley was like, he said it was impossible to tell because new babies were so wrinkled and red and cross and either cried or slept. So perhaps he was worried Hedley would have changed in a bad way. Or perhaps he was worried about the sickness in Rachel's head. Garfield had looked up *depression* in his dictionary but it had only confused him by talking about weather fronts and dips in the landscape along with *uncontrollable or clinical sorrow.*

The nurse's clock was electric, like the ones in school, so it didn't tick. Its second hand swept round so smoothly you couldn't really use it to count the seconds and it conveyed the impression that time was passing more swiftly. Something Garfield had learnt to resent in maths tests. Only the minute hand clicked. While Morwenna fidgeted beside him and Antony composed himself into stillness the way he did in Meetings, he watched the clock click from five to two to a maddening two minutes past before the nurse lifted the little upside-down watch on her starched apron front and announced, 'You can go in, now. Just present yourself to the nurse on duty in the ward you want to visit.'

'Which ward do we need?' Garfield asked as they approached a big sign listing all of them with arrows in all directions.

'Williams,' Antony said and led them up a big flight of boomy steps with no carpet on them.

'It smells,' Morwenna complained. 'I don't really like it.'

'Ssh,' Antony told her. They had to pass a man who was staring and not talking and she took Garfield's hand. She only did this when she was scared, which helped in a way because it meant he couldn't be scared too.

'Come on,' he told her. 'We're going to see Hedley!' But he flinched a bit when they passed a door where a woman was crying very loudly, like Morwenna did when she didn't get her way.

He made himself look into wards as they passed. In some, people were dressed and walking about or just sitting in chairs. In some they were all in bed. There always seemed to be either men or women. There was a room where everyone was really old and a children's ward with pictures on the wall, which he hadn't expected. He decided to start breathing as shallowly as possible so as not to draw the madness in.

'Williams Ward,' said Antony. 'Here we are. Williams Ward.'

The nurse there was young and really friendly. She crouched down so her head was the same height as Morwenna's nearly and said, 'And who've we got here?'

'I'm Garfield and this is Morwenna,' he told her.

There was a really strong smell of lavatories but not from the nurse, who smelled of fabric conditioner.

'Is that a fact?' she said. She had huge breasts, he noticed, so that she could probably read her upside-down watch without needing to lift it. 'Have you come to see baby Hedley?' she asked Morwenna. Morwenna nodded.

'And our mother,' Garfield said. 'Please.'

'Mum's a bit sleepy,' she said. 'So she might not chat much but she's been looking forward to seeing you both. I know she has. You're better for her than any pills. Soon cheer her up.'

She smiled at Antony as she stood and Garfield saw she had a great curvy bottom to match. He was surprised to wonder how it might feel to push his face into it quite hard or to take shelter under her bosom as under a great, soft-stacked cloud. She might have read his mind because she briefly laid one of her hands on the back of his head and let it slide down on to his nape in a way that gave him goosebumps and made him blush.

'You'll find her in the room on the end,' she told Antony softly. 'Down the ward and turn right. I'll go and fetch young Hedley from his cot.'

There was a Bob Hope film playing on the television and several women were watching it or pretending to. Their faces faced the screen but Garfield was sure their eyes were slyly turned on him as he passed. He hated Bob Hope films. They were full of jokes he didn't understand because everyone talked too fast and he associated them with nausea as they only ever seemed to be on when he was held home from school with a stomach bug. (He had heard it said that he had a sensitive stomach and was deeply ashamed of it.)

Morwenna was holding Antony's hand now, which must mean she was really scared and Garfield was briefly envious of the soft girlishness that would let her take such favours as her right until well past the age at which he had been told to be a big boy and stop crying and stop wanting to be held. Like Morwenna, he suspected, he really wanted to be carried high on Antony's shoulders, which was where he used to feel safest, but Antony had a bad back and wasn't supposed to do that any more.

A woman in a yellow dressing gown with a head that was much too big came up to them and said, 'You give me sweeties,' in a voice that was all wrong.

'I'm sorry,' Antony told her, 'we don't have any,' and passed on with Morwenna.

But Garfield had bought a mixture of Black Jacks and Rhubarb and Custards with some of his pocket money that morning. He had one Black Jack left and knew the woman knew it was in his shorts pocket because she wasn't moving away but was staring down at him. 'All right,' he told her. 'It's my last one, though.'

She took it from him and tore off the wrapper in seconds and threw it in her huge mouth. Like a frog's, her lips seemed to divide her head clean in two when they parted.

She gulped.

'You're supposed to make it last,' he told her.

She was holding out a fleshy hand again. 'You give me

sweeties,' she repeated and a dribble of liquorice spit fell on to her chin.

'It was my last one,' he said. 'I told you.'

He ran to escape her terrible stare and caught up with Antony and Morwenna as they were turning right at the far end of the ward. He glanced back to see if she was following. She had stayed where she was but she was staring and when she saw him look she twitched up her nightdress and he looked away fast but not quite fast enough.

There was a row of individual bedrooms off a corridor. They had brass numbers on the door and, when a room was occupied, little cards slotted into brass holders, with people's names on them. They made Garfield think of the jar labels in the larder at home, only instead of saying Dark Muscovado Sugar or Macaroni they announced their contents as Julie Dawson, Maggie Treloar or, in the case of room seven, Rachel Middleton (& Hedley).

It was funny seeing her called that because when she painted everyone called her Rachel Kelly.

'Why do all the doors have windows in them?' he asked.

'So the nurses and doctors can always see in,' his father said and gave the little cough that showed he was unhappy. 'So nobody can hurt themselves without someone seeing,' he added. 'Ready?'

Garfield nodded.

'Mummy!' Morwenna shouted and Garfield shushed her.

Antony peered through the window in Rachel's door, knocked twice, gave a little smile then opened the door and gently pushed Garfield and Morwenna in before him. 'Look who it isn't,' he said. He used a funny tone of voice, slightly wheedling, as though Rachel had stopped being a grown-up.

She was sitting in the room's only armchair, beside the oddly high-up window. 'Look,' she said sleepily. 'I have to sit on all these so I can see out.' She shifted slightly to reveal a great heap of telephone directories she had used to raise the chair's cushion by nearly a foot.

Garfield was shy of hugging her so, while Morwenna ran to jump on her lap, he jumped a few times instead to see what she was seeing, and caught a few glimpses of a lawn and trees and rosebuds. He was glad to see she looked fairly normal. She was wearing daytime clothes – a dark-blue dress covered in white spots – but she looked pale and somehow uncooked without her lipstick and there was something different about her eyes and she needed to wash her hair.

'What's wrong with your eyes?' he asked her.

'My eyes?' she asked slowly then understood. 'Oh. No mascara. Do they look terrible?'

He stopped jumping and dared to look at her full on. The directories made her so high she and Morwenna might have been on a throne. 'Not really,' he admitted. 'Just sort of pale. And weak.'

'Hello, darling,' Antony said and kissed her on the lips then sat on the end of her bed.

She had slowed down completely. Garfield was used to her being sharp and crackly and rather frightening because you had to think quite carefully what you said because she never missed anything and might pull you up short at any moment. But now she was so slow and placid she was frightening in a different way, as though her mechanism was winding down and no one else had noticed or thought to turn the key. For a whole minute they just sat in silence, Antony sad and watchful on the bed, she on the chair and Morwenna blissful and unquestioning on her lap. Like a ravenous cat given milk, Morwenna always became entirely focused on a pleasurable moment.

The room had no other furniture but a little chest of drawers with a vase on it and a heap of drawings Rachel had been doing with wax crayon.

'Can I see?' Garfield asked. You never looked at her pictures without asking, in case you had sticky fingers.

She stared at him and he could almost hear the glutinous plop as her mind closed over his question and drew it in. She nodded at last with a smile and he went to look.

Instead of doing the obvious view out of the window she had done the window itself, the panes of old, uneven glass, the flaking paint creamy with age, the damp-stained roller blind for blocking out the sun, and the arrangement of gutter, brickwork and drainpipes a little to one side. Then she had done her bed, over and over, with the rumples in different places and the sunlight in different places but the brutal black bedstead exactly the same each time, like a cage about something shifty and fluid. It was so unfair, he thought, that when he did pictures with wax crayon they looked like every other boy's wax crayon pictures but when she did them it didn't look like wax crayon any more. There were no pictures of the baby.

'I asked for pastels,' she said.

He was proud to know better than to think she meant sweets.

'But they said they were too messy,' she went on.

'Maybe I could bring you an old tablecloth and sheet to protect the floor,' Antony said but then the door opened and the nurse with the curvy bits came in with a pram.

'Who wants to meet their baby brother?' she asked and Morwenna slid off Rachel's lap to see.

Garfield was less obviously eager because men didn't show the same interest in babies as ladies did but actually he was quite excited.

'He's off in the Land of Nod,' the nurse said, 'but you can wake him at three if he's still asleep and give him his bottle. I've tucked it in there, behind his pillow. I thought you might all like a stroll in the sunshine,' she told Antony. 'You can take the service lift just outside here and get out to the garden that way. How are you feeling, my lovely?' she asked Rachel. 'Up to a walk?'

Rachel only did a sort of wincing smile by way of an answer but the nurse didn't seem that interested in a response and bustled off to see someone shouting *nurse nurse* from the room next door.

'Careful or you'll wake him,' Antony told Morwenna, crouching down beside her. Garfield drew near to look too. It was a big navy-blue pram almost like a boat with a fringed blue hood and a white inside. Hedley seemed tiny in it. Only his face and hands showed. He had dark hair that grew in a whorl and he had the smallest ears and fingernails Garfield had ever seen. He felt he had never looked properly at a baby until now. He turned round to look at Rachel but she was staring out of the window again.

'Can I touch him?' he asked Antony.

'Of course. Don't wake him, though. He looks so comfortable.'

Garfield reached out a forefinger and just grazed Hedley's cheek with his knuckle. The skin was warm and softer even than Morwenna's. Maybe because it was so new. He touched the back of his tiny fingers.

'Me,' Morwenna said. 'I do.' But she was too small to reach in unassisted so Antony lifted her almost inside the pram so she could touch too.

'What does he eat?' Garfield asked, smiling because he knew really.

'Milk,' Rachel said, focusing back on them.

'From you?' he asked, amazed at his boldness.

'It should be,' she slurred. 'But it's not safe. Too many pills in me now so he'd be drinking them too.'

'He has special baby milk,' Antony said. 'In a bottle. Shall we all go outside for a bit? Push him around the garden? Do you feel up to it, darling?'

Rachel said of course she did.

They went down in the service lift, which was fun as it left your tummy behind and had big metal doors that let you see the floors slipping by. Garfield would quite happily have gone up and down in it a few more times but didn't like to ask, although as it was his birthday Antony might have said yes.

The garden had gravel paths and very neat rose beds with very neat roses in them.

'I asked the gardener how he avoids black spot,' Rachel managed, 'and he said Jeyes Fluid. In solution. All over the soil in January.' She pushed the pram with Antony on one side of her and Morwenna on the other. 'You lead the way,' she told Garfield, though in fact there was little choice about where to walk and small chance of getting lost.

He followed the path, tuning in and out of his parents' horrible conversation. In fact it was all one-sided. Antony kept saying things like, 'Sarah and Bill asked after you on Sunday. They send their love,' which Rachel would answer with a sigh or a barely perceptible murmur. She wasn't fierce or rude, just sad and discouraging, as though each offering of news or good wishes merely caused her physical pain she was unable to describe. He wished Antony would give up. It was bad enough hearing Rachel sound so listless and miserable without him sounding all pathetic. She had not wished him a happy birthday, something so shocking he had to try not to think about it or he would cry.

Escape presented itself in the shape of a small play-ground area with a swing and a slide. Encouraging Morwenna to follow him, he ran ahead and used both in quick succession. The slide was babyishly low and short but the swing, tied to the bough of a big tree, had such long chains that he was soon able to make it fly so high that the chains went momentarily slack at the top of each arc and frightened him into swinging not quite so fiercely.

The others had caught up and sat on a bench nearby with the big pram beside them. He couldn't look at them too closely or he'd be car sick. Swing sick. But he snatched glances as he flew up towards the tree canopy and down again. He saw the baby had woken up. Antony lifted it from the pram with a knitted blanket all round it so that

you couldn't see its legs. It shook its arms though and
cried a bit so Antony gave it a drink from the bottle to
shut it up.

Garfield quite wanted to feed it too but he felt being
happy on the swing had become his job for the moment
so he kept swinging.

Morwenna didn't join him, although normally she liked
going down slides if the steps up weren't too high and
there weren't bigger children hurrying her from behind
or kicking her on the bottom. She seemed transfixed by
Hedley and was throwing him looks that mixed curiosity
with black resentment. As Garfield swung on she climbed
on to Rachel's lap, although Rachel was paying hardly
any attention to the baby. She wriggled and fidgeted until
Rachel held her as firmly as Antony was holding Hedley,
then she lay back in a kind of triumph, though still
throwing penetrating glances at her little brother.

Looking at the four of them it struck Garfield that he
somehow existed apart from them. They were a family,
a tidy family – woman, girl, man and baby boy – and he
was something else, something outside their tidy unit. By
pushing himself into their notice, by running ahead to
show off on the swing, he had accidentally excluded
himself. Where he ought to be was on the bench, snugly
in the midst of them, too old as oldest son to need a lap
but still belonging at the centre as of right. He tried not
to think about it in case he cried. He tried looking around
the garden instead as he swung.

There were other people out here. He spotted the people
from the waiting room, the man with the books, the
woman with the grapes, the haunted couple who had

looked so ashamed and unhappy. They each had someone with them now. The woman with the grapes had a man even older than she was. He was eating the grapes off the plate while she pushed him very slowly in a wheel-chair. The man with the books had left the books inside and was sitting on a bench with another man who was in stripy pyjamas and a tweed jacket. They were smoking and the book man was laughing as he told a story. The miserable couple had a boy with them: a big boy, a teenager, but still a boy. He had jeans and a T-shirt on and you wouldn't have guessed he was ill in his head at all. But then he looked straight over at Garfield on the swing, or seemed to, and his eyes looked totally blank, like two little chips of coal, and somehow you knew that if you could hear his thoughts they'd just be a sound like the washing machine made on a spin cycle and Garfield knew he mustn't meet his eye or he'd become the same.

To escape the boy's eyes and prove he didn't belong here, he showed off his new trick which was swinging standing up. It was quite scary but he knew he could do it. The trick was to keep a really firm grasp of the chains. That way you wouldn't fall even if your feet lost their grip on the seat. Rachel saw what he was doing but it was Antony who said, 'Garfield,' in a weary tone. He ignored them both by just smiling like a man on a circus trapeze. His sandals skidded on the plastic a little and the swing faltered slightly but then he was up, gloriously up, standing and swinging and proud. And because he was standing not sitting, it suddenly felt as though the swing was moving much faster and higher. He remembered what the older boys in the playground had taught him, that you had to bend your knees slightly then straighten them over and over to maintain momentum. And soon it felt as though he was almost reaching the horizontal, facing up into the tree one moment then facing down at the balding grass the next.

The sick took him by surprise. For a few minutes he was fine then suddenly he felt all hot behind the eyes and churny in his stomach and then he knew there was no time to slow down and get off. And then there was sick, arcing out and away from his mouth one moment, splashing all down his front the next.

Rachel actually cried out and Morwenna laughed. By the time he'd managed to stop the swing, he'd stopped being sick but he still felt as if he was going to be sick some more and it was all hot where it had spilled beyond his shorts and splashed down his leg. His head was filled with the sound of his own helpless gulping and his nose with the bitterness and stink of it.

Antony was there beside him helping him off the swing and leading him to the grass. 'Poor chap,' he said. 'Poor old soldier. Come on. Sit down. That's it. You need to keep very very still till it passes. That's it. Head between your knees and just breathe. That's it. In and out. Nice and slow. In and out. Look how still the ground is now. Poor chap. You overdid it a bit, didn't you?'

He held a big hand across Garfield's forehead, the way he always did if Garfield was sick on a car journey or in bed, and he wiped him clean with one of his big spotty handkerchiefs that smelled of peppermints and pockets and bunches of keys.

Gulping less often now, his insides settling, his nose

full of the frank reek of himself, Garfield continued to
sit with his head obediently resting on his knees, listening
to the voices as Morwenna took her turn on the slide,
repeatedly demanding first that Antony help her up the
steps then that Rachel watch her as she slid down the
slide. He made himself focus on the ants moving through
the miniature landscape of grass and twigs beneath his
legs.

If a blade of grass was a tree to an ant, what must a
tree be or a whole lawn? Perhaps, he thought, they simply
blanked out such vastnesses and, having no conception
of their own insignificance, could thus cope with life and
even be happy? Perhaps the trick was to aspire backwards, to the blessed narrowness of a baby's pram-bound
outlook and the more you saw, the less happy you could
hope to be? Perhaps Rachel was an ant who saw trees,
who couldn't help knowing how high it was to the top
or how far to the edge?

'Look at me!' Morwenna shouted again.

Garfield dared to raise his head and found the world
new-made. The midsummer colours of grass and sky and
rosebush and his mother's spotty dress seemed brighter
than before and the sounds, like the sights, seemed sharper.
He had experienced something like it when he was feverish
with first measles and then chickenpox, so hoped the
being sick was just from dizziness and not a sign of something more sinister, like tuberculosis.

'Look at me!' Morwenna was perched yet again at the
top of the slide, stout little legs stuck out ahead of her,
preparing to push off but Rachel wasn't looking at her.
She was tucking Hedley back into his pram. Morwenna's

voice acquired the shrieky edge she still used occasionally to bring a shocked silence to shops or bank queues. 'Look at *me*!'

Rachel stood abruptly, still not looking, and said, 'Oh for fuck's sake,' and turned away towards the hospital. They all watched her go at first, startled as much by her departure as by her words.

Then Antony broke away after her, leaving Morwenna unadmired and still on the top of the slide. 'Bring your sister, will you, Garfield?' he said and headed after Rachel, pushing the pram, which looked a bit funny because he was a man and the pram went all bouncy because he was moving a bit too fast for it on the gravel.

Hedley began to cry, bounced awake after his feed. Morwenna started to cry too and slid slowly down the slide to where Garfield was waiting for her. Ahead of them Rachel broke into a run, as if to escape them all.

Garfield watched her go, watched her pass a white-uniformed nurse who had just come out, and he realized he hated her. It was his birthday, something she had not even noticed, and because of her they were spending it in the worst way imaginable. Even being stuck in school would have been better. At least then he'd have had his friends around him. He didn't quite know how to describe it to himself but her illness and her running off like that seemed as blatant a bid for attention as the baby's wailing or Morwenna's shrill demands from the slide.

'There's no point,' he told Morwenna. 'They can't hear you and I don't care.' But Morwenna only cried the harder, grinding her fists in her eyes so hard it made him feel sore just watching her. 'Come on,' he said and pulled her gently upright before steering her before him by the shoulder.

The nurse was exchanging words with Antony who then hurried into the building after Rachel, still pushing the pram. The nurse rang a handbell briefly. All over the garden visitors started across the lawn towards her. She didn't bend down and say, 'Ah, what's the matter, then?' or anything like that as they drew close. It was sad but when she cried, Morwenna had the opposite effect on people of the one she wanted. She cried too hard or something. It put people off, even hardened their faces against her. Old ladies, who were quick to admire her pretty hair or pinch her apple cheeks when she was happy, grew shifty and looked about them for assistance, as though Morwenna's grief were a bad smell that somebody might think was theirs.

The nurse's face grew stiff and wary and she avoided looking at Morwenna at all. 'Your father said he won't be long,' she told Garfield. 'You're to wait in the car.'

'But I want to see Rachel,' Morwenna almost shouted because the crying was making her breath come in little rushes.

'Visiting time just ended,' the nurse said. 'You can see Mummy another day.'

Morwenna stood and stared at the door, as though will power alone might sweep the horrid nurse aside and open it for her.

Garfield gave a little pull on one of the shoulder straps of her dress. 'Come on, Wenn,' he told her. 'He'll soon be out.'

The car was never locked. The locks hadn't worked

for ages and Antony probably didn't think locked doors were Quakerly. Morwenna ran ahead and climbed in. She liked going in the car and he hoped the prospect of a ride would distract her but he had no sooner climbed on board in front of her than she kicked out at the back of the seat.

'Want Mummy,' she said, Mummy, not Rachel, and she started crying again only differently, quietly, just for him, so he would know it was real.

'I know,' he said, doing his best to feel grown-up. 'Me too. I miss her too, Wenn, but she has to be here for a bit as she's not well. She's not well in her head.'

'She *is* well!'

'No. She's . . . She's depressed and it's not safe for her at home. Not for a bit.'

But at this she started to cry loudly again, her public cry as he thought of it.

'Shut up,' he tried saying because she was making him want to cry too. 'Shut up! It's all your fault she ran in like that.'

'Nooo!'

'Yes it is, stupid. If you hadn't gone on and on about look at me she'd have stayed a bit longer. But you made her say fuck.'

'I didn't.' There was another thump on his seat-back and then the crying grew almost painful in such a close confinement so, after a few ineffectual and rather angry *pleases* he got out again and shut the door behind him.

He leaned on the bonnet, enjoying the heat of it through his shorts but taking care not to scald his bare bits. With any luck the heat in the car would send

Morwenna to sleep soon. He watched the other visitors leave.

The miserable couple drove off in a brown Austin Cambridge. They were arguing. He could hear, because their windows were open in the heat and they didn't seem to care. The grape lady waited at a bus stop just outside the hospital gates. She had the empty grape plate in one hand at her side. The other man just walked away so perhaps he lived in Bodmin.

'Sorry, Garfy.' Antony came back to the car. 'It got a bit much for her. Oh.' He noticed Morwenna's crying. 'And not just her. She didn't forget, you know. I think she wanted to have some birthday time with just you but then Hedley needed her and then Morwenna and then we ran out of time, didn't we? But she did this for you.'

He handed something over then opened the back of the car and crouched down to reason quietly with Morwenna.

It was a sort of homemade envelope but she had made it from the thick paper she used for doing watercolours sometimes. She had written on the front in the beautiful calligraphy she did when she could be bothered, when she had to write notices or place-cards or cards for an exhibition. MASTER MIDDLETON. She had explained to him once that he would always be Master Middleton until he was grown-up whereas any brother he had would have to be Master Hedley or whatever to show they weren't the eldest.

He peered inside just enough to see a flash of brilliant colour then decided to save it. Antony disapproved of children getting lots of birthday presents when there were some in the world who got nothing at all, so Garfield knew his birthday tea would not bring the lavish array of parcels and envelopes, of toys and games, he had watched non-Quaker friends open on their birthdays. He knew in his heart this was right. He had seen, and been faintly disgusted by the greedy heedlessness that came over children with too many presents, the way they tore one after another free of its wrapping without paying it the attention it deserved. But knowing something was right did not make it easier and a small part of him, the bad part presumably, always wanted to ask if that was all. In their family there tended to be two presents only, even at Christmas, one of which was nice-but-useful, like a dictionary or a box of crayons. The useful present was usually officially from Morwenna. His bad part wondered if the arrival of Hedley would mean one more present but not just yet. He knew greed was bad but presents weren't just about greed. They were about love too.

'Aren't you going to open it?' Antony asked as they set off for Penzance again. 'It looks pretty special.'

'I think I'll save it,' Garfield said.

'Ah,' Antony said in a pleased way that made Garfield think this was the right answer. Good boys saved and Garfield was good at it. He was saving for a Meccano set and had put half of his pocket money into a piggy bank for so long the piggy bank was nearly full. He had noticed too late it was the kind you had to smash to open, which seemed a wicked waste so he was deferring the evil by lining up a second, openable, plastic piggy bank he had found at a jumble sale for tuppence. He saved strawberries until the end. He made an Easter egg last for a week. He had learned to save good news, and jokes. He had learned that if you saved your anger rather than speaking it, it had a way of evaporating like smoke, leaving just a faint smell where before there had been flames.

Antony made an effort, even though he was a man. They had a birthday tea, that was actually high tea, with all Garfield's favourite food: sausage rolls and Welsh rarebit and the cake he and Rachel had invented last year which was shop-bought ginger cake with a bar of Bournville melted with some butter and spread over the top. He had seven candles and he made a wish before blowing them out: *Bring Rachel and Hedley home soon, please.* And he opened his cards first, then his presents.

He treated the thing from Rachel as a present and opened that last. The special present was a little model engine, a real Mamod one, where you used meths on cotton wool to boil water in a tank which drove a metal wheel or even sounded a whistle, if you wanted. Antony said they could use it to drive a Meccano windmill or roundabout once he'd saved up the money.

Garfield had slightly been hoping the special present would be Meccano anyway and felt a bit tight-throated in his effort not to let his disappointment show. The engine was very good – they would fire it up later once Morwenna had gone to bed – but it was just not what he had been hoping for so it would take a while for his hopes to rearrange themselves. The nice-but-useful present was a real leather satchel for school. This too was rather a disappointment. He had wanted one really badly a year ago, when several of his friends had them and all he had was a duffel bag which scrunched all his things in a heap inside. Now he would have preferred a briefcase like the ones the older boys carried.

Antony made him put the satchel on and walk up and down and look pleased with it once they'd adjusted the straps a little but even Morwenna stared at it with something like disdain. It *was* real leather – Antony encouraged him to smell it – and had his name and address on a little card like the ones on the hospital doors and a place for his pens and even a little compartment for house keys but its brown was too red and too childish and it was not a briefcase.

He washed his hands before opening Rachel's home-made envelope because he had chocolate icing on them.

She had made him a card by making a picture with wax crayons on half the paper then folding the rest behind and writing in it. It was a bit like the pictures she did with paint – an abstract, he had to learn to call them – only, being concentrated on to such a small space made it more intense. It was a series of orange blocks floating on a greeny-blue background but she had made the orange bits all slightly different shades, some brighter, some darker, some with deeper orange around their edges, some sort of wispy and less defined, as if there was a fog in front of them.

'Let me see,' Morwenna was whining. She didn't like it when it wasn't her birthday, which was only to be expected. He showed her, which silenced her more effectively than Antony's shushing, but he wouldn't let her touch.

He looked some more. Because they weren't all quite

NOTES FROM AN EXHIBITION

the same shade, the orange bits seemed to move forwards and backwards out of the paper as you stared. The one you focused on would hold still but then immediately one of the brighter ones came forwards a bit and your eye felt it had to flick sideways.

'You're honoured,' Antony said at last.

'How do you mean?'

'Well she's never done a picture for me.'

'She must have.'

'No.' He shook his head, mock-rueful, and smiled.

Garfield looked inside.

'For my darling Garfield,' she had written, 'On his seventh birthday with love from Rachel. Sorry I can't be with you. Blame young Hedley! This time next year the bearer of this card is to have me all to himself for a whole day to do whatever he likes . . . Don't forget!'

She had drawn three Xs. Then, perhaps as an after-thought because he was only seven and the picture was a bit serious and not at all like the other cards he had from his godparents and school friends, with their cars and footballers, she had drawn a cartoon. The Xs were on a sort of sledge and she was pulling them up to a sign-post which said Penzance 46 miles. She had drawn herself like a mad lady, with sticky-out hair and bare feet with big toes but you knew it was her because she was in her painting clothes and she had her nose. Beads of sweat were pinging off her in her effort to deliver the kisses and the reason the sledge was so hard to pull was that Baby Hedley and his pram were tied on to the back of it and the road was a bit uphill.

It felt odd getting something from her but not having

315

her there to thank. Antony was looking at him as if he expected something more so Garfield put it back in its special envelope and said he would clear the table while Antony took Morwenna off for her bath. She had reached the point where she was so tired she would probably grizzle herself to sleep.

Soon there was the usual splashing and wailing from the bathroom – she hated having her hair washed, especially by Antony who tended to get soap in her eyes and didn't understand that she meant it when she said her hair hurt. Garfield took the satchel and the picture to his room. He tried filling the satchel with books and pens and things, which made it look less new at least. He took the picture out and propped it up in the middle of his short mantelpiece where it glowed beautifully against the white paintwork. But it worried him. It was too vulnerable and too precious. He left it there to inspire him while he wrote her a thank-you letter telling her all the news he had been unable to tell her while he had been showing off on the swing and she had been preoccupied with Hedley and Morwenna and Antony.

As he wrote, he pictured her as a huge gingerbread woman and the rest of them as little dogs nibbling bits off her. No wonder she was ill. They must learn not to eat her all at once. They must learn to save her.

Making out a fair copy took a while because the letter was quite long in the end. He tucked the picture back in its envelope and hid it in his desk for safekeeping. When she came home again, when she was well, he would ask her if she could let him have a proper frame for it. He would pick his moment carefully.

The young porter glanced at the coins she had dropped in his hand. 'Thank you,' he said. 'Thanks very much,' and left, leaving Winnie to fret that she had either tipped him too much or insufficiently.

She shrugged off the worry: she was a foreigner so was allowed to get things wrong. The only thing she couldn't abide was being constantly mistaken for an American here, something an American would never do.

She unzipped her case and fancied she heard her clothes give a little sigh at the release of pressure. The case was her biggest, the one Josh had always used on their holidays together but where she had always borrowed over-

317

flow space. She was a lousy packer and had little idea how long she was there for.

She took in the room and saw it was as shabby-genteel as the hotel's reception area. The curtains were sun-faded, there were stains on the ceiling and there was one of those silly little kettles and a bowl of tea and coffee sachets where she would have welcomed a minibar. If she needed a drink she would have to enjoy it in public, in one of those big downstairs rooms dotted with people who looked so ancient and so rooted that she suspected they were permanent residents parked there by their families. She had heard the English did that.

The bed did not look promising – after a lifetime of sleeping with a much bigger man, her back was rarely in the right alignment – but at least the linen would be clean. She tugged aside the pointless net curtains – she was on the fourth floor and quite unoverlooked – to reveal the view of the bay and distant boats and felt immediately better. It was for the view and anonymity she had chosen a big old place like this over one of the boutique B&Bs Petey had researched for her. She was a city girl and did not relish interrogations over breakfast, especially in chichi surroundings, especially on this trip.

She unpacked her things, picked out the slacks and blouse she would wear and hooked them above one end of the bath before leaving the shower running on its hottest at the other in the hope of their wrinkles dropping out in the steam. Then she kicked off her shoes and lay on the bed, thinking to doze a little. The overnight flight from Toronto and then the little shuttle from Gatwick and then the hour's taxi ride from Newquay had left her physically shattered. She was too keyed-up to sleep, however, and her mind was spinning.

Close your eyes, at least, she told herself. *Listen to the sea out there. This is the sea She must have listened to. And swum in. And stared over.*

His e-mails hadn't exactly been chatty – he wasn't like some of the guys she'd bumped into online who barely had your name before they were giving you way too much information – so she decided he was simply one of those men who only spoke when they deemed it necessary. A Quaker. Her brother-in-law.

She got shivery when she thought back to it. All those years, through her mourning for Joanie, through her marriage to Josh, through her mother's quick last illness and her father's long decline, Ray Kelly had remained her private demon. Whenever another schizophrenic stabbed a complete stranger, whenever she heard colleagues spooking themselves with tales of blank-eyed psychos pacing empty hotels or driving deserted late-night buses, it was Ray Kelly's face that sprang to mind. If Josh was away on business, it was Ray Kelly she thought of as she remembered too late to draw the curtains or bolt the back door. She could not believe a person could have that traumatic an effect on four lives then disappear so entirely. Had she read about her killing someone else or being arrested finally or knocked down by a tram somewhere it might have lessened her bogeywoman potency and maybe made her banal or even pitiable.

Then, when Winnie had been idly searching for old school friends, to see her name there so starkly on the new genealogy postings with the note 'born Toronto late

1930s, lived Gerrard Street East, died this year', had taken her breath away.

Yes, she thought. *Yes! The mad bitch is dead at last!*

As for when she had clicked on the attachment tab and come face to face, not with blank-eyed Ray, that image so sickeningly familiar from the press coverage, but with darling Joanie, no longer rebellious and maddening but suddenly just young and vulnerable-looking . . . Winnie had doubted her own sanity for a minute or two then had to call in Petey, who ran the shop with her, and ask him to compare the photograph with the one she kept in a cherrywood frame on her desk and tell her, please, if he thought it really was the same girl on the screen.

Suppressing the urge to splurge there and then, to send Antony a great stream of wheres and whys and hows had been one of the hardest things but she found she was too choked by anger and hurt to be more than curtly careful in her initial response. Restraining Petey was harder yet; he had a tendency to wild overexcitement, which was why she hired him in the first place. And then to get those other photographs and suffer the twin convulsions of having Joanie age decades and raise a family in minutes then having her die all over again! It was small surprise if Winnie had been drinking by daylight for the first time since Josh's death.

Small surprise, either, if her memory had been working so hard dredging up things she had no wish to recall that she was having trouble remembering her own address, and twice this week had called herself Joanie when talking to strangers on the phone.

Her mother's illness had been short and merciful and

whatever terrible secrets she had nurtured went to her grave alongside her, buttoned up in her mock croc purse. Her father had taken far longer to die so had suffered more time for recriminations and longing glances over his arthritic shoulder at the paths not taken.

As his end approached, once he was being kept alive by machinery and the cancer was finally chewing at the parts that no ingenuity or donor could replace, he began to talk. Trapped in her dutiful vigil at his bedside, his only surviving kin, she had been obliged to listen. Years too late, years after it could do anyone any good, he began to talk about poor little Joanie and how bad he had always felt. Winnie loved him dearly, truly she did, but she could have finished him with a pillow right there.

Joanie had been raped, he said. That night when he and Mom had found Winnie with the drawings and Mom had raced her to safety, Joanie had been raped, repeatedly, by a whole gang of boys.

'Did anyone see?' she asked him softly, feeling a chasm open beneath her sweaty hospital chair.

'They didn't have to,' he said. 'One of the boys brought her home, saying he'd found her lying drunk on a bench on the street. But from the state of her it was obvious something had happened. She was bleeding and . . .' He broke off, overcome by weakness as much as emotion.

She gave him a sip of water from his beaker, hoping he would shut up now.

'I told her to get in a bath,' he went on, 'and clean herself up. And go to bed. When your mother came back she went in to her and Joanie told her and . . . And your mother told her not to be so disgusting. She said she was depraved, that those boys came of good families, families she'd be proud to have come to our house. Our shitty little house in Etobicoke.'

He took another sip of water and looked at Winnie as though he were already being pawed by other lost souls.

'Shush there,' she said. 'Shush now. It doesn't matter any more.'

But he had to speak. 'Your mother told me the same thing and I did what I always did with her and said *yes dear* and knuckled under. Joanie cut her wrists the next day, while we were in church. She was in the Clarke by lunchtime. And then she . . .'

Winnie soothed him as best she could but had to break off from her vigil to visit a hotel bar just along the street from his hospital because his nasty little revelation had made her admit what she had always known: the things her older self had been telling her younger self for years.

He lost consciousness that night and died when she encouraged them to turn his machines off the following week but he had one more story saved up for her when she came back from the bar, frantically chewing a mint.

'Your mother,' he kept saying.

'Yes?' she would prompt him repeatedly.

They made that little exchange about eight times and just when she thought that's all there was going to be to it, that he was maybe trying to say her mother had been good or that he'd always loved her or that she was waiting for him on the other side, he had a coughing fit then began the sentence another way.

'There's one thing I could never forgive her.'

'Yes, Dad?'

'She had another baby.'

'She did?'

'Joanie had a twin. It happens. Her twin died during the birth. Caught up in Joanie's cord. Not a thing that would happen now. And Joanie was a beautiful child. A cute baby. Perfect. And your mother told her. When she was, what, five or six could she have been? Could she?'

'Maybe Dad. What did she tell her?'

'She'd been a bit bad and your mother told her, and told her the wrong one had died. That was evil of her.'

Evil. The word so rarely on his lips. The word that even in church only got said once a sitting, during the Lord's Prayer. It buzzed in the room between them like a meat-fattened fly.

Which was just where Winnie'd left it. She couldn't take stories like those back to Josh to see his kind face wrinkle in the effort to understand. And now, twenty years on, that fly was out and bothering her again.

She and Josh had not been blessed with children. They had tried. They had tests. They had discussed and rejected adoption. Leastways, she had discussed and he had rejected it. He was funny about wanting his own and wouldn't go for the idea; she had to respect that.

There were advantages. She kept her figure. He kept his hair. They never had to go without interesting adult holidays and she'd had the freedom to build her own career after all and to put in three hours a week as a volunteer counsellor at the Clarke, helping distraught relatives work through their feelings at having a loved one join the wavering ranks of the mentally ill.

Josh's sisters had three apiece but their husbands took

them to Los Angeles and Chicago respectively, so they were never close. The time she had really missed motherhood, of course, was during Josh's bypass surgery and its failure. When there was no one to prop her up or cosset her.

In a curious way her little business had become her child, and her employees her family. Simple Gifts sold wooden furniture and household items and a small range of clothes and linens, all produced by Amish or Shaker communities. Housed in an old warehouse in Cabbagetown, the old Irish district whose fortunes had greatly improved, it had doubled in size since she first opened it with a single assistant and now had an Internet-based mail order side that had greatly increased its turnover. She was not quite a millionaire but what had begun as an indulgence, a venture in which Josh humoured her, had bought her a security. She was well past retirement age and had handed the running of the business over to her junior partner Petey, a sweet man who had come in as her first sales assistant straight out of high school. But she retained a desk in the office and came in almost every day because being home alone was lonely and boring. Something in the eagerness with which Petey had packed her off on this adventure told her it was time to cut everyone a little slack and try to be a merrier widow. Take cruises and stuff.

She sat up. She couldn't sleep, not with all those seagulls screaming outside, and she wasn't going to doze.

She reached for the phone and her diary, took a deep breath and rang him.

'Hello?' He didn't sound so old.

'Antony? It's Winnie MacArthur.'

'What?'

'Hello!'

'Sorry. Let me turn up the volume on this thing.' There was a deafening clunk as if he had dropped the receiver on a table then he came back on. 'Who is this?'

'It's Winnie MacArthur, Antony. From LongLost.com. Joanie's sister? Rachel's sister, if you like.'

'Oh. Oh yes. Hello. How are you?'

'Excited. Tired.'

'Ah. Sorry if I sounded a little distracted. We've rather a full house at the moment. My son Hedley's here, still, and my daughter, Morwenna, who isn't very . . .'

'Oh. Antony, you must say if it's not a good time to visit.'

'Why? Where are you?'

'The Queen's Hotel,' she told him. 'Just around the corner from you, according to my map.'

'The Queen's. I see. I thought you were calling from Toronto. Come. Of course you must come.'

'What. Now?'

'Why not? Just . . . Hang on a second.' She heard that clunk again. Evidently his phone wasn't cordless. And then there was the sound of a closing door. He picked up again. 'Sorry,' he said. 'I'm a bit deaf and I worry about shouting without realizing it and hurting people's feelings. Morwenna isn't very well, that's all. If she strikes you as a bit . . . Oh dear.' He sighed. 'Sorry. Life has been rather interesting.'

'It's a bad time. I knew I should have waited to hear back from you.'

'What?'

'I'll leave you in peace. We can meet another day.'

'No. Please come. I insist. I'll be looking out for you. But I . . . I haven't had a chance to explain who you are, that's all.'

'I understand. Sometimes I'm not sure *I* know who I am any more.'

'I beg your pardon?'

'Nothing. I'll be there in about half an hour, Antony.'

She had trouble hanging up neatly because her hand was shaking. Then she made herself roll off the bed (in the special way her latest back man had taught her), strip off her travelling clothes, retrieve the steamed ones, shower and dress before she could panic and change her mind. At least by calling round in the early afternoon she spared anyone the obligation to lay on any kind of meal.

It was a sort of terrace of charming houses, much older than the houses she had walked past along the seafront. He met her out on the street, so perhaps he was as nervous as she was. He smiled. She laughed. They shook hands and then he just looked at her.

'You're so like her,' he said.

'No I'm not,' she laughed. 'She was always so dark and striking and . . .'

'You're like who she became, then. Because I can see you were sisters.'

'Oh. Oh good. What a beautiful place. Have you lived here long?'

'I was born in this house.'

'Oh goodness.'

'After you. Please.'

NOTES FROM AN EXHIBITION

She walked through the unexpectedly subtropical garden to the pretty Georgian porch and through the open front door.

Used to the clean lines and calm paintwork of Simple Gifts and her house in Rosedale, the initial impression was one of a kind of crazy 1970s exuberance now frayed at the edges. Her mind had nowhere to settle. She had startled a shorthaired woman sitting on one of a pair of old brown sofas with her back to the door. As Winnie said, 'Hello. I'm Winnie,' she turned, stared at her with an expression she knew all too well from patients at the Clarke and slipped quickly past her and up the stairs.

'Morwenna,' Antony said quietly.

'I guessed.'

The woman had looked confusingly like a combination of how Joanie might have turned out and her early memories of their mother early in the mornings, without makeup. Perhaps illness had aged her but she looked at least twenty years older than Joanie was when Winnie last saw her.

A young man, clearly her brother, but cut of a sunnier cloth, was visible in a paved area at the back. He was talking excitedly on a cell phone.

'Jack, our GP, wanted to hospitalize her,' Antony said. 'But I wouldn't let him. I don't want her locked up.'

'Is she . . . ?'

'She turned up out of the blue. She's been wandering, staying all over the place for more than ten years now. She seemed quite calm at first but perhaps that was just the shock of learning about Rachel having died. Then she . . .' He sat at the bashed-up old pine table. Winnie sat

327

across from him. 'There's an old lido across the seafront from here. A sea-water bathing pool from the Thirties, you know?'

'I know,' she nodded, although she didn't.

'She took herself off there without warning one morning and tried to drown herself.'

'Jeeze.'

'Jack has got her medicated now but, well, we're all a little jumpy.'

Winnie could not believe she had managed to impose herself at such an appalling time. 'Maybe I should go,' she said. 'Gee, I'm so sorry.'

'You don't understand,' he said with a rueful smile. 'We're just happy to have her back where we can care for –'

'Hello?'

The young man had come in, tucking his cell phone back in his jeans pocket. He was a honey, in that poignant stage between being a pretty boy and whatever came next. Just Petey's type. He looked her straight in the eye and held out his hand. Just her type too, actually.

'I'm Hedley,' he said. 'How d'you do.'

'This is Winnie,' his father said. 'From Toronto. We've been e-mailing.'

Hedley glanced quickly from one to the other and for a second she could see he thought they'd met on some wrinklies' dating site.

'You knew Mum,' he said.

'Yes,' she said. 'I'm your long-lost aunt.'

'Oh my God of course you are!' He laughed, kissed her, hugged her and sat her down again. 'Let me put the kettle on. Have you had lunch? When did you get here? Antony didn't say anything.'

'Well it sounds as though you've had other things to . . .'

'Oh. Well. Quite. But still. Tea?'

'Yes please.' She chuckled.

He had that gift, Petey had it too, of being able to improve the atmosphere in a room simply by entering it. He busied himself filling the kettle, putting a cherry cake and teacups and little plates on the table. Nothing matched but it was charming.

'One good thing about a death,' he said, 'is not having to bake another cake for months. This freezer is *packed*! That was Oliver,' he told Antony. 'He and Ankie have driven down this morning. He was calling from Truro so they shouldn't be long. They'd been to that gallery on Lemon Street. Oliver's my hubby,' he explained.

'And who's Ankie?' Winnie asked and saw that his face briefly clouded over.

'Oh. She's . . . she's a painter friend.'

They had tea and cake and then Winnie opened her bag and took out the envelope of photographs she had brought them, of Joanie, of her parents, of their house in Etobicoke, of Simple Gifts, of her place in Rosedale, of their grandparents, of her Josh. An instant second family. She wrote down names for them, dates when she could recall them. She sketched out what she knew of the Ransome family tree. She told them they must come visit. Prompted by questions, she told them about the Clarke Institute and volunteering there and Joanie escaping it and managed not to cry, although she got a little choked up when she explained about Ray Kelly and the whole train thing.

There was what her grandmother used to call a *speaking silence* then, as the two of them took everything in. Even chatty Hedley fell quiet and his eyes looked full and teary.

'You must be very hurt and angry,' Antony said at last. 'At the way she cut you all out of her life.'

But before she could think of an answer they were interrupted by Hedley's phone chirruping and a video message coming through of the first trimester scan of his sister-in-law Lizzy's baby. Which of course made everyone happy and led to congratulation phone calls and Antony had to take the phone upstairs to Morwenna's room to show her the scan too, although there was really nothing to see but a blob with a heartbeat. Winnie knew he'd be asking her to come down and join the party and she'd be shrinking in on herself and saying no, not just yet. She badly wanted to be able to go up there and say hello and look I'm not so bad really and give her a big hug and buy her a ticket to Toronto for a nice long visit. Even offer the poor woman a job if she wanted one. But although her mind was upstairs with that stricken deer she had encountered on arriving, she sat with Hedley and slipped into counselling mode instead. She told him she knew it was hard for him because it was always hard when you wanted to help the one you loved and they sort of pushed you away but at least she was here at last and at least she was safe. And he gave her a long, tearful hug, which was nice of him as she needed it too by now.

Antony came down again, looking shattered, and Winnie thought she really should be leaving them, at least for today but then they started pulling out photographs for her to see and then suddenly this drop-dead gorgeous man appeared, a real silver fox, who turned out to be Oliver and so there was another round of introductions and a confusing explanation of how Ankie, who sounded kind of demoralizing, had insisted on being dropped at the airport suddenly which had held him up. Then there was more tea and she felt she badly needed the bathroom, less to use the john than to sit quietly in a calm space for a few minutes to give her poor jetlagged head a chance to catch up.

When she came out, Antony was loading the dishwasher and the boys had disappeared somewhere. She was an inveterate snoop so she thought to seize the chance of looking around the place before she started socializing again. There was a broad staircase, very light because of a tall, thin window to the back of the house with blue glass at the edges.

And then, of course, she came face to face with some of the paintings. She'd somehow guessed they were Joanie's even before she saw the signature – R. Kelly – that was exactly like the J. Ransome one she'd been working on in her teens, the same Greek E and neat underlining.

She knew absolutely nothing about what she thought of as modern art. On holidays with Josh they'd tended to home in on buildings rather than galleries, although she liked museums and museum shops. There was a big painting above the staircase and another on the landing. She could see they weren't *of* anything but the colours were fantastically intense, probably too intense to be hung so near one another. There was a blue like sea water over

331

sunny sand and a thin strip of orange you could almost feel like heat on your face if you stood near enough. She caught sight of other smaller paintings through open bedroom doors. (Morwenna's door – she assumed it was hers – remained firmly shut.) There were no pictures anywhere but Joanie's and Winnie sensed how her sister would not have made life easy for this kind family.

She came upon a little flight of wooden steps, a ladder in effect, let down from an attic room off one end of the landing. She started up there then stopped because Hedley was there with Oliver's arms about him but they sensed her and called her up.

'Sorry,' Oliver said. 'Haven't seen him properly for weeks.'

'We were just looking at these,' Hedley said. 'Come and see. Can you manage?' He held out a hand to hoist her up off the last few rungs. God alone knew how she would get back down.

It was a kind of lookout tower, like being in a lighthouse.

'Was this her studio?' she asked him.

'One of them. But look. This is what she was working on at the end.'

There were six pictures. The boys had arranged them in a rough semicircle which made the little room feel like a sort of chapel. Six circles. Only they weren't all circular. One was a sphere, like a burning sun, but the others seemed less even. Or perhaps it was an illusion? She had built up layers of paint in such a way that the longer you looked, the more colours seemed to emerge until it was like cloud lifting off a planet. One, which seemed murky brown at first, nothing like the intense canvases on the stairs, slowly revealed itself as having patches of bronze and even purple within its texture.

'Did she tell anyone what they were?' she asked tentatively, shy of revealing her ignorance. 'I mean, they're beautiful, really, but what was she trying to *do* here?'

'I think it's whatever you want it to be,' Hedley told her, still staring at the paintings and she saw how his waist had gotten enfurled by Oliver's arm again.

She heard another door open and the woman, the girl for God's sake, Morwenna appeared at the foot of the ladder thing.

Winnie smiled what she hoped was her least threatening smile. Morwenna stared up at her. It could so easily have been Joanie down there, an older, wounded Joanie, that Winnie had to swallow before she dared speak.

'Hi,' she said, her voice still cracking a little bit. 'Did you *see* these already? Come and see them. Come on up.' And she held out a hand.

NIGHTDRESS (c.2001). Brushed cotton. Lace.
This mundane but comforting garment is fashioned
in a style commonplace in Kelly's 1940s childhood.
Full length, in cream brushed cotton, its only impractical touches are narrow lace edging to the cuffs and
hem and a design of china-blue flowers around the
yoke. Some burnt umber oil paint (possibly from
Exhibits 60–69) can be seen on both cuffs and, clearly
displaying Kelly's fingerprints, near the hem at the
front. She remained loyal to this style all her life,
claiming it was warm enough to double as a dress
if she woke in the night and started painting. Later
examples, like this, had to be purchased from a
specialist mail order company.

For the first few days . . . Or was it weeks? She had lost
all sense of calendar time. For the first few whatevers she
was only allowed out of her nightgown to bathe, and
then only with a nurse in the bathroom in case she
drowned herself or decided to run naked down to one of
the men's floors.

Her mother had done her packing, so of course had
chosen the long, warm, sensible nightgowns she never
wore any more over the babydolls she had bought for
herself. She had tried asking for the other ones during
one of their visits but whatever chemical straitjacket they
had strapped her in made her tongue feel so fat and heavy
that her words came out mangled like a drunk woman's.

'I hate this Little House on the Prairie shit,' was what
she thought she'd said but her mother only looked
distressed and said,

'No, dear. Don't try to speak. We can just sit here a while and be nice and calm together.'

And calm she was, for what seemed like the first time in months. For that she did thank the drugs. Or the shocks. Whichever. Her fears had gone. And the baby. They would have drugged her and given her an abortion, of course. Everyone knew that had been going on for years. To corrupted daughters and wayward spinster sisters alike. So much easier than sending them to an aunt in Whaletown BC or wherever. This way if they had to say anything they could say she was taking a rest in the Clarke for her nerves.

'Such a clever girl, but her nerves wear her down sometimes.'

There was less shame attached to the Clarke than there had been. Quite smart people had been here. The Butterworth boy, the Claythornes' eldest. Even Angela O'Hara, that social meteorite.

She was relieved to be rid of it, monstrous thing. When it progressed from talking to her in her dreams to hissing its poisonous suggestions through her dress material and any number of layers in waking hours, she had become desperate. Pot didn't help so she tried getting drunk on top of it. And look where that had landed her. But she needed them to be honest with her.

As soon as they had stitched her and strapped her and given her a transfusion to replace what she had lost, but before they started her in the chemical straitjacket, they had let her talk to a shrink, a proper doctor. He was handsome and had one of those fantastic hero jaws, blue-black with five o'clock shadow, and a chin she wanted to brush with her fingertips. Married, of course, and too old for her but she could imagine her mother calling him, with that defiant innocence of hers, a fine, *upstanding* man.

He was kind but firm. He ran a battery of tests on her. She had to name the Prime Minister, and give the date, which she got wrong, and her mother's maiden name, which she got right, hooray. He made her look at ink blots and colour spots and tell her what she saw. He made her answer multiple choice questions like, 'You see a boy squash a worm under his foot. Do you a) feel sick b) laugh or c) feel nothing' or 'The house is on fire and you can only carry one thing. Do you rescue a) your favourite book, b) your favourite dress or c) your sewing machine.'

A social worker joined him. A woman. Sensible shoes. Not attractive. She asked her all sorts of questions about Havergal and her family and her parents and university plans and did she have a boyfriend and, oh well, did she have a *best* friend and, oh well, how about her sister. And so on.

Finally she got a chance to ask some questions herself so she asked them.

'You're not pregnant,' the shrink told her. 'There was no baby.'

So she knew at once what they had done. She tried to think back, through the throbbing at her wrists and her memory of the pain and blood, to work out when they had done it. Perhaps they had slipped an injection into her? Perhaps she had been out cold for hours and not known it?

At last they let her start getting out of bed for more

than the bathroom. They loosened the chemical strait-jacket so that she could walk on her own. Well, shuffle. Her steps, like her tongue, remained slurred and heavy. And they let her pull on a dressing gown and slippers to join the party of damaged girls and crazy ladies and women you'd change buses to avoid, all milling around. She wasn't allowed off the ward yet. Keeping her in the nightgown was their way of doing that. Other patients, properly dressed, were at liberty to move around the building more, even catching the elevator down into the podium to visit the self-service cafeteria overlooking College Street or, in the case of patients nearly ready to be discharged, actually to leave the facility and walk around in the neighbouring streets.

The floor she was on was high up, tenth or eleventh she'd have guessed though it was hard to count the floors of the nearby university buildings for comparison without the drugs making her dizzy. It didn't feel like a ward, not like where she'd been to have her tonsils out, because they had their own rooms off a corridor. Once she got up a nurse showed her how her bed turned into a sofa for sitting on during the day.

'Neat, huh?' she said. And it was.

There was a little closet, with hangers built-in so you couldn't use them to cut yourself and a little dressing table thing and a window that didn't open even a crack. (The windows didn't even break. She knew because there was one woman who kept hurling herself at them, given the chance. Not a fire extinguisher or a chair or something sensibly hard. Just her head.) The school-food smell never seemed to be quite ventilated out but drifted around the hallways, blending with the sharper smells of disinfectant, shit and disgusting pink soap.

She pulled on her dressing gown and her nurse, who was Marci with an i, showed her around. As well as the bedrooms – some of which were large and shared, she noticed – there were bathrooms and shower rooms, all kept locked, meeting rooms for group therapy and staff chats, Marci said, and on the other side of the tower, to the left of the elevators, a dauntingly large common room. Half the room was a cafeteria with a noisy metal screen that rolled up over the serving hatches.

'That's where you can do crafts and stuff when we're not feeding you,' Marci said. She was as cute as a kitten and had almost certainly dressed up as a nurse when she was little but never banked on ending up in a place like this with not a man in sight.

The other half had fifty or so vomit-coloured Naugahyde chairs arranged in a big rectangle. A TV was suspended from the ceiling in one corner and patients had rearranged the chairs to form a kind of movie theatre. There were windows everywhere, narrow and unopening, but at least they were there.

'So,' said Marci. 'You'll probably forget all this but it's on the back of your door in any case. Breakfast is seven-thirty, lunch is at a quarter to twelve and dinner's real early at five so we can go home and you can go to bed before it all starts again. All right? Weekends you can sleep in until nine. TV goes off at nine p.m. Medications are dispensed by one of us from a cart right here. That's three or four times a day. You're down for ECT so that

338

happens Mondays. Don't get up on Mondays. Don't have breakfast. Just stay right put, although you can go to the john, and we'll give you a sedative and wheel you down. You'll kinda lose a day but you'll get used to it.'

Sunday nights were thus blighted with the knowledge of what was to come. Some of the ECT patients, like the one with the obsession with tapping her knuckles on things and the one who wasn't house-trained and kept laughing, used to start getting wound up about it at about ten on Sunday night and their nervousness spread like a virus and the whole floor would get jittery. If there were going to be fights or breakouts or those terrible moments when orderlies – hey! Men! Hello, boys! – had to be sent for to sit on people, they tended to be on Sunday nights. She learnt to go to bed early on Sunday and would lie there listening to the flare-ups and shouts spread around her like panic in a monkey house.

And what people had always said about the deranged and full moons? It was all true.

The dread of the shocks was worse than the thing itself. They made her pee then sedated her then wheeled her off. She ached afterwards, though, and felt horribly confused and disorienta-ta-ta-ted. It was as though every Monday night she had to start all over again on the personality she had been slowly building out of little soft bricks all week. She knew they were hoping the baby would go, the idea of the baby – be burnt out of her by the shocks. She thought it had but then she'd wake on the Tuesday and there it would be. Hello, bitch. (It was a girl.) At least she reached the point where she could see that the baby was just that, an idea, which was sort of like it still being there but under a glass dome so she couldn't hear what it was hissing.

She didn't see the handsome shrink again, just the nurses, but they must have been told all about her because Marci with an i used to sit with her regularly and ask her questions that were caring but kind of searching too, like a mother going after your splinter with a sterilized needle. And she took notes, which wasn't very friendly.

'You know,' Marci said, 'you have a lot of unrealized creativity.'

Well, no kidding.

'I do?' Joanie said. She could manage short sentences by now.

'Did your parents stop you painting? Didn't they like what you did?'

'She didn't like me going to life class.'

'Huh?'

'Nudes.'

'Oh.' Much note-taking here.

'She wanted me to do nice paintings. Flowers and stuff.'

'If you weren't allowed to paint, I'd have thought all the need and the ideas would sort of swell up inside you until you'd burst.'

She didn't grant that tired attempt the reward of a reply but she let Marci show her where the 'craft stuff' was kept and she began to paint and draw again, anything to avoid being dragged into making hideous Christmas cards that would never be sent and baskets that would later be unwoven.

Drawing was a challenge here because pencils were too

sharp to be safe so she was only allowed crudely coloured wax crayons. She experimented with using the crayons under water paint though and painted over and over again the views of the streets far below, the endlessly re-ordered coloured blocks the parked and moving cars made, the shocking flare of an occasional brightly coloured dress or scarf weaving through a grey sea of tweed and gabardine.

After her initial horror of them, when venturing across to the day room felt like her first day at Havergal all over again, she learned that most of the patients could be ignored. They were a mixed bunch, from the very, very quiet to the off-the-wall loony but she soon detected a middle ground of wry, lost girls like herself, girls still young enough at eighteen or nineteen to be girdled in a family's disappointment as well as their own despair.

When they weren't being cajoled into handicrafts or group therapy – which was like the world's worst party with stilted conversation, no boys and no booze – they sought each other out to compare scars. She didn't warm to any of them however. They seemed to be using their depression and theatrical negativity as substitutes for the talk of dates and clothes and makeup and crushes that had been so mind-numbing at Havergal and the competition was as thinly veiled. My parents are worse than yours. My mother is more destructive. My suicide wasn't just an attempt! Huh, yeah but my outlook is so bleak it would kill you if I gave you even a tiny peek at it!

They got the message after a while that she was a stuck-up bitch and they stopped tapping on her door with their blunted nails or seeking out her lunch table and started talking about her in corners instead.

The one girl she did feel any kind of bond with was Ray. As tall and skinny as her and just as dark, Ray was eighteen but had been there for a staggering four years already. She was a schizophrenic, shut away for trying to kill her father with a pair of pinking scissors when he came after her in her room once too often. She only succeeded in taking his index finger off him, so he couldn't wave it at her any more. No one had believed her account of him attacking her, because she was always saying stuff. He was a janitor at a salt factory on the lake and could still use a broom with one finger less and a daughter who was crazy, so hadn't even lost his job which seemed unjust. But at least he could no longer get at her.

Ray heard voices and was so bad at taking her medication sometimes that Marci and the girls had to hold her down and inject her. She muttered to whoever was haunting her when she thought you couldn't hear her and she hated to meet your eyes straight on but that was fine. Joanie and Ray would sit side by side and, while Joanie painted or drew, Ray would tell her stuff she had learned.

Ray had a wild side and had learned that some of the orderlies would do things for you if you let them get fresh, like bring you beer or magazines or smuggle you out for a tour of the building. She had the layout of the Clarke down pat like any lifer. She knew about the locked wards – the forensic ones – on floor four, where the killers and criminals went while they were assessed for their fitness to stand trial and left locked up if they were deemed too crazy for justice. She knew about the juvenile wards and the unspeakably exotic gender reassignment clinic in the podium. She was naturally clever, Ray. She had graduated from high school by correspondence course and had read every novel in the hospital library. She also knew whole tracts of the Bible by heart but seemed to like Jonah best. When Joanie joked that they should slip down to the gender reassignment clinic to escape as guys, Ray laughed so loud and long the nurses came running as they thought she was having a fit.

Most of Ray's family had disowned her. Once a week her tiny mother came on her way to Confession and sat there crying for half an hour before Ray led her back to the elevator.

Joanie shared with Ray her old dream of escaping Toronto, escaping stifling, backward Canada entirely and heading somewhere warm and southerly, like Marseille or Malaga, where they could be wild and mad and artistic. Somewhere out of Hemingway or Mavis Gallant where they would fit right in. She only meant it as a dream. A dimly outlined but not quite lost part of her was still a well-brought-up, rigidly schooled Havergal girl. She would escape Etobicoke eventually and her parents but only into marriage or maybe a job and another Etobicoke, another suburb, another Canada. All she had been through had not quite stifled the confident girlish assumption of a husband, some day, and a sweet little screwed-up family of her own. When she was feeling brutal, when Ray was jabbering to herself about starlings talking code and radio waves in the bedsteads, she knew she would survive and pass beyond this and leave poor Ray behind to rot in Hell.

The nice nurses, Marci, who was *her* nurse but also Bobby and Pat, were pleased with her progress. (Pat

PATRICK GALE

thought the art was helping and would take the pictures up, or was it down, to the shrink for assessing.) But on bad days it seemed as though she had landed herself in a world where the rules had changed for ever and where simple expressions of frustration or passing sorrow became great black marks against her name, prolonging the sentence she was under.

They took her off close observation. They stopped coming to the bathroom with her. They let her mother bring in (the wrong) clothes so she could get dressed when it wasn't a Monday. But whenever she talked of her dreams or the future, Marci or Bobby or Pat would say, 'Now let's not run before we can walk. How about doing me another nice painting? Paint me your house in Etobicoke or paint me your mom and dad.'

Ray picked up on the dream of the warm south, however, and took it as some kind of promise. She was very sly about it. All she said was they had to have their passports or they'd never get free. Ray got her tiny mother to bring hers in. She was shameless, blinded her mother with science, said it was the law or something.

She'd had a passport since the Kellys went back to Ireland for her grandmother's funeral and a pilgrimage to Knock. Joanie didn't have one, having travelled no further than America, but she figured a driver's licence would be a start. So when it was her turn she made her sister get her that. Butter-wouldn't-melt-Winnie, who looked so scared to be visiting such a place it seemed only kind to give her something else to worry about.

'I've got nothing here that's me,' Joanie told her. 'It'll remind me who I am,' which seemed to silence Winnie's

344

questions. 'It's in my dresser,' she added. 'In the little drawer on the right.'

Winnie was obviously terrified of doing a bad thing but still sufficiently guilty and impressionable to do as she was told. She was such a Little Miss Perfect with her blonde cuteness and unambitious mind that she probably felt the Clarke wasn't far enough from home for her to be rid of this terrible blot on her eligibility for the life she felt she deserved. If a driver's licence got the two of them states apart, so much the better. Or was the poor child merely scared and guilty when it was proudly announced that she was now going steady with Josh MacArthur, who had just been made captain of the hockey team so wasn't going to enter his father's business just yet?

'I guess I'll be putting plans for secretarial school on hold,' Winnie breathed proudly and Joanie wanted to shake her and forgive her and weep and cry out, 'No! Run for the hills!' but all she could think of was the cool square of precious cardboard Winnie had just slipped her, and she responded so blankly her parents exchanged a look that said *not yet awhile*.

Ray was convinced the licence was all the Canadian authorities in New York would need to issue Joanie with a passport. Joanie didn't like to disillusion her but remained sharp enough to know having the thing back in her possession was just symbolic, a small but authoritative wedge between her and her tormentors. The fact was their consent would be needed along with the handsome shrink's opinion before she could go free and make use of it but she took to keeping it with her at all times. Unless it was a Monday.

She learned from Ray. She, too, became sly. Apart from the moment when the television came on, the only galvanizing times of day were meals and medication.

Even before the grilles were rattled up over the serving hatches they could hear food things being loaded into the dumb waiter floors below and would start lining up with their trays. The further gone among them even started dribbling, like Pavlov's poor dogs. The food was boring and fattening but at least it carried the faint possibility of surprise: a different colour Jell-O or – sign of summer turning to fall – a plate of grey or brown meat instead of steam-limped egg salad.

Medication also required a line to form but here there was no element of surprise, merely the rattling trundle of the meds trolley but it might have been an ice-cream truck in August for the eagerness with which most patients stopped whatever they were doing – even if this was merely staring at a patch of wall. Or perhaps the correct analogy was church, for many of them actually held their mouths obediently open as they approached and let whichever nurse was on candy duty place the pills directly on their tongue before handing them a paper cup of water to wash them down.

Just as she had been raised in a church where sticking out your tongue at God showed a lack of reverence and the wafer was placed in a politely cupped (and gloved) palm, so, from her first day in the pill line, her reflex was to hold out a hand and pop the pills herself. Pat or Bobby or Marci would always watch to see the swallow but they never asked her to open her mouth again to let them be sure. She learned by accident, when a pill snagged on a tooth once and nearly choked her, that it was simplicity itself to throw them into her mouth in such a way that she could hide them in a cheek. All she had to do then was gulp the water down through her teeth. The taste was vile and bitter however and it wasn't always easy to scoop the sodden pills out again. Instead she learnt to get her palm as hot and sweaty as possible first so that the pills would stick to it. She then pretended to put them in her mouth but, distracting the nurse with a rare, gracious thank you, would take the proffered paper cup with her right hand instead of left.

Ray often went missing in the evenings, especially at understaffed weekends, and was usually off on one of her illicit assignations with a kitchen porter or ward orderly. She was as horny as a mink. She didn't simply do it for favours. She was, she claimed, very highly sexed. She blamed it on the unnaturally high concentration of oestrogen caused by cooping so many women together in an airless space. She said it sort of floated among them along with the food smells.

One time, however, she was gone for two whole hours on a weekday. It didn't seem right to draw attention to it but as the day wore on Joanie started to wonder if perhaps Ray had escaped after all, and on her own. Like any boarding school, the Clarke was a vibrant rumour factory. Usually the rumour was along the lines of *Southern Fried Chicken tonight* or *Princess Margaret's changed her hair!* Just occasionally the buzz would be to do with a disappearance and would rapidly escalate, fed by fear as much as rebellious excitement, because so often an apparent escape proved to be no more than a hushed-up

suicide attempt and the patient would reappear, chemi-
cally manacled and, on one memorable occasion, with
both legs in plaster.

But Ray was suddenly back among them, quite
unharmed and certainly unsedated, in time for the afternoon pill line. The buzz abated as fast as it arose and,
when Joanie tried to ask her where she'd been, she only
got jabbering in reply about the patterns the starlings were
making in the park nearby. So perhaps Ray had merely
escaped for a walk in the snowy sunshine or a light-fingered
visit to the public library or a department store.

When the first policeman arrived, it was nothing
extraordinary. Policemen often accompanied new arrivals
or called in to check on patients who had been admitted
against their will. But then a second one showed up, with
a woman in tow. They asked questions of the nurses then,
with Bobby accompanying them to keep a watchful eye,
began to move around the ward attempting to question
patients. They were short-staffed that day – Marci had
flu – and Bobby was plainly harassed at the unexpected
extra duty and wanted them gone as soon as possible.

'You've been here all morning, haven't you?' she asked.

'Could be,' Joanie started to say but then changed her
mind. 'Yes,' she told her and realized the woman, who had
on a dark suit and looked petrified, was examining her.

'No. That's not the one,' she told the policemen and
they moved on but with a backward glance from the
woman who wasn't as sure as she'd sounded.

When they reached Ray, Ray was painting her cheeks
with blue poster paint and simply stared in answer to
Bobby's questions, so they spent little time on her.

The story emerged, as stories tended to, through the serving women at supper. There had been a hold-up at the bank a short way down the street. Using a toy revolver, afterwards dropped on the pavement, a young woman in white gloves and a headscarf patterned with poppies had persuaded a cashier to hand over the contents of her desk drawer. She left the bank at speed and appeared to jump into an uptown cab. However the headscarf was subsequently found on the handrail on the ramp into the Clarke.

The investigation descended into chaos as patient after patient now owned up to being the robber, excited by the sudden glare of attention. All closets and drawers were searched, mattresses lifted and many secret shames and irrational hoards were uncovered but no wad of banknotes. In the end it was decided that the thief had behaved eccentrically on purpose and laid a cunning false trail into the hospital before making her escape. The hawl had not been huge – a few thousand dollars – and did not warrant an expensive investigation.

The only after-effects were a brief tightening of ward security, with a nurse appearing from the nursing station the moment any patient lingered by the elevators and an even briefer surge in visiting families, as if parents and siblings wanted a share of the hospital's mild and temporary notoriety.

Ray woke Joanie just before dawn on a Sunday morning. She put a finger to her lips then whispered, 'Come on. Get dressed. Everything's ready.'

'How do you mean?' Joanie asked.

Ray was dressed for outdoors and had a small,

brand-new tartan suitcase with a zipper. She handed Joanie an identical one.

'You're serious about this, aren't you?' Joanie said.

Ray nodded.

'But I've got no money.'

'I've got money,' Ray whispered. 'Enough to get us to Europe I figure.' She unzipped her case and produced a brown-paper shopping bag stuffed with bills. 'Maybe even Tangier,' she added.

'Where did you . . .?'

'I sunk it in a pair of plastic bags in one of the john's tanks. Come on. Hurry. We have to get out before six-thirty. Don't forget your driver's licence. I already packed your art stuff. And hey, look. I got us winter boots.'

Joanie dressed, shivering with excitement and faint with early-morning hunger. She stuffed the suitcase to bursting with her clothes. She took her driver's licence from her dressing gown pocket and zipped it into the neat little compartment inside the lid. Then she joined her in the corridor. Ray made her take off her new boots so they wouldn't squeak on the linoleum then they slipped around to the day room the long way, avoiding the elevators and the nurse's station. One of Ray's conquests had left a serving hatch unbolted for them so they were able to lift it gingerly, wincing at the risk of it clattering, then slip through to the servery bolting it behind them. They avoided the service elevator in case it was alarmed. Ray knew her way through the staircases like a practised rat and they emerged through a fire door, among the dumpsters at the hospital's rear.

Then they ran. There was no real need for this. It was

a hospital, not a prison, and they weren't on a forensic ward but months of conditioning – years in Ray's case – made them react like fugitives. After two blocks Joanie started to laugh and had to stop running. She was slithering around in the snow in any case as Ray had bought her boots about three sizes too big. She couldn't quite believe this was happening and half-assumed their plan would run out of steam soon and they'd head back to the ward after a cooked breakfast in some café.

But Ray, who wasn't laughing, drew her on, still glancing about her for nurses and orderlies.

'Hey look, Ray, starlings!' Joanie said but got no response. 'I can't believe you held up a bank, Ray,' she added because the bit about the starlings was mean.

'I didn't,' Ray said, looking at her sideways the way she did. 'I don't know what you mean. New York,' she added in an undertone. 'There's an early train to New York.'

And Joanie realized she was serious, that this wasn't some crazy jaunt.

'I checked it all out,' Ray said. 'I went to a travel agency. We can get a boat to England from there. Or South America. What do you think? South America's warmer.'

'I don't speak Spanish. Let's go to England. Then we can get the boat train to France and keep going south.'

Joanie had no idea what a boat train actually was but people talked of them in clipped tones in English movies and it sounded glamorous and foreign and a long way from Etobicoke.

They caught a bus along Queen's Street then a car to

Union Station. The station was already surprisingly crowded and, quite suddenly, Ray's resolve began to drain away. She started to mutter under her breath, never a good sign. Joanie realized that in the outside world Ray was still pretty much a shy fourteen-year-old fond of her pinking scissors and wondered how long it would be before her medication wore off, assuming she had been taking it and was not, like Joanie, becoming sharper-sensed by dodging two doses in three while saving the rest for emergencies.

'I'll need to get our tickets, Ray,' she said gently, taking care not to look at her directly. 'Two one-way tickets to New York. Are you sure that's what you want?'

Ray was muttering to invisible enemies, making small, violent gestures as though to brush away crumbs or ants from the front of her coat. However she held out her case to Joanie with her free hand.

'Oh. You're sure?' Joanie asked. 'Thanks. You watch mine for me, OK?'

She left Ray with her suitcase, her mutters enough to scare away any thief, and sought out the ticket windows. She unzipped the case while she was still safely at the back of a line to slide a bill from the stash in the shopping bag. She tweaked a second one out and tucked it in her pocket for security. And another. If anyone caught her with all this loot, they'd never believe her story, not with Ray in her current state.

As first one then another passenger bought their tickets ahead of her, she asked herself the same thing she had asked Ray: was this really what she wanted?

'Miss?'

She didn't want her parents. After what they'd done they were as good as dead to her. Joanie certainly didn't want Etobicoke or anything like it.

'Miss?'

If she felt any pang it was unexpectedly for Winnie, for whom she found she still harboured an older sister's wary love. Winnie couldn't help being what she was.

'Next please, Miss!'

What the Hell! She could do the ladylike, Havergal thing and write her a letter.

She stepped forward and thrust a bill at the ticket-seller and asked for two tickets to New York. Perhaps she would go no further than there? Perhaps that would be enough? Perhaps she could enrol in an American art school or just hang around in Greenwich Village and find herself a life class to go to or at least some reefer.

Ray had stopped muttering, thank God, and pulled herself together again but she was plainly scared of the noise and the swelling crowds and Joanie saw she would have to take charge.

'Come on,' she said. 'We can get breakfast on board. There it is, see? Way over there on those last platforms.'

She led the way, pausing to buy them magazines because she felt in need of camouflage and it seemed like a normal thing to be seen to do. She found them a car that was still empty and would probably stay so as they had only a few minutes to spare. Ray refused to give up her case and sat hugging it to her as though there were something inside it she was scared of letting out.

Thinking to distract her, Joanie handed Ray a magazine and tried to read the other herself, hoping to settle

Ray by example. Out of the corner of her eye, however, she could see Ray hunched awkwardly over her case, flicking the pages much too fast for normality. Oh well, she thought. At least Ray would keep their end of the car empty for them. Joanie had not yet readjusted to life in the real world and was worried normal people would think her odd.

She looked away, staring out of the window at the men and women in the train across the platform from them. As it pulled out she had that confused sensation of being the one moving while they were staying put. Which made her think of all the times she had caught trains from there with her family. To visit her cousins. To visit Niagara. To weddings and funerals of people she hardly knew.

Her stomach was turning over with nerves now as much as hunger and she wondered if she would soon be feeing sick. It had been a mistake not to grab something to eat as they crossed the concourse. The dining car might not open for hours. There might not even be one on Sundays.

To calm herself she imagined how all this would one day be a madcap bitter anecdote: how celebrated artist Joanie Ransome once escaped a Canadian lunatic asylum with a crazy bank robber girl with a bag of loot and none of the right clothes and hopped on a train for Manhattan. She knew her future listeners would picture something wild and rough-edged, a louring Victorian asylum, two ragged girls hurling themselves into the open boxcar of a freight train headed south. This easy, almost genteel escape, hardly felt like an escape at all. But it was and when the whistle blew she found she had been digging her nails into her palms in the fear that someone they knew, some authority figure, some policeman, would fling wide the carriage door and stop them.

She became aware Ray was muttering again and shaking her head and hugging her suitcase tighter than ever.

'Ray?' she said, forgetting to look sideways at her. 'What's going on? Want me to put your case in the rack for you? Stay calm for me, Ray. Stay calm just till we cross the border.'

'I'm oh! I just! I just can't,' Ray said and for once she actually met Joanie's eye. 'I can't,' she said again, quite gently now, apologetically almost, then opened the door beside her and jumped out as they started to move. The door swung loose in her wake.

'Ray!' Joanie shouted. She dropped her magazine and hurried over to look down but the door slammed back in her face as a train arrived from the other direction, blaring its horn.

Ray had jumped down on to the tracks and directly into its path.

Further back in the train a woman screamed. There was no screeching of emergency brakes, though. The other train was braking already, being only yards from its platform but Joanie's train didn't stop. She was too shocked to do anything. She simply sat there, staring out at the tracks. Then, when the guard came running through and said, 'Someone jumped out as we were leaving the station. Was it from here?' a kind of instinct made her lie.

'I . . . I think she was sitting further up,' she told him, not needing to fake her shock.

On his way back through the train he asked to see her ticket. After he punched it and handed it back to her, she unzipped her case to slide her ticket safely into the little pocket with her driver's licence. She found herself staring not at her familiar, hated clothes and wash things but at several brushes, a bottle of turpentine, the useless wax crayons and a rather good box of oil paints Ray must have bought or stolen on one of her trips out. There was also a huge Hershey bar, the biggest money could buy, and a Gideon Bible, much of its text obliterated by Ray's insane annotations. Beside them lay the shopping bag stuffed with cash and a toothbrush so flattened and worn it would barely do for cleaning silver.

Feverishly she ransacked the case's zippered compartments and found a book of Charlie Brown cartoons, bubble gum, two new sketchpads and there, just when she was abandoning hope and imagining turning back, Ray's passport.

She grabbed it, zipping the case safely closed, and examined it greedily. Ray, it seemed, was short for Rachel. Rachel Kelly. There was only eight months' difference in their ages. Acquired for the trip to Ireland, it pictured her in usefully full-faced early adolescence. If Joanie wore her headscarf up and some lipstick and acquired some reading glasses she could travel all the way to England as a young woman mortified to be haunted by such an unflattering snapshot of herself in a larval stage.

When the dining car opened, she bought breakfast, although her appetite had vanished with poor Ray, and made herself eat nearly all of it. Her carriage filled up a little at the first stop. She read both magazines then locked

356

herself in the washroom to count every bill in the shopping bag. Then she was sick, then she felt much better although she bitterly regretted the hoard of skipped medication she had lost along with her driver's licence. In New York she would book a boat ticket – not steerage but not fancy either, this was money she would have to live off for a good while.

She could buy clothes and at the first opportunity she would see a doctor to get some Valium. Joanie Ransome was dead to her and her family now. She could face that with equanimity. But Rachel Kelly would need a little something to keep her on an even keel.

UNTITLED (1986). Oil on marine ply.

Contrary to expectations, Kelly did not suffer a mental breakdown following her son's death but some believe she produced this work instead. Setting aside the extraordinary Stones Sequence (2002) she was working on when she died, this is the last of her abstract works. It is monolithic and extravagantly large. She painted on what had been a barn door. She had to borrow Trescothick's much bigger studio to accommodate the panel and abandoned the rest of her family to live there while she worked on it. Initially the painting presents the viewer with a vision of black so intense it seems to absorb all the light in the room. As with Rothko's work for his Houston chapel, however, time spent before the panel reveals gradations in the darkness. But is this work abstract? Art historian Madeleine Merluza recently claimed it as the first, magnificent gesture in Kelly's late figurative phase; that it is, quite simply, 'a painting of a Cornish night, complete with trees and cloud-muffled stars and, deep in the darkness, a lane running from the bottom left of the canvas away to the top right-hand corner'. It is certainly impossible to stand before it for more than a minute and not feel one's eyes begin instinctively to search for patterns and shapes. Trescothick's theory was that Kelly 'needed to recreate in the viewer the sensation of her mind's desperate searching for meaning in the face of overwhelming loss'.

As Petroc began to come he saw stars: little, blue-white flashes. He shut his eyes, to black out the thin wash of light from the farmhouse, and found they were even brighter.

'Oh,' he said. 'Oh my word. Fuck, Bettany. Oh fuck! Sorry. I think I'm . . .' And then he came and it was a million times better than on his own with an old T-shirt and a head full of the busty girl from the chip shop. Actually he usually found himself thinking of a blonde woman who read the local news on television, who was sort of sweet but not a sex symbol or anything, not someone you could talk over with your mates. Now he wasn't thinking about her or anyone. He should probably have been thinking about Bettany, who was still rocking away on top of him with her amazingly uptilted breasts swaying in the moonlight and her meaty thighs clamped about him. It probably wasn't polite of him but he was thinking entirely of how good it felt and how long it was lasting and how he couldn't wait to try it again.

He subsided back into himself and smelled the moss and leaves beneath him and Bettany's sugary scent and the entirely new smell of her and him together which presumably was how sex smelled. She was still rocking away, eyes shut, apparently as self-involved as he had been moments before. Luckily he was still as hard as a rock inside her. In fact, if she kept this up he might even start coming all over again. He raised his hands and cupped the palms of them very gently over her breasts so he could feel her nipples rubbing against them. He had never felt breasts before, not even through a shirt. You had to call them tits with your mates but that never seemed right as it made them sound sort of small and silly and powerless when they were obviously very powerful indeed. They needed a longer word, with more syllables, like mammaries.

'Wow,' he said. 'Bettany. Oh bugger.'

'West End Girls' stopped playing for a second or two inside and the sound of people's voices was suddenly loud. Then someone put on 'Spirit in the Sky'. Troy probably, as he fancied himself as a sort of DJ and spent hours making compilations. And, as if it was the music that had tipped her over the edge, Bettany came.

He had heard about this, of course, about girls who made lots of noise or who went on and on and on. He heard smutty stories about girls using electric toothbrushes and spin dryers and girls who faked it. But Bettany was very restrained. She just clenched him, with her thighs and her insides, so tightly he thought she'd leave bruises, and her rocking got slower and slower and then she stopped. She opened her eyes. She had rather small ones, clogged with eyeliner, but he could see them shine. She bent down and gave him a quick kiss that tasted of rum and Coke. She had been swigging from a can of Coke earlier and he guessed she had tipped rum in through its opening. Her hair smelled of dope. They hadn't kissed much earlier, which was a relief because he wasn't sure he'd be any good at it and it struck him as the most intimate thing, in some way, perhaps because of using tongues. The rest was intimate too, naturally, but it was limbs and body parts whereas mouths were sort of where your personality came out.

She sat back on him rather heavily then stepped off him and almost lost her footing, which made her giggle. She was quite drunk. 'Whoops,' she said. 'Shit. You got a tissue on you, Pet?'

By a rare chance he had a proper handkerchief Hedley had brought him back from Italy. It was big and had famous Italian sights all over it, like the Colosseum and the Leaning Tower. He handed it to her.

'You sure?' she said and then used it to wipe between her legs. She sort of folded it up and handed it back. 'Souvenir,' she said. 'Where are my fucking . . . ? Oh.' She giggled. 'There they are.' She found her knickers, stepped back into them without taking off her shoes and tweaked them up under her dress.

Cold now, because she had left his middle sweaty, he pulled up his pants and jeans and stood too, tidying himself away.

'You're very sweet, Pet,' she said.

'Yeah?'

'That your first time?' She ran a finger down the front of his T-shirt.

'No,' he lied and hated his voice for sounding so young and wimpy.

'Oh,' she said. 'That's all right, then. It's just, well, we can't really . . . I'm sort of seeing someone else, is all.'

'Oh,' he said. 'That's cool.'

'No hard feelings?'

'Course not.'

'You sure?' she said, giggling some more and she rubbed the front of his jeans where his cock was swelling all over again and sort of bent sideways by his second-best pants which had shrunk in the tumble dryer.

'Get off!' he laughed, shoving her away, and she gave a sort of shriek and became just a mate's sister again.

'I'm getting another drink,' she said. 'You coming back in?' But the music had changed to 'You Spin Me Round', which he hated so he said, 'In a bit,' and she lurched away, having difficulty on the twigs and stuff in her heels. She had dressed up a bit tonight; normally she was in trainers.

Petroc tucked the damp handkerchief into a back pocket and walked the other way, circling the farmhouse and outbuildings at a distance, listening to the music, that wasn't too loud heard from outside, and watching the glimpses through the windows of people dancing or drinking or just standing around and shouting. He saw Morwenna, dancing the way she tended to, with her hands constantly snaking up above her shoulders as though she was dancing in a tube and the only way to move them was up. She had a cigarette in one hand and was either on Speed or E or wanting one to think she was. She had quite a habit, though he was the only one in the family who knew: Charlie, when she could cadge it. He'd seen her begging Es off Troy and overheard Spencer saying he liked the way they made her so horny.

He wandered, still circling. The Eurythmics came on and he saw everyone in the room sort of speeding up to match the music. He wondered where Hedley was and how soon they could leave without being rude or uncool. Petroc didn't like parties much and hadn't wanted to come only Morwenna and Hedley were clearly going and he couldn't stand being alone. He was no good at dancing, didn't like alcohol and loud music made his ears hurt. But these were all things you couldn't admit, like wanting a better word than tits. When the question of the party came up it was clearly an issue. Working at his desk on a model of a pilot cutter, he heard Wenn and Hed discussing it. Hed was saying there'd be hell to pay if Antony and Rachel found out they'd left him on his own and she said fifteen and three quarters was easily old enough to be left without a babysitter and what could go wrong.

Nobody knew about his fear of being in the house on his own because it never arose. Someone was always there and if they weren't he just went out with friends. He didn't need to be in the same room as people but he needed to know they were in the house somewhere, and always had. One of his longest recurring bad dreams involved being in his and Hedley's room and hearing the front door slam and whoever was leaving locking it behind them.

He was coming too, he insisted. Morwenna said he was still too young to drink and wouldn't know anyone there. But he was able to bluff with confidence, having a few mates in the sixth form now and said he had friends going and that even if Hed and she hadn't been asked, he would have been gatecrashing it. If they didn't take him, he'd only bum a lift, he cheerfully pointed out, with some mate who'd have been tanked-up on cider first. So they brought him and all went their own ways within minutes of arriving.

There was no food, of course, not even crisps, because food wasn't cool and the Youngs brothers lived like cavemen to the point where their own crippled father had moved out and lived in a caravan for a bit of civiliza-tion. Petroc came upon Mr Youngs now. He was sitting in a nylon deckchair in the caravan's open doorway, watching the world go by, listening to 'There Must be an Angel' and drinking beer from a glass.

'All right?' Petroc greeted him. He looked friendly enough and he was half-tempted to beg him for a bit of bread and butter and some cheese as he was so hungry.

But Mr Youngs couldn't talk properly and sort of mumbled in response, which made taking the conversation further a bit tricky. 'Lovely evening,' Petroc said instead and just stood with him companionably for a while and then left it at that.

The anxiety was returning that had never quite left him since Rachel announced, with no trace of excitement, that she and Antony were going to have to go to New York for a week. He wasn't superstitious, nothing remotely like that, but the announcement had left him with a growing dread that something bad was going to happen to her there. She'd be mugged or she'd have a bad turn and jump under a subway train or their plane would malfunction and catch fire. The others were so independent now – what with Wenn being in her last year at LSE and Hed having been to Italy on his own for two whole months – that it wouldn't have occurred to them to worry that their parents were away. They wouldn't worry about Rachel, at any rate.

Sometimes he felt as though he had grown up with a different mother to the rest of them. He knew about her being bipolar, how could he not with her regular trips for blood tests and the pills that had been cluttering up the butter compartment of the fridge door all his life. And the medication wasn't foolproof, not least because its success relied on her taking it and she was not a reliable woman. So he had suffered with the rest of them when she had bad patches or went a little crazy telling lies or spending money she didn't have or flying into her white-hot rages, which they probably all made worse by tiptoeing around her talking in soft voices rather than dealing with it and shouting *Oh my God there's a dangerous animal where our mother used to be!* But what with all the ageing hippies and potheads and sculptors and jewellery designers around Penzance now, she seemed to him to fit in pretty well, as an unusually successful eccentric.

But then, she seemed different to him because she had never had a real breakdown in his life, never been hospitalized with it, whereas Garfield and Morwenna and Hedley's childhoods had been overshadowed by regular crises so they had grown up thinking of her as mad first and their mother second. Whereas they knew the worst, having witnessed it, Petroc could only imagine it and had grown up waiting for it to happen again. This made him protective where the others were merely wary.

More recently he had started to notice her as a woman instead of simply as Rachel, and had begun to wonder about her marriage to Antony. This was a mystery to him: he so endlessly calm and forbearing, she so demanding and restless. If Antony suddenly cracked and set her free, said, 'All right. Go to New York on your own. Live in a studio. Do drugs! Take lovers!', if he refused to take any further responsibility for her, would she have jumped feet-first into the opportunity to run wild or would she have gone to pieces with no husband to nurse and nanny her? How much of her character was shaped by always being handled as though she might break?

Petroc came around the side of the house, to where the music was blaring out of open windows and the boys' knock-off disco lighting flickering across the dirty glass made it look as though the place was on fire. Couples were writhing about in two of the broken-down cars that always had feral cats in them by day. A boy he didn't know, with his T-shirt dangling from a back pocket, was being sick into an old tractor bucket, bracing his hands on its forks. In the far corner of the yard, Spencer was showing off his latest set of wheels to some friends who were clustered about it. He was gunning the engine pointlessly and demonstrating the crazy vigour of its sound system pounding out The Cure which, even at that distance, seemed easily as loud as the reggae now coming from the house.

Petroc spotted Morwenna at last. She was leaning on the jamb of the open front door, swigging from a plastic water bottle. She shone with sweat. She reached out a hand towards him theatrically.

'Baby brother,' she shouted. Her eyes were glittering and she looked madder than Rachel ever did. She ran a hand through his hair. 'Mop top,' she said. 'Where've you been?'

He shrugged, glad she hadn't seen him slope off with Bettany earlier. 'Bit noisy in there,' he said. 'It sounds better from the woods at the back.'

'What? Hang on.' She fiddled under her hair and tweaked out an earplug. 'Fuck it's loud!' she laughed. 'They'll have the police here soon even with no neighbours.'

'Yeah,' he said and yawned. 'It's a bit much.'

'You don't want to go already, Pet? It's only just gone midnight.'

'I wouldn't mind. It's full of tossers.'

'I said you wouldn't know anyone.'

'I do know them and they're tossers.'

'Christ you're only fifteen and you sound about forty-five.'

'Sorry,' he said.

She ran a hand through his hair to show she hadn't meant it. 'Maybe Hed can drop you back. I want to dance some more then we might head over to the Lizard. Spencer's heard there's a bit of a party happening on someone's farm down by Mullion.'

'Can I come?'

'No way. If you don't like this, you'd be completely miserable and a right pain.'

'So where's Hed, then?'

'I dunno. He danced a bit but I don't know where he is now. Shazz, have you seen Hedley?' she asked a girl who had just left one of the catty cars and had paused on her way back inside to light her cigarette off Morwenna's.

The girl glanced at Petroc then glanced at him again, in a way that made him feel as if he needed more clothes on. 'He was going in the barn,' she said. 'Last time I saw him.'

Morwenna gasped because the only reason anyone went in the barn was to have sex. Everyone knew that, which was one of the reasons Bettany had led Petroc into the woods instead. 'Who did he go in with?' she asked.

Shazz shrugged, taking a deep drag. She fired the smoke out through her nose in a way that must have taken weeks of practice. 'Dunno,' she said. 'Think he was on his own,' and she headed indoors.

Morwenna had started shivering. 'I'll be inside if you can't find him,' she said. 'I suppose we could always drop you off on our way, if Spence hasn't filled the car with his pet idiots . . .' She followed Shazz inside, already rocking her hips to 'I Wanna Wake Up With You'.

One of the pet idiots honked the car horn making Petroc

jump, which was absurd given all the other noises going on. He had to get away. He had never been good at waiting. One of the few things he disliked about coming from a largish family was the seeming impossibility of leaving anywhere fast, the second you'd decided to go. If he worried about the relative solitude he would face once Hedley as well as Morwenna had left home for good, he cheered himself by remembering how much more quickly he and Antony and Rachel could leave the house. Hed was a notorious last-minute changer of clothes and brusher of teeth.

What people meant by *the barn* was not the newer, open-sided one where straw was stored but a long, low, stone building which had fallen into disuse and disrepair, having no opening wide enough to admit a tractor with ease. An uneven flight of stone steps led up one end to the doorway that gave on to the old hayloft, a first storey whose treacherous boards spanned roughly a third of the building. In the cavernous space beneath lay stacks of plastic potato trays, a battle-scarred three-piece suite and several straw bales. The Youngs' old machinery still produced small, rectangular bales when everyone else was making the round ones that were too heavy for a man to carry.

Petroc had only ever looked in by daylight, excited and curious because this was a building whose reputation had reached him in school even before Morwenna decided to outrage their parents by casually taking up with the least suitable boy with the same postcode. There was old straw everywhere, inches deep, a heaven for mice and a hell for hay-fever sufferers. The doorway from the hayloft was letting in some moonlight so that even in the relative gloom of the lower room he could make out quite a lot once his eyes had adjusted to it. He could see or hear nobody and he realized that the place's reputation was probably a horny schoolkid's myth because not even a drunken idiot would have smoked in such a powder keg and any fool knew that most people liked to smoke after sex.

'Hed?' he said softly, anticipating the rustle of hastily rearranged clothes. But there was no response, just the competing musics from down the track and the revving of Spencer's customized Fiesta. There was a wooden ladder leaning against the edge of the hayloft floor. He tested it gingerly – most things being rotten in this place – and found it sound so took a few steps up to peer into the upper level. 'Hedley?' he said.

They were standing in the hayloft doorway with their backs to him, smoking a joint. It wouldn't have seemed a scene any different from the other little glimpses Petroc had been catching all evening, only instead of passing Hedley the joint bloke to bloke, Troy held it out for him, obliging Hed to lean forward slightly to suck at it. Moving forward slightly to take a drag, Hed stepped closer into the moonlight, revealing that he had nothing on below his T-shirt.

Until that moment, Petroc had been thinking to join them to cash in on the fun; he disliked the taste of alcohol but was curious about the effects of dope. So he was on the point of stepping off the ladder on to the hayloft floor when he saw he was an intruder and began to back off.

Troy saw him, however, and muttered something to Hedley who spun round then lurched down to the floor in search of his jeans and underwear, comically trying to keep himself decent with his shirtfront as he fumbled for them.

'Hey!' he stammered. 'We were just . . .'

'It's fine, Hed,' Petroc said. 'It's cool. I'm probably going to . . .'

'Are you OK?'

'Sure. I'm . . . Look, I'm heading home, that's all. Catch you later.'

He backed down the ladder as fast as he could. He was flustered at first of course, and could feel his face burning. Walking out of the barn and across the farm-yard and out to the lane, he avoided meeting anyone's eye because he wasn't sure what he might say. It was like when someone forgot to lock the bathroom door and you came suddenly face to face with them wiping their bum or shaving their legs: you couldn't help blundering in and they weren't doing anything wrong in there but it was impossible to say who was more embarrassed and it was equally impossible to know what to say. If you said nothing and just ran away it implied you'd seen some-thing unspeakable and bad, which was stupid, but if you just stood there and started speaking there was the danger it would turn into a conversation in which one of you was naked or inserting a tampon or something.

Once he reached the soothing darkness of the lane, however, and the music and sounds of people were begin-ning to recede, he slowed his pace and realized what he had just seen was a good thing. He found it hard to talk to Hedley about emotional stuff and this would spare them the necessity of an awkward conversation. He had guessed Hedley was gay weeks ago. A dim suspicion had been confirmed when Hed came back from Italy without once mentioning Italian girls, who were, after all, half the point of going there. In the seconds before he'd realized Petroc was watching him, Hedley had looked blissed-out which was good to see because he had been prickly and faultfinding, a bit of an old poof in fact, ever since he'd got back from abroad.

Petroc wondered if his brother and Troy had been doing their thing at the same time as he and Bettany had and then wondered if, by some miracle of synchronicity, Morwenna and Spencer had also been making out then, in the back of Spencer's car or even, like proper grownups, on Spencer's bed directly over the blare of the party. The idea of the three of them yards and yards apart but somehow linked by shared experience led to him unthinkingly doing what he had been taught to do in Meetings for Worship, holding each of them in turn, each pair, in the light of his mind.

He had compared notes with Morwenna once about what they did in Meeting and discovered that she imagined herself sort of holding the person in a warm light beam that fell on them from above. There wasn't any setting as such, she said, just soft darkness and, in the middle of it, this healing light. And her task, as she saw it, in praying for someone, was to use her mind like a sort of tractor beam in *Star Trek*, to hold the person at the centre of that light, almost as if she was toasting them on a Bunsen burner only it came down instead of up and did the opposite of hurting them. Somehow his version was completely different. There was still light – they'd had the same Sunday School teacher, after all – but there was a room, a totally blank box of a room, about the person. It wasn't much bigger than a lift and the light came from the walls of the room and the floor and ceiling and he had to make it bright enough to light the person until there were no shadows. What he didn't tell Wenn was that, when he prayed for people, they had always seemed to be naked, even Rachel and Antony. Not in a sexy way but like naked people in old paintings, where the nakedness was sort of truthful and a sign of vulnerability and innocence. When he pictured a couple naked, it made him feel protective towards them, as if they were children, made it seem less pushy to be praying for them without their knowledge or permission.

So it was quite natural to picture him and Bettany, who admittedly he found stayed rather blurred and in the shadows. He felt guilty and left himself out of the picture and tried, more successfully, to picture her on her own, sucking rum and Coke from a can and dancing a brave, self-involved dance, her eyes shut and her expression as open as when she had been rocking and riding earlier.

Then he pictured Hed and Troy kissing. But that was hard to do so he pictured Hed on his own, just happy, very happy, and relaxed and unHedleyish, as if a Hedley-shaped suit of armour had finally been lifted off him to reveal the real Hedley underneath, sexy and cheeky and not so worried about what people thought.

Then there was Morwenna, doing a dance for Spencer or maybe just for herself, with her hands snaking up above her head and smiling to herself as though she knew something good the rest of them would only find out later.

Praying for Garfield was difficult. It was hard to make him smile or relax as he seemed to care even more than

Hedley what people thought of him. He wanted to please so much it was almost painful. So Petroc concentrated on making the light so bright it almost blanked out Garfield's expression and he made the light Rachel's approval, which was what he sensed Garfield wanted best.

And this naturally led to thinking of Rachel and Antony. And they showed up in separate boxes because that was how they needed to be. So he made their light not just love and success but a kind of freedom too, from having to be parents and husbands and wives all the time. Seeing Antony on his own for once was a revelation. He was so practised at thinking of Antony as Rachel's minder, her guard even, at thinking of him sometimes as the thing that held her back with pills and peace and Quakerly carefulness from being her own wild self, that it was startling to understand the truth might be the other way around and that it was she who constrained Antony.

Petroc had reached the main road, almost without noticing how he got there. It was deserted, of course, but he still crossed with care as it was a notorious one for night-time accidents. Its hedges were regularly studded with improvised shrines of mouldering flowers and rain-soaked teddies. The dead were always young, all unproved potential and bad school photographs, tearing home from clubbing or a party. They were never the old and sensible.

Safely across the road he dived down the lane that led through Chyenhal to the edge of Paul. The first mile was one of his favourite stretches. Trees were rare in this bit of the world for some reason (like shallow soil or salty winds) but they thrived where the lane dipped around the edge of a damp valley for one magical stretch. They formed a kind of roof there, touching branches in a sequence of overhead arches that was thrilling when you flew beneath it in a car and looked up, because you were torn excitingly between the impulse to look up and watch the tree roof flying overhead and the instinct to look ahead, even though you weren't driving, to look out for what might be coming in the other direction.

By night, he saw, it became special in a different way. Your eyes soon adjusted to the darkness so that the trunks and branches showed black against the blue-black of the sky. Moving so much more slowly gave the trees time to form a room about you rather than just a roof. He walked in the very centre of the lane, looking up and about him and it was like walking through a natural church, full of the twitchings and rustlings of night animals and not remotely frightening as a real church in darkness might have been.

A car engine revved in the distance but this place felt so far removed that the main road might have lain on the other side of a pane of thickened, frosted glass. He found he had left all thoughts of family behind and, just as happened after the best Meetings, felt as though he had returned to his body to find it made new and doubly alert. He felt he could have sprung up a tree with the agility of a squirrel or flitted into the darkness beyond the hedges with the silent elegance of a moth. The engine sounded closer and he remembered he was no longer a virgin and would never be quite as young and naïvely aimless as he had been that afternoon.

AUTHOR'S NOTE

The Dame Barbara Hepworth who appears in this novel is a fictitious character loosely based on the real woman. In the construction of that fiction, however, I was indebted to first-hand accounts from Michael Sheppard and Elizabeth Anderson and assisted by Arwen Fitch at Tate St Ives.

Michael was one artist friend whose work and dedication triggered the novel. Another, less happily, was the Scottish painter, Graeme Craig-Smith, who lost his life to bipolar disorder.

Heartfelt thanks to Alexander Achilles, Mark Adley and Catharine Gale for furthering my understanding of bipolar disorder and the challenges of its treatment, to Simon Ewart, Margaret Chinn and Nancy Buchanan for teaching me about the Quakers as much by quiet example as through facts, to Barbara Gowdy and Rob Lindey for their invaluable assistance with the Canadian elements of the story, and to my editors, Patricia Parkin and Clare Reihill and my agent, Caradoc King, for their unwavering support.

Notes from an Exhibition was completed during a residency in Brussels in 2006 thanks to the generosity of Piet Joostens and Het Beschrijf.